I PUCKING LOVE YOU

PIPPA GRANT

Celebrate you!

Pippa Grant

♡

Editing by Jessica Snyder
Cover Design by Lori Jackson Designs
Cover Image copyright © Wander Aguiar

Tyler Jaeger, aka a dude in total and absolute hell

Two.

Chicks.

There are *two* chicks in this room. When Sparkle Hair invited me to sneak away from the bunny bar and upstairs to her friend's apartment, I thought we'd be playing hide-the-salami in the slam-bam-thank-you-ma'am kind of way.

All the makings of a good night. This should be heaven.

But Sparkle Hair is smiling a pouty smile and pulling me to the king bed in the bedroom adorned with Thrusters mementos where her friend, let's call her Super Tits, is reclining on her side and petting the black sheet under the Thrusters comforter while the *Rocky* theme song plays softly in the background. "Oooh, you found a rough one," she purrs, pushing her cleavage out.

I pinch myself, and it hurts.

Not a dream.

This is actually happening.

I thought I was picking up a puck bunny who can quote Aristotle for the night, and instead, I'm getting the Wrigley's Doublemint package.

Double the pleasure.

Double the fun.

Except for the part where my dick has died and is hanging in my pants like limp roadkill.

C'mon, Jaeger. Get it up. Get. It. Up.

"What's wrong, baby doll?" Sparkle Hair presses her boob to my arm. "Surprised?"

"In the best way," I croak out.

Super Tits climbs across the bed to press her boob against my other arm. "Have you ever had two chicks at once?"

Work, Wonder-Wood. Please work. "Ladies, all I care about is here and now. And here—" I wiggle my brows at Sparkle Hair "—and now—" I make kissy lips at Super Tits "—is my favorite place to be."

Sparkle Hair's hand drifts up my thigh. "Athena, he knows *differential equations*."

"Oh, god, that's so hot." Super Tits slides her knee over mine. "We only double up on the *smart* guys. Do you know why you should never talk to pi?"

Dammit. I *love* the smart bunnies. "Because he'll go on forever."

"Oh my god, I think I just came." We're all still clothed. Super Tits—*Athena*, apparently—is riding my thigh, her head thrown back. Sparkle Hair is doing a thing to my ear that would usually have me hard as marble while she plays with the button on my jeans.

But my dick yawns and rolls over.

Fuck.

I wish I could say it was fear that one of my teammates would catch us and kick my ass for being out past curfew, but let's be real.

I'm the youngest of six.

Pissing people off by doing what I want is what I do best. If I want to screw around with two bunnies when I'm supposed to be heading home after a game, I'm gonna screw around with two bunnies.

Curfew doesn't help my game. Breaking it doesn't hurt my game.

Ergo, on a normal night, *when my junk works*, staying with the bunnies is what I should do.

"Why don't mathematicians ever throw keggers?" Sparkle Hair purrs in my ear.

"Because you shouldn't drink and derive," I reply.

"Touch my pussy, you sexy beast." She rips my pants open, which is hot as hell, except for the part where Mr. Lazy Ass Disappointment in my jockeys has completely disconnected from reality.

Two chicks.

Two *smart* chicks who like math jokes and know what to do with their hands and I need a urologist, because there is *zero* movement happening south of the border, which—

"Oh."

"Hm."

Yeah.

Which they're both noticing.

Right now.

Sparkle Tits pulls my boxer briefs back, peers inside, and then both women scurry off me while I try to find words to convince them that what they're seeing isn't what they're seeing and that I'm into this.

That I am *so* into this.

"Sorry, Tyler," Sparkle Hair stutters. "We thought—"

"We don't take advantage of guys," Super Tits finishes.

"We can take no."

"We really can. No harm, no foul."

"When you came up here with me, I thought—"

"I mean, that's half of what you guys come to our bar for, right?"

"But if you're not into it, we get it."

"Totally."

"Completely."

"Two women at once is intimidating sometimes."

"Do you want one of us to leave? Or are you…?"

"No!" *Shit.* I drop my head in my hands. The weight of reality about the state of my lack of woody is making my head hurt, and I almost wish one of my teammates *would* come looking for me. "You didn't—I'm not—I want—"

I want my damn dick to work again like it used to.

"Too many hits to the head," I mutter.

"Oh, poor boo." Super Tits appears on the floor in front of me, looking up so I can't avoid her gaze without looking like a total asshole, and no, having a woman kneeling in front of me is still doing nothing in the crotch area. "Did it start after your concussion? That's not uncommon."

"*No!* That was—No. No, it didn't start after the concussion." Jesus. Am I really discussing this with these two?

And the concussion was eighteen months ago. Not yesterday.

I need a wingman.

I need a wingman more than I need my dick to roar to life.

Possibly an exaggeration, except for the part where I don't know exactly what would happen to my dick if he did roar to life, since it's been…

Let's call it a while and leave it at that, okay?

"So you could get it up right after your injury?" she presses.

"I was *fine.*"

"Can you masturbate?"

I can't keep track of which one of them is talking and

firing off all the questions, but that last one has me glaring at Sparkle Hair.

Because no.

No, actually, *I can't fucking masturbate.*

"Oh."

"Hm."

"Wow."

"That's…"

"Maybe one of us could rub it for you?"

"Yes! Either one. You pick. Bodies respond differently to self-touch than they do to being touched by a different person."

"I'd suck on you for a while if you thought that would help."

"Me too. For sure."

"Do your teammates know?"

I shove up off the bed and stuff myself back in my pants before all three of us start inspecting my limp, pathetic, broken weenie again. "*No*, they don't know. And I don't—I don't need *help*. Thank you. Just—just forget this ever happened, okay?"

They share a look, then both nod emphatically. "Yes!"

"Of course."

"I wasn't here."

"Neither was I."

"We don't know a thing."

"Never met you."

"Nope. Never at all. Though if you want to talk to someone, the doctors where I'm doing my internship are all *excellent.*"

"Oh my gosh, they really are. Dr. Jelani helped me work through my anxiety over taking tests, and now I'm on track to graduate with my microbiology degree next spring."

They won't stop talking.

It's like being in a room with my sisters, which is impressive, because I have four sisters, yet there are only two very, very smart bunnies here.

"I think we're overwhelming him, Cassadee," Super Tits whispers.

"He's had a rough night," Cassadee whispers back.

"Clearly," they say together.

"We fucking won," I grumble.

"Oh, honey, I know you did." Sparkle Hair—Cassadee, apparently—whips her phone out of her back pocket. "Listen, I'm going to send you my number, and Athena's number, and the number for Dr. Jelani. If you ever want to talk, we're here for you, okay?"

Athena—Super Tits—nods again. "There's no shame in working through your problems."

"Especially if it ensures this doesn't interfere with your game."

"We seriously love watching you play."

"Do you know how many people could've stepped into Ares Berger's skates when he got injured two years ago?"

"Like, no one else. Seriously. *No one else*. You're a god, Tyler."

"And we'd hate for this to be the reason you can't play."

"*I can compartmentalize*." Jesus. What if this interferes with my game?

Staying out late? No problem.

Having a broken dick that all the bunnies know about?

This could seriously mess with my confidence.

I blow out a breath and picture my sisters' faces where Athena's and Cassadee's are, and that helps.

Not with the soft dick situation, obviously, but definitely with the being-henpecked-by-bunnies situation.

My sisters would be doing the exact same thing.

"Can I ask the last time you got it up?"

Dammit. I forgot which one was which, and I don't know who asked that.

6

But I know that glaring at her like she's chirping shit at me on the ice makes me feel better.

Thinking back to the last time I got it up does *not*.

I know *exactly* when that was.

The *welcome back to hockey* party. September. Bunny bar. Walk-in fridge.

Brown hair. Fast words. Bright eyes. Curves. So many curves.

The woman who haunted my dreams for months. Teasing me simply by breathing.

Getting under my skin while staying a hair's breadth out of reach.

Until that night.

I'd tell you how many times I used to jack off to fantasies of her, but I refuse to admit how high that number is.

And my junk hasn't worked ever since.

"Hm," Athena says. Or maybe that's Cassadee.

The other one pats my arm. "Probably need to work through that."

"We weren't here."

"But I AirDropped you all the numbers. We're really good listeners."

"And we love the Thrusters. All of you."

"Happy to help."

"Anytime."

"With *anything*."

"But we know when to give you space too."

"Totally."

"Completely."

"Yeah. We're giving you space."

"Right now."

"Call us later!"

"Lock up when you're done!"

The two of them hustle out of the room. I want to kick something.

Punch something.
Maybe myself. In the junk.
That'll make it work again, right?
Fuck.
Just fuck.

2

Tyler

I WAIT ten minutes after Athena and Cassadee have left the apartment, then slink downstairs to the bar.

If we go out as a team after a game, we hit Chester Green's sports bar by the arena. But for curfew busting parties?

Bunny bar. All the way.

Getting in here is like getting into a secret society. The door's unmarked. If you can find the door, you still need the password to get in. If you break the rules, the password changes, and you're shit out of luck.

Not that there are many rules.

It's mostly *no means no, pay for your food and booze,* and *no fighting.*

The bunnies run their own brewery in the basement, they stock top-shelf liquor behind the bar, and they don't hand out menus since their kitchen is usually stocked to provide nearly anything the clientele here might want, and if they don't have it, they have ways of getting it.

I don't ask. No one tells.

It's another rule.

The décor is silver, pink, and black, with lots of glitter, lots of feathers, fuzz, and fluff, and chairs and loungers built for their comfort. A massive flag with the bunnies' adopted sorority letters, *Iota Feta Eta Pi*, hangs on a wall that's been coated with black glitter, and every time I see it, I think of a cheese pie, and then I get confused.

Feta isn't a real Greek letter.

I don't always understand the bunnies, but I'm sure they know what they're doing.

Connor Klein, our backup goaltender, and Rooster Applebottom, a defenseman the Thrusters acquired late last season from Oklahoma, are both breaking curfew too.

Rooster has a bunny on each arm at the bar, and Klein's sucking face with a bottle of whiskey on a couch. He started tonight, which means he most likely won't play again for a week or two unless something happens to Murphy, our first-string goalie.

"Jaegs! Whaddup, sucka?" Klein grins at me and salutes me with his bottle. "Coach's gonn' kick our ashes t'morrow."

Yep.

Probably will.

"Worth it," I grunt.

It's the party line. Gotta use it, or they'll figure out there's something wrong with me.

Rooster and his bunnies amble over. "You can buy energy drinks, but you can't buy memories." He thrusts his hips, wiggles his brows and then jerks his head toward the stairwell to the apartment I just vacated. "You boys wanna watch and see how it's done, you know where to find us."

Rooster Applebottom is the teammate we love to hate. All ego. All athlete.

The first to pay for everyone's meal and leave a three-hundred percent tip, and the first to throw himself in front of a puck to deflect it before it gets to Murphy or Klein at the net.

Also the first to announce he has the biggest dick of us all.

Coach knew what he was doing when he asked for that guy to fill some very big skates that retired at the end of last year.

One of the women giggles. The other's eyes flare wide and she bites her lip.

"Don't you worry, darlin'," Rooster whispers to her loudly enough for all of us to hear. "I'm actually lockin' the door so they can't hear us talkin' about all them musicals you want to tell me about."

He tips his cowboy hat to us. "Evenin', gentlemen. I'll be skating circles around you in practice in another few hours."

I look at Klein as Rooster and his dates head to the door.

His mouth's hanging open, head tipped back, while he snores.

"Screw this." I steal his whiskey bottle—he'll thank me at practice tomorrow—and carry it to Cassadee and Athena, who are now entertaining some guys from the team we spanked tonight. "Make sure Klein gets home, yeah?"

"Anything for you, Tyler." Athena blows me a kiss.

Cassadee winks.

At least, I think I got them straight.

And I'm getting out of here.

We all have to be at practice tomorrow morning—check that, *this morning*, as it's shortly after midnight—but I don't want to go home.

I don't want to drink. I don't want to talk. I don't want to screw.

I want—

Dammit.

I want a bucket of greasy fried fish and chips, because it's what my big brother used to take me to get every time he

11

came home on leave from the Marines and got annoyed at being hen-pecked by the four sisters between us.

My car's cold, thanks to the early November weather, and no, I'm not telling you what kind of car I drive, because yes, it very much feels like *compensation* tonight.

It gets me where I want to go.

That's all that matters.

That, and getting my ass to Cod Pieces before they close for the night.

Could I stay at the bunny bar and get fried fish and chips?

Yes.

Will I?

No fucking way.

I'm still stewing in my own misery when the bright neon sign with the armored cod and the storefront that looks like a medieval castle comes into view at the edge of a strip mall four miles the wrong direction from my downtown condo. I roll the window down, letting in a blast of chilly air and the scent of fries.

Just in time.

I holler my order over the sound of my engine, then pull around to the window to get my fish.

Debate calling my brother in Miami.

It's one AM. He and his wife recently celebrated their kid's first birthday, and I think they're working on baby number two.

If I call him in the middle of the night to bitch about how I can't get it up, he'll probably hang up on me, then tell our sisters.

And Mom.

She's a professional comedienne with her own popular Netflix special. There's no damn way I'm bothering West in the middle of the night for this.

I'll talk to the fried fish and call it even.

Has as much personality as West had before he married Daisy.

The window swings open. "That'll be fourteen seventy-three, please."

My car lurches forward before I remember to put it in park, and I gape up at the woman staring down at me. "*Muffy?*"

My brain is playing tricks on me.

It has to be.

Because there's no way the curvy, clumsy, smart-mouthed goddess who's haunting my dick is standing there wearing a Cod Pieces polo and hat.

But she is.

And I swear to god, her long brown braids are recoiling in horror as her whole face twists, her lip curling, her left eye squeezing shut, before she snaps herself together. "For the hundredth time today, I have no idea who this *Muffy* person is. My name is Octavia Louisa Beaverhousen."

Fuck me.

There are *two* of them? She looks exactly like Muffy. I'm not seeing things, and I'm not projecting just because I want my dick to work again and the bunnies made me think about screwing Muffy in the walk-in fridge at the bunny bar.

"Fourteen seventy-three, please." She turns away as she holds out a hand, twitching her fingers like she's waiting for cash or a card.

And that's when I see the tattoo.

Rufus.

Her cat's name. It's on her wrist.

Octavia Louisa Beaverhousen, my ass. This is Muffy.

"What the hell are you doing working here?" I hiss.

"Sir, please watch your language. This is a respectable fish kingdom, not a locker room."

I slap my credit card into her hand and briefly wonder if I'll ever see it again. "Does Kami know you're working here?"

13

Kami, our first-string goaltender's wife, is Muffy's cousin. They're both staples around the arena, though Kami's an utter angel, and Muffy is a matchmaking goddess of doom.

A sexy matchmaking goddess of doom who can quote *Dr. Who* as easily as she can quote *Schitt's Creek,* and who has the most gorgeous heart-shaped ass that I can't get out of my brain, but that ship sailed back at the start of the season, and I don't look back.

Don't we? my junk asks.

Is it wrong to junk-punch yourself?

We don't look back. My fascination with Muffy was merely because she resisted me for so long, rightfully so since we have mutual friends, and not because we're *interested.*

We don't get *interested.*

We do one-night stands with women we never have to see again, or who won't care when we move on to the next woman.

Women like Athena and Cassadee, who like sex for fun.

"Your cod pieces will be right up." Muffy flings my card back at me and slams the drive-thru window shut.

Screw this.

I whip my car around the corner, park, and hop out to stroll into the dining room, which usually has a fun Ren Faire vibe but tonight feels like a dungeon.

"Hi, sir, the dining room's closed, but—holy shit. You're Tyler Jaeger."

I nod to the teenager mopping the floor, who's probably actually college-aged, but he looks about thirteen, like all the college kids do these days, despite my own college years not being *that* long ago. "Just need to talk to Muffy."

"Your fish is frying," she calls from somewhere beyond the counter. "The dining room is closed. Go back and wait in your car."

"What are you *doing* here?" I yell back.

"Working."

"*Why?*"

"Because everyone needs a job, and every job is worthwhile. Please return to your car, sir."

"Quit calling me *sir*."

Fuck.

Did my dick twitch because she called me *sir*?

Or am I having a phantom hard-on?

I yank my waistband out and peer down at it, then remember *I'm in a public restaurant*, with a teenager mopping a floor behind me, and wonder if I actually drank something tonight and forgot.

I don't *think* I drank anything. It's November. I might stay out late at the bunny bar, but I eat and drink clean during the season, with few exceptions when I need a shot of Jack or a bundle of fish and chips.

Which means it's the Muffy factor driving me utterly insane.

And my dick is soft and limp as ever.

"What the *hell* are you doing?" Muffy's peering at me from around the fake stone column between the ordering counter and the kitchen, clearly horrified.

For the record, I did *not* whip my junk out. I gave *myself* a view of it, and no one else. "Taking you home," I reply.

"*Muffy*. You know Tyler Jaeger?" the teenager asks.

"No," she replies.

"If you need a job—" I start.

"I *have* a job. Clearly. It's for *research*, not that it's any of your business. And you will *not* speak of this to anyone, because whoever this Muffy person is doesn't deserve you spreading rumors that I'm her. Your fish is almost ready, okay? And then you can *leave*. Immediately. Also, leave a nice tip for D'Angelo, since you're getting footprints all over his clean floor. And if you ever, *ever* speak to *anyone* about seeing a woman you keep calling *Muffy* here, I'll tell Nick Murphy you asked to see my boobies."

D'Angelo laughs. "She's so hilarious."

Hilarious?

More like a walking disaster.

And if my junk wasn't already malfunctioning, now it's shrinking back into my body.

Telling Murphy, aka the Thrusters' number one goalie, aka Muffy's overprotective-to-a-fault cousin-in-law, that I asked to see her boobies?

Murphy is legendary for what he's done to his sister's ex-boyfriends.

He's mellowed since he got married, and even more so since his son was born, but I don't need to be the one to re-spark that wrath over something I said wrong to his wife's cousin.

Also, Muffy still trying to pretend she's not Muffy while threatening to have Nick disembowel me?

Classic Muffy.

See again, I've jacked off to thoughts of that smart, hilarious, nonsensical mouth more than once in the last year or so.

Back when I could still jack off.

"Is my fucking fish ready yet?"

"Don't use foul language in front of the crew, please."

She's still half-hiding in the kitchen, and I'm not having this anymore. I march myself behind the counter, making D'Angelo mutter a reverent *Whoa* behind me, and Muffy squeak out a protest in front of me. "What are you doing?"

"We need to talk."

"I'm none of your business."

"Tell that to Murphy. What the hell are you doing working here?" I know she dropped out of medical school pretty far into it a few years ago. She runs her own matchmaking service, which isn't all that great, but she does it. And she lives with her mom, who's terrifying on a completely different level. "If you need a job—"

"I *have* a job, which you're well aware of."

16

The fish smells stronger back here, and my mouth is watering. I can see it frying, with a red digital timer counting down. My fish and chips are almost ready. "Then why are you here?"

She's a manager.

She's a damn *manager*. Her nametag says so. She didn't pop in to Cod Pieces for *research* or whatever it was she said she was doing here. She's been working here a while.

"Go away, Tyler. We need to serve your fish and close up for the night."

"Bruh, yeah," D'Angelo calls. "I got a test in the morning. But can I get a selfie?"

The fish fryer beeps, and Muffy turns to lift the basket, and *fuck me*, my backstabbing dick is twitching again.

I pull out my waistband.

Shit.

He *did* grow.

Like not even half an inch, but he grew. At this point, I recognize *any* change in his appearance.

Is it the fish?

Or is it Muffy?

Or is it Muffy making me fish?

Or do I need to get my head scanned because Athena and Cassadee were right and I might have a neurological disorder preventing me from popping a boner?

"*Put your junk away!* Oh my *god*, do your neurons even fire in your cerebrum? What the hell is wrong with you?"

Jesus. She's hot when she uses big words to fling insults. "I'm not flashing my junk."

"You're looking at it!"

"I like it!"

"We all do, man." D'Angelo pushes his mop cart around the corner and slaps me on the shoulder, then goes deer-in-the-headlights and shrinks back. "Sorry. Didn't mean to touch you. Can I get a selfie? For real?"

PIPPA GRANT

Muffy shoves a bag at me. "Take the mother-forking selfie and *go away* so we can close up, please."

"I'll take care of it, Muff," D'Angelo says.

He smells like fish when he loops an arm around me and leans in to snap a pic.

I feel fish grease settling all over my skin and hair and beard, and I shouldn't have taken the bag the way I did, because instead of grabbing it by the top like a normal human, I let her set it in my palm and all of the just-fried fish and chips are still dripping oil through the brown paper.

I'll probably have blisters tomorrow. Pretty sure she was supposed to put it in a thicker paper tray or something before she dropped it in the bag to prevent this.

Probably I shouldn't poke a woman who's clearly not having the best day of her life.

She works at Cod Pieces by night and runs a terrible matchmaking service called Muff Matchers during the day.

She's probably had several not-the-best-days-of-her-life.

And yet I still wish I could go home and rub one out while thinking about her frying fish for me.

D'Angelo gets four selfies, pockets his phone, and then claps me on the shoulder again, except this time, he doesn't let go.

Nope.

The guy hits a nerve in my neck that almost has my knees buckling as pain rips through me from scalp to ankles. "Sorry, bruh. Hate to do this to you, but it's protocol. If you don't leave, I gotta go ninja on your ass. Can't have the boss-lady upset or she'll make me clean the toilets. You know? Then I go home smelling like a dead fish with diarrhea, and you can't get that smell out for *days*."

My body is breaking. Knees? Jell-O. Thighs? Overcooked noodles. Hockey ass? Quivering in pain.

I'm a badass on the ice, and this hundred-and-twenty-pound teenager is about to take me out with a little pressure on a point in my neck that I didn't even know I had. "You're a ninja?" I gasp.

"It's a hobby. You going?"

Dammit. "I'm going."

He releases the trigger point, slaps my shoulder, and does a thing with the mop and bucket on wheels that puts him out of reach and would make me have to step in dirty mop water to get to him. "No hard feelings, man. Gotta guard my manager, you know? Kick ass on the ice next game. I'll be rooting for you."

No *hard* feelings.

Jesus.

Nothing's hard anymore.

I should take my ass home, eat my fish and chips, and forget this ever happened.

Not so sure that's gonna work for me though.

3

Muffy Periwinkle, aka a woman who has it all together, really, if "has it all together" means "she's not dead yet."

IT'S NOT ACTUALLY HYPERVENTILATING if you're not choking on your oatmeal, right?

Asking for a friend.

Because I'm *certainly* not hyperventilating *or* choking on my oatmeal as I check my texts over breakfast.

Definitely not.

This is all fine. Totally fine.

"Muffy, you'll never snag a man if you make those fish eyes and pretend you're Rufus harking up a hairball every time you swallow a bite of oats, sweetheart," my mother says.

She's sitting across from me, dressed in a pink silk robe four sizes too big that's gaping in a way that's nearly showing off her nipples, which is pretty normal.

Normal's good.

Except for the part where I still live with my mother, who has a *Real Housewives of Las Vegas* soul in a *The Simpsons* life-style, and she's currently hosting an octogenarian criminal for

20

breakfast while they plot out how best to introduce her to his great-nephew, who has a fetish for women of a certain age.

Pretty sure the average person wouldn't consider that normal.

Also not normal?

A request from my med school BFF and silent business partner to go to her father's funeral.

The average person *might* consider that normal. People die. People have friends. People go to funerals for friends. But the average person probably hasn't been disappointing her silent business partner with a failure to turn a profit for three solid years.

Maybe I should change my business name. Who wants to hire a matchmaker who threatens to match your muff?

Although business *is* up the past few months. I'm possibly finally getting the hang of success, even if I side-eye my own methods sometimes and would absolutely deny them if anyone ever asked.

Won't jinx it by thinking I might turn a profit this year.

Success on any level is new. I'm still getting used to it.

"Muffy?" Mom repeats. "Do you need the Heimlich?"

Related: *Who names their child Muffy?* And don't start with *But, honey, it's short for Muffina.*

That's worse.

"I know the Heimlich!" our breakfast guest announces. "Learned it in the Army. Here, Hilda. Hold my cane. I got her."

Before I can whimper out a protest that I'm not, in fact, in danger of suffocating on my oatmeal, our friend William has dashed out of his chair like he's not eighty-three and is grabbing me by the boobs and pumping.

"I'm okay!" I gasp. "*I'm okay!*"

"You don't look okay," Mom says.

"Stomach ain't supposed to feel like that either," William says. "You got some lumps in it."

Neither of us tells William my stomach isn't lumpy.

I mean, it *is*, some, but he wouldn't know, because that's not where he's currently pumping me.

Mom winks at me. "At least it's some action," she whispers loudly.

I bolt sideways out of my seat so I don't knock William over, upending my bowl of oatmeal all over the vinyl floor, which Rufus, my so-dumb-you-can't-help-but-love-him mutt cat, promptly dives into like he's Scrooge McDuck and it's a pile of money.

Or like it's a pile of poo and he's that kind of a dog.

"*Rufus*!"

He peers at me like I'm the dumb one, yowls, and then flips over to start bathing himself with his ass still planted firmly in the pile of oatmeal.

Mom and William share a look. They both shake their heads, grab their coffee cups in sync, and force bright smiles at me while William settles back into his own chair.

"It's an auspicious start to the day when you spill your oatmeal," Mom declares.

"I spilled my oatmeal the very morning a sniper missed me by two inches when I was fighting the war," William adds.

Mom grips his gnarled knuckles. "You brave man! And to think if you hadn't spilled your oatmeal…"

His weathered face takes on more wrinkles as he squints thoughtfully. "Or maybe that was the morning I got married. Getting harder to remember what's what up in the ol' ticker." He taps his head, like that's his ticker, and I wonder how much I could make if I sit at a light-rail stop downtown and play a kazoo for cash.

Surely enough to take a few dimes off my student loans. Or maybe enough to be able to afford a closet to rent somewhere else.

Do people rent out their closets?

I'd ask some friends, but I've already gotten in trouble asking friends for help.

See also: My silent business partner has asked me to attend her father's funeral.

Back in Richmond. Where I spent almost four years studying at Blackwell College of Medicine.

Yep. I'm gonna puke.

I do stuff like spilling my oatmeal and getting my boobs Heimliched by old men on a regular basis. I've been trying to run a matchmaking service called Muff Matchers for a few years now. I hang out with criminals and my mother. I work basically sixteen hours a day, have screened half the men in our lovely city of Copper Valley, which sits to the east of the Blue Ridge Mountains in southern Virginia, and rejected all but about seven of them as potential suitors for my clientele for reasons that range from being rude to the staff to telling me that a woman who's larger than a size four doesn't take care of herself.

Yes, while talking to me.

Related: I am definitely above a size four.

My point? I have a very high tolerance for the unpleasant.

But going back to Blackwell?

Where *The Incident* happened?

No.

Even my therapist would tell me this is a terrible idea.

But if there's one person I can't say no to, it's Veda. She's believed in me for *years*. Our first year of med school, she was the only one with the patience to sit with me and quiz me for hours over the biochemistry class that I struggled with hardcore. When I left school, she was the only person to reach out and check on me, and she's probably one of the best friends I've ever had who isn't related to me.

We text at least weekly, and every few months we meet for lunch or dinner halfway between here and Richmond. Occasionally she comes all the way over here, and we do drinks and complain about our jobs and our families and our dating lives, and tell each other that we're fabulous, even though we know we're not.

She pushed me to start Muff Matchers when I started telling her about my idea, offered investment money to help me get it off the ground, and she's never asked a single thing of me in return.

Until now.

And all she's asking is for something a friend would do, so naturally, I can't refuse.

You don't leave your friends hanging in times of need, and if I'm who she needs for support during her dad's funeral, in Richmond, with all of his colleagues and current and former students from Blackwell, where he was the dean, then I'll be there.

What's the step after puking?

I might have to do that.

"Muffy, I know you like partying, but if it's going to leave you green in the gills every morning, maybe you should cut back to two or three nights a week instead of five or six," Mom says.

"Especially since she won't let you go along," William says to her.

"Right?"

They both roll their eyes.

If Mom knows I'm not partying, but instead working as a night manager at a fast-food fish restaurant, she's doing a good job of keeping up appearances.

And if Tyler Jaeger rats me out to my cousin, he's dead.

My job at Cod Pieces isn't exactly what it looks like.

Unfortunately, Tyler Jaeger *is* exactly what he looks like.

A spoiled hockey player who'll flirt only long enough to get what he wants, then get out as quick as he got in.

And I mean that in every way possible.

"Don't step in the oatmeal," I tell Mom and William. I

grab my phone, tuck it into my bra, and remember I haven't yet put on a bra when my phone clatters through my shirt and lands on my cat in the oatmeal.

Rufus streaks off like a demon, bouncing off the walls and leaving clumps of oatmeal everywhere.

So maybe I'll be playing kazoo at the light-rail stops to pay for the cleaning I owe Mom in her house now.

And a new phone case.

This one will be caked with oatmeal in all of its cracks until my phone's dying day, and that assumes its dying day isn't today, which is a distinct possibility considering there's probably oatmeal creeping up the plug-in jack.

At least I can't answer Veda's text. Positive side, right?

Not immediately, anyway.

And that's good.

It means I have time to come up with a plan.

Not *much* time—the funeral's on Monday, with a viewing Sunday night—but some.

Maybe I can fake appendicitis. Or an accident that leaves me in a full-body cast. Or my own death. With my contact list, surely I can find *someone* who knows how to get me new identification and can hook me up with a ride to a tropical island where I can sleep on the beach and pay for food by bussing tables at a greasy spoon.

Or maybe I need to finally face my past and do for Veda what she's always done for me, which is to be there when needed.

But first, I need a shower and to head out to work.

My clients won't match themselves, and if I don't meet a few new men, I won't either.

Tyler

PRACTICE IS A BITCH.

Klein doesn't look like he's hurting at all for all the shit he drank last night, but my fried fish and chips are sitting in my gut like I'm as old as my brother, who's retired from the Marines and about old enough for a mid-life crisis, instead of a well-oiled machine of hockey greatness with the false sense of immortality that those of us not yet thirty are blessed with on a normal day.

Rooster's skating laps around all of us.

Duncan Lavoie, our team captain and one of the oldest guys on the team, is at the top of his game, despite giving me *I know you stayed out past curfew* glares every time we pass each other on the ice.

He was fun my rookie year. But then the old captain retired, Lavoie took over as the team leader, and now he's Mr. Wet Blanket.

He needs some quality time at the bunny bar.

The married dudes on the team are all doing their married

dude thing, hanging out together and talking shit about whose kids and wives are the best.

Meanwhile, I woke up in the middle of a dream that Muffy was giving me a hand job, even though her hands were fried fish pieces, and I had the closest thing to morning wood that I've had since—

Fuck.

Since Muffy and I hooked up.

This is why you don't hook up with chicks you're actually friends with, idiot, my junk reminds me.

I tell it to shut up. Muffy and I aren't friends.

We merely know how to be friendly when we're around each other.

After practice, I'm throwing things into my locker, debating going to lunch with Klein and Rooster, when Lavoie sits down next to me.

He's in a towel and nothing else, which is pretty normal for the dressing room, but he shouldn't be giving me that look if he's not in full pads.

It's the look of *I know something's bothering you, and if you don't work it out, your game's gonna go the way of your dick.*

My shoulders bunch. I'll take the shithead out if he says anything wrong right now.

"Wanna talk?"

My molars crack and my dick snorts with bitter laughter. No, we don't want to *talk.*

He leans forward, casually draping an arm over his thigh. "Your game's about as fine as it usually is, and I saw your whole family on the news yesterday and they looked happy, so I'm gonna go out on a limb and guess this asshole attitude is about a woman."

First, still don't want to talk.

Second—what was my family on the news for? "Maybe I miss my sisters."

"You wanted to be on a yacht with all four of them, plus

27

your sister-in-law, serenading all the passing boats with your favorite disco songs?"

Hell. West marrying a billionaire party girl heiress with a heart of gold in Miami is both the best and worst thing to ever happen to my family.

Lavoie's grinning. "I can't keep your sisters straight, but one of them flashed the Coast Guard."

"Did *not* need that mental image."

Rooster pauses next to us. "She single?"

"They're all married, asshat, and even if they weren't, you'd only be going near them over my dead body."

"Uh-oh. Cranky Jaeggy's back." Klein sits on my other side. "Ares know you got the thorny side of a rose up your ass?"

"Go easy on him, partner." Rooster, also in nothing but a towel, props a leg up on the bench, letting his junk hang out. "Had a rough go of it getting overwhelmed with *two* willing ladies last night."

"Did not." Jesus. I'm a six-year-old again.

"Is this about Muffy?" Klein asks.

"What the hell?"

He shrugs. "You had a boner for her for most of last season, then the two of you got all cozy that time she showed up at the bunny bar, and now none of us have seen her since."

"Is Muffy the one with the hot mom?" Rooster asks.

Lavoie shoves him. "That's disgusting. Put your junk away."

"Dude. Get your eyes checked." Klein's making a face like he wants to puke.

I can't make my own face stop twisting in horror. "I really hope you're thinking about a bunny."

"Muffy's not a bunny?" Rooster switches legs on the bench, but we can still see his dick dangling under his towel. "Huh. That's a good bunny name."

"No, man. She's the matchmaker. Muff Matchers?" Klein's still making faces, but he's not gagging anymore.

Rooster snaps a finger. "Yeah! That one. With the hot mom. She set me up with this chick who could quote Aristocrates or something right after I got here."

"If you don't quit calling her mom hot, we're telling Murphy," Klein mutters.

"Not saying I'd tap that. Just saying she's got confidence. That's hot."

I grab my coat and shove my arms in it. "You have issues."

"I ain't the grumpy-grumplebottom here. I'm a simple hockey god who knows the best things in life come to those who believe. We live in magical times, my friend. Internet sex *and* make-your-own-funnel-cake kits exist."

Rooster slaps me on the back and heads across the dressing room to his own locker.

Lavoie looks at Klein, then at me.

I make the *don't ask me* gesture, turn, and run into Ares Berger.

If we're all hockey gods, Ares is the king of all of us. They call him The Force on the ice, and I'm pretty sure they'd call him the same even if he were a smaller man.

As it is, he's six feet, nine inches, and over three hundred pounds of hockey-loving muscle and heart. I got called up from the minors when he was injured two years ago, and *nothing* will make a man get better faster than knowing he's trying to fill Ares Berger's skates.

The fact that I'm still here, playing at the top echelon of pro hockey, instead of being sent back down to the minors when he got better, is a miracle I'm grateful for every day.

Okay, *most* every day.

Today, I'm pissy. Not even gonna deny it.

"What?" I grouse.

He doesn't talk. It's an Ares thing. And he's gotten quieter

29

since his identical twin brother retired this past summer—
again—after playing his final season with us.

But Ares doesn't have to talk.

He taps his temple. Then taps his heart. Then glares at me.

Yeah.

I get it.

Get out of my head. Let my heart guide me. Yada yada
baloney bullshit that worked pretty damn well for two years,
since the first time he told me the same when I was floundering right after getting here to Copper Valley and the
Thrusters.

"Tomorrow," I growl at him like he's not the guy I respect
the most on the team, and like I don't care what he thinks
of me.

Ares Berger is my hero and my mentor. I should not be an
asshole to him.

He lifts a brow.

Probably means I'm about to find myself dangling by my
ankles while he holds me up and tells me to my face to quit
being an ass.

"Dick broke?" he asks.

"Motherfucker." The bunnies talked. The fucking bunnies
talked.

He taps his head again.

And right when I think I've escaped any more Ares
wisdom for the day, he lifts me by the waistband of my
training pants, squishing my useless dick in the process.

"Intervention?" Murphy calls while I thrash about, trying
to get out of Ares's grip without causing permanent damage
to my nuts.

Half the dressing room snaps to attention.

"Intervention!" Klein whoops.

And it's suddenly crystal-clear that an atomic wedgie will
not be the worst part of my day.

5

Muffy

BY LUNCHTIME, I've been stood up, laughed at, and had my ear talked off by a guy who's probably as good at day trading as I am at muff-matching, despite all the arrogance in his story about how he made a thousand dollars last week.

I'm also out sixty-three dollars and riding a caffeine high after seven back-to-back screening sessions where I might have stretched some truths of my own—like sharing my real name—for the purpose of doing my job. And all to decide maybe one of the seven men I met so far today would be worthy of a trial date with one of my clients.

But on the plus side, it's time for my weekly Muff Matchers support group.

I'm gathered with five other women, three of whom are current clients, at a café next to one of those make-your-own-stuffed-animal places hosting a birthday party for a bunch of very loud preschoolers. The sounds are drifting through the shared wall, making Julie, the manager there who's joined us for lunch, twitch like she's still in the store.

Julie's boyfriend dumped her at her family's Independence Day cookout. She called me the next day, and after nine failed dates including one that ended with an ambulance on site, I re-evaluated my entire process, closed down the open applications on my website for men to apply, did something I swore I'd never do, and two weeks later, Julie and Gustav started dating, and they've been together for two months now.

Sometimes matchmaking is about letting the universe do its work.

Sometimes it's about seeing something in a client that no one—not even the client—has seen before.

And sometimes it's about finding creative ways to identify the right guy for a client, because the end justifies the means.

Julie still comes to my client support group meetings, because she was short on girlfriends outside of work. I like having her since she's a success story, and I don't have many, so I need to use what I've got, though things are improving.

"How's everyone doing today?" I ask after we've been served. I send motivational emails to my clients daily, so I know a lot of the answers already, since they tend to email me back.

Still, talking and emailing are different.

"Sick of men," Maren mutters. She's an environmental engineer that I've been trying to match off and on for a year. She's also my biggest source of guilt in my business since she's also of my cousin Kami's closest friends, as is Alina, the woman next to Maren, who's a cellist. Alina isn't a client like Maren is, but she comes to the support group meetings anyway.

I have hopes of bringing her over to the Muff Matchers side.

And, you know, of not letting her down when it happens.

"Oh, no," Julie says. "What happened?"

"I was putting gas in my car this morning, and this guy at the next pump started telling me how I should do it."

"No!"

"Yep."

Eugenie, who's a massage therapist at the spa four stores over in the strip mall, snorts over her Reuben sandwich. She's also not a client, but she joined our lunch dates after overhearing us a few weeks ago. "Did he try to explain to you how a hybrid engine works too?"

"*Yes.*"

Maren punctuates the word with a snort, and all of us groan.

Phoebe, who's a contracts manager for the city, lifts her glass of tea. "To clueless mansplainers. May we never date them, never raise them, and find creative ways to reject them."

I flinch a little. I've set most of my clients up with mansplainers—and worse—before, including one who was so bad that he mansplained mansplaining before a server intentionally dropped a plate of mashed potatoes in his lap. But my screening methods are improving, so I toast with them.

"How's your job going?" I ask Phoebe. "Any word on the promotion?"

"Not yet, but I should hear soon."

"You've got this," Julie tells her.

"They'd be stupid to pass you over," Maren agrees.

We spend the next hour talking jobs and friends and family and dates, offering encouragement and support to each other, with me taking various notes in my master Muff Matchers notebook, and steering the conversation when necessary, but it's not really necessary.

These women lift each other up all on their own, and they help each other feel deserving all on their own too.

I know I could do the same for each of them, but this way, they get extra friends, and they don't have to worry I'm only telling them what they want to hear because they're paying me.

In theory.

I don't actually see payment until I make a match.

Possibly I should rethink that, but it's the fee structure that lets me sleep at night.

Phoebe's phone alarm goes off shortly after two. "Gah. Bridesmaid dress fitting."

Maren, Alina, and Eugenie groan.

"Prospects for a date?" Maren asks her.

They all look at me.

I smile brightly like I have as much confidence in me as they do. "Want me to find you a good-enough date?"

And that's when it hits me.

I know what I need to do to survive going back to Richmond.

I need to take a super hot, athletic, rich date.

There's not much time between our late lunch and my next appointment, but when the ladies leave, I hop in my car and point it toward a house that is not my own.

It's a lovely Victorian in a private neighborhood with large mansions on huge lots, populated with smart, successful, occasionally famous residents who donate more money to charity every month than I usually see in a year.

In other words, it's not a neighborhood where I fit in.

But it's where Kami lives, and she's my favorite cousin in the entire universe, and she'd still be my favorite cousin even if we weren't related.

There are three things you need to know about Kami.

One, she's this adorable, brown-haired, brown-eyed, kind, sweet, smart, petite-ish, big-hearted animal lover.

Two, she's been in love with Nick Murphy, her best friend's older brother, basically since high school, and she pulled a total baller move last year that had him crawling on his hands and knees begging her to love him for like a month, which is the coolest thing I've ever seen in my life.

And three, she has the cutest baby on the entire planet.

Naturally.

Despite Nick being the baby's daddy.

I pull my car to a stop in front of the house that Nick bought her as his final *please take me back* gesture, which I can't be mad at him for, since the house came with room for their pet cow-dog, and he got lucky in that Kami's always wanted to live in a Victorian mansion and that was the kind of house for sale when he needed a few acres for farm animals too.

Long story.

There's an Escalade parked in the driveway, which means Ares Berger is probably here as well, but it's not a big deal. Ares doesn't talk, so he won't repeat anything he's about to overhear.

And it's time for me to spill my guts to Kami.

Some of them, anyway.

I bang on the front door, hear a subtle *moooo* in the back-yard, and take that as the cow-dog giving me permission to go in.

And would you look at that?

The door's unlocked.

"Kami?" I whisper-shriek, in case the baby's sleeping.

"Muffy?" comes my cousin's louder reply from the living room.

I bolt for the sound of her voice. "Kami! Kami, I need Nick."

She's still in her scrubs from work—she's a vet, naturally —as she rises from the rocking chair, baby cradled in her arms, like she just finished feeding him. "You...need Nick?"

It's a strange request. I get it. If I had a leaky toilet or I needed something off a high shelf, Nick wouldn't be my first choice. Ever.

Not because he's not tall or capable—he is—but I have a

stepladder. Also, never trust Nick Murphy around a toilet. It's a rule.

Which means I wouldn't trust Nick for other home repairs either. Or most anything else.

Nick, the dark-haired, green-eyed, prank-pulling goal-tender for the Thrusters, pokes his head in from the dining room. He's eyeing me like I'm an alien being who shouldn't be trusted around his wife and baby, which is probably fair. He nods, still wary. "Muffy."

"I need a fake date to a thing on Monday morning. Can you glue on a super thick villain mustache, use a fake earring, wear color-changing contacts, and answer to *Renaldo* for a day?"

He blinks once at me, slides a look to Kami, and disappears again.

So I turn back to my cousin, who's now eyeballing me like I have finally gone off the deep end.

For the record, I once set her up on a date with an octogenarian criminal—yes, yes, the same one my mother was having breakfast with this morning who Heimliched my boobs—so it does actually take a lot for her to think I've lost my marbles.

"*Please*?" I drop to my knees and clasp my hands. "Please talk him into being my fake date. I won't kiss him, I won't touch him except to possibly take his elbow since that's something a date would do, and I won't talk on the drive there or back since I know it would annoy him. I'll even spring for his hotel room Sunday night since it…doesn't make sense…to drive in Monday morning. I only need him to make me look good. Like I'm not a total disaster."

"Muffy, you're not—"

"I live with my mother, my matchmaking business is improving but it's called *Muff Matchers*, and we all know there's only so good it can get after that. I have student loans that the authorities will probably ask *your* kids to repay for me someday, and I also found a really weird mole behind my knee this morning that had me freaking out until I showered and it came off because it was a smudge of ketchup. Ask me the last time I had ketchup. *I don't know.* I don't know. I don't know when I had it or how it got under my pants. I am the very definition of a total disaster. And I *cannot* go to this fu— thing with these people who already saw me at my very worst without looking like a million bucks, and the only way to look like a million bucks is to stand in its shadow, so *please*. I need Nick. For *one* day."

Kami bounces in place and pats the baby's bottom while she frowns at me, the back of her head reflected in the mirror over the mantle, also bouncing, and I swear her ponytail is frowning at me too. "You're going back to Blackwell."

The name of my medical school makes me cringe, but I push on. "Veda asked me. She has this…ceremony thing… and she asked me to be there to support her. I owe her everything." I know. *I know.* A funeral isn't a *ceremony thing*, but if I tell Nick I need him to be my fake date to a funeral, he won't go.

This is even worse than asking someone to be a fake date to a wedding.

At least at a wedding, you get cake and it's okay to gossip about other people's drama, which is why I'm willing to help clients find maybe not the perfect guy, but a good enough guy to take to one. At a funeral, it's like all hushed whispers and you can only say nice things. It's a rule.

Plus, at a funeral, there are so many more tears, and it takes a special kind of date to pull off being there *just* for a funeral.

Maybe that's the next step for Muff Matchers.

Maybe I branch out into temporary dates for funerals.

And maybe I'm utterly insane.

Kami glances toward the dining room. I can't see Nick, so

I don't think she can either, but I'd guess he's listening in, and she probably thinks so too. "A ceremony for Veda?"

"She's being...honored...for her work with... You know what? I got tied up working with a client who has this huge list of little awards she's won over the years this afternoon and I'm having a total brain fart. But the point is, Veda's the reason I started Muff Matchers. She's the only friend I have other than your friends who tolerate me because you're awesome and they'd do anything for you—Maren and Alina say hi, by the way—and so I'll do anything for Veda, including going back to Richmond and Blackwell just because she asked me to. But I really don't want to go alone, so can you *please* talk Nick into going? Or maybe Nick *and* Duncan? Showing up with two hot hockey-playing bodyguard dates is way better than one."

"Muffy. My friends do not *tolerate* you. They love you. You're hilarious and fun and you tell it like you see it, except for right now, when I'm pretty sure you're hiding something from me."

The baby burps in agreement. Kami catches a bubble of spit-up before it lands on her clothes, which is a skill I don't expect I'll ever learn in my lifetime, even if I someday have a baby, which is also unlikely.

On the off-chance that I could find a guy I wanted to marry and have kids with, I'd still know where half that child's DNA would come from, and cursing another human with my genes seems like a cruel and unusual thing to do to an innocent baby. "Can you please loan me your husband and a few of his friends for a day and a half for no reason other than that I wouldn't ask if I wasn't desperate?"

"Are you sure Veda would be okay with you stealing her spotlight by bringing a harem of hot dudes as your dates?"

"That's a really good point. I should ask her. And I get what you're saying. I shouldn't accidentally set myself up to be the center of attention. I'd rather get sucked into a wormhole so I never have to go there again, and if I could go in a magic suit that makes me invisible, I would, but also, I can't be Veda's support if I'm having my own personal crisis without a human brown bag."

"Human brown bag?"

"Someone to hyperventilate on when it's all over."

I frown.

I probably shouldn't have said that part out loud. Nick's surprised me with how good he can be with diapers and puke, which Kami did a *lot* of when she was pregnant—the puking, I mean, not the wearing of diapers, though I've gotta tell you, I wouldn't have judged that either considering the number of times she had to pee every hour those last three months.

But back to Nick.

Puke and diapers? Yes.

Hyperventilating Muffys?

Probably not.

"Or maybe he can suggest someone else on the team to go? What about Duncan all by himself? He's got his life together and he's adorable with those curls and those eyes, and he's not quite as well-known around the world as Nick after all of those pranks and presents last year. Or Connor! I'd take Connor. There are like, *zero* pictures of him on the internet since no one ever cares about the backup goaltender. I'd take Ares, too, but it's not like he can go in disguise, except maybe unless he disguised himself as Zeus, but if there's a single person in the world who doesn't know who the Berger twins are or who would still think either of them is single, I'd be shocked. Plus, again with the upstaging thing. There's no way I could ask Ares."

"You know the guys have practice on Monday morning, right? Sunday too. They still practice on their days off between games."

"One guy can't get a single day off to go support a friend

in need? We can leave after practice on Sunday. They don't practice all the way until night on a Sunday, do they?"

She winces. "Muffy, I—"

"I'll do it."

That voice.

I know who that voice belongs to, and it has my shoulders bunching up to my ears so high that if I were in a onesie like the baby, I'd have to pull my underwear out of my butt.

"What about Rooster?" I say to Kami like The Voice didn't speak. "If I took Rooster, people wouldn't be looking at *me*, and then I could be there for Veda?"

"I said I'll do it," Tyler Jaeger repeats.

If I don't look at the wide arched doorway between the living room and the dining room, he doesn't exist, and he's not making the offer, so instead, I give Kami my best imploring *please don't make me answer him* look.

She half-squints back at me with the universal looks of both *what the hell is wrong with you?* and also *beggars can't be choosers, Muffy. Maybe you should take your octogenarian criminal friend instead.*

And then she stabs me in the back by turning to face Tyler straight on. "That's so kind of you. Muffy accepts."

Tyler

THERE'S nothing quite like a woman trying to look past you as if you're not two hundred pounds of solid muscle standing right in front of her to make a guy realize there might be a reason for his complex.

His *and* his dick's.

"I have no idea what you're talking about, Kami, but I think you should see a doctor if you're accepting dates for me with ghosts," Muffy says as she scrambles off her knees, making the pink bag slung across her body shift, clanking the contents inside it.

What does she have in that thing, coffee mugs?

Knowing Muffy, it's more likely cans of silly string and Magic 8-Balls.

She's in jeans, a Muff Matchers hoodie, a light jacket, and a layer of something that smells like panic, and she's clearly not interested. "I need a real man in corporeal form to do this, but if you can't help me, I'll go—*hey!*"

Yeah, it's juvenile, but I'm now holding her scrunchie high

above my head while her hair flops out of its ponytail and frizzes to her back, except for the smoother portion that was held against her scalp. I point at her. "You. Me. Outside. Or we're talking about last night in front of Kami too."

"There was no *last night*."

"Whatever, fish lady."

Kami makes a noise between a cough and a snort, and I wonder if she knows about Muffy working at Cod Pieces, or if she assumes I'm making a vulgar insinuation about Muffy's muff.

Whatever.

It works.

Muffy lifts her head high, bumps into me as she stalks through the wide doorway to the dining room, then through to the kitchen, where Murphy, Berger, Lavoie, Klein, and Frey are debating god only knows what over a cheese platter—yes, a *cheese platter*—and past them all to the back door.

Their idea of an intervention was stuffing me full of dairy and suggesting women I should hook up with to work off my frustrations.

The fuckers *know*. They know I love cheese, and they know my dick doesn't work. I don't know how Berger knew, but then, Ares is Ares.

He just *knows*.

And when he decides other people need to know, then other people know.

"Don't do anything out there that'll scare my dogs," Murphy says as I follow Muffy.

"Your dogs will get over it," Lavoie retorts. "Fixing Jaeggy takes priority over a moment of trauma for pampered pups. Or cows."

Frey, who's a real-life prince of a small country north of Scotland in addition to being one of the best right wings the Thrusters have ever had, smirks like he always does. The cheerful asshole has one of those faces stuck in a permanent grin. "Especially if it makes him quit scowling like a sheep with an intestinal disorder all day. I miss his smile. Don't you, Murphy?"

I leave them all with double-fisted, one-fingered salutes and step out into the chilly, overcast late afternoon.

Four chickens bawk at us from a pen near the back of the garage. Kami's dogs ignore us as they chase each other through the yard. Muffy marches to the back fence where two cows, which Murphy calls his other dogs, raise soft eyes at her.

The first one moos, then the second one joins in.

If you'd told me two years ago that Nick Murphy would move out of his swanky downtown condo and into a house on the line between city and suburbs with a big enough yard to keep farm animals, *for love*, I would've asked how hard you hit your head.

It'd be like telling me that I'd one day want to get married and have kids.

You want a guy to stay single for life, give him four older sisters with no verbal boundaries.

Would I like a woman in my bed every night?

Yes.

At the cost of living with what my brothers-in-law live with?

Not a chance.

I love my sisters. They're great. My nieces and nephews? Awesome too.

In small doses.

Being able to leave the house on my own when my sisters start talking about the trauma of childbirth has been the greatest gift of adulthood. I was a surprise several years after Mom and Dad thought they were done, so yeah, I've heard a lot when I couldn't leave.

Second-best?

Until recently, it was being a hockey-playing sex god. And I'd like to get back to the *having sex* part of adulthood.

The last time my dick worked was when I hooked up with Muffy. So I'm retracing my steps, going back to whatever went wrong, and I'm fixing this.

I stop next to her at the fence, where Sugarbear, the all-brown cow, is rubbing her muzzle into Muffy's hand. The other cow, a brown and white rescue named Tooter, snorts cow snot at me, turns around, and drops a load.

Muffy looks at me, then does that thing with her eyes where they go unfocused so you know she's not actually looking at you, and then looks back to the cow. "Thank you for your kind offer, but I've decided I don't need a date after all. You can get back to your Havarti party now if you'd like."

One, the next time I have people over, I'm serving cheese and calling it a Havarti party.

Two, what the hell is her problem? "Did I do something to offend your majesty?"

"No. But I don't date-date, so I figured ghosting you after that thing in the walk-in fridge at the secret club was the kindest gesture I could do for you. I mean, it's not like you don't have your pick of women."

She's lying. Not about me having my pick of women—that part's true—but about the rest of it.

And the idea that she's lying because I did something to ruin her trust makes something roil in my gut.

Not the marrying kind here, so it's not like I'm heart-broken if she doesn't want to see me anymore. But women don't usually actively avoid me either, especially women who felt weirdly like my friend before we hooked up, even if I refuse to admit that we might've been friends, and a walk-in fridge isn't the strangest place I've ever had sex, so that's clearly not the problem. Also, as much as my sisters can irritate me, I'd defend the shit out of every last one of them *and* their best friends, even the annoying ones, if a guy ever so much as insulted a single one of their fingernails.

Never mind if he actually hurt her.

I clear my throat. There's no good way to ask what I suddenly have to ask, but it *was* dark in the fridge, and I could've missed something with all the teeth chattering. "Did I force myself on you?"

"What?" She spins and looks at me, eyes wide. "No. *No.* I wanted—I was a willing participant. I just...don't want to anymore. With you. I'm one-and-done. Boom. We're over. Sorry. Should've warned you. You can go back to your business now."

One and done.

Jesus Christ on a goat.

I'm hardly a paragon of commitment, and I make no secret that I don't do relationships, but this is extreme. Why the hell wouldn't Muffy—oh, hell.

Oh, hell no.

"It wasn't good for you?" I sputter.

Her face goes the same shade of maroon that I put on every game day. "Of course it was. It was very good. The best I'd ever had."

Fucking fucknuggets.

It wasn't good for her.

"We're doing it again." Jesus. Where did that come from? I can't *do it again.* I can't even *get it up.* "This time I'm eating your pussy. All of it. Like seven times."

"That's a very kind offer, but no, thank you."

"*That's a very kind offer*? Are you serious? I offer to go down on you, and you come back with *that's a very kind offer*?" Holy shit. "You faked it."

She cringes like it's her fault, and I want to hit something.

"You did. You faked it." I look down at my dick and silently ask him if he knew.

Can't see him through my pants, but I think he rolled his

eyes and asked me how long it was going to take me to catch up.

And now I'm wondering how many women have faked it.

How many of them have I left unsatisfied, thinking I was master of the female body when really, I was a notch on a bedpost, and not one worth the time it would take to scratch that notch in?

Shit.

My dick knows we suck, and he's given up on life. No more nookie for us. He's done. Called it quits. Told me to go do other things that I do well, and leave the orgasm-making to dudes who know how to actually play a woman's body.

Wait.

That can't be right.

I'm fucking awesome.

"Have you ever...you know...with another guy?" Maybe it's not me.

Maybe it's her?

But if it's all her, why do I feel like I'm going to throw up all my cheese?

Her face contorts and the maroon stain spreads down her neck. "And this conversation is officially over. Goodbye, Tyler."

"Hold up. I think I deserve an answer here."

Sugarbear moos at me, which sends the chickens squawking all over again, and then the dogs—the actual dogs —come running over while Muffy tries to step around all of us. "Um, no, actually, as my therapist constantly reminds me, the only person I owe anything to is myself."

My sister Allie uses her therapist's wisdom all the time too. If Muffy thinks she can *my therapist* her way out of this conversation, she's wrong. "Then could you do me the honor of telling me if I need to work on my game, or if this is maybe not all my fault?"

"That's a conversation for you and your own therapist. And possibly your former conquests."

Dammit. Allie hasn't used that one on me before. "Why do you need a date to this thing so badly that you'd ask to borrow Nick in disguise?"

"I appreciate what you're trying to do, but I need to get home and change before I'm late to my next appointment."

"Cod Pieces?"

"Client. My job at Cod Pieces is complicated, and I'm not explaining it to you. I'm a matchmaker. I match muffs. And I need to get back to it."

"Great. You're hired." *What the hell am I doing?*

"I choose my clients. I don't pick you."

"Why not?"

"You don't fit what my clientele is looking for."

"What are they looking for?"

"Matches to their misfitness." She finally turns to face me again, and she gestures up and down my body. "You're a highly-paid, naturally-gifted, attractive professional athlete who can carry on conversations about solar panels, DNA, and Shakespeare. You play Pokémon and watch *Dr. Who*, which puts you on the geeky side of a sliding scale of personality types, but considering your profession, it adds depth to your character rather than pigeonholing you. Also, you could probably make three phone calls and get a chance to hang out on the set of *Dr. Who* if you wanted to, which means you operate on a completely different plane of existence than my clients who might still live with their parents, have a stutter, lack fashion sense, or miss social cues. You don't think the ideal woman exists because you don't want to settle down, and if you *did* think the ideal woman existed, she'd probably be a size two, love to run through the mountains with you on a spring morning, spend the afternoon drinking kombucha at a coffee shop while you debate if Wayne Gretzky or Stan Lee would be a better dream dinner companion, and then go to a baseball game in the evening as much to be seen and support fellow professional athletes as because you want to actually watch the game. Also, she'd give the best blow jobs, she wouldn't mind trying butt stuff, and she'd appreciate when you make her breakfast in bed but probably never tell you that your scrambled eggs are too runny for her taste, because she's so grateful you'd lift a finger to try. Sound about right?"

Not all of it, but too much of it. I do like my eggs runny. "I'm not a superficial asshole who only cares about size. *And* my sister Staci used to stutter, and my sister Keely has the worst-smelling feet of anyone you've ever met, but I still love them both. I'm *not* surrounded by perfection. I'm real as fuck."

I don't add that I fucked her too—her being Muffy, not one of my sisters—and she's not anything like the perfect puck bunnies she described—who don't exist, by the way—because she'd probably throw back that since I *don't* want forever, I'm not all that picky.

And she'd be correct.

She nods. "You're right. You have everything together."

"Exactly."

"So you have no reason to need to be my fake date to a fu —few things, and no reason to sign up for Muff Matchers' services."

"And that's exactly why I'd be your perfect date. We screwed. You ghosted me. We have zero future romantically. No one will mistake me for one of your clients. And we can still be friends. I'm hot as balls and every other woman there will be jealous you have me on your arm." What am I saying?

What the hell am I saying?

And why is Muffy looking at me like she's a squirrel and there's a garbage truck barreling down the road at her and she doesn't know if she should go left or right, but she knows she'll get squished if she doesn't decide?

She makes a vague gesture with her arm that might be *I'm*

trying to distract you or it might be some kind of weird help signal and she's hoping Kami's watching from the window to come save her.

Seriously, it reminds me of my sister Brit's *Who shall rescue me from this wanker?* gesture that she created after my sister Staci set her up with a friend's brother and no one realized he'd made it his life's mission to be the world's grossest photographer.

You don't want to know. Trust me.

Muffy blinks twice, sucks in a loud breath, and then nods. "Okay. Great. I'll text you the details."

"Do you still have my number?"

She mumbles something that might be a yes or a no. I can't decide.

"No problem. I still have yours." I whip my phone out and text her, and her phone audibly dings in her pocket.

So she didn't change her number.

That's good.

"Anything else I need to know before we do this?" Other than that I'll have a few hours alone in a car with her to convince her to tell me exactly what it was I did wrong so that I can figure out how to fix my broken dick?

"Don't you have practice on Monday?"

"I'll get out of it. We can leave right after morning skate on Sunday."

Her squinty doubtful face tells me she knows it'll be an uphill battle for me to convince Coach to let me out of practice.

And that almost has me smiling.

I do like a good challenge.

"Great." She doesn't sound like it's great. "I have to go. Thank you. It's very kind of you to come with me to Veda's thing. Dixie! Tyler has treats! Get Tyler!"

Kami's cocker spaniel takes a running leap to dive at my crotch while Muffy weaves around the other two dogs and heads back to the house. I *oof* and try to calm the dog down, watching Muffy's hips swing the whole time.

She's infuriating and fascinating and perplexing.

And I want to be done with her, but the truth is, I don't think I can.

Not when I think I need her to help me solve my little problem.

7

Muffy

IT TAKES me longer to get ready for my meeting and then my shift than it should, because I'm hyperventilating about taking Tyler with me to Veda's dad's funeral.

On the one hand, we've hung out off and on for a year, he's seen me naked—kind of, I mean, since it was sort of dark in the fridge—and we've screwed, which means faking intimacy shouldn't be difficult.

On the other, despite my assertion to him that I didn't want to hear from him, *he ghosted me*.

The sex was ho-hum. Whatever. It happens, right? Doesn't mean it would've always been ho-hum.

But he didn't call.

He didn't text.

He didn't use the *contact me* form on my website, which I know he knows about, to drop me an email.

He didn't ask about me. If he had, Nick would've told Kami, who would've told me. I mentioned the *kind* part, right? Kami doesn't press, but she does have eyeballs, and if she thought I wanted to hang out with Tyler and he wanted to hang out with me, she would've mentioned if he talked about me.

She didn't.

Which means *he* didn't.

I might've claimed I ghosted him, but that was my wounded pride talking.

Better to be the one who walked away, right?

And now, I'll probably have to tell him why I left med school, because other people who know—or at least strongly suspect some vague version of the truth—will almost certainly be there, and while I seriously doubt any of them spend any time thinking about me on a regular day, I don't know if any of us will be able to look at each other without me thinking about why they're practicing doctors now and I'm not.

And if I'm going to hyperventilate before we make it through the doors to the funeral parlor for the viewing, much less to the graveside services the next day, Tyler deserves to know why.

But, since I'm running late, this is a problem for tomorrow.

Or Sunday.

Sort of like booking two hotel rooms is also a problem for tomorrow.

So I finish getting dressed, call to Mom that I'm heading out to dinner and a party with friends, and I take off to attempt to succeed at my dream job.

I mean, the dream job I found after I gave up the dream of being a surgeon. And let's be honest here, does anyone who knows me think I could've actually been a surgeon?

Surgeons have their lives together.

I don't.

Plus, *Dr. Muffy Periwinkle*?

Please.

No one would've come to me for anything anyway, except possibly to inspect their stuffed animals' upset tummies after a tea party.

My therapist says the name is what you make it, not what makes you, but *I* wouldn't have hired me. And now I'm filling a niche need in the world for special people who don't know what they're worth, even if it's a struggle, and even if I've had to get creative in finding potential dates for my all-female clientele. I have a purpose. It's not in physically fixing people's hearts, but in emotionally fixing people's hearts.

I call Veda on my drive to check in and see how she's doing and reiterate my promise to be there on Sunday, which I have to do over voicemail since she doesn't pick up.

Not surprising.

She's planning a sudden funeral for her father, whom everyone thought would live to be at least two hundred years old, after he came down with salmonella poisoning. And I'm pretty sure she has complicated feelings about all of it.

She and her dad weren't all that tight since he refused to accept that she's bisexual and always thought she should be working harder and succeeding faster than anyone else, but publicly, she was his pride and joy for following in his footsteps. We bonded over mutual father issues.

And that's all I have to say about that.

My client arrives at our meeting mere seconds before me, which I know because I pull into the parking lot at Cod Pieces in time to see her walking through the door.

Fingers crossed that my instincts are spot-on with wanting to introduce her to D'Angelo. Since I started here two weeks ago, I've had a lot of time to talk to him, and if ever there was a good candidate for Muff Matchers' first male client, it's D'Angelo. People are forever asking him if he plays basketball since he's a tall Black guy, but he has as much interest in team sports as an armadillo has in fashion. His parents enrolled him in tae kwon do classes when he was ten to try to help smooth out his klutziness, and he's here at Copper Valley University with an undeclared major and a serious love of all things *Star Wars*. Also, he's a few years older than his fellow freshmen, since he worked at the family business while his grandpa was sick instead of enrolling straight into college after high school.

This match is my best chance at making a match without having to stretch into questionable territory for digging up male prospects.

I toss a Thrusters hoodie over my Cod Pieces polo and grab my messenger bag, which has a Muff Matchers new client box inside it, and I scurry into the dining room.

Lauren, the day manager, waves at me and taps her watch with her eyebrows raised in question. I point to a table and mouth *I'll wait* and *I have a meeting* at the same time, which is most likely impossible to interpret, since I think I actually mouthed *I'll meet a waiting*, which makes zero sense.

But since she's a client and the reason I'm here, she speaks Muffy well enough.

She's an engineering student in her third year at CVU, and she only works here as a manager because she's worked here so long that she makes more than she would filing papers for the admissions office. The night manager quit unexpectedly while Lauren and I were having a meeting about potential prospects, and since I worked at a Cod Pieces in high school, it was easy to offer to help her out for a few nights.

And honestly? Making a little extra cash isn't a bad thing. This job might be the only reason I make my student loan payments this month, hence why I'm not asking her if she's found a replacement for me yet.

And fish and chips four nights a week?

I'm possibly here for this.

Okay, I'm definitely here for this.

Just like Tyler was last night.

Also, now I'm thinking about him again.

I'll be your date, Muffy.

Why?

Why the *hell* would he do that?

Better question—who else can I find to take to the funeral so I can let him off the hook?

And why do I keep picturing Tyler stepping between me and my former classmates and professors, or whispering something in my ear that makes me laugh, or offering to bench press the casket when someone else's date tries to prove he's stronger than my hockey-playing, Aristotle-spouting, Pokémon-loving, one-night date?

Tyler would totally do that.

I've *seen* him.

Granted, he was being spurred on by his teammates and had had enough alcohol to flatten a non-hockey-playing person, plus, it was a fake casket at a Halloween party, but he did it.

Also?

He's a professional hockey player with a super famous, billionaire party girl sister-in-law. Tyler's in the gossip pages a lot. Everyone will know who he is. There'll be zero doubt that I have an *actual* hottie by my side, and we *do* know each other well enough to sell the idea that we're dating.

My client interrupts my internal musings by setting a powder-blue Cod Pieces tray on the table between us, and I pretend I don't want to lean over and inhale the amazing scent.

You'd think a year of working here in high school would've ruined fried fish.

Nope.

Still love it.

I paste on a bright smile. "Hi, Brianna. Thanks for meeting me here."

She's twenty-five, also a freshman on campus with an undeclared major after recently leaving the Army, and worried she's too stubborn and not feminine enough to find a man.

We could literally be besties, but it probably wouldn't be healthy for either of us to continue to stew in our lack of direction in life.

Not that I'm lacking a direction.

I'm simply lacking actual skill at any direction I've tried, until a recent string of small victories with Muff Matchers that were entirely more difficult than they should've been.

Brianna sits, bends, and sniffs deeply over her fish, which is wrapped in foil stamped with Sir Pollock, the Knight Fryer, the franchise's well-known cod mascot. "Oh, baby, come to mama. I missed you while I had to fit into a uniform."

Confession: I slept with Tyler Jaeger because he looked at me the way Brianna is looking at her fish.

And not just once.

The looking part, I mean. Not the sleeping part.

Every time I saw him from the time Kami hooked up with Nick a year ago until Tyler and I got together at that secret club, he would look at me like he wanted to lick me from head to toe. And then he'd talk to me.

Hey, Muffy, had any cognitive stimulation lately?

You play Pokémon Go? Trade you Pokéballs.

Muffy, need your opinion. Does this shirt make my arm muscles look too big?

I still can't believe *that* was the line that had me pulling him into the kitchen and hiding in the walk-in refrigerator before the chef spotted us the night Maren took me to the secret club.

Or that a guy with an actual six-pack took his shirt off *for me*, showing off his tattoos *for me*, hoisted me up against a shelf full of boxes of tomatoes, and then popped an actual boner that size *for me*.

Not that it got better after that—it didn't, really, and I don't know why I thought it would—but still.

It was probably my fault it wasn't great. I didn't exactly tell him what I liked or didn't like, or why I didn't know what I liked or didn't like, or maybe I couldn't get out of my own head, or maybe, I don't know, most guys are overrated?

That's what they say, right? That women fake it all the time?

It's not like I've never had an orgasm. I *do* masturbate.

And yes, my mother's caught me at it before, and no, I don't want to talk about *that*.

"Would it turn a guy off if I licked something like this in front of him?" Brianna asks.

She's still sniffing the fish like it'll get better with age, or maybe like she needs a private minute with it.

As much as I love fried fish too, I'm honestly a little uncomfortable. And not because I was visiting that memory where Tyler Jaeger was into me while I'm supposed to be concentrating on a client. "If a guy walks away because he can't handle you enjoying your food, then you deserve better than him."

She frowns. Her pale skin is dusted with a thick layer of freckles, and her glasses are smudged like she's gotten up close and personal with the fried batter already. Her hair's still cut short, and like me, she's not exactly a waif.

Pretty far from it, actually. She fought to be allowed to wrestle in high school, and she kicked ass.

"I'm not what most guys are into." Her shoulders are drooping, and I want to hug her.

"Who wants most guys? That's why you're here. To find something better than *most guys*."

"But can you *really* do that? How do you find the guys who are better than most other guys?"

With a lot more work than I wish it took.

People like Brianna deserve love as much as people who look like they have it all together, and believe me, I know *plenty* of people who look like they have it all together, but underneath it all, they're a mess.

Or they have been.

Even Kami was a disaster for a bit last year, and she's one of the kindest, smartest, prettiest, most-together people I know.

Also?

She doesn't think she's all that pretty or smart. She *does* know she's kind though. I love that she owns it.

"Are you willing to give a few guys a chance?" I ask Brianna.

She frowns again, picks up her fish, bites into it, and moans.

And moans.

And moans.

I squirm, because this is starting to feel like being on a porn set, and not gonna lie, I'm getting a little warm in some spots. One of the day shift people drops a bucket or something that clatters loudly, and a customer walking to the counter turns to stare at us, trips, and falls onto another customer at a different table.

It's *When Harry Met Sally*, fried fish edition.

Mental note: add *she's a moaner* to Brianna's file.

Other mental note: do real people actually moan like that during sex? Is it ever *actually* good, or is it a myth that women tell men because a large portion of the female population has a biological need for babies and so they *pretend* it's good so that everyone gets what they want? Have we been so trained to coddle men's egos for so long that no one actually knows if there's legitimately good sex out there?

Brianna slumps back in her seat with a blissful smile on her face, her shoulders relaxed, one leg cocked out funny from beneath the table. "You're single too, aren't you?"

I clear my throat and stifle the urge to wipe my forehead with a napkin.

That question is the worst.

How do you know how to set me up with someone when you can't even set yourself up?

It's not what she asked, except it's usually what people mean.

Time for my standard answer. "You know how you sometimes have that friend who'll be like, *does this rash look weird*, and you tell her to go to the doctor, but if you have a rash on your own skin that looks weird, you write it off, because of course it's fine and it'll go away on its own in a few days?"

"Fuck, yeah. Actually, I've got this skin tag on my toe, and I think it's growing. Do you think I should see a doctor?"

"Can't hurt, right?"

She nods and eyes her fish again, and once again, I'm back in that fridge with Tyler squeezing my ass while we played tonsil hockey and yanked off all of our clothes.

He moaned sort of like Brianna when he came too, now that I think about it.

And now I need a shower before my shift, which sucks, because *the sex wasn't all that great*, but here I am, getting hot and bothered at the memory.

Maybe if we hadn't been in a thirty-five-degree fridge?

No, it's probably more that Tyler's ego is bigger than his skill. I *know* that's a thing.

Brianna points at me with her half-eaten fish stick. "Wait. We were talking about you being single."

"Right. I'm that friend who'll tell you to go to the doctor but refuse to do it for myself. It's easier to have clarity for other people, and I *like* making other people happy, so I'm okay with being single, and it doesn't interfere with my ability to help you. If anything, it makes me more objective about the men I screen for you since I have no interest in them myself."

Which is good, especially considering how I'm meeting men to screen these days.

She's still frowning while she takes another bite of fish. "Oh my god, this is *so good*. I would date this fish. I would take this fish to bed. Have you tried this? Here. Have a—no, you know what? I'll give you ten bucks to get your own."

"That's okay." I wave her off as she reaches for the wallet in her back pocket. "I can afford my own fish, I promise. And I'm going to find you a man who makes you moan as much as that fried cod does."

Her eyes go round. "Oh, shit. We're in public, aren't we?"

"Don't worry. I've seen worse here."

"Muffy! Dude! You're here early too." D'Angelo swings through the door and stops at our table, holds out a fist, and we do our usual bump-slap-shake routine, which we both miss at least one step of, and we end up staring at each other for a split second before cracking up.

We are such dorks.

I hope that doesn't turn Brianna off.

Probably not, considering she's looking at him like she was looking at her fish a minute ago. A piece of cod dribbles out from between her lips. I make a quick *wipe your mouth* gesture, and she jerks to grab her napkin, bumps the table wrong, and spills her Coke all over both of us. "Oh, shit."

"I gotcha." D'Angelo leaps into action, grabbing a leftover stack of napkins on the next table and helping me attack the mess with the fervor of a guy who doesn't want to mop the floor twice in one night.

"Sorry," Brianna stutters. "Sorry. I—you're gorgeous."

His brown eyes glow with the kind of warmth that makes him one of my favorite people. "Aw, not next to you. You okay? Didn't get any on you, did you?"

She shakes her head.

"D'Angelo, this is my friend, Brianna." I smile at both of them.

Brianna gapes.

"Hey, Brianna. Nice to meet you." D'Angelo smiles back, and I congratulate myself on my instincts.

Brianna needs the kind of guy who's a little protective, a lot of good humor, and a dash of hard work, and D'Angelo has been bemoaning his lack of courage to talk to girls lately.

They'll become friends, realize they like each other as more, and *boom*.

It'll be my first all-organic match, no side scheming required.

He tilts his head at a stunning woman behind him. "And this is Willa, my girlfriend."

Girlfriend?

Girlfriend?

Since when does he have a girlfriend?

"We hooked up last night," he adds in a whisper to me.

Oh, fuuuuuuuck.

Muff Matchers fails.

Again.

I'll find a guy for Brianna.

I will.

My bad for thinking this time might be easier.

Tyler

IN THE THREE days since I told Muffy I'd be her date to this thing, I've almost backed out twice an hour, but my dick is still playing dead, and Nick cornered me after the game last night and told me Kami doesn't have details, but some shit happened to Muffy to make her leave medical school, and if I do anything to make her life difficult today, I'll wish getting an atomic wedgie on my way to a swirly of death was the worst thing looming in my future.

So here I am, pulling up to a two-story house with faded siding and patchy dead rose bushes in need of pruning in an older neighborhood in Copper Valley, hoping Muffy comes running out so I don't have to talk to Aunt Spanky-Spanky— ah, I mean Muffy's mom, who has an unfortunate self-given nickname in the locker room—before I play the gallant gentleman who saves the woman who faked it the one time we hooked up.

Yeah.

I want karma points for my dick.

My overnight bag is in the trunk. Coach let me out of practice tomorrow after making me do extra sprints and shooting practice today and promise I'll be there for every charity event he wants me to do in the next month. I'm in a suit, as requested, since we're apparently going to a pre-ceremony reception tonight basically as soon as we check in, and I'm ignoring the bruise on my side from a puck that snuck between my pads at the game last night.

The front door opens as I'm stepping out of my car, and —*shit*.

It's Muffy's mother.

I scramble for my phone, put it to my ear, and make the *one minute* gesture.

My phone screams out an old Bro Code song in my ear, and I drop the damn thing.

Jesus.

Do all my sisters have to have awful timing? I fumble with it again, drop it twice, and then send the call to voicemail.

Staci can wait.

Also, for the record, I don't usually listen to boy band songs. It's simply an appropriate ringtone for my sister.

Muffy's mother is marching down the steps.

Shit again.

I give up pretending I'm on the phone, retrieve it from the asphalt, and stand back up to look at her over the roof of my car.

Best to leave the beast between us. "Morning, Ms. Periwinkle. Muffy ready?"

She's in knee-high leopard-print boots, baggy black leggings, and a ruffly orange blouse that she's belted at her waist. She's making pouty lips as she reaches my car and strokes the hood of my red Maserati GT convertible. "My, my, you're certainly taking Muffy out in style today, aren't you?"

"I—yeah."

My phone dings six times in rapid succession, which

means my sisters have re-activated our group chat text. The call from Staci—who doesn't usually participate in the group texts—probably means I'm on a gossip page somewhere.

Awesome.

And by *awesome*, I don't actually mean *awesome*.

"Ooh, it's a four-seater." She peers in the window. "I could come along."

The last time I was around Hilda Periwinkle, she asked if she could get a selfie with me licking her face so her online friends would know that she wasn't lying when she told them that she got busy with half the Thrusters in the off-season.

And I didn't know if she was joking or not.

I do know that hanging out with Hilda Periwinkle will not improve my broken dick situation. And neither will any of the text messages continuing to blow up my phone. "Is Muffy ready?"

"She's still in the shower. Why don't you come on in? I did a boudoir shoot with my dear friend Aubrey Innsbruck, and I got the proofs this week. You could help me decide which one you like the best?"

You have to admire her confidence.

But I still don't want to see anyone's boudoir photos. Not Hilda's. Not any of my sisters'. Not my mother's.

Again with the *not helping the broken dick* situation.

"I—I'm sorry, Ms. Periwinkle." I wave my phone at her in the crisp morning air. "Family situation. I need to check these—"

"Mom, leave him alone."

I can't see Muffy, but I can hear her. She's—oh.

There she is.

Window. Second floor. Peering through a screen.

"I don't like you going off on overnight dates with men I don't know," Hilda calls back.

"You asked if he'd show you his *pee-pee* at Kami's wedding last year. You should be more worried that I'm going on an overnight date with a man who knows you. He might not bring me back."

Hilda gasps.

"I'll be down in a minute, Tyler. Please ignore every syllable that comes out of her mouth, and *do not* agree to see her new pictures."

"I have them on my phone." Hilda circles the hood while I pretend I'm not backing away to circle my trunk and keep the car between us. "You've heard of Aubrey Innsbruck, haven't you? He's renowned in art circles for his creative interpretations of the human body."

I don't know what that means, and I don't want to either. "My sister's twins are having tonsillectomies today and I really need to check in and see how they're doing."

"*Both* twins?"

"Yep." No. Not at all. They had their tonsillectomies about three months apart in the spring. Also, I don't think doctors schedule tonsillectomies on Sundays. "They're identical."

They're fraternal.

And hilarious for being so small.

"I didn't see that on Daisy's social media."

There are a ton of upsides to having Daisy Carter-Kincaid as a sister-in-law.

This is not one of them. "There's a lot of stuff Daisy doesn't post about our family on her social media. We like our privacy."

Hilda winks. "*Some* of you do. I saw Daisy's boudoir photos from a few years back too. *Hoo*, mama. I'm lifting my weights so I can look that good."

For the record, I don't look at Daisy's old boudoir photos either. My brother might have over a decade on me and be a retired Marine, but that doesn't mean he's gone soft.

Far from it.

Looking at his wife naked or nearly so?

Bad idea.

Bad, bad idea.

No matter when the pictures were taken.

The front door flies open. "Mom, Rufus is in your closet."

Hilda shrieks. *"Why did you let him in there?"*

"I didn't! You left it open!"

Hilda darts for the porch.

As soon as she disappears inside, Muffy's shoulders droop and she squeezes her eyes shut, but only for a minute before she pastes on a smile and walks the short distance to my car.

I eyeball her as I take her small suitcase and fling it into the trunk. She's in a black dress that lands just below her knees, a fluffy light blue coat on top of it, with her hair back and makeup on and her bag slung across her body again, and it strikes me once again that Muffy's one of those unique women who manages to be steal-your-breath pretty in unexpected ways.

Which still isn't making my dick do anything other than sit in my pants like he's having a drink-beer-and-watch-ESPN-while-lounging-on-the-couch kind of day. "Is your cat really in your mom's closet?"

"No. He's trying to eat the fake goldfish on the aquarium channel in the living room. Get in the car. We need to go before she tries to come along."

She doesn't have to tell me twice.

She doesn't wait for me to get her door either, so I dive into the driver's seat in time for her to swing her purse into the backseat, miss, and smack me in the face with it instead.

"Ow!"

"Oh, *shit!* Fuck! Shit! Oh my god, I'm so sorry! Are you okay? Did I get you in the eye? Can you drive? Can you see? Did I knock out a fake tooth?"

I open my jaw wide to stretch my nose while my eyes water. "Had worse. What the hell do you keep in that thing?"

"Chocolate and brass knuckles."

"Brass knuckles?"

66

"No. But I do have like seventeen dollars in change in case we hit toll roads, plus my favorite candle that I give out to all of my clients when they sign up for Muff Matchers. Oh, crap. I'm sweating. Do I smell like fish? I swear I smell like fish when I sweat these days. Do I need to drive? Seriously, not to be pushy after I assaulted your face, but my mom will be back out as soon as she realizes Rufus isn't harking up hairballs on her fur boots, and I really don't want her coming with us today. I, erm, don't have enough hotel rooms for that. Actually, the entire city of Richmond doesn't have enough hotel rooms for that."

My phone dings a bunch again.

I blink to clear the last of the sting, crank the engine, toss my phone in the cup holder, and glance at her again.

On second peek, she doesn't actually look like Muffy.

She looks like a professional, dolled-up version of Muffy who might start talking about the stock market or the abstract meaning behind a literary fiction novel or offer to take my coat and show me to a special waiting room?

I glance down at my dick.

He doesn't seem to realize that's a fantasy about getting a blow job before a business meeting.

Also, *a fantasy about a business meeting*? I don't do business meetings.

Even for blow jobs.

And Muffy isn't making innuendoes either. Plus, she's right. We don't need her mother tagging along.

"What was it like growing up with her as your mother?" I ask as I peel away from the curb, now with my phone hooked up to my stereo system, which is announcing every text message from my family.

"Normal? Do you ever really know any different than what you grow up with? My friends were all embarrassed by their parents too, so it's not like I realized her lack of filters are different from other people's lack of filters. Do you always get this many text messages? Holy crap. Your phone hasn't stopped with the notifications since I got in the car."

"Thirty seconds ago."

"At least a minute. I *know* that's not normal. Is there an emergency or something?" She grabs my phone out of the cupholder as it dings three more times with my car stereo unable to announce who's texting before another incoming text arrives.

"It's normal."

"This many messages is normal?"

"Yep." Only sometimes. Like when the twins were both having tonsillectomies basically one after another. Or when we found out Brit was having twins. And when West accidentally co-inherited a baby with Daisy last year. And when my dad was in the hospital for kidney stones while Mom was on an East Coast tour and I had to take him to the hospital and Mom wanted updates of the funny stuff to use in her show, and so my sisters started making shit up.

Muffy holds my phone to my face.

"I can't look when I'm driving. It's fine. It can wait."

"Just needed your pretty mug to unlock it with facial recognition. Holy crap. Are these bunnies? Do you have a group text with bunnies?"

I snatch the phone out of her hand, because I *do* have a group text with Athena and Cassadee, who are giving me unwanted but probably necessary advice.

Yes, I told them I was going out of town with a woman I was interested in.

No, they didn't have any advice I plan to take.

"They're my sisters," I tell Muffy, "and whatever it is they're up to, neither of us need to know. If it's an actual problem, my brother will—"

"*Incoming call from Westley Snore-Man Jaeger,*" my car system announces.

Fuck.

If there's an actual problem, my brother will call. And there he is, right on time.

I hit the button on my steering wheel to answer. "Not alone, West. What's up?"

My brother's voice comes over the line. "Javi had a vasectomy Friday and ended up in the ER overnight with complications."

Muffy stifles a cough, but when I glance at her, she looks more horrified than amused.

"He's fine now," West adds. "Staci's leading the charge on the broken balls jokes. But I thought you'd want to know. Plus, someone's starting a pool on how long before you and I get fixed."

"Did I mention I'm *not alone*?" Talking to West about my brother-in-law's vasectomy complications in front of Muffy is exactly what I want to do this morning.

Jesus.

She'll think all of us have broken dicks.

The bastard chuckles. "Hello, Tyler's friend."

"Ty's with a friend?" Daisy's voice carries through in the background as Muffy says a tentative hi back. "Like a woman-friend? Or do I need to set him up with—"

"I'm hanging up on both of you now," I announce.

"Mom's taking donations for a care package," West says.

He audibly stops himself like he's realized what he just said.

I pinch my lips together.

Muffy snorts. "He said *package*," she whispers.

West coughs. "We take care of all of the packages in need in this family."

Jesus. Thank fuck he doesn't know what's up—or not—with my equipment. "Goodbye, Westley."

"Send Mom money, crankypants."

"Is there actually a point to that?" Considering Daisy's net worth and how much she loves to do random acts of kindness, I suspect Javi's balls are in good hands.

Figuratively speaking.

"Daisy's forbidden from contributing. So, yes," West replies.

"I'm doing my own thing," Daisy calls.

"Do I want to know?" I ask my brother.

"Don't ever have complications from a vasectomy," he replies.

I kill the call, then hit the power button on my phone as I steer us out of the neighborhood.

Muffy and I both don't say anything for an entire block.

I don't know what she's thinking, but I know what I'm thinking.

If my sisters find out my dick doesn't work, they're gonna send it a damn *care package*. And I don't think I want to know what would be in it.

Nor do I want to know what extra-special thing my creative, rich, no-filters sister-in-law would do separately.

"Who's Javi?" she finally asks.

"Brother-in-law."

"Is he—"

"If he wasn't going to be okay, West would've said so. He's Mr. Responsible. All-business. All the time." Probably *not* all the time, though, now that he's married to Miami's biggest ray of partying sunshine. She has a *ball pit room* in her mansion. With trampolines.

I glance at my crotch.

Still no movement. Normal, though. My brother's sex life doesn't usually do it for me.

It'd be nice to fantasize about my own sex life and get a boner though. I'd take that.

Muffy shifts in her seat and looks at me. "So, yeah, my childhood was pretty normal."

I cut a glance at her.

She grins.

And I cede the point.

Given all the things I've heard my sisters say at the dinner table over the years, I have no room to judge Hilda. If my childhood was normal, then so was Muffy's.

Also, Muffy grinning?

Fucking adorable.

This is going to be a good trip. It'll fix me. Everything will be absolutely fine when we get back to Copper Valley tomorrow afternoon.

I can feel it.

9

Muffy

THERE'S nothing like being trapped in a car for three hours with a man who doesn't know the full story of where we're going or why to make a woman get the nervous sweats. Especially when our date has already started with me smacking him in the face with my handbag and a discussion of his brother-in-law's vasectomy issues after my mother most likely offered to show him pictures of herself nearly naked.

I keep telling her that it's basically harassment, but she's lacking the critical pieces of her brain to understand that not everyone is as open with bodies as she feels the need to be these days.

I'm peeling out of my coat before we've left the Copper Valley metro area. "Nice game last night."

Tyler grunts.

We haven't been alone really since the walk-in fridge hook-up thing—not if you don't count the cows and dogs as company the other day at Kami's—and we've only seen each other maybe three or four times since then, with two of those times being in the last week, and the other time or two being super awkward with me spending half the time avoiding looking at him and the other half of the time wondering why he was avoiding looking at me.

There's some perspective that comes with knowing each of us expected the other to make the next move after our time in the veggie locker.

I should tell him what he's in for today.

And thank him.

And not question why he's doing this, or why I agreed to let him. I tried to visualize myself going alone, and in the end, I couldn't do it. Every time I thought about seeing *him*, my confident visualizations would fade into the dust and my eyes would fly open while I breathed through a simulated panic attack.

Possibly I should've faced all of this a long time ago.

Or I should be faking Montezuma's revenge or something right now.

I shift in my seat again. "Thanks for coming with me. I... used to go to college in Richmond, and leaving was...difficult."

"Medical school, right?"

"Oh. Kami told you."

"Why'd you leave?"

"Flunked out."

He makes one of those faces guys make when they're annoyed, or when I used to ask if they'd like to be on my prospect list for Muff Matchers.

I don't ask anymore. My pool stays wider when they haven't specifically said no.

"No, you didn't," Tyler says.

"How do you know?"

"You're too smart to have flunked out."

"That was a few years ago, and also, medical school is

hard. Maybe I didn't do well under the pressure. Maybe I don't test well. Maybe—"

"Did you actually flunk out?"

"Better question—how fast does your car go? And can I eat road trip snacks in here, or are you the type who doesn't want to get your interior dirty?"

A wicked grin flashes over his handsome face. "You can get my interior as dirty as you want."

That was *not* supposed to make my belly drop like I'm on a roller coaster.

Accept that we had a misunderstanding post fridge sex? Yes.

Sign up to do it again, since clearly we communicate so well? No. "Good, because I have powdered Donettes in here." I reach into the backseat for my bag, which is like a *Mary Poppins* bag. More fits in than you'd expect.

Tyler flinches.

"I swear I won't hit you in the face again. Or do you really not want powdered sugar all over your seat?"

"How often do you hit people in the face with your purse? Is that actually why you left medical school?"

"Yes. I was at the movies. It was dark. I went to the bathroom in the middle of the show, and when I got back to my row and tried to get back to my seat, I tripped and smacked the university president in the mouth with my purse. He expelled me because I gave him a bloody nose."

He takes a hard left to get on the interstate ramp, and I grab the *oh, shit* handle to keep from falling on top of him, which is awkward since I'm still half in the backseat, reaching for my purse on the floor, which is also making my boob rub his arm.

Oh, god. Solid hockey arms. You wouldn't think it would require that much muscle to lift a hockey stick—they're not *that* heavy—but Tyler's arm is hot steel against my squishy boob, and also, I probably need to go up a bra size, since my breast is threatening to pop out.

"Sorry," I stammer. "Donette?"

"I don't eat sugar during the season."

Right. Of course not. I get to be the lumpy one, and he gets to be the fit hockey jock with buns of steel. "Thank goodness fish and chips are okay."

Another flinchy face. "Yep."

Ooh. A mystery.

Good.

I'll wait to tell him we're going to a funeral until we hit Richmond. "You *don't* usually eat fried foods during the season."

"A guy's allowed a cheat day."

"You were in a bad mood. What happened?"

"Nothing."

Total mystery. Something happened. "Did you have another group text with your sisters?"

"No."

"Oooh. You were at Duncan's house for the after-party, weren't you? Did something happen there?"

His brows do that thing that tells me he has no idea what I'm talking about. "How do you know about Lavoie's party?"

Better question—where was he that he doesn't know that Duncan had a party? "Kami told me. What happened? Did you find out he uses your face on his dartboard? Did Rooster steal your phone and send inappropriate suggestions to your sisters? Did you fall asleep and wake up with shaving cream in your ears? Did you proposition a bunny and she turned you down?"

"Yep."

"You weren't actually at Duncan's party, were you? *Oh my god*. You weren't invited."

"Are you going to talk this much the whole drive?"

"You keep telling me you have four sisters. You're not

used to this?" I can't believe he wasn't invited. Maybe it wasn't a party. Maybe it was what the players with kids and wives *call* a party, but it's really them sitting around talking about what it's like being in their thirties with responsibilities.

I could see not inviting Tyler to that kind of party, but Kami loving it. She *did* say Ares and Manning and their wives and kids were there too.

Tyler answers my question about his sisters by cranking the stereo, gripping the wheel with both hands until his knuckles turn white, and staring at the road straight ahead.

And I go silent, wondering if he was actually at that secret club that Maren took me to the night Tyler and I hooked up.

I say *secret club* like I don't know it's the bunny bar, because I don't like to think about Tyler at the bunny bar. If I had a lot more confidence and a smaller butt and no hang-ups about sex, I'd like to think I'd fit right in with the bunnies.

I *love* the bunnies. They're smart and kind and killer businesswomen, putting their sisterhood ahead of even the hockey players they claim to love. It's weird to me that they know their friends might also sleep with the same players they sometimes sleep with, but it's also kind of a thrill to think about being so utterly free and open about sex being a fun adult activity. There's no stigma to it. No name-calling. No backstabbing.

If one of them *does* get serious with a player, they all talk about it, and everyone knows that player's off-limits. If a player gets too clingy to one of them and makes them uncomfortable, they kick him out.

It's like the best kind of power. No one's putting them down. No one's putting them in a corner. They're stronger because they're together.

They're living life on *their* terms.

Whereas I can't even tell Tyler why I want a date.

Or what the date actually is.

So instead, I settle deeper into my seat and pull out my

phone and work on scheduling out a week's worth of motivational and supportive emails to my clients, plus do a little pre-screening of potential matches for them, pausing occasionally to look out the window.

I like the drive to Richmond. Lots of pine trees to keep things green even when the rest of the trees have lost their leaves.

But I also don't like the drive to Richmond, because I know what's waiting for me there.

Haunting old memories.

Some good memories too. I had friends. I liked my classes. We had our favorite bars and restaurants.

But it all ended with one terrible idea with an even worse outcome.

That seems to be the story of my life, though I still have hope that Muff Matchers is on the right path.

Once I've finished my work, I make it through two songs and half a dozen Donettes before I reach over and turn the volume down. "What's the most embarrassing thing that's ever happened to you?"

He slides a look at me that lingers longer than it probably should, given that he's flying down the interstate at ten miles over the speed limit. "Hold on. Let me dig deep into my buried memories to relive something painful since you asked completely out of the blue."

Sarcasm seriously makes him so hot. So does that flat, blue-eyed glare. And the beard. I am completely digging the beard.

Not that I'll be telling him that.

I probably shouldn't poke at the bear, considering he's doing me a huge favor.

And considering he's doing me a huge favor despite me telling him sex with him wasn't all that great.

I should probably also tell him I thought he ghosted me instead of me taking all the credit for doing the ghosting, but

77

it's easier to make him not like me than it is to admit he hurt me. "I just...I remember getting embarrassed over this little thing once when I was in medical school. That's all."

His eyes shift again, and it's like I'm looking at Tyler Jaeger, number ninety-one on the Thrusters, in his zone on the ice, ready to kick ass and take names.

I want to take my coat off, but I already have, which means I can fan myself and let him see he's affecting me, or I can pretend I'm not sitting here breaking into a sweat and ignoring the way my body's tingling again despite all the ways I was disappointed the last time we were close and friendly.

"Someone embarrassed you?" The words come out rough and annoyed, and I don't know if he's annoyed because he doesn't think I can handle being on the receiving end of a joke, or if he's annoyed that I'm talking when he wants to listen to music, or if he's annoyed that someone embarrassed me.

Considering our discussion the other day was plenty embarrassing for both of us, it's probably some combination of not wanting to talk and not really caring if I've ever been embarrassed.

Everyone's been embarrassed. It's not like my embarrassment is special or more embarrassing than anyone else's, except for the part where my most embarrassing moment could've gotten me on the kind of daytime talk show that gets ratings for catfights and unexpected paternity test results.

"Never mind." I reach back into the bag of Donettes.

"Does your friend know you got embarrassed?"

"Which friend?"

"The friend with a thing? The friend who's the reason we're going today?"

"Oh. Veda. Right. Yeah. We were tight. Like, if we'd been on a hockey team together, we would've been Ares Berger and Manning Frey tight. If we were candy, we'd be toffee and chocolate. We used to study together in this back corner of the library and we called it *the hole*. We'd meet there before big finals or whatever, when we really needed to concentrate and study, and no one ever wanted to go along to a place called *the hole*, so we had it all to ourselves, especially after we put the sign on the door labeling it as *the hole*. She'd tell me about who she was dating, and I'd tell her about which new Ben & Jerry's flavor I tried after I stayed up late studying on Saturday nights."

I wasn't a great student, even if I *am* excellent at deflecting questions.

I wasn't a *bad* student, but I wasn't at the top of my class either. See also: I didn't get hired for a residency and wasn't sure what I was going to do after that final year.

But I believed if I made it through medical school, I really could help people. That it's not all about *you heal a broken bone by setting it*, but also about *why were you doing what you were doing to break your bone and what can we do to help anything else that might be wrong?*

I wanted to be the doctor who listened.

The one who got to know her patients.

The one who knew it wasn't only a broken arm or a bad kidney sitting on my table, but someone with a story.

"What's this thing for Veda today?" Tyler asks.

"It's a, erm, celebration of accomplishments. With a big… reception…before the ceremony."

I get another *what the fuck is wrong with you?* look.

Legit.

I'm lying to the man about the fact that we're on the way to a funeral, because I'm still afraid he'll bail if I tell him the truth, and I'm not doing a very good job of it. Even I don't believe me.

I mean, I wouldn't if I didn't already know I was glossing over the most important details.

So I do what any rational person in my position would do.

I shove two powdered sugar Donettes in my mouth at once, which makes one of them stick like glue to the top of my mouth.

I can't answer a question if I'm giving myself a headache by trying to pry a donut off the roof of my mouth with my tongue.

Tyler slides me another look.

He sighs the same way I've heard people sigh when encountering me and my mother our entire lives.

And then he cranks the radio up again.

Probably for the best.

Also?

I'm pretty sure I owe him big time.

10

Tyler

WE'RE two hours down the road and my dick and I are still debating what to say to Muffy about me leaving her unsatisfied at that party.

I don't want to *talk* about it.

I want a chance to do it better. But he's not cooperating. And the idea of staying overnight in a hotel with her isn't helping. Especially when she's made it clear she reserved two rooms.

You and your broken dick are not welcome to play in my garden is the message, loud and clear.

"Restroom!" she suddenly exclaims, pointing to a sign on the road as she snaps her head up from her phone, which she's been working on nonstop since not telling me why she has to go to Richmond.

"Seriously?" I mutter.

"Yes!"

There's a hint of desperation in the word that has me cutting a glance at her. "Are you sick?"

81

"No."

She's sweating and squeaking one-word answers.

"Okay. Okay. Restroom."

You don't grow up road-tripping to various cities where your mom's having a show without learning some people have bladders the size of a walnut. My dream used to be to go an entire six-hour road trip without stopping once.

Scratch Muffy off the list of people I could take with me.

But I also won't be the guy who refuses to stop. Not like I have plans she's keeping me from.

I pull off the interstate and pick a gas station. As soon as I stop at the pump, she darts out of the car and dashes for the shop, almost trips on her heels, straightens, and makes it inside.

If she's sick, we're turning around.

Oh, shit.

What if she's *carsick*?

Nope. No way. She was fine until five minutes ago. We even had a little debate between her playing on her phone and me dialing the radio sound back up about whether *Calvin & Hobbes* or *The Far Side* was the greatest comic strip ever written.

Oh.

Wait.

She ate an entire bag of Donettes and has been staring at her phone half the trip.

She might be carsick, but there's probably a reason for it.

"Hey, man, anyone ever tell you that you look like Tyler Jaeger?" a guy at the next pump says. Our cars are facing opposite directions, and I can see his back window, decorated with those stick figure families that tell you how many kids and dogs the guy has, except all of his stick figures are versions of Thrusty, my team's rocket-powered bratwurst mascot.

Nice.

Still, I shake my head, playing it low-key because these days, I never know if people recognize me as a hockey player or as Daisy Carter-Kincaid's most famous, most single in-law. Technically, my mom's more famous than I am, but she's not young, hot, and single.

Also, please note: Being Daisy's most famous in-law is akin to *I went viral on social media once for a TikTok video of myself admiring the shape of a fried egg while high*. Playing hockey isn't on the same continent as Daisy's level of fame. Possibly even in the same galaxy. "No. Who's that?"

"For real? Man, you look *just* like him."

"Must be a pretty great dude."

"Not really. Hockey player. Fourth line material, you know? He's no Duncan Lavoie."

Ouch. "Don't follow it."

"Seriously? Wow. The resemblance is uncanny. Take my word for it. You could pretend to be him and charge people for selfies." He snort-chuckles. "Probably suit up for a game and do as good of a job too."

"I'll keep that in mind."

Muffy's not out when I finish topping off the car—another old habit I picked up from Mom's touring days when we almost ran out of gas a time or two—so I move it to a parking spot by the door and go inside looking for her. Not looking forward to busting into the women's room to check on her, but turns out, I don't have to.

She's in the candy aisle.

"That whole bag of Donettes wasn't enough?"

Her entire body goes visibly stiff before she turns a glacier-melting scowl on me. "*Some* of us stress eat, *okay*, Mr. Fish-and-chips?"

Did I stick my foot in my mouth? Because I feel like I definitely stuck my foot in my mouth. "Did you throw up?"

And now she's giving me the *are you a shapeshifting worm who digs up my flowers for fun?* look. "No."

83

"You looked sick."

"You look lovely today too, Tyler. Your beard really makes your neanderthal stick out." She snatches a pack of gummy bears off a hook and marches past me.

The guy who was at the next pump pauses at the end of the aisle, looks at me, then at Muffy, then back to me. "Holy hell. You *are* Tyler Jaeger. I didn't mean what I said about that fourth line thing. I—"

"Keep supporting the Thrusters, man." I clap him on the back and step past him to follow Muffy, who's snagging breath mints and two king-size candy bars from the racks under the checkout counter. "I got this."

"I can pay for my own junk food," she mutters.

This is exactly the problem, my dick tells me. *You're an idiot when it comes to Muffy.*

"Should've taken that shot in the second period last night," the cashier tells me.

"Shit happens."

Muffy pays for her stuff and marches out of the shop, with me trailing behind like a puppy. She stops short on the sidewalk outside, squints at the pump I used to fill up the Maserati, spots my car to her left, and keeps marching.

It's on the chilly side today—thank you, November weather—and she didn't put her coat back on after wiggling out of it back in Copper Valley, so I have a very clear view of her curvy ass hugged tight in that black dress.

Anything? I ask my dick.

She's just not into us, he replies with a yawn.

And that's why I'm here. To fix it. Figure out where I went wrong, what I can do better, and get back out there. So I climb into my car and start the engine while Muffy sits there clutching her bag of snacks.

"Thank you for coming with me," she says stiffly.

"What friends do," I grunt back.

Friends.

I'm friend-zoning myself.

And the weird thing?

Of all the women I've fooled around with, I probably like Muffy most. She's funny. She's unpredictable. She's creative.

So are most of the women I hook up with, if I'm being honest.

But there's something about Muffy that's different too. In a good way. Fresh. Unexpected. Always something of a puzzle, which is basically irresistible to me. She has this air about her that says *I care about people and want them to be happy, but I won't let you close because you are not yet to be trusted.*

Somehow, I don't think leaving her unsatisfied at the bunny bar is scoring me points on that last bit.

The weird part is how much I care, and not because my dick has been broken ever since.

Fine.

Fine.

We were friends. She's a woman. I'm a man. And we were friends.

We settle into silence, her clutching her candy but not eating it while she goes back to working on her phone, me driving and pretending I'm listening to the radio, and we hop back on the interstate.

By the time we roll into Richmond, neither of us has said three more words to each other.

But now that she's looking away from whatever she was doing on her phone, taking in the scenery around us, her face is pasty and sweaty again, and I don't know if it's from all those Donettes that I would've given my left leg to eat with her, if it's because staring at her phone makes her nauseous in the car, or if it's because of whatever happened the last time she was here.

Or maybe she's coming down with an actual bug.

"Take the next left." She's squeaking like a mouse as she studies the map on her phone, which I can see now.

Off. Off. Off. Off. Off.

She was hiding the phone from me until we hit the outskirts of Richmond, which makes me wonder if she was playing *Candy Crush* and didn't want me to know, or if she was working on top secret Muff Matchers business.

"How much further?" I ask.

"Six blocks."

Six blocks?

I don't see anything university-ish anywhere. I thought we'd be near the campus.

Maybe it's in six blocks.

Or the hotel is.

And maybe I've had three hours in the car with her to ask her what I could've done better when we hooked up, and I've been a complete and total chicken shit.

That's the whole reason I'm here.

To find out what Mr. Disappointment in my jockey shorts and I need to do better so we can function as one again, but instead, I've managed to offend her over her choice of road trip food and she's basically refusing to speak to me.

We hit a stoplight three blocks down the street.

Muffy's breathing so heavily that the windows are fogging up.

That's not normal. "What the fuck happened the last time you were here?"

"Nothing."

She's lying. "Muffy—"

"I have to tell you something."

"Look, if you just got one hotel room, I don't care."

"No, that's not—"

A horn honks behind us, cutting her off. Light's green. I lift a middle finger to the honker and take my time hitting the gas. "What happened?" I repeat.

She looks down at her lap and scrubs hard at the white spots on her black dress, left over from her Donette binge. "I really don't think anyone's going to say anything about it, but if you hear weird stuff—well, one, remember it's me, and two, sometimes people exaggerate, and three, if you could do that thing where you glare at someone like you're planning on gnawing their leg bone for dessert, that would be great, and I'll owe you free services at Muff Matchers, okay?"

"I don't want free services from Muff Matchers."

"Right."

Fuck. Again. "I didn't mean—"

"No, it's okay. I'm a terrible matchmaker. I know. I *am* getting better, but I get it. You need to see a track record longer than three matches to believe it. Well, four, but I don't like to count the first one because it was so easy and they basically did it themselves."

"Muffy—"

"You can find a parking spot anytime now. We're close enough."

"The hotel doesn't have a parking lot?"

"We're...not going to the hotel first. No time. The reception...thing is starting."

I pinch my lips together and remind myself I volunteered for this. What difference does it make if we go to the hotel first?

None.

If I were planning to camp out on the bed and binge watch *SpongeBob SquarePants*, which is *always* showing on hotel TVs, I would've stayed home.

I'm not wiggling out of whatever it is I promised Muffy I'd come here for just because I haven't gotten up the nerve to ask her if she can have a talk with my dick and promise it that it's still worthy of performing.

Street parking is full, and I don't see any parking garages or parking lots immediately. We get stopped at another light where a dozen people all wearing black are waiting to cross the street. "What's this reception for again?"

She crinkles the bag in her lap. "Veda and her family and this...thing."

Two people dressed in all black walk past my car.

Four more people in all black are strolling down the sidewalk across the street.

There's a funeral home two buildings behind us.

My heart doubles down and I get a tinny taste in my mouth. "Oh, fuck, no."

Weddings and funerals.

Weddings and funerals are the *only* two things you have to be at to support a friend.

And maybe baptisms or bachelor parties, but Muffy's definitely not taking me to a bachelor party. And there's no way we're here for a wedding.

We'd have a gift.

Even if it was a second-hand gift from Hilda, which is a terrifying thought.

"You're taking me to a *funeral*?" I spit out.

"I didn't think anyone would come with me if they knew why I was really here. And if you don't want to go in, that's fine. I'll—I'll go in by myself. I'll man up, okay? I'll get over myself and everything that's put me into therapy for the past four years. Maybe I'll find a few new clients."

The car is too small. The car's too small, and my shirt's too tight, and the tinny taste in my mouth is turning to cotton. I try to swallow while I find my tongue. "Your friend *died*?"

"No! No. Veda didn't die. Her dad did. And this really is a celebration. She only went to med school because he made her because he's—he *was* the dean, and he wasn't a very good father. So she's free of him now, and she can do whatever she wants without judgment, but she still has to get through everyone telling her what an awesome person he was, plus, he was her dad, so there are complicated feelings. Listen, if there's one thing I know, it's shitty fathers, and one day, I'm gonna be asking Veda to do this exact same thing for me. If

88

this were anywhere else but *right here* in Richmond with all
the people I used to know at Blackwell, I'd be all over it solo.
But it's here, and—Tyler? Are you okay?"

A funeral.

She's dragging me to a damn *funeral.*

Nope.

I am not okay.

11

Muffy

SO THIS IS GOING WELL.

I have a date who judges me for eating sugar and who looks like he might hyperventilate. The line to get into the funeral home for the viewing is six thousand people long. And I've already spotted three former classmates.

Part of me wants to squeal, hug them, and ask how they're doing, where they're working, and what's new, because I did like most of my classmates back in the day. Or at least, I didn't *dislike* them. I just didn't know them as well as I knew Veda.

I liked them enough to want to ask how they're doing. That says something.

But I can't.

I'm *that* failure.

And being here is making my pulse race and my mouth dry and it's like I can see the auras of everyone who ever believed in me when I decided to go to med school, and they're all telling me what a horrible disappointment I am.

I push it all away and look at Tyler again.

I'm wearing a hat with a black veil that my mom had in her closet, and so far, I don't think anyone's recognized me, but if he passes out, people are going to notice, and then they'll want to know why I'm wearing a funeral hat when no one else is, and it'll be obvious I'm super uncomfortable, and while I don't think anyone actually thinks about me, ever, I can't stand the thought that I'll be whispered about once again.

Or, worse, that *he'll* be here, and someone will point me out to him, or someone will point him out to me.

Not that *anyone* should know *who* he is.

At least, I hope not. I didn't even tell Veda. Ever. She still doesn't know, which means no one should know.

Still, it's a lot.

Possibly too much.

"It's fine if you want to go back and wait in the car," I murmur to Tyler, even though the words make adrenaline spike so hard that I get a pounding in my temple that makes me wonder if I should see a doctor about a stroke.

Lucky me. I'm surrounded by them.

"You're not going in there alone," he mutters back.

He doesn't even know *why* I don't want to be alone, but he's sticking with me. Two points to Tyler.

I forgive him for being judgmental about what I eat. And after growing up with a dad who'd constantly ask if I went up *another* size and a mom always dieting until she had gastric bypass surgery a few years ago and lives for that moment she steps on the scale every morning to see that it's still working, yeah, I'm sensitive about what I eat.

Also, eating an entire bag of Donettes probably wasn't my wisest decision on a road trip.

My stomach *does* actually hurt from that too right now. Not that that's why I made Tyler stop for the bathroom.

I made him stop because I had a mini-panic attack at getting so close to here.

Definitely should *not* do that again.

I reach for his hand and squeeze it, and a jolt travels up my arm and pings from my shoulder through my abdomen like it's a pinball machine. "Thank you."

He squeezes my hand back. "You don't even want to know what you're gonna owe me."

Sex. He's going to demand repayment in sex.

And now I'm going to puke.

I really am.

Possibly because had I not eaten an entire bag of Donettes, and if we left the lights off, I'd be willing to try sex with him again tonight.

Maybe.

Is it appropriate to have sex while on an overnight trip for a funeral?

"Are you okay?" he murmurs.

"Peachy."

"Liar."

"It's a viewing for my friend's father. Of course it's uncomfortable. But we'll get through it, and it'll be fine."

"This is ridiculous. We're both getting out of here." He tugs on my arm, but I tug right back.

Do *not* underestimate a woman with birthing hips, which is what my mother called them after my father started making comments about the time I hit puberty. It lowers my center of gravity and makes it harder for muscular jocks to move me.

But apparently Donettes don't give me the right kind of energy, because Tyler's succeeding in tugging me when I *know* I should be able to resist.

"I have to be here for Veda," I hiss. "I promised."

"Then why are you meeting her *here*? Why didn't you meet her someplace before now? Why aren't we already inside?"

"I didn't know it would be so crowded."

"When's the last time you even saw this friend? I've never heard of her before."

"A month ago, for lunch, which we do regularly, and you haven't heard of her before because you and I aren't besties and I don't tell you everything."

He squeezes his eyes shut.

What is it about frustrated men in suits that makes my nipples perk up?

The line moves, and I shuffle with it.

Tyler shuffles with me.

"I thought you ghosted *me*," I whisper.

"What?"

"After that...thing...we did at that club. I thought *you* ghosted *me*. I know I said I did it to you, but...that wasn't my intention. Not at first. I thought you'd call me, but you didn't. I know you don't do relationships, but we were friends, Tyler. We were friends, and you didn't call."

He squeezes his eyes shut again and doesn't answer *again*.

So that either means bad timing with telling him, or it means he *did* ghost me.

Whatever.

It's not important.

What's important is being here for Veda.

I pull out my phone and send her a text letting her know I'm here. Then I nudge Tyler like I didn't just confess to being incredibly insecure.

Again.

"While we're waiting, you should check on your brother-in-law."

He mutters something to himself.

Pretty sure it's about how he should've known better. Or that if I'm involved, of course this will be a disaster.

"At least you don't have to worry about any of my relatives asking when we're getting married," I whisper.

"What about your friend?"

"She knows me too well to think you're anything other than a very kind person doing me a favor."

He stares me down.

I squirm.

I've seen Tyler Jaeger laugh. I've seen him smirk. I've seen him flirt. All of them with me, though the flirting, I'm positive, was merely a kindness and not an actual attraction, like the sex in the club's fridge was a thing to do that was easy and convenient, and it didn't mean anything.

But until this moment, I haven't actually understood why he's such a great hockey player.

Being on the receiving end of that intense, focused, no-nonsense glare is making me wish I were padded up for battle.

Or possibly in a different state.

This is even more intense than the glare he gave me in the car.

"Why are you friends with people who don't think you're attractive enough to bring a real date to a funeral?"

My phone buzzes. "Veda knows I don't date. It has nothing to do with being attractive."

He folds his arms over his chest. "You don't date, but you still spent time thinking *I* ghosted *you*? When every time we've ever seen each other, it was because *you* were on *my* turf? At the arena? Or at Chester Green's? Or Nick's house?"

"Nick's house is also Kami's house. And who keeps track of *turf*? That's ridiculous."

"And you never texted or called me either."

Clearly, we're both to blame, and this is why misunderstandings suck. One of us needs to say sorry, then maybe the other one will say it too.

Or maybe not.

I PUCKING LOVE YOU

"Oh, look. Veda's asking me to sneak her a margarita. *This* is why we're here. C'mon. Let's go find a liquor store."

I tug his elbow.

He grunt-sighs the long-suffering grunt-sigh of a man frustrated with a woman, but he doesn't argue, which is a relief.

Not a relief?

Running headfirst into someone cutting in line.

The scents of licorice and pipe smoke fill my nose. Wool scratches my cheek. Dread fills me from the feet up like someone's pouring concrete into my blood, and I freeze as my eyes connect with his.

His weathered face twists into annoyance. "Watch where you're—do I know—oh, fuck."

"*Gerry*," the woman with him snaps. "Language. We're at a *funeral*, for shit's sake."

I can't blink. I can't move. I can't even breathe.

I'm back in a dark hotel room, trapped, half-naked, waiting, like I promised I'd be, except it's not some rich douchebag from the football team coming to claim what he's paid for.

It's my middle-aged rheumatology professor.

My *married* middle-aged rheumatology professor.

"Excuse us," Dr. Richardson's wife says. "Eyeballs, Gerald. Straight ahead."

The wall of wool disappears. The scent fades. And the whispers start.

Or possibly they don't, but I feel like I'm this giant blob covered in boils that everyone's pointing at and trying to stay away from, lest my extreme discomfort cooties infect them too.

My ears are burning. My lungs are coiling themselves into a ball. My eyes are so hot they're melting. All the Donettes I ate threaten to make a reappearance.

And then a hand settles on my shoulder. "Muffy?"

Tyler's voice filters into my brain. I gasp.

Air. There's air, and I can breathe it, and it's fresh and clean and flowing into my lungs, and I'm fine.

I'm totally fine.

My feet feel like bugs are crawling inside them, my knees are lit firecrackers about to split into a million pieces, and my stomach is threatening to turn itself inside out, but I'm fine.

Or maybe I'm not fine.

Tyler wraps an arm more firmly around me. "C'mon. Liquor store. *Now*. Veda needs you."

He doesn't ask.

I don't offer.

He just gets me out of there, supporting me while I figure out how my legs work again.

But I know he *will* ask.

And I probably owe him an answer.

It's but a matter of time.

12

Tyler

You did this to yourself, idiot.

Rule number one of knowing Muffy Periwinkle: *Nothing* is ever exactly as it seems.

I let myself think I'd get a chance to be alone with her, work out whatever's wrong with my junk, and that everything would go back to normal after this trip.

Nope.

Because who needs a date to *a thing*?

Of fucking *course* this is a *funeral*. With a woman who thinks *I* ghosted *her*.

Jesus.

I hate funerals.

I hate funerals more than I hate losing, more than I hate all the complications that go with relationships, and more than I hate listening to my sisters talk about their cracked nipples and perineal tears at the dinner table, *combined*.

"Who was that guy you ran into?" I ask as we walk down an alley back toward the cave of doom, also known as the funeral home, laden with a few four-packs of single-serving margaritas and two new Yeti tumblers full of ice.

"Can we maybe focus on Veda right now?"

"No."

"Her father just died."

"And you nearly had a panic attack running into a random old guy on the street. Are you going to have more panic attacks when you see more people? What the hell happened the last time you were here, and what the hell kind of friend is this Veda person for wanting you to come back here?"

If anyone asks, I'm in full protective mode over Muffy, and this has nothing at all to do with the level to which I hate funerals.

I'm not trying to re-channel my energy.

That's my story. Don't challenge me. I know how to use a hockey stick.

"Do *not* talk crap about Veda. She's my hero."

"Does she fly?"

"She's the first person who's ever believed in me."

That gets my attention, and I cut a look at Muffy in time to see her eyes widen and her hand fly to her mouth. Either she didn't mean to say that out loud, or she's never realized it before.

Maybe both.

We stop outside the back door to the funeral home, facing a row of hearses, which makes my skin crawl. "Your parents don't believe in you?"

"My mom's a bit of a spotlight-stealer, in case you haven't noticed, and my father only thinks you're worthy if you're young, rich, skinny, and pretty, which is one thing my mom's never gotten over and is also one hundred percent the reason she had gastric bypass surgery a few years ago. She's *still* trying to stick it to him for leaving her." She pulls her phone out and texts someone.

Probably Veda, telling her we're at the back door to the funeral home.

I sincerely hope they don't have any bodies delivered while we're standing here.

And now I'm shuddering.

That's perfect. Exactly the image I want to project.

Scary hockey player terrified to be at funeral home.

I try to work up something to say about Muffy laying out all of her family's dysfunctions and psychological issues, but I can't.

Because I'm at a damn funeral home.

"Veda says to come on in and meet her in the first room to the right."

I can do this. It's like heading into a game. Objective is winning. Winning is delivering a margarita to the mourning.

Focus.

I can do this.

I tuck the two Yetis between my arm and my abs. My hand barely shakes when I reach for the door and turn the knob.

Do they do all the *things* to the bodies in this room we're going to?

Or do they have a secret basement?

How big of an elevator would you have to have to move gurneys and caskets between floors?

I'm gonna throw up. Shit. I am. I'm gonna hurl.

Muffy steps past me into the hallway, which is neither dim nor bright. It's neutral, like the light is trying to not impede on anyone's experience of being in a *funeral home*.

Pictures line the neutral-colored walls, but I don't look at them.

Logically, I know they won't be pictures of dead people —*Look at all of our satisfied customers!*—but illogically, my balls are sweating and my pulse is racing and I need something forty billion times stronger than a margarita.

I'm gonna need a horse tranquilizer.

Please.

Let me wake up tomorrow when all of this is over.

"First door on the right," Muffy murmurs to herself.

First door on the right. Don't look up. Don't look down. Don't focus. Follow Muffy. Don't concentrate. Don't breathe.

What the hell is that smell, anyway?

Is that flowers?

Dead flowers?

"Here." Muffy turns left, I follow, and *oh, fuck me*.

That's a body.

That's a dead body. Straight ahead. Laid out in an empty room.

With a dog.

There's a dead stuffed poodle, head cocked, staring straight at us, while sitting on the chest of a dead elderly woman in a pink glitter casket.

They're both dead.

Dead-dead.

Why do they have to elevate the bodies in the caskets so you can see all the deadness?

And why is this room empty? Why aren't there people in here?

Am I hallucinating?

Is that actually a dead lady?

Am I having a horrible dream?

Am I dead?

Is this how it all ends, with me trapped in a room with a dead body?

And is she *actually* dead?

And the dog too. If that dog moves—

It'll be Grandpa 2.0.

I am okay. That body is dead. Death is part of life. That person is not coming back to life.

I am okay.

That's not Grandpa.

"Tyler?"

Tyler? Tyler! Oh my god, Grandpa came back to life! How long have you been sitting here?

All I can see are my grandfather's eyes.

They took him off life support.

He died.

Everyone cried.

Everyone left.

I stayed.

And then *Grandpa came back to life.*

Fuck me.

I need to sit down, but hell if I'm sitting in this room.

Muffy's voice is tinny in my ears. "*Right.* I went left. Whoops. C'mon, Tyler, this way. Hey, Tyler? Oh my god, are you going to faint?"

I am *not* going to faint.

I'm not.

I'm a badass hockey terror. I don't faint.

But everything's going blurry at the edges of the room.

The dog's still staring at me, its head cocked and its tongue hanging out, but *still fucking dead.*

"Oh my god, that's seriously disturbing," Muffy says.

The casket jumps.

Swear to fuck, it does. It *jumps.* The dog jiggles. The body jiggles. I scream.

And then the world goes black.

13

Muffy

THERE COMES a point in every dreaded trip back to your college town for a funeral when you give up counting all the ways things are going wrong and start wondering when you should call a biographer or a Netflix studio executive and offer them your life story for a train wreck biopic.

Pretty sure we're there.

The funeral director was all kinds of nice while helping revive Tyler, and also *super* apologetic over accidentally backing into the casket while he was trying to get the lectern in place for that viewing for his other customer—customer? Patient? Whatever—to start later. Basically, either of us can have a funeral for free if we happen to die in Richmond now.

I got to drive Tyler's car from the funeral home to the hotel, and I'm pretty sure that's only a minor ding in the bumper from where I hit that concrete log thingie at the front of the parking spot at the hotel. What are those even called?

Whatever it is, it should really be two inches shorter.

Also, Tyler only twitched a little when my credit card was

declined when we checked in and he had to offer his instead
—no, I don't want to talk about it—but the twitch could've as
easily been because there was also no record of me booking
two rooms.

Only one.

And the rest of the hotel is full with—you guessed it.

Funeral guests.

So now, we're in a single hotel room with a double bed—
yes, a *double* bed, not a queen, not a king, but a lone *double*
bed—while he sits on the ugly green and brown comforter,
the top two buttons in his shirt undone to reveal the white
undershirt, sleeves rolled up to show off his tattoos, glowering at the fish and chips I got him from the local Cod Pieces
with my seventeen dollars' worth of coins on our way here.

Veda arrived not long after I texted her the room number,
and I'm attempting to not ogle Tyler while my best friend and
I huddle over the small round table smushed next to the bed,
sharing the margaritas.

She ditched the viewing after faking menstrual cramps
and is the brightest part of my evening.

Completely, one hundred percent worth running into Dr.
Richardson to be here for her right now.

"I am *so* glad you're here," she tells me again.

I hug her tight, loving the way she smells like cardamom
and cinnamon. "I'm so gladder *you're* here."

"No, you're not."

We make eye contact, and we both burst into snort-filled
laughter.

"To not being here!" She lifts the massive Yeti tumbler
Tyler bought at the liquor store, takes a long gulp, then passes
it to me.

The other one got left at the funeral home, because I didn't
realize it rolled away when he hit the floor.

Whoops.

"To not being here!" I echo.

Tyler gives both of us the death-eye, which is what I'm calling it every time he looks up from his fish and chips on the bed and glares at us for being happy in the midst of all of this.

Also, is it hot in here, or is it just him?

Probably just him. He *came to a funeral with me* despite clearly having issues with death, and he *definitely* knew what he was in for by the time we saw that casket.

That's sexier than all the orgasms in the world.

Possibly I have weird standards.

I hold out the Yeti to him. "Alcohol?"

"Not during the season," he mutters, like I didn't see him drinking at Manning Frey's annual Halloween party a few weeks ago when he didn't realize I was there since I was hiding inside a giant blow-up chicken costume, and he goes back to his fish.

Maybe it was juice or water?

Or maybe it doesn't matter. I still got to see him bench press a casket, so I really did *not* expect him to pass out.

I guess it's different when you know it's fake versus knowing it's real?

Veda leans over and pats his leg. "Thank you for being here for Muffy."

He grunts, not at all charmed by Veda's sweet voice and gorgeous face and warm smile.

I want to hug him and apologize, but I'm also not eager to get close to him, considering he has reason to basically hate me for the rest of my life and if I were him, I'd be plotting how best to handcuff me naked to the shower curtain rod before leaving me here to find my demise on my own.

And now I'm thinking about myself naked, and Tyler, who's a million times more attractive right now than he was back when I thought he was an attractive hockey player who sometimes talked to me like we were equals.

I make myself focus on Veda. "How are you? Has it been awful?"

She wrinkles her nose. "Yes and no? I don't think it's fully processed yet. It wasn't even two weeks ago that we were having dinner and he was lecturing me about how I wasn't being aggressive enough with expanding my practice, and now it's like…"

"You can finally make yourself happy without anyone else's expectations in the way?"

"Yes. I know he wanted what he thought was best for me, but it was never what *I* wanted for myself."

Her brown eyes get shiny, and she shakes her head and dives back into the margarita. "This is weirdly good for pre-mixed."

"It's the company," Tyler says gruffly.

"Yes!" Veda beams at him. "Must be. Tell me something happy. How did you two meet?"

"Oh, we're not—" I start, but Tyler cuts me off.

"Muffy called Nick Murphy a neanderthal in geek-speak at a bar one night after a game, and I was hooked."

Veda's eyebrows bunch. "Who's Nick Murphy? What game?"

"Hockey," I supply. "Remember my cousin, Kami? She married the Thrusters' goaltender, Nick Murphy, last Christmas."

Veda bounces in her seat and smiles at Tyler. "You play for the Thrusters? That explains why your neck's as wide as your head. I was guessing maybe football, but I can see hockey."

"You don't follow hockey?" he asks her.

"We root for Washington."

He rolls his eyes. "Better than Florida."

And now Veda's frowning. "*We*. Holy shit. I can root for whoever I want to root for."

"Ooh, you can!" I take the margarita from her. "I can get

you a list of the cutest mascots or the teams with the hottest players."

"Sitting *right here* with a rocket-powered bratwurst mascot and a hot thick neck," Tyler mutters.

I ignore him, mostly out of self-preservation, because now that Veda pointed it out, his thick neck is *also* super attractive. "Or you could turn into a baseball fan, or MMA, or even like, monster truck rallies if you wanted to."

"What about softball? Are there professional softball leagues?"

"Oh! I know! You could become a soccer fan! Copper Valley has The Scorned—they're a women's soccer club—and they're *amazing*. Plus, Tyler could probably introduce you to some of the players. Sportsers know sportsers, don't you, Tyler?"

She shakes her head before he can answer. "I'm not meeting people right now."

"Oh, no. Did you—"

She waves a hand like she doesn't want to talk about her dating life, which could mean anything from *I broke up with someone recently* to *the rest of my family doesn't want to know I'm currently dating a woman* to *I'm dating someone with commitment issues*.

"If Tyler judges you, I'll kick him in the nuts," I whisper to her, and I'm mostly positive he doesn't hear me.

Or he's thinking I'd have to catch him first, and he knows exactly how many Donettes I ate this afternoon.

She laughs. "It's not that, I promise. Enough about me. Tell me about Muff Matchers."

"It's great!"

She tilts a brow at me.

"Okay," I sigh. "It's still super slow, though I *did* make *three* matches since August, I'm expanding my network of men who pass my new standards testing, and all of my clients are making friends with each other and the Muff Matchers support group and newsletter keeps getting better, and we have people with us now who aren't even clients. Yet. Still... It's just..."

"Hard to overcome years and years of stereotypes to find the people who see past what looks like less than perfect while convincing women who are told from birth that they're not worthy that they actually are and should have standards?"

"*Yes.*"

Tyler's watching me over his fries.

I don't think he pigeonholes me as a loser, but then, he's not kicking Veda out and trying to talk me out of my clothes either.

If anything, he looked relieved when she showed up.

Yet I'm still sitting here thinking he's the hottest thing since that egg white omelet that Mom accidentally set on fire yesterday.

"Maybe you change tactics?" Veda says. "Maybe you concentrate more on the support group and newsletter aspect? God knows women like you and me could use a shot of confidence when it comes to what makes us attractive."

Tyler chokes on his fish.

Not hard to understand why. Veda's flawlessly gorgeous. A socially respectable size six, D-cups, clear skin, shiny black hair, big brown eyes, pillowy lips, eyebrows that behave in whatever the latest brow style is, and the world's most perfect nose, which she's decorated with a single small diamond stud.

She also has the most gorgeous rose tattoo on her ribs, which he doesn't know, but I suspect he'd like to.

She and I share a look.

He has no idea, she's telegraphing.

Men are so superficial, I telegraph back.

I take a long gulp, then turn my clunky, not-so-comfy hotel chair so I'm angled toward him as well as Veda. "Tyler, when you were growing up, did your parents ever tell you that you should play hockey less and concentrate on your grades more?"

He pulls a face. "Youngest of six. I got to do whatever I wanted, and my sisters bitched about it despite going out of their way to make sure I knew they adored me too."

"So your parents didn't tell you you'd never be a neurosurgeon if you didn't ace your third-grade science project on the life cycle of frogs?" Veda asks.

"And they didn't burn your Halloween candy in the fireplace because it was better for your hips long term?" I add.

"And they didn't tell you that the neighbors' kids got better grades than you three quarters in a row when you got A's and they got A plusses?"

"And they didn't ask if you were sure you wanted to wear your hair that way, and maybe you shouldn't smile so big when your teeth made you look like a horse?"

"And they didn't tell you to join chess club instead of being a cheerleader?"

I whip my head around. "Oh my gosh, you wanted to be a cheerleader? I didn't know that!"

Veda's smiling again. "My school colors were sky blue and white and the uniforms were *so* cute. And the cheerleaders always had those ribbons in their hair."

"I wanted to be the top of the pyramid but my dad always said no one else would be able to lift me!"

We stare at each other, and maybe it's the margarita, or maybe it's emotions, but suddenly we're hugging each other and crying.

"My dad wanted me to take horseback riding lessons and learn to play polo so I could go to an Ivy League school," Veda sobs. "When I got rejected by all of them, he never looked at me the same again."

"When my parents got divorced, my mom took me on giant shopping trips and tried to make me wear the cutest clothes but my shoulders were too wide for the cute tops and I always muffin-topped out of the cute shorts, and one time, I *muffin-bottomed*. My *thighs* had rolls under the jean short cuffs."

"You're perfect exactly the way you are, Muffy."

"Any man or woman would be so lucky to have you, Veda."

"Same, Muffy. *Same*."

"Why is it always two chicks?" Tyler mutters.

At least, I think that's what he mutters. When I lift my head and peer through the blurriness at him, he's dumping his fish and chips in the trash and pocketing his wallet. "Get up. We're getting out of here."

"Why?" I ask.

"Where are we going?" Veda asks.

"Like, leaving Richmond leaving, or leaving the hotel leaving?"

"I have to be at the funeral in the morning or my uncle will disown me." Veda cocks her head. "Actually, I don't care if he disowns me. I think the only thing he's leaving me is his pet fish and a few more insecurities, because *he* thinks I should've been a lawyer and gone into politics, and I'm allergic to aquariums. Let's hit the beach. I'm not allergic to sea life. Only sea life kept in buildings."

Tyler presses his palm into his eye socket.

He's seriously hot, standing there looking like he wants to strangle someone.

And it doesn't lessen the hotness factor that I'm pretty sure the someone he wants to strangle is me.

"We're getting dinner," he informs us. "And while we're there, you two are going to sit there and tell each other good things about yourselves and then we're all getting drunk. Or possibly drunker."

Veda squints at him. "I get to say good things about Muffy?"

"No. You get to say good things about yourself. And Muffy gets to say good things about herself. And I get to suffer through it all in my vodka and steak. And if either of you tell me you're vegan or fruititarian or potato-tarian, or you only eat cocktail shrimp or watermelon soup or whatever, tough shit."

"He grew up with four older sisters," I whisper to Veda. "Something tells me this won't be the first time he's had to do this."

"He's seriously hot in the protective kind of way. You should really think about dating him for real," she whispers back.

He glares at her.

"Told you she'd know you were only doing me a favor," I say to him.

"It's not that Muffy's not hot enough for you," Veda says. "She doesn't date. And I *did* want to know how you met because it's just as interesting when friends who'll go to funerals with you meet as it is when lovers meet."

A muscle ticks in his neck, which really is as wide as his head. I hadn't noticed until Veda pointed it out, since his beard technically makes his face wider than his neck, but she's right.

He has a very thick neck.

"Ride's here," he grunts.

I grab my shoes and shove Veda's at her too. "C'mon. Let's go get dinner."

"But *not* anywhere my father or his friends or colleagues would go," she says quickly.

"Deal."

14

Tyler

WE DRIVE ten miles south of town to a busy exit off the interstate with a popular chain sports bar not far off the main drag, and now I'm trapped in a booth with Muffy and her friend Veda, who are breaking all of my rules and saying nice things about each other but nothing nice about themselves while I chow through a steak.

The bar's playing the Washington-Denver hockey game on one screen, the LA-New York basketball game on another screen, and the Chicago-New England football game on a third screen.

I could easily lose myself in any of the three, but instead, I'm paying attention to the women.

Neither of them have said a word about me passing out at the funeral home.

Not exactly. Muffy did give me very specific looks while she made that side trip to Cod Pieces before we got to the hotel, like she *knew* that was my comfort food, and that, more than anything, has me in a mood.

Muffy Periwinkle is not supposed to take care of me.

She's too flighty for that.

Or is she?

She *is* the same woman who once texted me after a game to ask me to go to Chester Green's and "accidentally" bump into a specific table where she overheard a family talking about how I was their favorite player, and they came all the way in from Chicago for the game, and wouldn't it be cool if I showed up at the hockey bar?

Another time, she saved Klein from a bunch of pissed-off fans by pretending to be his angry pregnant girlfriend, speaking only in some kind of French-Russian accent and using broken English to accuse him of leaving her out of his planned orgy, which left them feeling incredibly sorry for him instead of angry.

And then there was the time we were playing darts at a party at Lavoie's house and I swear she threw the game for the sake of my ego.

Must've been beginner's luck, she'd said with a shrug when she couldn't hit the board anymore.

Her methods might be weird, but until she came shrieking into Murphy's house the other day, begging for a date, she's not usually asking for things for herself.

Tonight?

Yeah. Tonight she's definitely in need of *something*.

And I want to know why.

She and Veda are doing that silent communication thing my sisters do sometimes, and I'm positive Muffy's told her friend to not speak a word about when they were in med school together here, because every time one of them says *Blackwell* or *school* or anything else related to education, the conversation abruptly stops, and they switch to the weather or Muff Matchers or Veda's family practice or stories about their parents.

Mostly Muffy's mom and Veda's dad, since Veda's mom

apparently died when she was young, and Muffy's dad moved away when she was in grade school after her parents' divorce, and she got very creative in finding ways to avoid going to her assigned weekends with him.

Plus, there are *endless* stories to tell about Hilda Periwinkle.

I've only met the woman a handful of times and also have stories from every single time.

Makes sense.

Also, no, I don't want to talk about any of them. The woman has even fewer boundaries than my sisters, and that takes skills that I'd prefer to avoid.

Once I'm done with my steak and on to my third beer, I turn my phone back on and catch up on all the messages from all day long about my brother-in-law's vasectomy issues.

He's fine now. Back home. Resting with more ice.

But I have a private, one-on-one text message from my sister-in-law asking if I'm okay and threatening to bring the whole family into it if I don't answer her *immediately*.

Shit.

"Bathroom," I grunt to the women.

I'm dialing Daisy before I've left the table, on my way to the brightly lit parking lot in the chilly evening.

Feels good to not be boxed in.

"Tyler! You're alive!" Daisy cheers after picking up on the second ring.

"What exactly were you planning on telling my family if I didn't call you?"

"I heard you passed out at a funeral home. West's packing our bags. If you're going to pass out and die, you couldn't pick a better place than a funeral home, but I'm really glad you're not dead. At least, not yet. What are you doing in Richmond? How did you know Professor Harris?"

Professor Harris.

That must be Veda's dad. I don't actually know her last

name. Or maybe that's the funeral guy and she thinks I hang out at mortuaries three hours from my place for fun. "How do *you* know Professor Harris?" I counter.

"I don't. I know Barry, the funeral home director. Long story. It involves a hippo and a stun gun mishap on a vacation in an undisclosed location. But not a stun gun used on a hippo, to clarify. Anyway, he recognized you and texted me to ask me to let him know how you're doing. So, are you okay?"

"I'm *fine*. Don't come. I'm doing a friend a favor."

"A *girl* friend?"

The idea of Muffy as my girlfriend doesn't make my balls retract fully into my body, which may or may not be a bad sign. Clearly, I'm out of my normal element, and it's affecting my brain. "Don't you dare start…"

"West, Ty's okay," she calls. "He says not to come because it was all a plot to score points with a woman. So we're still going, right?"

"I forgot to eat. Got lightheaded. Passed out."

"And screamed," she says helpfully over West's answer in the background about if they're still coming, which I can't make out clearly. "Who's your friend?"

"We're not discussing this."

"I can ask your sisters."

"And I can clear out my bank account, ditch my phone, use cash to fly to an obscure tropical island, and never have to see any of you again." Which would be boring as hell, but I'm not telling her that.

"Aww, sweet boy. You're forgetting there's basically nowhere you can go that your brother won't find you. He loves you too much to let you disappear and not look for you, and I love him too much to not give him all the resources he needs to succeed. Actually, he probably loves you more than your sisters do. You know if they knew what I knew, they'd be all over a group message by now, but he's very politely asked me to not tell them until you say it's okay. Also, I love you too much to do that to you. So. Tell me about your girlfriend."

"She's not my girlfriend."

"But you want her to be."

"No, I don't."

There's a beat of silence. Then, Daisy does what she always does.

She finds the drama.

Do *not* underestimate a woman who spent her twenties alternating between high-powered board rooms and party yachts. "Oh my god, something weird happened between you two!"

Yeah. Something weird happened. And right now, I want to march into that restaurant, pull Muffy out of her seat, kiss her senseless, and tell her she deserves better than what the world's given her, which is also weird.

I'm no champion for anyone unless I have to be, and *have to be* is limited to the women I'm related to. More often, their husbands. "I'm hanging up now."

"That wasn't a denial."

"I have two women in mourning waiting for me. They shouldn't be alone. Lots of alcohol. Lots of regrets. Lots of bad decisions coming. It'll be like Allie after Fox canceled *Firefly*. Or like Keely after Keebler quit making those magic middle cookies. Ask West. It's bad. My services are needed. And there are two of them. I need to go."

I'm not really exaggerating. I can see the women through the wooden slat blinds, and they're hugging again. Muffy's face is splotchy.

And I want to put a fist through her father's face. Her mother's too.

I can rarely find pants that fit well. My ass and thighs are huge. Side effect of all the skating. Hockey butt's a thing. There are web pages devoted to shots of our butts.

So the shopping thing they were talking about?

I get it. Clothes that fit are hard to find when you're not a fashion-industry-approved size.

Except I'm celebrated for my shape, and Muffy was made to feel ashamed of hers before she'd fully developed.

That pisses me off.

My mom uses my struggle as a bit in her shows sometimes, making fun of her mom-hips and talking about borrowing my shorts and jeans since those are clearly socially acceptable.

Everyone laughs.

It's not funny.

Also not funny?

There are *two women hugging*, both very attractive in their own ways, and my dick *still* isn't playing.

I was *on a bed*, inches from two women sharing a margarita and also hugging, and *nada*.

Maybe I don't need to retrace my steps and get my boners back.

Maybe I need a doctor. I wonder if any of Muffy's former classmates became urologists.

"Where are you staying tonight?" Daisy asks.

She's heiress to a real estate empire that she was heavily involved in running until last year, including hotels, and we're *not* staying in one of her family properties tonight, despite the fact that I know there are several in the area. Not that she'd judge me one way or another, but I don't want to discuss it with her. "Hanging up now. For real."

"No worries. I can track your phone. Expect cookies wherever you are. Oh! Or *cotton candy*! Wouldn't cotton candy be awesome? I wonder if you can get vodka-infused cotton candy? I'll have to make some calls. Hug your girl-friends for me. Funerals suck, though the last one I was at actually gave me West and Remy, so maybe they're not all that bad?"

That's Daisy.

Never a boring or conventional conversation, and she loves her random acts of kindness.

"Weather here sucks. Stay in Miami," I tell her, and then we hang up.

The weather doesn't suck.

I love this weather. It's a little warmer than a hockey rink. Overcast so the city lights reflect off the clouds. Mother Nature is wrapping us in a cold hug and promising more winter is on the way.

When I get back inside, Muffy and Veda leap apart.

They're both sniffly-nosed and red-eyed, though Veda looks like she's ready to snap a man in half.

I sigh and wave over our server. "All of the desserts," I tell him. "One of each."

"You got it, Mr. Jaeger. Can I get a selfie? *Huge* Thrusters fan."

I oblige him and smile bright for the camera, then climb back into the booth across from the women. "You gonna let me help you take care of whatever it is that has you so pissed off?" I ask Veda.

I'm done asking Muffy.

She's made it clear she won't tell me.

But I know this game. When one won't tell, you get on the other's good side.

Veda wipes her eyes with a napkin. "There's nothing to take care of."

Someone's foot brushes my calf under the table.

I jolt.

My dick lifts a sleepy head.

Whose foot is that? Is it Muffy's? Or is it her friend's?

Whoever's it is, it's not stopping.

It is definitely rubbing me on purpose.

And my junk is tingling like it's waking up.

Hell. *Shit.*

That better not be Veda's foot.

If I'm getting my first semblance of a woody over Muffy's friend, my life is basically over. It's a rule. You don't take one woman to a funeral and then bang a different mourner, even if she's the head mourner.

But we're raising the flagpole! my dick cries.

You could do two chicks! my balls chime in. *One for each of us!*

Jesus.

My balls are talking to me too.

I have issues.

So many damn issues.

15

Muffy

I'M NOT DRUNK ENOUGH.

I *want* to be drunk enough, but I'm not, not by a long shot, and now we're back in our hotel room, just me and Tyler and an inky-dinky bed and a whole bunch of elephants that we're tiptoeing around.

"You can have the bed," I tell him.

"And you'll sleep where? The bathtub?"

"It's on my bucket list."

He scrubs a hand over his face and opens his mouth, but I cut him off.

"I get that you're trying to be nice to me, but the truth is, you're doing me the hugest favor in the history of favors, and I was an asshole for not telling you that we were coming for a funeral, and so I would very much appreciate it if you'd take the bed, if for no other reason than I know how important sleep is to athletes and I really like the Thrusters to win so I need you to sleep well tonight, then sleep well tomorrow night, and then kill it on the ice Tuesday night so that I don't have to have any lingering guilt about anything that goes down here, okay?"

"Do you actually breathe when you talk, or do you have secret gills somewhere?"

I flinch.

I don't want to, but I can't help it. It's habit.

And now he's doing that see-right-through-me thing where he looks ready to whip out a sword and slay dragons. "Talk," he orders.

"I have a new client and I was going to set her up with D'Angelo from Cod Pieces but he started dating someone the night before I introduced them."

"Talk about *talking*," he growls. "Does someone tell you that you talk too much?"

Did someone take a blowtorch to my cheeks, or am I having a weird reaction to alcohol tonight? "Tyler. I'm a woman. Someone is *always* telling me I talk too much."

He crosses his arms and glares, but he also goes a little pink in the cheeks above his thick beard, which is adorable.

I'm gonna go out on a limb and guess he's told his sisters they talk too much a time or two in his life.

But the idea that he's realizing it's rude because he doesn't want people telling *me* I talk too much is making him a little more attractive, and I can't have that.

Tyler Jaeger doesn't want me.

But he's here, isn't he?

I flick a hand at the room phone. "I'll call down to the desk and ask for extra blankets and pillows. It'll be like camping in a bathtub, plus, after a day in heels, it'll feel good to have my feet elevated."

"You're sleeping on the bed."

"*You're* sleeping on the bed."

"We're *both* sleeping on the bed."

"There's not room."

"That's another thing—your parents are dicks. *No one* gets

to judge you based on how you look or what size you are. *No one*. You know what's important? How you feel. *That's* what's important. Fuck everyone, *especially* your parents, for telling you otherwise. If Donettes give you good energy and make you happy, eat the fucking Donettes, okay? Now *get ready for bed*, and *get in the fucking bed*, and go to sleep."

His chest is heaving and those bright pink spots are growing over his beard. Fists clenched and tendons straining in his neck like he's holding himself back from punching the wall. And I want to throw myself at him and kiss him until I can't breathe.

I won't.

I basically can't.

Even if I thought he did want me, I've rejected him every possible way I can reject him. I don't get to kiss him.

I surrendered that privilege when I didn't try to contact him either after the thing in the fridge.

And I've never regretted anything more than I regret not being able to leap at him and kiss him until we're tearing each other's clothes off and trying that naked carnal humping thing again.

Not because I'm especially horny—though I'm getting there—but because no one has *ever* defended me to myself quite the way he is right now.

And until this moment, I didn't know anyone needed to.

"I—" I start, but he brushes past me with another irritated noise, grabs his duffel bag, and slams the door to the bathroom.

"Get ready for bed, Muffy."

Bed.

Right.

Sleeping.

With Tyler next to me.

Nope. No way. Nuh-uh. I'm sleeping in the bathtub. I am *not* sleeping in the bed next to him. For starters, because I like to sleep in a T-shirt and panties, and I don't trust myself to not touch his bare leg with my bare leg. Next, because I've never shared a bed with a man overnight at all.

Ever.

And finally, because I like him.

I like him.

But I don't like anybody. Not like that.

And why don't you? a voice that sounds very much like Tyler's pissed-off growly voice demands in my head. *Because you've been absorbing all the subliminal messages from your parents for years that only thin, quiet, successful people deserve love?*

Dammit.

I've cried seven oceans already today. I ran into Dr. Richardson, and he recognized me, and I recognized him. Veda's lonely and I want to help her, but I can't because I know I'll let her down the same way I've let so many other clients down. I took Tyler to a funeral without warning and he *passed out*.

Today is *not* a good day.

But there's this little flower of light struggling to poke its head out of my heart, a warmth that I don't understand or recognize, and I think it's because Tyler Jaeger doesn't see me as a size fourteen disaster who still lives with her mom, has a failing matchmaker business that's only miraculously still hanging on, and who's in very real danger of defaulting on the student loans that she'll never pay off.

He sees me as a person worthy of being friends with.

Or at least worthy of help.

And he's under absolutely no obligation to feel that way.

Nor is he anywhere near the top of the men I know whom I would've expected to volunteer to help me.

I swipe at the streams leaking out of my eyes and falling on my boobs and dive for my luggage. I should've hung up tomorrow's dress when we first got here, but I didn't, because

I didn't want to open my bag and show off all my underwear and Slimzies in front of him.

I yank out my usual overnight T-shirt, remember it has a giant Thrusters logo on it, and silently debate with myself if Tyler will think that me wearing his team's gear is an indication that I'd be more interested in telling people I had sex with a hockey player than it was that I was into him as a person, or if I'm seriously overthinking this because I've been a Thrusters fan basically since birth, since I was born cousins with Kami, whose parents have been Thrusters fans forever too, and Tyler has nothing to do with it.

Then I re-think everything I've been thinking and understand why he asked if I have gills.

Fish have gills.

He knows I've been pulling a few shifts at Cod Pieces.

Was he making a joke and I took it way too personally?

The bathroom door opens, and I slam my luggage shut lest my Slimzies make Tyler turn into a cringing puddle of man-wimp. Body-shaping underwear can do that sometimes.

Or so I hear.

And then I see him.

He's in a skin-tight T-shirt—the fancy kind that athletes wear—and gray sweatpants and bare feet, his hair mussed, his blue eyes weary but still alert, those tattoos peeking out from under his sleeve and traveling down to his forearm, and if my mouth knew how to form words, it has now forgotten.

He tosses his bag into the small closet alcove, glances at me gaping at him, and stands there, holding my gaze, like he's asking me a question that I should know the answer to, except I'm not sure I'm reading the question right.

Someone knocks at the door.

He does one of those closed-eyed sighs like he knows who's on the other side, but I fly past him to answer.

Everything inside this room feels stupidly intense right now, and I don't know why, and I don't like it.

A distraction? Yes, please.

Maybe Veda came back.

Maybe she wants me to stay at her house.

Maybe— "Holy shit. That's a lot of cookies."

"Compliments of a random stranger," the front desk clerk says as he hands me a platter almost too wide to fit through the doorway.

Tyler makes a noise.

Poor guy.

All that temptation.

I shove the cookie tray back at the clerk. "Can you leave them in the lobby for everyone here to share?"

"We have sixteen more trays in the lobby, ma'am."

"Oh. Um, maybe the next hotel over would like some?"

Tyler reaches around me and grabs the tray, lifting it over my head since he can't squeeze it past me without dumping it over. "Take the cookies, Muffy. Every hotel on this block probably got hit." He makes another noise, then mutters, "And the funeral home too."

"Dead people can't eat cookies."

His eyes lock with mine, and the next thing I know, he's doubled over, laughing into the cookie tray.

I shrug at the clerk, thank him, and shut the door.

Tyler slides down the wall, sets the cookie tray on the floor, sticks his head between his knees, and laughs.

And laughs.

And laughs.

"Jesus," he finally wheezes.

I slide down the opposite wall and watch him.

I'd eat a cookie, except I had both peanut butter pie and a chocolate mousse for dessert and I'm stuffed.

Actually, I put the chocolate mousse on top of the peanut butter pie, and I'll basically never eat another dessert in my life that will ever top tonight's dessert.

"Have you...have you totally lost your marbles?" I whisper to him.

"Yes."

His laughter is petering out into little chuckles that are somehow both sexy and adorable, and I have to spend the next ten hours alone, in this dinky one-bed hotel room, with this man.

"Why are you here with me?"

"Because my dick broke after I had sex with you, and I'm trying to fix it by figuring out where I went wrong."

Now it's my turn for the weird noises.

He quits laughing.

Makes eye contact with me.

Then leaps up from the ground. "Kidding. You should see your face. Everything's fine, Muffy. I'm here because I'm a nice guy, and there are cookies on the floor because my sister-in-law is a pain in the ass, and we both need to sleep if we're going to help Veda get through tomorrow and everyone whispering about how she skipped out on her father's viewing."

"I broke your penis?"

"No."

"Tyler."

"What happened the last time you were here?"

I should tell him. I really should.

But part of me wants to seduce him. See if the hard-on of wonder will make a reappearance, or if his penis really is broken.

Except I've eaten more than a hippo today, I still smell vaguely like fish and chips because I've absorbed it into my body and I can't get rid of it between shifts, and Tyler failing to get an erection if I stripped in front of him would be more about me and less about him.

Also, my stomach is so full, there's a reasonable possibility any physical exertion would make me burp—or worse—and that would basically be the absolute utter end of me.

I make myself stand up too. "Do you want the window or the bathroom side of the bed?"

"Bathroom."

"Oh. Do you get up a lot in the middle of the night?"

"It's closer to the door so I can leap up and battle off the invaders who'll sneak in at two AM to try to kidnap you."

"I can't tell if you're joking or not."

"Good."

Good? I huff out an irritated snort, but mostly, I'm irritated with myself.

He's a nice guy. Occasional attitude problems. Thought I was sexy enough to want to have sex with me in a walk-in refrigerator in the dark a couple months ago.

And now he knows I'm a total, complete basket case, right when I'm realizing there's more to Tyler Jaeger than I gave him credit for.

And *this* is why I never date.

By the time I realize I can board the ship, it's already halfway across the ocean, going from a dirty shipping port to some tropical paradise.

16

Tyler

MUFFY DOESN'T TOUCH the cookies.

I don't know if it's self-consciousness or if she's full, but she sets them on the corner table, leaving them wrapped in their plastic wrap, then digs around in her suitcase and disappears into the bathroom.

And because Daisy is Daisy, the platter is wider than the table it's sitting on.

I strip off my shirt and climb into bed, propped up against the headboard. As far as hotel rooms go, I've slept in worse. Hate the pillows here though. We only have one each and they feel as fluffy as flat rocks.

But instead of dwelling on how my neck will feel in the morning, I text Daisy, because it's less stressful to text Daisy than to wonder what the hell happened between Muffy and that Gerry guy that she ran into while we were standing in line at the funeral home, which isn't my drama, and I want it out of my head.

• • •

TYLER: Are you serious right now? How did you get seven thousand cookies delivered all over Richmond with two hours' notice?

BRIT: Aww! It's Tyler! He lives! Why are you in Richmond?

ALLIE: I didn't send cookies. That sounds like Daisy.

KEELY: Definitely Daisy. Ditto to the Richmond question. How far is that from Copper Valley? And which Richmond?

BRIT: Did you know there are like ninety Richmonds? He could be in a foreign country.

TYLER: Ignore that message. It was for Ares. He's in Richmond playing pranks on random people.

ALLIE: *gif of Carol Kane screeching LIAR! in *The Princess Bride**

BRIT: You need to work on your lying game, T.

KEELY: *picture of her friend-finder app with Tyler's location highlighted in Richmond, Virginia*

ALLIE: What Keely said. We all know you're in Richmond.

. . .

Daisy: Guys, go easy on him. He was at a funeral.

Brit: OMG! Who died? Was it open casket? You okay, Ty? Did you see dead people?

Keely: Better question: did anyone come back to life?

Tyler: *middle finger emoji*

Brit: *gif of a troll saying SOLID BURN*

Tyler: *gif of a dude saying FUCK YOU ALL*

Dad: I've got a lovely buffalo coconut in my butt.

Brit: Seriously, Ty, who died? And are you okay?

Allie: Why didn't you tell us? You know we wouldn't have let you go to a funeral alone.

Keely: That's exactly why he didn't tell us.

Daisy: Don't worry. West and I are on the way.

. . .

TYLER: Why do I even talk to you?

KEELY: Because you know we'd have your back in the zombie apocalypse.

ALLIE: I really didn't think Keely would be the one to follow in Mom's footsteps, but there she goes with another not-dead grandpa joke.

BRIT: OH MY GOD. Tyler. It's a woman, isn't it? You're dating someone! Who is she? What's her name? When do we get to meet her? Are you bringing her home for Christmas? Is she a bunny, or is she someone else? Wait! Wait! Are you dating one of your teammates' sisters? OH MY GOD. You're dating the coach's daughter and you're trying to make a good impression, aren't you?

TYLER: *picture of a skinny white guy with big glasses* Haha! Psych. I stole this phone. This is me. I'm Bernard. You guys sound like fun. Will you adopt me? I'll send you my real number.

DAD: That's a funny Grand Canyon of a vagina, Tyler, my favorite son, god of the sun and moon, he who bangs best.

DAD: Grand Canyon of a vagina.

. . .

130

Dad: WHO CHANGED MY PHONE TO INSULT YOUR YO-YO MA'S SEX TAPE?

Dad: BEEEEEEEEEEP.

Keely: OMG, I'm wheezing.

Allie: My favorite part of this is that Tyler's going to get blamed for changing the autocorrect setting in Dad's phone. Again.

Brit: I can't believe no one changed "joke" in his phone before now.

Dad: I CAN STILL SEE YOUR MESSAGES.

Keely: Let's hope Ty's new girlfriend doesn't tell jokes, or Dad might autocorrect insult her vagina too.

Tyler: Wow, this family is really inappropriate. I like it. So will my mom. I'm thirteen.

Brit: You tried that last year, Ty. Same fake selfie and everything. We're not buying it.

• • •

Keely: Also, if you don't want us to ask about your girlfriend, the best course of action is to stay silent in group texts.

West: I can confirm this battle strategy. *thumbs up emoji*

Allie: OMG. West. It was YOU! You changed Dad's phone, didn't you? It's always the quiet, serious ones.

Brit: Don't let him distract you, Allie. We're talking about Tyler's dating life.

Keely: It's like eleven at night there. If he had a girlfriend, he'd be getting busy with her, not texting with us.

Brit: Good point. You need advice, T? We're here for you.

Keely: I can call Staci and type in her opinions. I'd do that for you.

Allie: No, don't bother Staci. She's been waiting on Javi all day.

Dad: That man's poor balls.

Brit: Hey, Tyler disappeared again.

• • •

DAISY: Maybe he's having happier balls than Javi is.

THE BATHROOM DOOR OPENS, and I hit the power button on my phone. Part of me is pissed that I hit the wrong conversation in text and ended up getting ambushed by my sisters, and the other part of me is pissed that I wasn't the one who changed the settings in Dad's phone to mess with the word "joke."

That should've been a no-brainer with Mom being out on her *Does This Joke Have Ketchup On It?* tour.

Also, I'm not leaving my phone unattended the next time I'm home.

Maybe I won't take my phone at all.

Except it was very helpful in getting us around Richmond tonight. Can't use apps to get rides if you don't have a phone.

Muffy steps into view from the short hallway, looks at my face, then my chest, and twists her head up and away so fast she probably snapped something in her neck.

She's in a Thrusters t-shirt that hugs her breasts.

No bra.

Plain black pajama shorts. Curvy thighs. Adorable knees.

Adorable knees?

Fuck.

I have a problem.

Was she the one playing footsie with me at the restaurant?

Or was that Veda?

Had to be Muffy, unless Veda's into hitting on her friends' dates of convenience, and I didn't get that vibe off her.

She hustles to her side of the bed, shoving her dress into her luggage quickly on the way, hits the light on her side, and eyeballs her pillow.

This bed isn't remotely big enough for me by myself, much less two human beings.

I pointedly shift until my hip is right at the edge, then gesture to the space left.

Yeah, I'm a dick.

She has like three inches.

And if that's three inches, I used to have two-foot boners, back when my junk worked.

"The switch is by the door!" She darts back to the door, fiddles with the deadbolt and the chain, then plunges the room into total darkness.

Two seconds later, there's a clank, then— "*Ouch*!"

"Watch out for the furniture."

"Thank you, Mr. Obvious."

She grips my foot, then yanks her hand away. "Sorry. It's dark."

"I noticed."

The bed creaks and sags as she sits on the other side of it. Sheets rustle. The bed shakes.

Her leg brushes mine and jerks away just as fast, but not fast enough.

My dick has just gotten its second jolt of juice in under two hours. It's like watered-down apple juice, the stuff my sisters give to their kids, instead of high-octane, full-strength energy drink, but I will literally take any movement at all in the cock area right now.

"Could you maybe be a side-sleeper so you take up less room?" she whispers.

Could I? Probably. "What's it worth to you?"

"Never mind. This is fine. We're adults. We can accidentally touch in our sleep, and the world won't end. Thank you. I don't think I've said that enough. I really appreciate that you were here for me today, and I'm sorry that I didn't tell you we were going to a funeral. I didn't think anyone would go if they knew it was for a funeral. But if I knew you didn't like funerals that badly, I would've told you. I swear."

It's weird how a not-simple *thank you* can make you feel like a complete slug. Probably because she keeps thanking me like if she doesn't, I'll sneak out of here in the middle of the night and leave her to go alone tomorrow. "That's what friends are for."

I definitely would not be here if I'd known this was a funeral. I've successfully avoided funerals for over twenty years, and going to a stranger's was not in the life plan.

But I won't abandon Muffy.

I can't.

I like her too much to want her to suffer on her own.

Dammit.

"Are we friends?" She's still whispering like she's afraid her mother's down the hall and might overhear us.

I flop onto my side to face her, making the entire bed shake and the headboard rattle against the wall. "I don't know, Muffy. Are we? You have secrets. I have secrets. We had sex. It was bad for you. You tricked me into coming to a funeral. Your friend played footsie with me all through dinner. Does that—"

"Veda was playing footsie with you too?"

I smile into the darkness.

So it *was* Muffy.

"No. Only you. Just checking to see how you would've felt if I was into her."

"Do *not* hit on Veda. She got out of a long-term relation-ship a month ago, and now she's—never mind."

They must've talked a lot while I was on the phone with Daisy, because I was under the impression Muffy had no idea what Veda's relationship status was.

"Muffy?"

"What?"

It's so easy to get a huffy *what?* out of a woman some-times. "I'm yanking your chain. I'm not into Veda."

"Oh."

"And you're welcome."

She takes a big breath, like she's about to say some-thing profound, then sighs. "We should get to sleep.

Funeral plus long drive home equals sucky day tomorrow."

The bed shakes and the headboard rattles the wall again. My eyes are adjusting to the darkness, and I can make out the curve of her neck, up her shoulder, down her arm, over her hip.

I wonder if she usually sleeps on flat pillows and hard beds, or if she'll wake up refreshed tomorrow.

"I had a bad experience with a not-dead body when I was little," I hear myself say.

I don't mean to, but given how much I've asked her to tell me today without giving her anything in return—other than passing out at the funeral home—it only seems fair to confide in her.

And maybe I need to change tactics if I want her to talk to me about whatever it was that happened to her here, and maybe I need to do something nice for her if my dick is ever going to work again.

The sheets rustle as she half-turns toward me. "Not-dead?"

"My grandpa had a zombie moment. The whole family was there at the hospital with him. Kidney failure. He flat-lined. Everyone cried. The nurses unhooked all the machines, and everyone left, but I stayed because it was sort of morbidly fascinating. Until he...well, he came back to life. He rolled over, gasped once, looked me straight in the eye, said *DIE!*, and then he died again. He might've said *Ty*. I don't know. I just know he died, again, with his eyes and his mouth open, staring straight at me, and it was the fucking scariest thing I've seen in my entire life. My mom thought my dad had me, and my dad thought my mom had me, and they left me at the hospital, so I had to sit outside the room with a hospital security guard while they tracked my parents down. When they transported my grandfather's body out of the room, the whole thing was shaking like the casket did tonight, and I—I don't like death, okay?"

"Oh my god."

"I don't watch zombie movies. Or movies where there are corpses. I can't even make it past the first sequence in *Up*."

"Oh my god," she whispers again. "So at the funeral home —with the casket moving—you basically—"

"Man down. Yeah."

"I'm so sorry. I should've told you where we were going. I didn't know." She strokes my face, then freezes like she's realized she's touching me, and she jerks back. "Sorry," she stammers again.

I'm sorry too, because I wouldn't mind if she kept touching me, but I've been giving her all the right *leave me alone* signals. "I knew where we were going by the time we got back to the funeral home."

"But what were you going to do, wait in the car?"

I don't answer.

I *wanted* to wait in the car.

But when Muffy ran into that guy and went the same pallor as my dead grandfather, there was no way I could bail on her.

You don't abandon friends just because you don't want to come face-to-face with a dead body.

Even when you don't know what the whole story is with why they don't want to be there in the first place.

If she'd said *I don't want to go to a funeral*, that's one thing.

Who doesn't get that?

But there's more to this story.

"It's my turn, isn't it?" she says in the darkness.

"Are we taking turns?" *Are we friends?* Do I want to be friends with Muffy?

Holy hell. I think I do.

But she's suddenly still as *actual* death.

Not kidding. I'm starting to sweat.

After a moment, she takes a deep breath. "I was drowning in student loans and credit card debt and I didn't get matched for a residency so I didn't have any idea what I was going to do for a job or money or if I'd ever be able to be a doctor at all, because without a residency, you can't become a doctor, so I auctioned off my virginity and then couldn't follow through because—just *because*—and then I was so mortified that I left town and never came back. I didn't even get my clothes from my apartment. I just went."

No small part of me is nodding along, thinking *this makes sense because it's Muffy*, but *who does that?* "Seriously?"

"No more talking. And if you *ever* repeat that to Kami, or anyone, I'll—okay, I don't know what I'll do except for probably move to another state, without my clothes again, and start over with a new name, which I can do, because I *am* friends with senior citizen criminals who can help with that sort of thing."

It's weird to have a woman in my bed, on the verge of tears, and not have an overwhelming impulse to leap away. "Why did you..." I trail off, because I can't make myself form the words to ask the question I want to ask.

I couldn't ask my sisters the same question.

Not that any of them ever would've done what she did. I don't think.

"I got the idea from a book," she mutters. "And I'd lost a bunch of weight because of stress and I was hot for once, and then my mom found out how much I owed and that I hadn't found a residency, and she was researching how to sell a kidney, or other things you don't want to know about, and I think she was serious, especially when she started asking how much kidneys weigh so she'd know how many pounds would come off immediately, so I knew I needed to make some fast cash, and it was what I had, so I decided to see if anyone would bite. Sex is pretty clinical when you get right down to it. Tab A, slot B, right? What's the big deal if it's nothing more than going through the motions? Except I couldn't—I swear, Tyler, if you tell a single soul—"

"It was the guy you bumped into before the viewing, wasn't it?"

"No."

"Muffy."

"I need us both to believe me right now, okay?" she whispers.

I want to hit someone. Or something. Specifically that professor. "Was that *his wife* with him?"

"*Tyler*."

Fuck. Just *fuck*. "I'm not going to tell anyone."

"Thank you."

"You never told Veda?"

"She knows about the auction but she doesn't know who showed up or what happened after that. No one does except me and that person. No more talking. I only told you because we were doing the friend thing and confessing things that won't exist in the morning. Plus, some people at the funeral tomorrow might remember that the auction was a thing and say something, even though I tried to be totally anonymous about who *I* was through the whole thing, which I don't think I did very well, and I didn't want to look like the kind of idiot who doesn't tell her date about the dumb stuff she did in med school, even if nobody knows what happened the night that…the winner…came to collect his debt. And I'm probably moving to Montana as soon as we get back to Copper Valley."

My sister Britney got engaged in college to this total dick who always stared at her ass and tits, even when they were visiting us, right in front of my dad and me, but never West, since he was off in the Marines, which explains why the guy's still alive today. When the jacknugget broke up with her, she spent two weeks crying in her room at home. I remember wanting to punch the guy, but I also remember wanting to punch her.

PIPPA GRANT

Why was she broken-hearted over some asshole who didn't deserve her?

The only thing she'd done wrong was to fall in love with a dick, and for the way he treated her, I couldn't see why it was worth it.

She told me I'd never understand how women felt about their own self-worth.

She was right.

And now I want to punch Muffy's parents again. Anyone who whispered behind her back in school. Or ever. That dude she ran into, who better *not* be the guy who tried to buy her virginity.

Oh, fuck me.

"Muffy?"

She flops around in the small bed, her legs brushing mine, her elbow connecting with my gut and making me *oof*, until she's facing away. "We should go to sleep."

"You weren't...you know...when we..."

"I said *go to sleep*, Tyler. Don't make me get up and smear cookie crumbs in your sheets."

Dammit.

"Muffy—"

"Shut up."

Catching up, you idiot? my dick says with a yawn.

She was a virgin.

That night, in the fridge at the bunny bar, she was a virgin.

17

Muffy

I'M in the middle of a dream that I'm drowning in regrets in a hot ocean when I wake up to the realization that Tyler Jaeger is spooning me.

No wonder I'm hot.

He's like an ocean. An ocean of lava. And he's surrounding me.

Also, his hand is cupping my breast, and my nipple is *very* much enjoying the human contact. My other nipple is aching for attention too, but my stomach feels like I ate barbed wire and drank gasoline last night, which is overriding my sudden curiosity over whether Tyler also wakes up with morning wood.

If he does, he's not poking me with it.

Is my butt in his crotch?

Is that why I can't feel it?

Was he serious about his penis being broken? Did I actually break his penis? Is my vagina the curse of death? Does it have superpowers that render men impotent?

Or was I that bad at sex?

Oh my god, I told him about Dr. Richardson.

Will he remember? Can I tell him I made it all up because what happened was even worse?

Would he believe that?

Probably not.

Does it get worse than *I tried to auction my virginity and couldn't follow through when my married rheumatology professor showed up in the hotel room?*

I mean, I guess it could be worse if I murdered him and covered up the crime, but that actually *is* out of character for me.

Someone bangs on the door. I'm so deep into my head that it scares the crap out of me, and I scream and fall out of bed. I don't know what Tyler does, but I assume he's moving too, because the headboard rattles, sheets go flying, and there's a *thump* and a "Fuck!"

I scramble to my feet, forget about the cookie tray that's larger than the table crammed close to the bed, and send the whole thing flying upside down, courtesy of my head hitting it wrong.

Tyler's limping to the door in nothing but white boxer briefs, muscles, and tattoos. He must've stripped out of his sweatpants sometime while I was sleeping.

"Are you okay?" I pant while I scurry to save what I can of the smushed cookies under the tray.

"Fucking wall. Fucking door. Fucking—*Jesus*. Are you *fucking kidding me*?" He unhooks the slider and wrenches the door open.

I drop the cookie tray again and yank my shirt down.

My short bottoms too. They were riding up my ass.

"What the *fuck* are you doing here?" Tyler snarls as Daisy Carter-Kincaid sashays into my hotel room with an adorable little boy on her hip.

Daisy Carter-Kincaid.

Oh. My. God.

I don't often read the gossip pages, but it's hard to not know who she is. And there's a big difference between knowing that Tyler's brother married her and seeing her in all of her blue-haired, gold glitter jumper, holy-hell high heels of glory.

"Watch your mouth," says a male voice that sounds like Tyler's but a little deeper. "And put some pants on."

"She's seen worse," Tyler snaps back.

"I'm just glad he's alive," Daisy says. "Oh! Hi. You must be Tyler's friend. I'm Daisy. This little guy's Remy, and the big guy who's about to put Tyler in a headlock is West. I think you talked to him on the phone yesterday. What's your name, sugarplum?"

"Her name's Muffy, and if you crack a single joke, I'll... *Dammit.*"

The other man in the room looks a lot like Tyler, but older, with shorter hair and a deeper tan, and he's definitely more amused. "Still can't think of a thing you could do to horrify her, can you?"

"I still can't believe she married *you*, you big stick in the mud," he mutters.

Hoo boy.

Tyler's boxer briefs don't leave anything to the imagination. And Daisy's still holding out a hand to me, and her nails are— "Oh my god, are those *mermaids* on your nails?"

She twists her hand to show me. "Aren't they adorable?"

"How long did that take?"

"About one naptime. Completely worth it."

The little boy on her hip doesn't look old enough to walk, or maybe he is. I don't know. I'm bad with baby ages, but he's holding onto his own sippy cup, so he's clearly older than Kami's baby. He's smaller than Ares Berger's baby, but then, Ares has big genes. It's not a fair comparison, and it leaves me with no idea how many months the little guy might've been on the planet so far.

"I'm Muffy." Which Tyler already told her, but I suddenly can't think of anything else to say.

"Lovely to meet you, Muffy. The family got concerned when Tyler's phone dropped off our friend-spying app yesterday, and when we heard he came to a funeral…"

"Yeah. Sorry about that."

Daisy's shorter than I thought she'd be. You hear about celebrities and think they're all seventeen feet tall, but even in those heels, she barely comes up to my chin. And she's winking at me. "Don't apologize. You must be special if he's going to a funeral for you."

Tyler swings the door open again and points to it. "You have proof of life. Go away."

"Breakfast?" Daisy says.

He sighs.

I glance at the clock.

The little boy babbles and pumps his legs, which makes every adult in the room smile at him.

"We're next door," Daisy announces. "Room service in thirty minutes. Be there or be hungry."

No way. Nope. Not happening.

I'm not getting out-classed by Daisy Carter-Kincaid before ten AM.

For a second time, I mean. "I have to call my friend. She shouldn't be alone this morning. So I should—"

"Bring her along, sweetie. There'll be plenty. Any friend of Tyler's friend is a friend of ours."

"Daisy—" Tyler starts.

"Enough, peasant." She smiles broadly at him, and I swear the entire room lights up with fireworks because she's that brilliantly gorgeous. "Breakfast, or my feelings will be hurt."

"Can't have that," Tyler's brother says with a shit-eating

grin. "Also, put pants on, or I'm sending pictures to the rest of the family."

They leave as fast as they came in.

I should pick up the cookie tray again. Or at least try to. But instead, I gape at Tyler. "How—"

"Pointless question, Muffy. It's Daisy. There's always a *how*. And don't ask *why didn't she just call* either. Not her style when she has a private jet and wants to get somewhere." He pauses on his way to the bathroom and looks me up and down, his gaze finally settling on mine. "You okay?"

Am I okay?

I confessed my worst secret to him last night after I took him to a funeral home where he passed out because of childhood trauma, and my best friend from college has to lay her father to rest today.

I'm probably not supposed to be okay, and my therapist would tell me that it's okay to not be okay today. But I paste on a bright smile anyway. "I'm great."

He studies me until I want to squirm. "Shower?"

"Yes."

"Excellent." He wiggles his eyebrows, which makes my nipples tighten.

"Oh! Oh, no. I mean, not together. You go ahead." Awesome. My panties are suddenly soaked too.

Why am I saying no?

Right.

Because he probably knows I have exactly zero experience with shower sex, and I really don't want to be naked in front of him in the light right now.

I'd probably fart.

And I've caused enough trauma to the poor man already in the past twenty-four hours.

Not even.

He sighs, shakes his head, grabs his bag, and disappears

into the bathroom. "Not like there won't be enough food next door whenever we get there," he mutters.

"Wait. We're doing that? We're having breakfast with your family?"

"If my options are a breakfast buffet in this hotel or whatever Daisy's having catered to her room next door, *I'm* having breakfast with my family. You're welcome to come along. Or you can stay here. Or call Veda. Have her join us. West and Daisy won't mind. Or do something completely different. Whatever. But I'm going to shower, and you can join me if you want to make it fast, or you can wait your turn and risk missing out on all the bacon. Doesn't matter to me. I'll leave the door unlocked."

And now I'm confused.

Is he offering to take a shower with me and have sex, or to shower quickly together to save time?

Does he like me?

Does he not like me?

Did we have a moment last night?

Did I dream the whole thing?

Is he in denial because there were feelings involved?

Am *I* in denial because there are feelings involved?

Why are men so complicated?

Or was he actually serious when he told me I broke his penis?

And speaking of dicks, I think I'm actually done being embarrassed about what happened when I left med school.

I think I'm *pissed*.

And I don't know why, but I have a feeling it has to do with one very sexy man currently getting naked on the other side of that bathroom door.

Did Tyler Jaeger, clean-eating athlete supremo with buns of steel and arms of wonder, actually lecture me last night about how I'm perfect exactly the way I am?

And that anyone who would shame me for it should go to hell?

I think he did.

But you know what's crazy?

I think I believe him.

I *shouldn't* be ashamed of my body. I shouldn't be ashamed of doing what I felt I needed to do to pay down some student loans. And I shouldn't be ashamed that my married professor bid on me.

He was wrong.

I can't control what he did.

But I can control what I do. And how I talk to myself. And how I let myself feel.

And right now, I feel like being brave.

Taking a chance.

Seeing if this Tyler Jaeger who's here this weekend is more than just a guy who'll take any available woman.

If he *likes* me.

And I think he does.

Would he have told anyone else about what happened with his grandfather? Would he have stuck around after the funeral home last night and still be planning on going to graveside services with another woman today?

I kinda don't think he'd do it for any of his hockey buddies.

Or possibly even his sisters.

But he's here. Being not just a date, but my champion.

Screw it.

I'm doing this.

I'm being brave. I'm taking a chance. I'm being bold.

I'm going to do what I'd tell my clients to do, and I'm going to march myself into that bathroom, strip off my clothes, and climb into the shower with him.

He invited me, right?

He *wants* me to.

And even if it's only because he's horny and I'm a girl, do I care?

Probably.

Okay, yes.

I want him to want me like I'm someone better than any other girl.

I take one step toward the bathroom.

Then another.

And another, until I'm standing at the door.

I hear the shower turn on.

It's now or never.

So I pull off my Thrusters T-shirt and fling open the door as I launch my shirt into the room at him.

The door connects hard with something and thuds to a stop. Tyler yelps, straightens, and grabs his bare ass, and *oh my god*.

Oh my god.

I flush so hard I get an instant headache as I slam the door shut again.

My face is on fire.

My scalp too.

Even my hair.

I think my *hair* is blushing.

I'm standing here with my boobs hanging out after accidentally ramming a doorknob up Tyler Jaeger's ass.

Maybe there's a reason I was a virgin until the night of the walk-in fridge at the club.

And maybe that reason is me.

Tyler

NEVER, ever, ever let me think that things couldn't possibly get more awkward.

Somehow, passing out at a funeral home, telling her about my zombie grandfather, and snuggling her with a broken dick all night is *still* not the end of the awkward.

Now, we're sitting at a comfortable table in a high-scale suite while the train wreck gets worse, unable to look at each other since she tried to join me in the shower.

Not that we discussed that that was her intention.

Pretty clear given that I caught a glimpse of her tits and found her shirt on the bathroom floor once my ass quit aching.

This'll be a fun one to explain to the team doctor. *Yeah, it's bruised because I almost got a prostrate exam from a doorknob.*

And speaking of exams—

"Oh my gosh, you're both doctors!" Daisy's saying to Muffy and Veda, who made the fatal mistake of telling Muffy that *anything* would be better than breakfast with her own family this morning, and is now sitting with the four of us as the fifth wheel in a married-couple-plus-two-spare-wheels-already situation.

"Veda's a doctor," Muffy tells Daisy. "I didn't finish school. I'm…"

Say something, Jaeger. Say. Something.

Save her.

"She's a matchmaker," Veda interjects with a bright smile. "These crepes are delicious. I didn't know they served crepes here."

Knowing Daisy, she brought along her own personal chef to take over the hotel's kitchen. I'd question if these are actually the hotel's plates and linens except for West's no-nonsense approach to everything that's basically the opposite of his wife's.

Also knowing Daisy, discussing crepes won't distract her from the more interesting discussion of Muffy's career. "Fruit salad's better," I interject. "You try the pomegranate mango salad?"

"A matchmaker!" Daisy claps her hands. "That's such a cool job. How many couples have you matched?"

"Daisy, is Remy supposed to be stacking those blocks?" I ask.

He's one.

Of course he's supposed to be stacking blocks in the corner after leaving his breakfast mostly untouched. He probably already had breakfast.

How do I know?

Because every time the grandkids come to stay at my parents' house, they're always up at the crack of dawn, being fed their breakfast by adults who look like there's not enough coffee in the world to help them recover from a parenting hangover.

But that's not the point right now.

Right now, the point is that West is giving me the *what in the ever-loving world is wrong with you?* look.

No doubt it'll quickly morph into *Oh, your girlfriend sucks as a matchmaker?* look, and I don't want that look, since Muffy gets enough shit in her life for everything else, so instead, I accidentally spill my orange juice.

On purpose. "Oh, shit."

"Watch your mouth in front of the baby," West growls.

"Shit. Sorry. Forgot. *Shi*—sorry."

Everyone's diving for napkins, and Muffy's job is temporarily forgotten.

I don't actually know how many people she's matched, but I know it's not many—three, did she say?—and I know her recent string of successes with the other parts of her matchmaking business isn't enough to give her the kind of confidence she needs if she's going to succeed long-term.

"You drunk?" West asks me.

He's mainlining coffee, which isn't much of a surprise considering they flew in from Miami last night, and he's not the night owl his wife is, and see again—parenthood destroys your will to live without caffeine.

"We all have accidents," I tell him as everyone leaps into action making sure the orange juice doesn't make it to the carpet.

"I spilled water all over the professors presiding over my board exam," Veda says.

Daisy nods. "I accidentally smacked a prince in the face with a vodka bottle once."

I point to her. "If Daisy can try to take out the future leader of a country, then I don't think I deserve any shi—*crap* for spilling a little orange juice at breakfast."

But West is still scowling at me. "Says the man who spends at least an hour during every family cookout following Keely around and asking if she needs a towel yet."

"She's needed that towel more times than she hasn't. Have

we *ever* had a family cookout where Keely didn't spill or drop something?"

"Do you do mixers with your clients, Muffy?" Daisy asks. "I can't think of anyplace more likely to have klutzy people than matchmaking socials. People get so nervous."

"My clientele is already special enough that we don't risk nerves in group date settings," Muffy says. "But we do have support group meetings with my clients, and I usually email them all daily, if I can, or whenever I find motivational things that really resonate with me."

"She's doing the world such a favor." Veda beams at her. "She specializes in misfits and socially awkward people."

"That's amazing!" Daisy sits back in her chair as we finish cleaning the orange juice. "The world is so lucky to have you."

Muffy smiles, but it's pained. "That's what I hear."

Once again, I want to shove my fist through someone's face. I don't even know whose face this time. Her parents for making her so insecure? Whoever told her that auctioning her virginity was a good idea? Whoever didn't select her for a residency?

Whoever rejects her clients on a regular basis?

Myself for probably being one of those people who make her feel inferior, and also for probably rejecting her clients at some point?

Daisy refills Muffy's mimosa. "Do you get invited to the weddings? I love weddings."

"Weddings are great," Muffy agrees. "Yours must've been beautiful."

"It was at a drag queen brunch. Didn't you see the pictures?" Veda starts to blush. "I mean, they *were* in *People*. And my office stocks *People*. Of course I saw the pictures. It looked so fun."

I poke West. "And I forever get to say that my boring,

stodgy old brother got his picture in a gossip magazine for getting hitched by drag queens."

"Are you boring?" Muffy asks him.

"As stale toast," he confirms.

"Would you have matched us?" Daisy's beaming again. She's basically always a bundle of sunshine, and it's not usually annoying, but today it is.

"Does it matter?" I ask.

But Muffy's already answering for herself. "Not unless either of you are completely socially inept."

"I can't dance," West offers.

"That doesn't make you socially inept."

"His track record with women prior to Daisy should've," I offer.

And then I dodge, because I know when I'm about to get a plateful of scrambled eggs in my face.

Plus, dodging means I accidentally fall out of my chair, and look at that.

Pain shoots over my bruised ass, but we're not talking about Muffy's job anymore.

Also, she's bending over in her chair and looking at me for the first time since we got here.

It's bad that I'm almost grateful we had a doorknob mishap.

If we hadn't, she might've found out my wood is still missing.

"Are you hung over?" she asks.

"He's attempting to get out of seeing more dead bodies," West replies for me.

"Nerves," I agree. "I'm a disaster."

"When he was little, he decided to start a pet-walking business because he wanted to buy flashy new skates, and for once, Mom put her foot down, so he needed his own cash. But he tried to walk all of the dogs at once, and he ended up tied to a neighbor's tree since all the dogs wanted to pee on the tree and they all kept circling it and getting their leashes tangled. Everyone came out and took pictures for half an hour before anyone thought to go get our parents or sisters."

A real smile touches Muffy's lips. "Seriously?"

"I wasn't tied to the tree. I was *pretending* because everyone wanted pictures. I was hugging it and hamming it up for a crowd. There's a difference."

West snorts. "I got video. He couldn't move. *And* Mom made him throw away his shoes. The dogs didn't all have good aim."

Muffy holds out a hand. "C'mon. Get off the floor before you get jam on your pants. *I'm* the one who's supposed to be a disaster this morning. Not you."

"You're not a disaster."

She holds my gaze, silently calling me a liar.

I scowl right back at her, silently telling her she's been listening to the wrong people.

Her eyes narrow, and I get the feeling she's not calling me a liar, but she's accusing me of something else.

No idea what, but whatever it is, it's unflattering.

"Are you getting up?" she finally asks.

I eyeball her hand.

What would she do if I pulled her down here and kissed her?

Would she kiss me back?

Do I want her to?

Who am I kidding? Waking up wrapped around her, that warm, perfect breast in my hand, is the most action I've had in weeks, and yeah, I want more of it.

So I yank on her arm.

But she yanks on my arm at the same time, and I have seriously underestimated Muffy.

She's got game.

She's also got better leverage.

Screw that.

I shift on the floor, plant my feet, and tug again, but she's already braced her own feet, and she's using her thighs to anchor herself, and my ass is suddenly sliding across the floor.

She's strong enough to pull me across the carpet.

Jesus.

That's seriously hot.

I double down. She's gonna sit.

She adds her other hand to her grip and adjusts her stance, and fuck me.

She's winning.

"Are you two playing tug-of-war with just your hands?" West asks.

Daisy claps. "Kinky."

"If one of you breaks a bone, I'm not setting it for you," Veda announces. "I'm also not treating bloody noses or concussions. I'm off duty today."

"Mama?" Remy says.

Little guy's adorable.

"Let go, Tyler," Muffy mutters while everyone else coos over Remy. "Last thing we need is the team hearing a girl tore your rotator cuff and put you in rehab for the rest of the season."

I'm probably in danger of needing rehab for my bruised ass, but I refuse to admit that to her. "Why are you being so stubborn?"

"Because I know what you're doing, and I want you to stop."

Glad one of us does.

All I know is that I want to pull her into my lap and kiss her.

And I don't know why.

Also?

There's still not much action in my junk, so this makes even less sense. "What am I doing?"

She rolls her eyes. I yank one last time, except this time, she twists her hand so that it slides right out of mine, and I plop back onto my ass on the floor.

I stifle a grunt as more pain shoots through my tailbone.

Muffy goes pink.

Veda eyes her, and the two of them do that silent communication thing again, and it ends when Veda carefully pats her mouth with her linen napkin and puts it on the table. "Thank you so much for breakfast. I need to go finish getting ready for the funeral and to dash a few relatives' hopes about what's in my father's will."

"Did he have any other children needing guardians? Are you in danger of accidentally inheriting them?" Daisy asks as she lifts Remy and spins him in a circle.

Veda's clearly well-versed in celebrity gossip, because she doesn't blink at the mention of how the little guy came into all of our lives. "No, but now I wish he had some creepy dolls or something that he wanted my uncle to look after."

"Does he like creepy dolls? What's his address?"

"Do *not* answer that," West tells Veda.

Muffy's setting her own napkin aside too. She ate maybe a third of her plate, and now I'm wondering if she was too self-conscious to eat in front of my brother and his socialite wife.

"I need to brush my teeth and go help Veda," she says to the room at large. "Thank you so much for everything. This was fun."

Daisy smiles brightly at her. "You'll have to join us the next time the family invades Copper Valley for one of Ty's hockey games. Or ride along the next time they play in Florida. I love hosting the boys for parties after their games."

"No pressure if you're not interested," West adds to her with a head nod toward me. "We'd get it. But you're still welcome."

I ignore the subtle jab that I'm no fun to hang out with.

"It was nice to meet you too," Muffy says to West. "I hope you enjoy Richmond today."

"Do you need any extra guests at the funeral, Veda?" Daisy asks. "I'm *very* good at distracting annoying family members. All I need is the obituary and a general timeframe when your father might've taken a trip where I might've possibly met him, and I can be the life of a party."

I shoot West a look. Who the *fuck* volunteers to go be the life of a party at a funeral?

He shrugs, but he's clearly hiding a smile.

"Are you serious right now?" Veda asks her.

West turns that smile onto his wife. "Daisy's life mission is to improve other people's lives."

Veda and Muffy share another look.

"Not to sound rude," Muffy says, "but if you come, can you pretend you don't know us?"

Daisy winks. "Only if you promise to let me take you out for drinks next time I'm in Copper Valley."

19

Muffy

TYLER'S IN A MOOD, and I know I should care, because it's probably my fault—funeral, awkwardness, his bruised butt, you name it—but I don't.

He might be holding my hand as we stand graveside behind Veda and her uncle in the dreary November morning, and it might be stupidly reassuring since Dr. Richardson is right across the casket and keeps looking at me, but I still don't care that he's in a mood.

I thought he didn't care that I'm a disaster, and that he found me attractive despite all that, but clearly, I was wrong.

If I embarrass him, then he shouldn't have taken me to breakfast with his family.

I embarrass myself plenty.

I don't need to carry the weight of his embarrassment too.

Plus, *why* is Dr. Richardson staring at me again?

I paid him back what he bid on me. I didn't even tell Veda who met me in that hotel room. If he's going to cause a scene—

A woman starts singing a funeral song, and I've been paying little enough attention to the service that her sudden acapella performance makes me jerk.

Tyler leans down like he's going to ask if I'm okay.

But that's not what he asks. "Why is that asshole you ran into yesterday staring at you?"

"What asshole?"

"I told myself I wouldn't pry, but if I need to take him behind a headstone and beat the shit out of him, squeeze my hand twice."

I choke on an unexpected laugh at the image of Tyler grabbing Dr. Richardson and trying to stealthily beat him behind one of the wider headstones in this cemetery, like any of them are small enough here that no one would notice a two-hundred-pound hockey player beating a sixty-year-old man.

But then, considering the Daisy Carter-Kincaid factor, it's likely no one really would notice. People can't stop stealing glances at her.

Naturally.

She's utterly stunning in her black dress, and she'd stand out even without the blue hair and massive sparkly sunglasses.

And she's *behind* Dr. Richardson, for the record.

He is *not* staring at her.

I'll bet she and Tyler have some secret signal that would prompt her to pull her flask out of her cleavage and pretend she's trying to be subtle about taking a hit off of it so that everyone would watch her while he leaps across the casket, grabs Dr. Richardson, and pushes him behind that taller, but still not very tall, tombstone a few rows back.

Not that I'd ask Tyler to beat anyone up. Especially at a funeral.

Especially when I'm starting to want to beat him up myself.

It was my fault for thinking that auctioning my virginity

was something I could follow through with, and for not considering that a faculty member might be the one to win me instead of one of the preppy trust fund students.

But yeah, I'm totally squicked out at the fact that he keeps staring at me.

And now I'm wondering how many other students he's slept with. Or tried to sleep with.

And if his wife knows.

Tyler lets go of my hand, then clamps his arm around my shoulders so tight that I get a weird pull in my hips and have to adjust my stance.

Across the casket, Dr. Richardson goes pasty white. He looks down quickly and steps closer to his wife, who makes one of those *back up and give me space* looks and steps away from him, running right into Daisy, who pulls her flask out of her cleavage—really wasn't kidding about that—and offers it to Mrs. Richardson.

If I hadn't tried to take a shortcut to paying off some of my student loans, I could be here right now as an actual medical doctor.

I could've stayed in Richmond an extra year, done a few more classes, taken on a research project, found a different job in a medical field to stay in the industry, and tried again for a residency the next year.

I could've been through that residency by now. I could've been starting a practice like Veda did last year.

But instead, I'm floundering, trying desperately to help eight women find the love of their lives.

Eight.

I have *eight* total clients, and two are pro bono cases who don't know I'm trying to find matches for them, because everyone deserves love.

You can't make a living off of eight clients.

At least, I can't. I can't even find dates for my eight clients without working outside normal matchmaker boundaries.

I PUCKING LOVE YOU

Of course Tyler's embarrassed to introduce me to his family under circumstances that suggest we're something more than friends.

I could've made something of my life by now, and instead, I'm the woman who didn't have the courage to go back to my college town solo.

His grip on me tightens as the song comes to an end.

The funeral director says his closing words and thanks everyone for coming.

Which means it's probably about time for them to lower the casket into the grave.

I glance up at Tyler.

He's staring straight ahead, jaw visibly clenched.

It's hard to stay mad at him for being embarrassed by me when I know being at a funeral is physically uncomfortable for him for *other* reasons beyond the normal funereal discomfort.

"It would be really nice if a bird swooped in and pooped on the casket right about now," I whisper to him.

"If I never hear the word *casket* again for the rest of my life, it'll be too soon," he mutters back.

A couple people I don't recognize are the first to break ranks as the funeral director messes with something at the head of the casket. So maybe it's not a thing to stay and watch the casket get lowered?

I really don't know.

I don't do this often.

Once folks realize other people are moving away from the grave, more follow.

Some pause to offer condolences to Veda.

Others slip away.

And then there are the mourners who angle closer to Daisy.

Dr. Richardson's wife leans over and says something to her. Dr. Richardson checks out Daisy's cleavage in her black dress, and his wife hits him with an elbow to the gut.

She's not even looking at him, and she still knew what he was doing.

"I am *never* getting married," I murmur.

"Same."

I would absolutely get married. One hundred percent. No question.

But not until I found a man that I knew with absolute certainty loved me for everything I am, and everything I'm not, and everything I could be, and everything I could never be.

And not until I could love him back with everything inside of me.

So, basically, I'm never getting married. There's not a single person on this earth that I could ever trust that much.

The casket begins its descent into the ground, and the mourners still gathered all pause, like they, too, have realized maybe they made a faux pas.

Tyler shudders, so I wrap an arm around his waist and squeeze.

To his credit, he doesn't ask if we can get out of here.

But then, he probably knows I'd tell him *no*. Until Veda's done, I'm here. "If you want to go back now, I can hop a bus later."

"I'm not leaving you here without a ride home," he mutters.

"I could ask Daisy to fly me over."

He winces.

And suddenly I'm mad at him all over again.

I know I shouldn't be. He had to ask for a day off practice to be here today, and it's not like the coach randomly hands out *get out of practice free* cards. Tyler gets paid a crap ton of money to play hockey, and that means he's expected at every practice unless he's dying, injured, or ridden with contagious cooties that could wipe the whole team out, and even then, he's supposed to be there for his team however he can.

Plus, *funeral.*

He *really* doesn't want to be here.

Still— "Am I that embarrassing?"

"What?"

"Don't play dumb, Tyler. You spent all of breakfast trying to make sure no one talked about me and what I do and how terrible I am at it. You *spilled your orange juice* so your brother and his wife wouldn't figure out that I'm basically a failure."

"*What?* No. I thought—"

"That I couldn't handle talking about my own business, which I do *every day*, with your very successful sister-in-law?"

"Muffy—"

"Never mind. It doesn't matter. Thank you. Again. For being here. I know you hate funerals, I know I should've told you that's what this was, and I know I shouldn't have burdened you with *anything* that I burdened you with last night, and I—"

"Stop saying *thank you*," he hisses. "This is what friends do. And we're friends. And I'm not embarrassed by you. I didn't want—"

"Muffy? Oh my god, Muffy, is that you?"

My shoulders hitch up to my forehead as I slowly turn to face Connie Bragowski.

Doctor Connie Bragowski.

Who clearly doesn't care for the sanctity of the moment of having Veda's dad lowered into the ground, and who apparently might have a new last name, if the stunning man in the custom-tailored pinstripe suit and million-dollar hairstyle standing next to her is any indication.

Maybe he's her fake funeral date.

"Muffy! Oh my god, it *is* you. I told Hendrick that there was *no way* you were back after you basically ghosted the *entire school* after you auctioned off your virginity, but *oh my god*, here you are! This is Hendrick. Hendrick Meyer. Yes, of *those* Meyers. We got married last summer." The annoying skinny cow shoves her hand in my face so that I can see a diamond ring the size of the Titanic surrounded by diamond chips the size of large tugboats.

Tyler steps between us before I can say a word. "Hi. Tyler Jaeger. I'm Muffy's boy toy. Offered to be here for fun, not because I have to be for risk of pissing off the ol' ball and chain. We're hooking up with one of my teammates for a threesome later. You follow the Thrusters? Heard of Rooster Applebottom? Guy's *freaky*. But we don't fuck around with married people. Sorry. Can't invite you."

I choke on air.

Connie goes completely silent.

Hendrick clears his throat.

And everyone who was watching the casket get lowered turns to stare at us.

"Oh, shit, did I do that awkward thing again?" Tyler looks at me and rolls his eyes. "Babe, you gotta tell me when I'm supposed to keep the handcuffs out of the cemetery."

I try to talk, but all that comes out is a strangled noise that sounds like I'm a mooing cow.

Yeah. I sound like my cousin Kami's "dog."

Tyler grins and slides a hand to my ass. "Alright. If you insist. I'll wear the bridle this time."

Connie gapes, then abruptly turns on her heel, trips—mental note: the grass is soft and I should not attempt quick turns in my own heels—and face plants while her husband watches.

"C'mon, sexy pants." Tyler squeezes my ass. "Let's go pay our respects to the lovely doctor."

Instead of steering me toward Veda, though, he spins me into his body, grabs me by the back of my head, and slams his mouth over mine.

Oh god. Oh god oh god oh god.

I am *not* a good kisser. I've had exactly three boyfriends in my entire life, and two of them were when I was in high school, one of which was freshman year, when we thought *dating* meant passing notes in class, and he was only my boyfriend in my head and never actually knew I thought he was my soulmate for six weeks, three days, and four hours.

Kissing practice?

My mother only thinks I have it because I try to out-outrageous her at every opportunity, and also because I have to tell her I'm going *somewhere* when I leave for all my shifts at Cod Pieces. I'm all talk.

But Tyler is all action.

And *oh my god*, is he action.

It wasn't like this in the fridge. In the fridge, he was handsy and only a little kissy after the first attempt got awkward, plus it was all over so fast, but now?

His lips are hot and aggressive, and I can't keep up with what he's doing with them, but I don't think it matters, because if I quit thinking and let myself go, my body knows.

My mouth knows.

My hands are gliding all over his chest, over the thick, warm fabric of his white shirt, under the wool of his outer coat, my fingers taking in more solid muscle than they've felt since I was poking cadavers in my med school days, which is *not* something I want to think about while Tyler's grinding his pelvis against mine and devouring my mouth with his and desecrating this entire cemetery.

Thank *god* Veda's family aren't religious.

Why can I not get out of my own head?

Because you know he's faking it, Muffy.

I sigh and my whole body sags in defeat, which Tyler apparently takes as a sign that I'm fully surrendering to his kiss, because he deepens it even more.

And *oh*.

Oh, my.

Is that a petrified bratwurst in his pants, or is he just happy to be kissing me?

And is that *me* that I smell, or are other people getting turned on watching us make out?

Am I an exhibitionist?

Holy hell. My panties are soaked. My nipples could cut glass. And I'm thrusting my tongue into Tyler's mouth like there's an ice cream cone waiting at the back of his throat.

Tyler Jaeger is a kissing god.

I did *not* realize this the night of the private club fridge incident.

But he is. Everywhere his hand roams, my nerves spontaneously light themselves on fire. I want to strip out of my dress and beg him to lick me from head to toe. I want to ride him like a mermaid riding a dolphin and drown in this intense feeling of being a sexy, desirable, untamed woman with her whole life together.

Am I unbuttoning his shirt?

Oh my god.

I'm unbuttoning his shirt.

"Hate to break up the party," a voice that sounds like Veda says somewhere in the hazy distance, "but if you two don't quit pawing at each other, I think my uncle's going to have a heart attack, and one funeral in a week is quite enough with me."

Tyler freezes with his tongue in my mouth.

I squeak.

Kind of.

Oh my god, I can smell myself. I really am turned on.

I need to change my underwear before I can ride home in the same car as myself for the next three hours, never mind riding in the same car as Tyler.

How, exactly, does one unentangle her tongue from someone else's when there's an audience?

Not asking for a friend.

Tyler abruptly pulls back, wipes his thumb over the saliva left dangling on my lip, and clears his throat. "Sorry, Veda."

"Oh, no, don't apologize to me." She grins at him. "I've never seen Connie Bra-cow-ski silenced so quickly. That was glorious. You're forgiven for being an ass at breakfast. Thanks for coming to my dad's funeral."

I wipe my mouth too, but it doesn't scrub off the feeling of Tyler kissing me. "What else can we do? Need anything else? We don't have to leave for…what? Another hour or two?" I look at Tyler, immediately wish he had the decency to look like someone who wasn't just kissing the stuffing out of me on top of a grave, then look at the ground. "When did you tell the coach you'd be back?"

"Team meeting at four."

"Oh, no, then you should get going," Veda says. "Thank you so much for being here. And for the margarita. And dinner. And breakfast." Veda hugs me tight and drops her voice. "Oh my god, Muffy, that was the hottest kiss I've ever seen. If you don't do something about that and give me all the details, I'll basically never forgive you."

"We should tell Daisy we're leaving," I reply.

"Not a chance," Tyler says. "She's in her zone. We go over there, we'll be partying on a riverboat for the next three days."

"Seriously?" Veda grins at him. "That's an option?"

He shakes his head, also not looking at me. "Two years ago? Definitely. I was there. Now? No chance. Disgusting as it is, she's way too into my brother, and he's not much of a partier."

"If he ever decides to throw a three-day riverboat party that he lets her plan, let me know."

Tyler laughs, and my vagina fangirls like a middle-aged woman at a boy band reunion concert. "You got it."

Neither of us say a word on the way to his car.

I don't ask if we can stop somewhere so I can change my panties.

He doesn't ask if I need any more Donettes.

And when he opens the door for me, he doesn't touch me.

Instead, he looks down at his phone.

Right.

That kiss?

It was all for show.

And this favor?

It's over.

20

Tyler

I HAVE A BONER.

And not just any boner.

It's like my first boner after my junk developed and I found my buddy's dad's anime magazine collection and stole an issue with one of the hottest anime girl drawings to look at with a flashlight under my sheets, spanking the monkey and not understanding why I had that infernal ache in the pit of my stomach when it felt so good to yank on my dick.

I have a boner so hard I actually feel physically ill.

And I'm supposed to drive three fucking hours like this.

Gratitude. I should have gratitude. My dick is no longer broken. He's fully capable of standing up for himself. But it's so hard I'm nauseous.

I could text West. Tell him Muffy and I need to "talk" and I need his hotel room for twenty minutes.

He'd know I was asking for space for a booty call.

I wouldn't care.

It'd be quicker than checking into another hotel. More efficient. Even if there's traffic between here and Copper Valley, I'll be back in time for the team meeting if I can use a pre-paid hotel room.

Or we could find an abandoned parking lot and bang it out in the back seat.

I cut a glance at Muffy, who's staring straight ahead as I pull out of the cemetery, lips drooping, eyes sad, arms crossed over her chest in exactly the right way to offer a hint of cleavage at the top of her dress, and my boner grows another inch.

Not a good sign for my performance if we *do* stop.

Or maybe it *is* a good sign. Maybe she needs comforting.

"You need a bathroom or anything?" My voice is rough and also higher than normal. It's like I'm sliding backwards into puberty again.

Muffy doesn't seem to notice. She keeps staring straight ahead. "No, thank you."

"Food?"

"I'm full, thank you."

"Want to change?"

She twists in her seat to face me. "Thank you for being basically the perfect date for Veda's dad's funeral. I'm fine. It wasn't as bad as I thought it would be, but it could've been, especially if you weren't here. Thank you for worrying. That's very kind of you. But I'd prefer to get on the road. I need to get back to work on helping a client get a first date, which isn't going well, if I'm being perfectly honest, and it makes me mad, because she's this awesome person with the biggest heart and a great sense of humor, and she's so *real*, but she's not conventionally pretty, and everyone judges her by her shoulders."

Is this a trap? Is this one of those times when she's actually talking about herself but pretending she's talking about someone else, and I'm supposed to tell her I find her very attractive, both inside and out?

Do I find her attractive?

Or do I simply like that I was right, and the solution to getting my boners back was to go back to the woman who took them away from me?

Holy shit.

Muffy's a witch.

She heaves a loud sigh and flings herself back into her seat.

I clear my throat. Right. Didn't reply for too long. And she's probably not talking about herself. She did that plenty in front of me with Veda last night. "I could ask a few guys on the team to take her out."

"Thank you, but that's not necessary."

Translation: I've met your teammates and I think they're all superficially judgmental assholes, just like you are, Tyler Jaeger.

I'm not a superficially judgmental asshole, which I'd think she'd know by now, so why am I calling myself one?

And yet I still have a raging hard-on.

Shit.

Is this like one of those things I should call my doctor about?

Or is it the reflex boner after weeks of no boners?

"Do you want me to take her out?" I ask.

It feels like the wrong question, but I don't know what else to ask.

Her answer is equally wrong. "Do you want to get married?"

"*No.*"

"Then no, thank you. My clients are looking for long-term, committed relationships."

She doesn't sound angry or irritated by any of this.

She sounds tired and defeated.

Much like my junk was until that kiss.

How many guys has she kissed like that?

Was she a virgin when we banged in the bunny bar kitchen?

She's thirty, I think. Maybe a year or two older? I don't actually know. The odds of her being a virgin seem slim.

But at the same time, I've never heard her talk about a boyfriend. I've never seen her with a date, and she's been pretty vocal about not dating. And if she was a virgin in her final year of med school, she was at least—dammit, math is hard when I have the boner from hell—okay, I don't know how old she would've been, but I know she would've been through at least four years of college and at least two or three years of medical school—or four? I don't know—which means she made it past the prime virginity-shedding years with her v-card still intact.

Jesus, this woody hurts.

I shift in my seat to try to relieve some of the pressure.

Distraction.

I need a distraction.

And not a distraction that involves thinking about funerals, friends dating married guys, my family, or anything other than getting to know Muffy a little better. "What made you get into matchmaking?"

There's a long pause while Phil Collins sings softly in the background.

Phil Collins?

One, who changed my radio station?

Two, how did I know that's Phil Collins? I don't listen to *Phil Collins.*

"I want to help people," Muffy says quietly. "Especially the people who are usually overlooked."

I glance at her. She's staring out the window at the row of stores we're passing on our way out of Richmond. "Help people find love?"

"It's the greatest power on earth. Can you imagine what the world would be like if we actually loved each other the way we pretend to? I can't fix the world. I can't fix their bodies. Clearly. Medical school drop-out and all that. But if I can help one person who feels *different* find someone who loves her the way she deserves to be loved, then I can change *her* world. And I don't always get it right." She snorts quietly. "Okay, I *often* don't get it right. I could write a book about all the awkward dates my clients have had because of me, though I'm getting better at making sure that doesn't happen anymore. But I hope I'm also showing all of my clients that they can love themselves. That they're worthy of love. And that their needs are as important as anyone else's."

Now my dick isn't the only thing uncomfortable.

My chest is feeling some tightness too. "That's pretty cool."

"It would be if it worked," she mutters.

I've seen Muffy sassy. I've seen her confident. I've seen her not give two shits and I've seen her tell off people to defend her friends.

Hell, she's told me off a time or two. Not that many days ago inside a Cod Pieces, actually.

I even saw her scared this weekend. Angry, too.

But I've never seen her defeated.

"You have a higher calling," I say. "A purpose. That's cool."

"What's a purpose without results?"

"You got Kami and Nick together."

"No, I didn't. Kami would've found herself other dates on dating apps with or without me, and Nick would've come to his senses all on his own. He *did* come to his senses all on his own. I was a tool in her belt. I wasn't the magic. *She* was the magic."

"But she trusted you."

"Above all things, Kami is kind, and she called me because she didn't want my feelings to get hurt if I heard she was using a dating app. You don't have to pretend I'm a good matchmaker. I've made a fine art out of failing for a long time, and I know it. I'm okay with who I am, because I keep trying, and that's what's important."

I floor the gas pedal as I hit the on-ramp to I-56. Muffy is *not* okay with who she is, and she doesn't even know it. "You said you've made a few matches lately."

She makes a face. "A few isn't anything to write home about."

"Tell me three good things about yourself."

"What?"

"Three good things. Tell me."

"I'm no longer in Richmond, I'm not my mother, and I can burp the alphabet."

"Seriously?"

"No. I accidentally burfed once at a dinner party my dad was hosting for his boss, and I've made an effort to never burp in public again. Private either."

"Burfed?"

"Burped and barfed at the same time? Like when you think it'll be a quiet burp that you can subtly stifle, but then stuff comes up? Like a shart in your mouth? *Oh my god.* This is *exactly* why I can't get a date, isn't it? You kissed me. We slept in the same bed together. We've had sex. We ghosted each other. And now I'm talking about sharts and burfs."

"You have a name for it. That's hot."

"Don't mock me."

"I'm serious. I like made-up words."

"When they're about bodily functions?"

"I also like that you're not afraid to speak your mind. You care enough about your friends to get physically and emotionally uncomfortable to be there for them. And you want to make the world a better place."

She's eyeballing me again. I can feel it, and it makes me want to squirm.

With good reason, given what comes out of her mouth next.

"Why don't you ever want to get married?"

Is it hot in here? Or is it that she's going right for the balls? "I grew up with four sisters. That's enough for one lifetime."

"Being married would be like living with your sisters again?"

I open my mouth to reply, and nothing comes out.

They talk about childbirth seems like a dumb thing to say. So does *they nag me*.

I love my sisters. They're all great.

But I wouldn't marry them.

Still, I'm not a big enough idiot to suggest that the four of them encompass every personality of every woman in the world.

Plus, West also nags me, so I know it's not only a sister thing.

So why don't I want to get married?

Heartbreak and expectations.

"Yes. That's exactly it," I finally say. "It'd be like sleeping with my sisters and listening to my sisters and fighting with my sisters."

"So you're afraid of commitment."

"You know what it takes to be a low-ranked draft pick, spend years playing minor-league hockey and still never give up on that dream of making it to the top tier of the pros? *Commitment*. I'm not afraid of commitment. I'm *here* because of commitment."

"Commitment to a job and commitment to a person are two very different things."

"Not really."

"Yes, they are. You *know* you can only play hockey for so many years, and then you'll retire and find a new job. Maybe it'll be sports-related. Maybe it won't. Maybe you won't find a job at all and you'll go somewhere with a low cost of living and raise goats for fun. Your teammates will change over the years. Maybe your team will change too. The only thing that'll stay steady is that you'll strap on your pads, lace up your skates, grab your stick, and spend your days getting paid to chase a puck on the ice until your body gives out or you get tired of it. Commitment to a person, though—that's a lifetime. And that person? They'll love you back. They can hurt you, or they can complete you, and some days they might do both in a span of a few seconds. When that person's sick, *you'll* feel sick. When they get life-shattering news, you'll feel it so deep in your gut you know it'll never leave. When they're happy, you'll feel the sunshine and rainbows. The game? The game doesn't love you. It won't be there for you the next time you have to go to a funeral. It won't throw you a surprise birthday party. It won't know when you need a hug or someone to talk to, and it won't keep you warm at night."

"You don't know the game the way I know the game." I'm sweating. She's right.

"Maybe not. But I know fear of commitment when I see it. And you, Tyler Jaeger, are afraid of commitment."

"So?"

"So maybe don't try to diagnose what's wrong with me if you're not willing to put the time in to figure out what's wrong with you."

"Why does not wanting commitment have to be *wrong*? I like myself fine the way I am."

Yeah, that's why we're malfunctioning, idiot, my junk offers.

It doesn't get to talk, because it's still a raging stiff rod of *someone pet me!*

"Good," Muffy says. "Because I like myself fine the way I am too, broken and incapable and everything."

"You're not broken."

She eyeballs me and doesn't answer.

"And I wasn't embarrassed by you this morning," I add.

"I didn't want *you* to feel uncomfortable. You sit here and talk about being broken and incapable, and I didn't—fuck, Muffy, *I* feel like a failure next to Daisy sometimes, and I didn't want you to feel judged or insignificant or unsuccessful when you *are* doing something pretty cool with your life."

More crickets.

But my mouth won't quit moving. "Were you still a virgin the night we hooked up?"

I know. Shut up, Jaeger. Throw it in reverse, back it up, swallow the words down, don't let them come out of your mouth.

But I want to know.

I *need* to know.

"This isn't Regency England, and I'm not the kind of girl who made chastity vows."

"Your first time should be special no matter what."

"Who died and made you king of sex rules?"

"Veda's dad."

"Oh my god."

I choke on a laugh.

Yeah, that was probably inappropriate.

Muffy halfheartedly shoves my arm. "Veda's dad was this stuffy academic guy who only ever wanted to talk about the importance of the grading system and how big of a dick parking ticket traffic cops were. Veda's mom died when she was three, and she grew up with a dad who'd make eyebrows at every skinny woman who walked past him and then forbade Veda to be anything other than a woman who liked men, like he had the market on being attracted to women in the family. I saw him choke on a burrito once, and Veda told me she'd accidentally walked in on him getting busy with his secretary and saw him making that exact same face. If that's who you want making the sex rules, then pull over and let me walk home."

Jesus, I have a problem.

My boner isn't at all affected by *any* of this. He's still raging down there. It's party central in my pants. "The one thing everyone in high school talked about more than anything else was the state of people's virginity. It's ingrained in our culture to care about it."

"Maybe I don't."

"You auctioned yours off and couldn't follow through with it. You care. You thought you didn't, but you did."

She goes silent.

I pound the button on my stereo to switch stations, because now Whitney Houston is singing, and I don't mind Whitney Houston, but I'm not feeling like dancing with anyone right now, and it's annoying me.

Pearl Jam.

Better.

I tap my thumb on the steering wheel, feel every beat in my boner, and concentrate on the traffic around me as we fly down the highway.

Until Muffy mutters a very soft sentence a few miles later. "So what if I was?"

And here I thought I couldn't possibly get any harder.

Why. The fuck. Is my dick. Obsessed. With *Muffy*?

Because we like her. Catch up.

"Do-over," I say before I can stop myself. "Thursday—no, out of town. Saturday. Saturday night. You. Me. Dinner. Do-over."

"That's very kind of you, but—"

"It's not *kind* of me. I have something to prove here."

"So you want to have sex with me just to prove that you're good at sex."

"Yes."

"And it has nothing at all to do with you liking me or being attracted to me or wanting to see if having sex with me, *again*, after being my date *to a funeral*, with a whole lot more baggage than I expected showing up and making things hella awkward for both of us, might demonstrate that there's some-thing between us?"

This is exactly why I'm never getting married.

Mind games.

Traps.

Or possibly she has a point and I don't want to admit it.

Am I afraid of commitment? Is she right?

Or is it really that my sisters soured me on living with women forever?

And possibly one or two girlfriends in high school and college who got way too close, then dropped me like a puck that sprouted spikes in their hands?

My first girlfriend dumped me because things got super awkward when I introduced her to my family before our date to my junior year homecoming game.

My second girlfriend didn't so much dump me as she listened to her brother when he forbade her to ever look at me again, and then he tried to beat the shit out of me before practice.

Related: It astonishes me every day that Nick Murphy's sister is married to Ares Berger and the team didn't implode when they hooked up.

And I don't date seriously anymore.

Just not worth it when I know the ultimate payoff to rela-tionships.

"I want you to know it can be good," I tell Muffy. And I need to see a doctor. My dick really isn't supposed to strain like this.

Plus, Muffy's looking at it. I hid it at the cemetery. I've been doing my best to block her view with my arm. But there's no hiding Junior. He's being an exhibitionist.

"So your own needs have nothing to do with this?" Muffy asks.

"I could hook up with any woman I wanted. So, no. My own needs have nothing to do with this."

She snorts softly and goes silent.

And a text message thread with my family plays out in my head.

Who needs actual messages when I know what they'd say?

KEELY: *Smooth, idiot. Tell her how many other women you want to bang.*

ALLIE: *Maybe you can tell her how many other women you're bringing home for Thanksgiving too?*

BRITNEY: *Women love a man who brags about how hot he is and how many women he can get. Serious turn-on. Maybe you should tell her you're smarter than the average hockey player too.*

DAD: *Tyler is never getting laid again. Whoa! Autocorrect got this one right!*

KEELY: *I'm pulling Staci in, and you KNOW she doesn't do group texts.*

STACI: *I'm only here to reiterate that you need to plug your mouth back in to your brain, muzzle yourself for the next millennium, and hope that the gossip rags don't hear about this.*

DAISY: *Go easy on Tyler. It's hard (heh) to be a guy with a broken penis and then realize the only person he can get it up for is the only person he not only fails to impress every time, but also actively pushes away every time.*

KEELY: *Fear of commitment.*

ALLIE: *Well, duh. He takes us for granted and he knows it.*

BRIT: *Any other woman definitely wouldn't put up with him the way we do.*

STACI: *And they don't have to love him like we do, and they definitely won't love him when he gets old and retires from hockey and has a monumental identity crisis.*

DAD: *He has redeeming qualities. Like his beard. He gets that from me.*

DAISY: *Also, he has to compete with West, who's basically perfect, and he has nothing going for him other than his hockey career, if he can manage to stay pro and not get demoted back to the minors.*

MUFFY RUSTLES NEXT TO ME.

I cut a glance toward her and see her pulling a pack of Oreos out of her purse. She starts to open them, notices me watching, and shoves them back in her purse.

My jaw clenches on its own, and my grip tightens on the steering wheel.

Is it any of my business if she's self-conscious?

No.
But do I want to fix it anyway?
Yes.
That's not normal.
I have a problem.
And it's bigger than my boner.

21

Muffy

I'M TRYING VERY hard to not look at Tyler's erection and instead concentrate on what I need to do when we get back to Copper Valley.

Namely, shower quickly and manage my time very well for two appointments I have back-to-back early this evening that I booked myself as we're heading out of Richmond.

The funeral's over. Time to think ahead. Get back to business. Make a few more matches. Get a few more referrals. Set reminders to check in on Veda every day this week, and schedule lunch with her one weekend soon.

Find out why my mother thought she needed to charge *my* credit card for her boudoir photo session, thus maxing it out, and figure out how I'm going to pay Tyler back for gas money and the hotel bill.

Ponder why Tyler would've made a joke about his penis not working if it's clearly working fine.

Although, is that actually his penis? That's a long erection.

Long-lasting, I mean. But yes, also long-long. Lengthwise.

Is it hot in here? Someone needs to turn the heater down.

Like he's reading my mind, he reaches for the control and yanks it down. "Why don't *you* date?"

I flinch. I hate when the tables are turned. "Trust issues."

"That's a reason to not get married. *Not* a reason not to date."

"I get to have whatever reason I want to not date."

"I dare you to go on a date with me."

"Been there—"

"Nope. Nuh-uh. Not hooking up at a bar where we ran into each other. Not being tricked into going to a funeral together. Not having breakfast with my brother and his family. A *date*-date. You and me. Alone. On purpose. Saturday night."

If Tyler's anything like his teammates, he'll take me out to a fancy restaurant where I *could* pronounce things on the menu even though no one would expect me to be able to, and I'd still probably break a bunch of unspoken rules, like laughing too loudly at a joke that isn't funny, or putting my elbows on the table, or accidentally mistaking the tablecloth for a napkin when I don't look clearly as I reach for my lap and standing up and pulling everything off the table when I need a bathroom break, or turning down wine when it's expected that everyone who goes into the restaurant pays for hundred-dollar bottles that you can get for thirteen at the liquor store.

And while it's nice to think about being pampered with a treat like that, I can never enjoy my meal knowing what a dent the final bill would make in my student loans.

Not that I expect a date to offer me peanut butter and jelly and a check for my monthly loan payment instead, but I'm still aware of it.

And then there's the kissing problem.

Kissing leads to touching, touching leads to clothes coming off, and the truth is, no matter how many hours of therapy I've had, I still hate the idea of being completely and totally naked in front of a guy.

I went through with having sex with Tyler in the walk-in fridge at the bunny bar because the lights were off and the flashlight on his phone only worked so well and I'd been wondering if he was into me for a while, and I wanted to.

But doing it again?

I've been telling myself the payoff isn't worth the effort, but the truth might be a little more than that.

The truth might be closer to *I'm afraid he'd be good at it if I let him.*

And if he were good, I'd want more, and he…wouldn't.

He steers the car off the interstate at an exit with nothing more than a closed auto repair shop sitting within view on either side of the road.

"What are you doing?"

"Solving a problem." His eyes are flashing, and his beard is twitching like his jaw's clenching and unclenching.

I glance at his crotch again and the way his cock is straining his pants.

Is he—is he going to jack off behind the building?

Crap.

That should be disturbing, but my panties just got wet. Again.

He whips the car into the crumbled parking lot and around to the back of the building, out of sight of the interstate.

I shrink into my seat, gripping my phone in front of me like it has some kind of force field that'll keep me from what-ever tumultuous emotions have him scowling like the Thrusters are down five-nothing going into the third period, and he has something to prove.

As soon as he puts the car in park, he yanks his seatbelt off and turns to face me. "I like you."

"I'm sorry?"

"I said, I like you."

"I know. And I'm sorry."

"Dammit, Muffy. *You're likeable*. You're obnoxious and you're opinionated and you're bull-headed. You act like you have your life together when it's painfully obvious you don't, and it's nearly impossible to help you until you're at your breaking point."

My face is curling into a horrified glare, and my fingers are doing something similar. "I thought you *liked* me."

"I *do*. I *like* all of those things about you. It's sexy as hell to me that you're not easy. You're not predictable. You're not boring. You're different. I like that. *I like you*. Okay?"

I blink at him. "Oh my god. *Am I a shrew?*"

"Oh, fuck me." He squeezes his eyes shut and drops his head to the steering wheel. "You're not a *shrew*. You're *you*. I've met your mother. I know what you live with every single day. You don't fit any mold of what's conventional or expected, which puts you at a disadvantage in this ridiculous world that rewards people like Daisy for being able to afford the right clothes and makeup and hair dye, and punishes you for not being able to do the same, but you're still *trying*. You still believe good things are possible for other people who don't meet modern standards of brains or beauty or whatever. But you're fucking infuriating in refusing to see that good things are possible for you too. So let me be one damn good thing in your life, for one damn night. Okay?"

I really am a shrew.

I hide behind all the forces that shaped me and tell myself I can't be anything more.

That I don't *deserve* more.

Three years of therapy haven't made it as painfully obvious as Tyler's making it right now.

But three years of therapy have reinforced the idea that I can change if I want to. That I can choose to believe in myself and step over to the other side, where I *am* worthy of having a date with a guy who'd drive a couple hundred miles to pass out at a funeral home for me.

Except there's a reason I don't like Tyler.

I like him too much, and that makes me vulnerable.

It wasn't one little moment of him being attractive at a bar that had me giving in to temptation that night.

It was him tossing me a puck before a game last year, with a grin and a wink that didn't immediately put me on the defensive for wondering if he was setting me up for embarrassment later.

It was him sitting down next to me at Chester Green's one night and asking if I'd read any good books lately, then having an actual conversation that suggested he reads books regularly.

It was randomly running into him at a coffee shop downtown and him taking the seat across from me like we were friends to talk about which Pokémon we were still hunting for, when any other guy on the team would've nodded, grunted, and run like hell to go drink his coffee anywhere else besides with me.

I kept telling myself that he was just a nice guy. That he wasn't into me. That he would've done the same for any other teammate's cousin-in-law, except Tyler Jaeger isn't that kind of a saint.

He wouldn't be here if he didn't like me.

And he's going out on a limb, risking me rejecting him.

So I resist the urge to close my eyes, and instead, I make myself look straight at him. At his disheveled hair. His twitching beard. His eyes, sparking with blue fire. His parted lips. The way his chest is rising and falling like he's been sprinting on the ice.

"I like you too," I whisper.

I've never said those words out loud to a man before. *Never*. And I know he's not offering a relationship—he wants *one date*.

He's made that crystal clear.

But I'm not panicking like I thought I would.

Am I raw and exposed and a little uncomfortable for admitting to him that I like him?

Yes.

Except over it all is this sense of freedom.

I just told a man I like him, and he didn't laugh. He didn't point and pull a *gotcha*. He didn't whip out a hidden camera and threaten to send it to the national news so the entire world could mock me for thinking that I, Muffina Alexandra Periwinkle, would be worthy of the attention of an attractive athlete with his life together.

Instead, he's leaning into my space, his fingers brushing my cheek as he tilts his head and goes in for a kiss.

It's not like the kiss in the cemetery or the sloppy whatever-it-was before we banged in the walk-in fridge.

This one's slow.

Deliberate.

With his beard tickling my cheeks and his lips hot and firm and his tongue slowly but steadily teasing me into parting my lips so that he can show me an entirely new world.

Like I'm the very last Oreo cookie in existence, and Oreos are his favorite, and he wants to make it last as long as possible, savoring every last little bit, experiencing it fully.

I don't think Tyler Jaeger likes me. I think he *like*-likes me.

And maybe he wants a quickie in the car to relieve what looks like a very uncomfortable situation in his pants.

Or maybe that's actually a can of squeezy cheese.

Squeezy cheese?

And possibly this is why I don't have romantic relationships.

Why do women even hire—*oh*.

Oh, my.

Tyler's hand is drifting from my jaw, down my neck, and I

didn't know a full-body shiver prompted by a man's touch could make my clit pulse like that.

It certainly didn't that night we went all the way at the club.

But this is different.

None of what I've put him through since he picked me up yesterday has been easy or convenient or comfortable. He should be making me sit in the backseat while he blares his music so loud that our ears would ring for days, since that would be preferable to putting up with each other one minute longer.

But instead, he's kissing me like he needs me to know that I matter.

That I have value.

That he sees me, and he likes me anyway, and he wants more of me.

I trust him.

And that's more arousing than how well he kisses, where he puts his hands, or how well he uses his equipment.

I follow his lead and let myself touch him, my hand lingering first on his forearm, radiating with heat, and then up, soaking in the feel of thick muscle beneath his shirt.

And touching him is turning me on every bit as much as having him touching me.

Every bit as much as him kissing me.

Every bit as much as this new, heady feeling of believing that he *wants* me.

I'm doing this.

I'm going to have sex with Tyler Jaeger, in his car, in this parking lot, because if I don't, I might implode.

I want him.

I want him.

I shift in my seat, intent on climbing into his lap, and he abruptly pulls back, chest heaving. "No."

One simple word.

189

And that tower of self-confidence that was growing inside me crumbles.

He grips me by the chin. "Don't go there. I know what you're thinking. Do *not* go there. Right now, I want to rip your clothes off and eat your pussy and make you scream my name until you're hoarse, but not here. Not like this. The next time I have you naked, I'm doing it right. You deserve something special. Understand?"

Oh. "This…isn't no?"

"This is me being a saint." He's holding me captive with a gaze that's ordering me to not look away, not squirm, not crack a joke and retreat back into myself. "You deserve better, Muffy. You deserve better."

He lets go of my chin, flings himself back into his own seat, and growls.

He *growls*.

It's like taking a lit match to my panties.

Poof. They're on fire. In the good way.

But he's buckled back up, putting the car in gear and pulling the car back out of the parking lot before I can put my scrambled brain cells back together to say something, *anything*.

Weirdly, though, I don't feel awkward in the silence.

I feel *glowy*.

And Tyler's squirming in his seat while he visibly adjusts his erection.

Mine, my pussy whispers.

For a little while, I whisper back to her.

"You ever read the *Wheel of Time* series?" Tyler asks.

It's completely inconsequential, yet not, and I'm suddenly smiling bigger than I would if scientists invented calorie-free brownies.

He's not a fling, or a hook-up, or whatever.

He's also a friend.

I hope nothing changes that.

2 2

Tyler

MY POOR DICK is so tired.

He finally gave up the woody about fifteen minutes from Muffy's house, though I'm wondering if that has more to do with knowing we might run into Hilda rather than him running out of steam.

And now I'm a little worried he'll be too tired to stand up again.

But not as much as I'm suddenly worried about letting Muffy out of my car.

Richmond feels so far away now, which is making everything that happened there feel far away too.

Like it wasn't real.

But it *was* real, and I'm not ready to let Muffy go, which is more disconcerting than facing dead bodies.

And that's a realization that'll take time to unpack.

I like Muffy more than I hate dead bodies.

We coast to a stop in front of her house, and I swear she twitches at the sight of it.

Or maybe that's me.

"Oh, look! Rufus is waiting." She grins back at me as she points to the front window, where her cat is licking its own butt in the windowsill. She turns back, and the cat disappears.

Pretty sure it fell off the windowsill. That didn't look intentional.

She sighs. "He does that at least twice a week. You'd think he'd learn. Thank you, again, for coming with me. I won't tell anyone about anything. Promise."

"Saturday night."

Her face flushes, but she smiles at me, and *fuck*.

She's adorable when she smiles like that. It's like hope and joy got together and had a face baby.

"Saturday night," she says with a nod.

She reaches for the door handle and slips out of the car before I can snag her for the kiss I desperately want.

What the hell is going on with me?

No idea.

Other question: do I even care what's going on with me?

Nope, I decide.

I pop the trunk and climb out to get Muffy's suitcase. The minute my foot hits the pavement, Hilda's voice carries over the yard. "Muffy! You're back! Just in time. I cleaned out my closet. Can you believe I still had a whole wardrobe of size sixteens in there? I put them all on your bed since they're too big for me, but I think they'll fit you."

Muffy's smile freezes. Her shoulders start toward her ears, then go back like she's caught herself having a reaction to her mom's words, and that's it.

That's fucking *it*.

I slam the trunk without getting her suitcase out. "Get back in the car."

She visibly jolts. "What?"

"I said, get back in the car. You're not staying here." I've heard people talk about blood boiling, but I never really knew what that meant until *right now*. I'm so furious, I'm about to pop an artery.

Muffy's gaping at me.

"Don't stand there fishing it up," Hilda calls. "Kiss the man. That's the only way to reel 'em in, sweetie."

I point to the car and ignore the fact that my finger is shaking.

Rage.

This is what rage feels like.

I thought I knew rage. I've been betrayed before. I've been shit on before. My former best friend gave me a damn concussion on the ice eighteen months ago because I hooked up with his sister once. You damn well better believe that pissed me off.

But this?

This is body-consuming, furious, raging *rage*. "I swear to holy fuck, Muffy, if you don't get in that car and away from that horrific woman, I *will* kidnap you. *No one* gets to treat you like that, and don't tell me she doesn't know what she's doing, or that she has her own issues, or that she means well. *You* know what she's doing, and she's *not good for you*. Get in the car. What else do you need inside?"

It takes a hot second, and she doesn't answer me, but she does sink back into the car.

She *hadn't even shut her door*.

Her mother got her with a one-two punch of insecurities before she could even shut the fucking car door.

Her eyes are as round as a hockey puck as I close her in the car. Lips parted. Cheeks stained bright pink on her high cheekbones.

I don't know if she's horrified or turned on, and I don't care.

Hilda peppers me with questions that I ignore as I stroll up the walk, past her, and into the house. I have no idea where Muffy's room is, but that's the only thing I don't know.

I know she needs clothes. I know she'd probably like her cat. I know to grab the box of tampons under the sink in the bathroom, and no, it doesn't bother me in the least, because my sisters have talked about way worse than tampons over the years.

Dammit.

This is the moment having four sisters has trained me for.

And you know what?

For the first time in my life, I'm grateful as hell.

It takes two trips.

One for the clothes, and I don't mean the massive pile of clothes on her bed. I mean all the clothes from her closet and drawers that I can fit in the three reusable grocery bags I find scattered on her floor.

And one trip for the cat.

I grab him by the scruff and carry him outside, knowing I'm not getting his litter or his food or his toys, but also knowing that's the easy stuff.

I wrench Muffy's door open, shove the cat in her lap, and march around to the driver's side.

Hilda's actually fallen silent and is gaping at me while I rev the engine, then peel away from the curb.

I'm gripping the wheel too tight. Breathing too hard. Clenching my jaw so tight it might not ever open again.

We're well out of the neighborhood and halfway to downtown before Muffy speaks. "There's a shortcut to Kami's house if you turn right on—"

I cut a glance at her that has her falling silent.

She's not moving in with Kami.

23

Muffy

Is it normal to be both so horny you might spontaneously combust and also on the verge of a total meltdown?

On some level, I know that it's all kinds of wrong to enjoy being kidnapped by a broad-shouldered, angry, testosterone-fueled hockey player of doom.

But I'm here willingly.

Physically, anyway.

Emotionally, I'm pretty sure I'm butt-naked in the hot seat in the middle of a crowded restaurant while a hibachi chef twirls his tools all around, playing a drum beat before flaying me alive.

I said hot seat?

I meant right there on the griddle.

You deserve to have your body worshipped the right way. Say something nice about yourself. I won't let her treat you this way.

Tyler Jaeger is my hero and my nemesis all at once.

I haven't been in therapy for years to not know that my mom isn't exactly healthy for me.

Every time my therapist would broach the subject, I'd tell her I worked enough hours and had an active enough social life that I didn't see Mom *that* much. Or that I couldn't afford to live somewhere else. Or that I felt like working through my issues with Mom was more important than abandoning her. She's funny in her own way. And I know she's only worried about my weight because she wants me to be healthy.

She loves me. I know she does. But she doesn't have a lot of self-awareness when it comes to how her words land.

But possibly I'm making excuses so I don't have to tell all the people in my life who think she's funny and that it's fabulous that she lets it all hang out that I don't, in fact, have the same relationship with her that they do.

Or possibly so I don't have to admit how terrified I am that if I move out, I'll fail.

Again.

I'm holding Rufus tight on my lap so he doesn't hop into the backseat and do something I'd regret and have to pay to clean up.

Unlike most of the drive from Richmond to Copper Valley, which was both simmering with tension at the unspoken expectation of what we plan to do on our date Saturday night, and also super fun as we talked about everything from fantasy novels to the worst sports moments of all time, right now, there's only tension, and I'm not sure it's the good kind.

Tyler's not speaking.

He's just breathing.

Loudly.

Angrily.

His knuckles are white, and I hope he's not going to have to hold anything when he gets to his team meeting this afternoon, because he's probably cutting off enough circulation to his fingers to cause some stiffness in the joints.

I know exactly where we're going a few blocks before we get there, and it makes my stomach drop.

His place.

We're going to his place.

I haven't been here before, but I've heard Kami talk about going to Schuler Tower and running into Beck Ryder—the former Bro Code boy band guy and underwear model who owns the building and lives in the penthouse—when she and Nick dropped by Tyler's place once to drop off something he left at the arena.

My stomach drops again when we pull into the parking garage across the street from Reynolds Park.

"Thank you," I whisper.

He grunts a response.

Rufus yowls.

I wince.

Tyler doesn't react at all.

Instead, he whips the car into an open numbered space that I'm going to assume is his assigned spot, throws the car into park, kills the engine, and pops the trunk.

He still doesn't say a word as he climbs out, but he also doesn't slam his door.

And he comes around to open my door too.

Rufus eyeballs him, eyes wide, ears back, and I grab him a little tighter.

I have two choices.

One, I can start listing off every other person in the world who would take me in for a few days.

Or two, I can acknowledge that Tyler already knows all this, and I wouldn't be here if he didn't want me to be here, even if he's angry, and he's probably not angry with me unless he gets off on self-torture and will be telling everyone the horrible story of how he's stuck with a roommate with a needy cat.

I don't think he's the kind of dysfunctional who would take us in just to bitch about us and make himself out to be the victim though.

I think he's mad at my mom.

For me.

This dress was always a little tight in the boobs. More so since I've gained a few pounds. But now, with my heart swelling so hard and fast at Tyler sticking up for me and insisting on getting me out of my mom's house?

I'm about to split seams this dress doesn't have.

And that's *before* he grabs *all* of our luggage from last night, plus the bags he gathered for me at Mom's house, all in one trip, and still has enough of a hand free to hit the button on the elevator.

Confession: there's this group on the internet that's all about women—mostly moms—carrying in all of their groceries in one trip, and I sometimes spend hours scrolling through the pictures and stories, fascinated at how they can move while loaded down like that.

Seeing Tyler do the same with our luggage?

The man cannot get any hotter.

We step into the elevator, and I briefly wonder if I could zip Rufus into a suitcase—very temporarily—so that I could leap on Tyler and kiss him until I can't breathe.

I want to have elevator sex with him.

I want to have elevator sex with him *right now*.

I'm getting up the nerve to hit the stop button when the doors open.

He hustles me out of the elevator, down a hall, around a corner, and stops in front of apartment 708.

While he digs his phone out and uses it to unlock the door, Rufus squirms.

Tyler shoots my cat a look, then swings the door open and gestures us inside.

We almost get tangled in the middle of the bags he's carrying, and I am definitely caught up in the subtle scent of hotel soap that I didn't notice on him as much in the car as I do now.

He follows us inside and lets the door swing shut. When it seals with a bang, Rufus leaps out of my arms, lands crooked next to the door in a houseplant that resembles a small tree, then plops into the dirt in the elegantly simple pot.

Tyler eyeballs the cat, then glances at a large aquarium full of brightly-colored fish. He briefly squeezes his eyes shut before grunting something that I interpret to mean *follow me*.

I don't pretend I'm not gawking at everything as I trail him through the apartment. The living room is done in tans and browns, and I'm almost positive the floor is bamboo. In addition to the fish tank, Tyler has a wall of family photos, and there's a gas fireplace beneath a massive television, with a lone stuffed Thrusty the Bratwurst mascot sitting on the mantle.

His furniture is understated and positioned around red Turkish rugs.

He has bookshelves. And books. And candles.

We pass the kitchen, which is shiny and clean except for a bamboo bowl of oranges, a stand mixer, and a crock of cooking utensils and salt and pepper shakers next to the stove, which has a teapot on the back left burner.

Then it's down a short hallway past a bathroom and into a large, airy bedroom.

Tyler marches into the attached bathroom, which is way fancier than the attached bathroom of a guest room should be. There's a double sink. A soaking tub. A separate shower. A little alcove for the toilet. And another door leading to a closet that's clearly already in use with his own clothes.

Either the man has a ton of clothing, or he's moving me into his own bedroom.

Does this apartment have a guest bedroom?

I hope so.

I want to know Tyler *wants* me.

There's a reading lamp on the nightstand, and a book with a bookmark sticking out of it. Plugs for phones. A very cozy-looking maroon chair by the window with a throw blanket haphazardly tossed over the back.

Scattered coins and a picture of his parents on the dresser, plus a sticky note on the mirror that's curling up at the bottom, like it's been there forever.

Tyler is my favorite sibling, it says.

Clearly, there's a story.

Also clearly?

This is his bedroom.

I eyeball the bed.

It's neatly made with a quilt that looks like it could've been made by someone's grandma, but probably wasn't. More likely, one of his sisters got it for him.

He strides back out of the bathroom, stops, and we stare at each other until it gets awkward.

That doesn't actually take all that long.

Maybe three seconds.

"Don't put up with anyone who treats you like shit," he says gruffly. Then he pats his back pocket—wallet check, I'm sure—followed by his front pocket—phone check, definitely. "I have to go. Make yourself at home. Eat whatever. The doorman's bringing up a litter box. Tell him what kind of food you feed Rufus. He'll get that too."

I nod like being left alone in his apartment after everything we've been through in the past twenty-four hours isn't awkward and weird.

And then it hits me. "My car," I blurt.

I have two appointments tonight, plus I need to drop off Brianna's Muff Matchers welcome kit that I forgot to give her last week, which is thankfully in my trunk, because if it wasn't hidden inside the box labeled "jumper cables," my mom would...

Let's just say she'd borrow things and leave it at that.

Tyler hands me his keys. "Use mine."

Use mine.
Holy crap.
I think we're in a relationship.

24

Tyler

I RETREAT from my apartment as fast as I came, stopping on my way out of the building to ask the doorman for the favors I already promised Muffy.

Did I just accidentally make her my girlfriend?

I know she'll figure out fast that I have two spare bedrooms, and I could've put her in either. I gave her the keys to my car. I sent her an authorization to unlock my door with her phone.

I didn't just make her my accidental girlfriend.

I made her my accidental *live-in* girlfriend.

The six-block walk from my place to Mink Arena goes too fast, and it's still over an hour until the team meeting starts.

I could hit the ice. Work out some frustrations.

Head up to see the front office staff. Ares's wife works in marketing, and there's a solid possibility he'd be in her office. They might have some good advice.

But what do I ask?

Does Muffy think we're dating?

Nope. Not gonna ask that. Ares's wife is friends with Kami, and therefore friends with Muffy. They'll talk.

For all I know, they already are.

Which means my follow-up question—*how do I know if my dick is working again, or if it was a fluke?*—isn't something I'm talking to Ares and his wife about either.

Not gonna lie. The old man in my pants is tired after all that bonering on the way home.

Dammit.

I need the bunnies.

I'm texting them as I walk down the hall, asking Athena and Cassadee all the questions that I don't want to ask my teammates, when I hear my nickname.

"Jaegs!"

"Jaeggy, man, you're back."

"So you survived the funeral. Good. How's your head? Coach is gonna kill you."

Rooster, Klein, and Lavoie converge on me, since I was the dope who walked to the players' entrance at Mink Arena instead of going in the front door to avoid my teammates.

I scowl at all of them.

Rooster grins under his cowboy hat. "Don't get mad, now. We got your back. Ain't gonna ask why you needed sniffing salts. But we wouldn't be friends if we didn't make sure you're okay."

"I'm asking," Lavoie says.

"And then I'm asking how things went with Muffy." Klein wiggles his brows.

I almost throw a punch.

But for what?

"I kidnapped Muffy and made her move into my apartment when we got back, and now I don't know if she's staying, or if we're dating, or if she's gonna take my car and drive to Kansas or Vermont or somewhere that's basically anywhere but here and never talk to me again."

I wait for my body to recoil in horror that I put it all out there, but instead, mild relief settles into my bones.

I can't talk to my sisters about this without drama—and yes, I'm ignoring a billion texts that have my phone regularly buzzing in my hand, none of which are Athena or Cassadee texting me back with answers—and while I could talk to West, he's still in his honeymoon phase with Daisy and everything in his world is all *women and children are the best thing to ever grace this earth*.

Or possibly I'm afraid if I tell my brother that I might be falling for Muffy, it'll be more real than if I tell my teammates and the bunnies that my relationship status is currently *it's complicated*.

Duncan sighs. He grabs me by one arm. Rooster gets me by the other. Klein leaps ahead to open the team lounge door.

"When you say *kidnap*..." Lavoie mutters as they march me inside.

"I didn't shove a bag over her head and stuff her in my trunk. I ordered her to get back in the car and then packed a few bags full of her stuff, got her cat, and took her to my place instead of letting her live with her mother one more day."

Klein snorts. "Dude, that's not kidnapping. That's *saving*."

"Muffy's the one with the hot mom, right?"

All of us glare at Rooster, but Lavoie's the only one to speak. "Say that again, and I'm calling Zeus Berger myself for ideas on making your life hell."

"ZB! I love that guy." Rooster whips a Sharpie out of his back pocket. "Started carrying this to sign the fans' foreheads like he used to."

Lavoie stops, but Rooster keeps going, which makes them yank me like the rope in tug of war.

Connor's gaping at Rooster. "Dude. That's not... You don't... Fuck, man. I heard a rumor Zeus and his wife are thinking about moving back here—don't tell Murphy, it's a surprise—and you can't take his thing. He'll kill you. And not like easy kill you, but like, master of torture kill you. You can't steal his signature move."

He's right.

Ares's twin brother is devious. Both of them are. Ares just hides it better.

And if you pick on one Berger twin, you're going after both of them.

Rooster Applebottom clearly knows no fear, because he merely grins wider under his cowboy hat. "Dude retired. He's old news."

"Been nice knowing you," I tell him.

"Yeah, back to a problem we can solve." Klein looks at my crotch. "Still having performance issues?"

"No." Maybe. Shit.

"Muffy know?" Lavoie asks.

He's all business with a hint of sympathy, and suddenly everything's okay.

My teammates have my back. They're asking about my dick because they care. And if I tell them to have Muffy's back too, they will.

"She has her own problems," I reply.

The team captain nods once. He's divorced. I don't know details. Happened before I got called up. But I know it means he had in-laws and there was a time in his life when he put someone else as number one above hockey.

Klein pulls us through the foyer and fully into the lounge. Frey and Murphy are already there, both with their families. Frey's daughter is toddling around between the well-loved couches. Murphy's burping his little guy while the women laugh about something.

But they all stop when we walk in.

"Tyler!" Kami gives me the universal look of *are you okay?* "I knew something was weird about Muffy's date request, but I swear, I had no idea it was for a funeral. I probably should've known it was something bigger than a *ceremony thing.*"

My phone buzzes six more times in my hand, all my sisters.

Guilt creeps over my skin, heating my scalp and face.

I have *two* awesome families. My sisters might drive me nuts, but they're *there*. All married to great guys I could call for backup on anything in an instant. Not that I'd need to. West would have my back first, if Daisy didn't beat him to it.

And then there's my hockey family.

Any given moment, I have literally dozens of people I can call for anything from joining me to grab a bite to eat to helping bury a body, *plus* I'm texting puck bunnies for relationship advice.

Muffy has her mom.

Sure, she has Kami too.

But her mom negates the Kami effect.

Fuck that.

Muffy's getting my family.

I'm dating her.

And if she doesn't know it yet, that's okay. If she doesn't want in yet, that's okay too.

But I *will* date her.

I'm gonna date the shit out of her.

Muffy Periwinkle's gonna know she's worth something.

Whether she likes it or not.

Muffy

IT TAKES me longer than it should to shower at Tyler's place.

I'm off my routine. I don't know which shampoo I should use. He doesn't have conditioner. It takes me a while to sort out which bag has clean underwear and a nice enough outfit to wear for my screenings this evening. Plus, Rufus keeps trying to gnaw on one of the oranges in the bowl in the kitchen, and I don't know the best place to put the litter box that the doorman delivers right as I'm finally naked in the bathroom.

Also?

Tyler has guest rooms.

Not one.

Two.

And one of those rooms is decorated in bright colors and stocked with Legos, blocks, board books, and dolls.

He's a bachelor prepared for his sisters and their kids to stay with him.

Swoon.

Or possibly he secretly has kids of his own that no one knows about.

Unlikely, but there's safety in pretending he has bigger secrets than that he's scarred for life because of his zombie grandfather.

Otherwise, I'll start asking questions.

Things like *how long is he expecting me to stay here?*

Which is really *how long until he gets tired of the chaos of having me in his very neat and tidy home?*

I can't solve that one, so instead, I rush through a shower —yes, I *am* picturing him in here with me, *without* me accidentally assaulting his butt with a doorknob first—grab his keys, and head out for my first meeting, doing my damn best to not think about Tyler expecting me to sleep in his bed with him tonight.

Meeting one is a bust—the guy spends the entire time staring at something behind me in the coffee shop, and when I check to see exactly what's behind me when I leave, I realize it's a brick wall.

He literally would've rather talked to the brick wall.

And it's not a fear of eye contact thing.

He made *plenty* of eye contact with everyone from the barista to the firefighter who came in for a to-go order for the station.

I'm willing to overlook social awkwardness. My clients are all on the socially awkward side too.

But something felt abnormally off, so he gets a pass, and I'm also really glad I'm using aliases as I screen candidates.

Candidate number two is a lovely gentleman who lets me buy my own coffee at a separate coffee bar several blocks away from the first, but offers to grab it for me when the barista calls my name. He makes eye contact, tells me about his nieces and nephews, and makes me wish I were having coffee with Tyler instead.

And I completely wig out on him when Maren walks in the door.

I'm talking diving-under-the-table, pulling my coat over my head, mumbling something about needing to go to the bathroom and then locking myself inside the men's room wigging out.

While I'm hiding, my phone rings.

And the name flashing on my screen makes me cringe hard enough that I give myself a headache.

I still answer it though. "Hey, Kami."

"Muffy? Where are you and why are you whispering?"

"I'm backstage at an indie rock concert at the amphitheater."

"Did *you* fall and hit your head this weekend too?"

"No, I'm in the middle of something, and I don't want to talk about it."

"I saw Tyler. He said you moved in with him."

I make static noises with my mouth. "I ca —*squaawaabasssshhhhaaa*—think I—*swishswishswish*—later."

She doesn't immediately call back when I hang up, but someone starts knocking on the door, so I wouldn't answer even if she did.

Yes, I moved in with Tyler.

But I don't know what it *means*.

I unlock the bathroom door, peek past the startled gentleman trying to get in here, spot Maren looking at her phone while she waits for her coffee, and realize my only option is to dart through the little kitchen area and burst out the back door.

"Sorry sorry sorry," I mutter, jacket pulled up over most of my face, as I brush past the afternoon manager. "Bad date. I'm gone. I'm out. Sorry."

My heart's basically in my uvula by the time I'm halfway down the alley, realizing I'm completely turned around and I have no idea where Tyler's car is.

I am the worst live-in not-girlfriend *ever*.

Also, I really hope Rufus isn't chewing on any plants.

I log into the app I pretend I don't have on my phone and send a message to Roger, my "date," and tell him something came up and I had to dash, but would he like to meet my friend Phoebe?

Tyler's car is still in the garage near my first screening date, so I hoof it back there, calling my credit card company on the way to tell them my card was stolen, and asking them to please send a new card to Tyler's address.

It's better than the truth.

My mom thinks I'm way more successful than I am, so she borrows my card from time to time and dorks up my already lack-luster credit.

Not that it matters.

Since I'm over my limit, they decline to replace anything, though they take note of my new address and promise to send all my billing statements there, and they put a freeze on the old card.

So when I get to Cod Pieces for the evening support group with my clients, I'm in the dumps. I'm not working tonight— not frying fish, anyway—which means I can relax and enjoy dinner without leaping up every time the doorbell or drive-through buzzer go off.

Brianna hands me a paper birthday crown when I slide into the booth by the window where she's waiting with Phoebe. "You look sad."

"We saw you on the news." Phoebe's also in a Cod Pieces birthday crown.

I know it's neither of their birthdays, nor is it mine, but some days call for crowns, so I put my own on too. "You...what?"

"You were at a funeral this morning?" Brianna prompts.

Phoebe nods. "And with Daisy Carter-Kincaid there. Are you really dating her brother-in-law?"

"I—we—it's complicated."

Brianna nods. "I know you said you don't date, but if you like him, and he likes you, go with it. Sometimes you have to take a leap, you know?"

My two clients don't have a lot in common. While Phoebe's into business, Brianna seems to be leaning toward studying something in science. Phoebe does water aerobics and takes cooking classes for fun. Brianna's considering joining the weightlifting team at CVU and she knits while listening to poetry when she needs to chill.

Phoebe grew up in a small town in the Southwest.

Brianna grew up in an apartment downtown here in Copper Valley.

But they're both peering at me with warmth and sympathy and a willingness to listen.

So what do I have to lose?

Both of them as clients?

"We're friends, and I didn't tell him I was a virgin before we hooked up a couple months ago, and neither one of us want a long-term relationship because we both have our own hang-ups, but...I like him."

"Muffy!" Phoebe lunges for my hands, bumps my tray, and sends my fish and chips sliding into my lap. "Oh, shit."

I leap up, picking everything up. "It's okay. It's okay."

"Got your back, Muffy," D'Angelo calls from behind the counter.

"No, no, it's okay. It's—"

Oh, shit.

Brianna's crying.

She's *crying*.

I lunge across the table to hug her. "Don't cry. It's okay. *It's okay*."

"I'm a virgin too," she wails. "I thought I was the only one, but I'm *not*. I'm not alone."

The entire restaurant falls silent.

I think even the shop next door goes silent.

Phoebe visibly tenses, then looks around at every last customer, finishing with D'Angelo behind the counter.

Most people go back to their fish.

Brianna hasn't seemed to notice. I keep patting her back and telling her all the ways she's amazing and that she shouldn't judge herself for any part of her sexuality or experience level while D'Angelo continues to stare at us.

I have zero idea what he's thinking, and I hope it's nothing that means I'll have to break up with him as friends.

But I would in a heartbeat.

After a minute, he frowns thoughtfully, turns, grabs the basket of fish and chips that slide down the chute, adds a fried pie, and carries them out to us.

Brianna wipes her eyes quickly, pushes me back, and stares at her lap.

"Hey." D'Angelo lightly bumps her with a fist on the shoulder. "You're a mother-freaking rock star. Got it?"

She mumbles something that sounds like *banana gargle toilets*.

"Chin up," he tells her. "Anyone says anything wrong here, you and me are taking out the judgmental assholes together. 'Kay?"

She flashes an embarrassed smile at him.

He grins back. "Good. You're in my biology class, aren't you?"

She nods.

"Study group. Second-floor student lounge, right above the lecture hall. Wednesday. Noon. If you're free, join us."

She nods again.

And I'm relieved I don't have to take him out, because I saw him take Tyler down last week, which means my odds of success aren't good.

Also?

If Brianna can put herself out there and make a commitment, even for a study group while she waits for me to find the perfect man who's worthy of her, maybe I should consider trying it too.

26

Tyler

MUFFY'S not in my apartment.

It's almost ten, and there's no Muffy. No texts. No calls. No cryptic notes left anywhere.

I know she said she had stuff to do tonight too, but I don't know what it was. Pretty sure it's not working at Cod Pieces, because her uniforms are still in the bags I grabbed from her mom's house.

But I'll take it as a good sign that all her stuff is here. Plus, her toothbrush is out in my bathroom, which feels weird, but not wrong.

Not like I'd expect a woman's toothbrush in my bathroom to feel.

Her cat's also still here. Rufus and I are having a stare-down, him from my kitchen sink, ears slicked back, eyes wide, his weird brownish-tannish fur puffed up so he looks like his face is one of those craft pompons my sisters' younger kids glue to their art projects.

I snap a picture from my spot at the edge of the kitchen,

then send it to West with an accompanying question. *Does this look normal?*

He and Daisy don't actually know how many cats they have, but it's a lot. She adopted an entire shelter after a photo shoot gone wrong in her mansion not long after Remy landed on her doorstep.

"I'm coming to get a glass, and it's above your head, okay, cat?"

He jerks and lunges like he's attacking a dust bunny on the side of the sink, then lifts his head and looks at me again, mouth open like he's skated a few laps and is gulping oxygen.

He's freaking hilarious.

West doesn't answer, but I hear the telltale click of the door lock, then shuffling, and a moment later, the door swings shut with its normal bang.

The cat rowls and leaps for safety, but he doesn't account for the faucet and dives headfirst into it.

Before I can move to check on him, he's using the oranges in my fruit bowl as a trampoline to leap to the top of the fridge.

All of the artwork from my nieces and nephews that I've stored up there rains down as he scrambles to get purchase on the edge of the refrigerator.

I grab my thickest oven mitts and dart for the cat. Not hard to see what's coming next.

Rufus Superman-ing it off the top of the fridge and landing in my trash can.

"Calm down," I order as I reach for him.

He scrambles again, switching directions on the flying papers, and sends an old Valentine's Day card coated in glitter straight at me while somehow managing to get enough traction to leap up onto the cabinets instead of falling into the trash can.

This should be an improvement.

But one, I have glitter falling into my face, and two, he's trying to climb into the vintage brown and tan pitcher that I insisted I wanted from my grandma's estate merely because I knew Keely wanted it and she was royally pissing me off.

It's one of those weird pitchers that's wide at the top, narrows in the middle, and goes wide again at the bottom, which means the cat's butt is now hanging out of the pitcher, back legs spinning.

The pitcher's toast.

Oh, hell.

Shit.

Keely will kill me if that pitcher gets broken.

I vault myself onto the counter and grab the damn thing by the handle—the pitcher, of course, not the cat—pull it down, and dump the cat back on the counter.

Just in time for Muffy to walk in.

She's in jeans, a Thrusters hoodie, and her fluffy blue coat. Her hair's cascading in soft curls down her shoulders, and if she's wearing makeup, it's light.

Her gaze darts to Rufus as he leaps into the trash can —*dammit, cat*—and then to me, standing on the counter, wearing oven mitts decorated to look like lobsters and holding an ancient pitcher without enough room to get down gracefully on my own.

She bites her lower lip, and I go hard as granite so fast I feel it in the bruise on my ass from this morning.

If she notices, she doesn't let on. "Sorry about Rufus. He's—"

"Hilarious," I finish for her. Mostly because I know the trash is empty. I took it out before I left to pick her up yesterday.

She blinks. "You think my cat's funny?"

"Yes. And also not stealthy enough to eat my face while I'm sleeping. Best kind of cat to have."

Her lips spread in a full smile, the same one I've seen her

use so often at Chester Green's after a game, or when she's talking to Kami and their friends, and I want to kiss her.

I want to kiss her just to kiss her smile, and I don't care if it doesn't go anywhere but kissing.

"Um, do you need help? I can grab a stepladder if you tell me—" Her gaze travels down, pausing halfway down. Her eyes flare wide, and she visibly swallows as they darken.

Yeah.

No hiding that woody.

And if she's not horrified, what am I still doing on this counter?

I leap down and tilt the trash can so Rufus can escape and wreak havoc elsewhere.

Muffy's watching me.

I like Muffy watching me.

I also like that she's not moving away as I cross the kitchen to her. "You smell like fish."

Her smile blooms again. "You like that."

"I do." Look at that. I'm smiling back at her.

"You put me in your bedroom."

She says *bedroom*, my dick blows a kazoo in celebration.

Figuratively speaking, of course. "That a problem?"

"No. I mean, we handled it fine last night, didn't we?"

Shit.

What does that mean? *I liked cuddling with you?* Or *we managed to not have bad sex again?*

"About Saturday," she says. "When we talked about Saturday—you know, the date thing?—we didn't know...I mean, we didn't plan on me spending any time at your apartment. So are we still doing this date thing on Saturday? Or—"

Fuck it.

I'm kissing her.

No more talking. No more awkwarding. Just kissing.

Except I miss her mouth, because Rufus shoots into the

217

kitchen like a bat out of hell, dragging Muffy's pink messenger bag with him.

She ducks away and lunges for the cat, missing as he bounces off the bottom cabinet under the sink. "Rufus! We're guests. We have to behave."

I lunge for the cat too as he gets close to me. "My nieces and nephews have done worse. I found one pooping in my house plant last time they were here."

Rufus dashes out of the kitchen.

We both follow, since the bag's wrapped around his neck.

"He sleeps twenty-three hours a day and spends the last hour trying to maim himself," Muffy pants.

I accidentally check her into the wall as we both try to run down the hallway. "Shit! Sorry. You okay?"

"Padding. I'm great. *Rufus!*"

I'm a romantic disaster, and the cat just took out the lamp in one of my guest rooms.

I am *not* getting laid tonight.

But that cat?

That cat's getting caught.

I dive for him as he streaks back out of the bedroom, manage to snag the messenger bag, but Rufus doesn't stop.

Muffy shrieks.

The cat makes an unholy noise that's cut short as the handle tightens around his neck.

Fuck.

Fuck fuck fuck.

I just killed Muffy's cat.

Muffy

WHEN I ADOPTED RUFUS, I couldn't understand why he'd been at the shelter so long when he's utterly adorable.

But it took about forty-eight hours for me to get it.

Rufus is the cat version of me if I were a little klutzier, a lot more YOLO, and completely lacking in any natural sense of self-preservation. If he understood English, he'd leap out of an airplane without a parachute because he'd heard cats always land on their feet.

"He's fine," Kami tells Tyler once again as she snaps her travel vet bag shut, which I'm pretty sure she has specifically for Rufus.

We're sitting in Tyler's living room, my cat in my lap, sleeping off his near-death-by-bag experience, Tyler himself pacing the room in front of the aquarium that I double-checked Rufus couldn't somehow get into before I left earlier, and in need of having his heart rate and blood pressure checked.

And he probably has a few extra bumps and bruises too.

I stroke Rufus, who's purring so loudly as he sleeps that the neighbors downstairs can probably feel the vibration, and ignore the subtle smirk Kami's wearing.

She drove across town after bedtime on a work night so that Tyler could sleep tonight knowing that Rufus's neck was completely and totally fine.

She probably thinks she's helping me get a booty call.

Or Tyler.

But I doubt that's the entire reason she's heading for the door so quickly, now that Rufus has been declared fine.

"Thanks for coming," Tyler says gruffly.

She smiles at him with her brilliantly kind Kami smile. "It's Rufus. I expect this at least once every few months."

"He tried to climb into a glass of milk once and gave himself diarrhea," I offer.

And then I wince.

Hey, Tyler, let's talk about body waste and then bang.

"My personal favorite was when he tried to eat a bag of yarn," Kami muses.

"Not the yarn," I agree quickly. "He wasn't trying to eat the yarn."

"No, he was eating the burlap bag it was stored in," she explains.

"We were all together for Thanksgiving anyway, so Kami didn't have to drop anything for him that time."

"He hated the taste after he got the first bite off and walked around dry heaving for what felt like an hour before we figured out he had a bit stuck at the back of his throat."

"Kami's an angel."

"Rufus is lucky he's lovable when he's not testing the limits of his nine lives."

"Yolnt."

They both squint at me.

"Like YOLO? But for a cat? You Only Live Nine Times? That's Rufus's motto. I should get him a collar with it."

Kami laugh-sighs.

And Tyler's shoulders drop below his chin for the first time since I got back to his place.

But all too soon, Kami's gone, undoubtedly heading home to a hero's welcome from Nick, which will probably involve happy naked time for them, and it's just Tyler and me and my cat left here, and I want to hug him—the guy who whisked me away to his downtown sanctuary, I mean, not Rufus—except I'm suddenly feeling very, very shy.

Screw it.

If my cat can be brave and adventurous and accidentally try to maim himself on a regular basis, I can work up the courage to stand up, meet Tyler on his way back from walking Kami out, throw my arms around him, and kiss him.

And I will.

I *am*.

I'm setting Rufus aside. Standing up.

Looking at the man who's looking back at me with that mix of *are you sure you're okay?* and *I worry about you for more reasons than a normal man should worry about a normal woman* in his flickering blue eyes.

He knows why I left med school.

He knows I'm average. I don't finish at the top of anything, unlike him, who has two championship rings tucked away somewhere.

He knows I have insecurities and weird relationships with my parents.

And he's still meeting me halfway, eyes locked on mine, determination written in the set of his lips.

He lifts a hand to stroke my hair. "I'm taking you out for breakfast tomorrow."

That's all it takes.

One growly sentence from a stubborn, overprotective, sexy man-beast, and I'm flinging my arms around his neck and pressing my mouth to his.

A rough groan comes from his throat as he takes charge of the kiss.

Every cell in my body flashes to life. My brain threatens to spell out all the reasons this could go wrong, so I hit the *off* switch, part my lips as he flicks his tongue over them, and let myself believe.

I'm attractive.

I'm sexy.

I'm worthy.

I'm *wanted*.

His beard tickles my face while his hand slides down my spine. I want him to touch me everywhere, all at once, and I want to touch him everywhere too. My fingers thread through his barely-long-enough hair. My other hand explores the thick cords in his neck, then the broad expanse of his chest.

He walks me backwards out of the living room and down the hall to his bedroom, his arms solid around me, his hands settling right above my ass, his thick, hard length pressing into my belly, our feet sometimes tangling, which makes both of us giggle as we're still kissing.

My heart is fluttering harder than a hummingbird in a hurricane.

The backs of my knees touch the bed long before I'm done kissing him, but he breaks away as we stop.

I whimper.

I do.

But it's barely a half whimper before I go mute again, because Tyler's pulling his shirt off, and holy mother of fried fish.

I want to bite his shoulder. I want to lick his tattoos.

I want to leave my mark on every inch of him.

He tosses his phone on the floor like he doesn't have it in him to aim for the bedside table, and then he leans in and goes vampire on my neck. "I'm going to strip you naked, eat your pussy, and make you come so hard you'll forget time exists."

"O-*gurp*," I gasp.

O-gurp? *O-gurp?*

He already has me halfway to forgetting how words work.

He was all talk last time too, a snide little voice in the back of my head whispers.

I ignore it.

That Tyler and this Tyler are two different people.

This Tyler is sliding his hands under my hoodie while he does a magic trick with his teeth and his tongue on a spot below my ear that I didn't even know existed.

It's like I've been dipped in a pool of straight pleasure.

Everywhere he touches, my nerves explode in exquisite joy. My panties are wet. My nipples are pebbled so hard, my breasts have goosebumps.

I want to explore his body, but it's all I can do to cling to his shoulders, the heat of his skin seeping into my hands and leaving my palms itching for more but completely ignorant of how they're supposed to work.

He guides one arm out of my hoodie and the T-shirt underneath. Then the other arm.

He doesn't catch my chin on the fabric when he pulls it all over my head like I do half the time, and when my hair frizzes with static electricity, an honest, unguarded smile blooms over his face. "You are the sexiest kind of fucking adorable."

He smooths it all down, kisses my forehead, then down my nose, brushes my lips with his, setting my entire face aglow with the combination of hot lips and tickling beard, and then he's guiding me back onto the bed, nibbling on my neck, crawling between my legs, and worshipping my breasts with his mouth.

I'm still in a bra—a massive, white, double full coverage granny bra—and I've never felt sexier than I do with Tyler thumbing my nipples through the fabric and licking my cleavage.

"Good?" he asks.

I grunt out an incoherent response, grab his head, and push it back to my breasts while I fling a leg around his back.

Would it be wrong to rub myself against his abs to get off?

Nope, I decide.

He slides a hand under me, unhooks my bra, and tears it off with his teeth.

"*Oh my god*," I gasp.

He gathers my breasts in his large hands, thumbs still teasing my nipples, pushes the girls together, and licks the underside of my breast.

My hips buck.

He does it again, going all the way up to my nipple and sucking it into his mouth hard enough that I feel a jolt of lust ping from deep in my breast and straight to my throbbing clit.

"Oh, god, *Tyler.*"

"Delicious," he murmurs, his words tickling my overly sensitive skin while he licks and kisses and sucks on the very neglected part of my chest, pinching and teasing and sucking on my nipples while I fling my other leg around his ribs. My clit is tingling and begging for the attention it's not getting with this angle. My vagina is aching. He could probably make me come just by telling them they're both beautiful.

I'm chanting his name.

He shifts, his fingers trailing lightly down my ribs as he kisses a line from my breasts to my navel.

I try to suck it in, but does it matter?

His tongue dips into my belly button while he gently unhooks one of my legs, and then he's tackling the button on my jeans.

I'm still gripping his hair.

Are these my tight jeans?

Is this about to get awkward?

Does he— "*Oh my god*," I gasp again.

It's like he knows when I start thinking too hard, and he knows my nipples are my brain's *off* button.

Nothing else matters.

Not that he has to tug to get my jeans off.

Not that I'm suddenly exposed and bloated and I can't remember if I shaved my bikini line.

All that matters is that he's kneeling above me, parting my knees, spreading my legs to gaze down at my most intimate parts, his eyes hot and dark and hungry while he licks his lips.

Tyler Jaeger wants to eat me out.

He bends to capture my lips in a searing kiss, like he's claiming me, like he's saying *you are my prize and I am here to collect every last drop.*

He strokes me from my opening to my clit, and I whimper and almost come off the bed.

"Tell me what you like," he orders, and then his mouth is on me again, but this time, he's licking me between my legs, his hands on my inner thighs, holding them open while he draws lazy patterns with his thumbs, his tongue going places no man has gone before.

Sure, I've touched myself.

But getting myself off and trusting someone else with my body are completely different.

I didn't trust him that night at the club.

But tonight?

Right now?

I would trust him to guide me across a tightrope while I'm blindfolded.

Which might be exactly what he's doing with my body.

Every lick is heaven. When he sucks on my clit, I see stars. I'm gasping his name. Probably a few other things too. I can't actually hear myself.

Everything is shut down except my pleasure centers, and

they're lit up brighter than the sun, concentrated between my legs, where everything inside me is coiling so tight that I'm almost in physical pain.

"C'mon, Muffy," he whispers to my clit, his breath landing on my exposed, swollen skin like the flutter of a butterfly wing. "Come for me. Let go. Come for me, baby."

He grazes me with his teeth, and I shatter.

I think I scream his name.

My hips are bucking out of control, my thighs straining while the most powerful orgasm of my life rips through me.

I think I'm levitating.

And he's still eating my pussy, coaxing my exposed nerves higher and harder as the waves of pleasure crash and crescendo in my core.

I can't feel my feet.

I don't know my name.

I don't even know what a name is.

I'm one with the universe, and I'm holding the entire universe in my pussy all at the same time.

I am the Big Bang.

I am love. I am fear. I am religion.

I am the goddess of every orgasm to ever exist.

I am clearly hallucinating, but *oh my god*, this is—this orgasm is the supreme, ultimate pinnacle of human existence.

"Oh my god, am I dead?" I gasp as my body settles into soft aftershocks.

Tyler presses a soft kiss to my very center, then to each of my thighs. "Yes."

"Good. That is definitely how I wanted to die."

28

Tyler

ONCE AGAIN, my dick hurts so bad that I wonder if it's possible to break it from overextension, but honestly?

I wouldn't care.

I'm laying with my head on Muffy's belly, her taste on my lips, inhaling her spicy scent, while she runs her fingers through my hair.

And I don't think she realizes she's doing it.

"Is it normal to see the Milky Way when you come?" she asks.

"The candy bar or the galaxy?"

"The galaxy made up of the candy bars."

"Maybe. I see planets made of pizza when I come."

Her breath is evening out, and my head bounces on her stomach when she laughs. "What kind of pizza?"

"Chicago deep dish. Pepperoni, sausage, olives, mushrooms, and banana peppers, with extra cheese."

"Oh my god. I think I just drooled. Can we get one of

those now? *Oh my god*. It's like sex is marijuana. It gives me the munchies."

I chuckle and kiss her soft skin. God, I love her.

Oh, fuck.

Fuck.

What the fuckity fuck?

"I should offer to munch on you but I can't move," she says. "Can I offer to munch on you when I can move again? I've watched YouTube videos. I know what I'm supposed to…"

She trails off with a yawn, and a moment later, a soft snore escapes her lips.

Her hand slides off my head and flops to the bed.

Yep.

She's out cold.

I should move. My legs are hanging off the bottom of the bed. The cat's climbing onto my ass. I need to rub out this boner.

Convince myself I'm confusing oral sex with love and that Muffy's simply a good friend.

But I don't want to do any of that.

I want to stay right here. With her belly as my pillow and her breathing as my music, knowing I'm the only man whose name she's ever screamed, the only man to ever make her come.

Rufus kneads my ass, his claws digging through my jeans, and he hits the spot over my tailbone where Muffy clocked me with the door this morning.

Jesus.

That was *this morning*.

Maybe that's why I don't want to move.

Long day.

But that's not it.

That's not it at all.

Truth?

I just want to be with Muffy.

It's all I've wanted from the first time I noticed her hanging out at Chester Green's.

Her kind of special speaks to something buried deep inside me that I haven't let out in years.

Rufus hits my bruise again, and I lift my head to glare at him.

He makes eye contact with me, misses my butt with his next attempt at kneading, and falls off me.

Muffy mumbles something about snowplows and chicken feathers, then shivers.

She's completely naked except for her socks, her skin whisker-burned where I kissed her, goosebumps popping up in patches. I push off the bed, and she instantly rolls to her side, curling in, shivering.

It's not normal to want to take care of someone else as much as I want to take care of Muffy.

But grabbing a blanket and draping it over her doesn't feel like an obligation.

It's not something I resent.

It's a privilege.

She smiles softly in her sleep, and I take that image with me into the bathroom after I kill the lights in the bedroom. That, and the memory of her face, lips parted, head thrown back, chest rising and falling as she screamed my name.

The taste of her orgasm on my tongue.

Yeah.

I'm totally rubbing this out in the shower, yanking on my cock and fantasizing about driving into Muffy. Taking her bent over the bed. Fingering her while she soaks in my tub.

Letting her tear my clothes off the minute I get home and banging her against the door.

I want to worship her gorgeous breasts.

I want to feel her come around my dick.

I want her to cradle my balls and suck me so deep into her mouth that I can feel the back of my throat.

And I want to eat her for breakfast every day for the next week.

Month.

Year.

I come with a blinding force, clenching my jaw so I don't make any noise and wake her up.

My knees almost buckle, and my thighs are shaking.

I haven't climaxed in almost two months, and it's every bit as painful as it is euphoric.

My dick still works.

And it's not on a hair trigger.

I rush through the rest of my shower, towel off, and head back to the bedroom completely naked.

Muffy's still curled up in the middle of my bed, so I climb in, wrap my body around her, and bury my nose in her hair.

She sighs and wiggles her ass into my crotch. "Rhinestone panda."

I can love her.

It's like a friend thing.

Right?

Right.

No biggie. We'll be friends who love each other, quietly, without saying the words out loud.

And have sex.

And don't get married or have kids.

Perfect.

29

Muffy

I'M DOING my best to very quietly make myself breakfast in Tyler's kitchen, which is proving difficult.

One, my phone won't stop blowing up.

My mother wants to know if she should tell William to bring over his old wedding china so she doesn't have to buy me a new set when I get hitched to Tyler, because of course she's going there.

Kami wants to know how Rufus is doing and when I'm going to talk to her about whatever the hell happened in Richmond.

And four of my current clients, plus three more women who regularly join us for our support group meetings, want to know why I haven't mentioned that I'm dating a professional hockey player, because they definitely want details, and is it true that Rooster Applebottom has some sort of magical penis that would be worth trying out at least once, even if he's not long-term relationship material, because they would absolutely be up for meeting him if I could set that up.

PIPPA GRANT

Also keeping me from getting breakfast is the fact that I can't locate an egg-flipper anywhere, which is getting awkward since I already cracked two eggs and they are *definitely* at the need-to-be-flipped stage.

"Rufus, find me a flipper," I whisper to my cat.

He ignores me and pushes his food bowl along the half-wall separating the kitchen from the dining room, making the scraping noise that only porcelain against tile can produce.

My phone buzzes again in rapid succession, and I wonder if this is how Tyler feels every time one of his family group texts starts.

It's a lot to keep up with.

But most importantly, I need to flip my eggs.

Without a flipper.

"Screw it," I mutter to myself. I've watched Food Network. I've seen chefs flip eggs without a flipper by doing that thing with the pan, so I'm gonna shake the pan and flip the eggs that way.

"Think coordinated thoughts, Rufus," I whisper.

I grab the pan by the handle, jiggle it a little to make sure the eggs are free, flick my wrist, and— "*Dammit.*"

You guessed it.

Egg all over the stove, dripping over the cast iron grates.

"Seven out of ten," Tyler says behind me, startling me so bad that I shriek and drop the pan, which lands crooked on the stove, then tumbles to the floor less than an inch from my bare foot, spilling the rest of the egg that wasn't already on the stovetop.

"Not a serial killer," he says dryly. "You're safe."

While I scurry out of the blast zone of the hot food, Rufus leaps onto the goopy eggs and slides into the oven.

I wince. My heart's still in my throat, my phone's buzzing incessantly, and I've made an absolute disaster out of Tyler's kitchen after he put me to sleep with the orgasm to end all orgasms last night.

With all that exertion he put into it, I thought he'd sleep another hour or two. Especially with how very dead to the world he was when I left the bedroom ten minutes ago.

And now that he's awake, I don't know how to say *thank you for the best feeling of my entire life and I'm sorry I fell asleep instead of trying to reciprocate.*

Falling asleep after he went down on me feels very on-brand though.

It's one hundred percent something I'd do, and look at that, I did it.

I point around the kitchen. "I'll clean this up. And get you more eggs. I couldn't find—"

He steps behind me, wraps one arm around my waist, and uses the other to reach into the crock of utensils on the counter and produce an egg-flipper.

"—That," I finish lamely.

Is it wrong to feel like a disaster and not care at all because you're suddenly realizing that the guy whose place you're demolishing has a mighty oak in his pants that's poking you in the butt?

Asking for a friend.

And yes, I'm my own friend. Most days.

His fingers drift lower on my belly. "I'll clean it later."

"Tyler?" I whisper.

"Hmm?"

"Are we dating?"

"Yes."

I've never wanted to date anyone before, but there's a grown woman inside me twirling and shrieking with joy right now.

Play it cool, Muffy. Play it cool. "Okay."

"Just okay?"

No, not just okay, my vagina yells. *This is fucking fantastic!*

I press my ass back against his crotch. "I mean, good. Great."

He replies with a kiss to my neck.

My breasts get heavy, my nipples tighten, and my clit pulses in anticipation.

"Tyler?"

His lips continue their path down to my shoulder. "Mm?"

"I'm not wearing panties."

That tree trunk in his pants twitches against me. His hand momentarily stills, then slips into my sweatpants.

Okay, *his* sweatpants.

I totally raided his closet.

And that's my last coherent thought before his fingers find my clit.

He circles the nub while sliding his other hand up my shirt to tease my breast.

Sensations rocket through my body, ecstasy skating over my skin while he strokes my pussy and caresses my breast. I gasp and grab the counter for support. "Oh, god, you're good at this."

"Spread your legs for me, Muffy."

I do, and he slips a finger inside me. "Fuck, you feel good," he breathes in my ear. "So hot and wet."

I'd reply, but words have once again abandoned me.

Instead, I close my eyes and find a rhythm with my hips, riding his finger and pressing my butt into his morning wood and arching into the hand fondling my breasts.

"You snuck out of bed," Tyler says in my ear as he matches my rhythm with his hands. "I wasn't done with you."

And just like that, another orgasm rocks through my core.

I throw my head back. "*Tyler!*"

"That's it, Muffy. Squeeze me. Come harder. Let it all go."

He pinches my nipple and all the sensations crash higher and faster. I'm pushing my ass so hard into his crotch that I'm probably damaging his lovely thick length, gasping for breath, gripping the counter tight enough to leave marks, and I don't want to stop.

I don't want to let go.

I want to live in this pulsating bliss of orgasming around his fingers for a few more minutes.

Or hours.

Or days.

Just me and Tyler and my cat, naked and touching all the time.

Laughing. Talking. Sexing.

Like a real relationship.

A full-body shiver races through me as the last vestiges of my orgasm fade away.

I open my eyes and almost shriek again.

Rufus is sitting on the counter, and we're nearly eye to eye.

Oh, god.

Tyler probably thinks I was making eye contact with my cat while he was fingering me.

"My eyes were closed," I gasp as I sag against him.

He kisses me on the top of my head. "Mm-hmm."

I twist to face him.

He's grinning. It's a smug, self-satisfied, amused, sexy as hell grin that should be obnoxious and off-putting, but it's so *Tyler*. "Told you I could do better."

I glance down at his tented pajama pants, then lift my eyes slowly over his bare stomach and chest. Insecurity rockets through me—I will *never* be as fit as he is—but he strokes my ass and pulls my belly against his hard cock, leaning in to capture my lips as my gaze lifts to his face, and nothing else matters.

Just this bone-deep desire to be closer to him.

I've had two life-changing orgasms in a matter of hours, and I want more.

I want *all* the orgasms.

But more—I want *him* to get all the orgasms too.

And the idea of giving him as much pleasure as he's giving me—that's every bit as much of a turn-on as he is.

So I take charge of this kiss. And I slide my hands down his pants to squeeze his bare cheeks.

He growls low in his throat, a raw, primal sound that has my pussy aching in anticipation already again.

He likes me.

He wants me.

It's time for me to step fully outside my insecurities and show him I feel the same.

Tyler

I CAN DO THIS.

I can use my magical peen to give Muffy the orgasm of her life.

Me and the Wonder Stick are in this together. We're not panicking. We can do this. We've climbed this mountain before.

But never with the stakes quite so high.

She's kissing me like she's found the meaning of life, one leg wrapped around my hips. I grab her ass and boost her all the way up so she's cradling my dick between her thighs, and *fuck*, she feels good.

She tastes good too.

And the scent of her arousal?

Fucking intoxicating.

It's game on. Performance of my life.

I can't do her against the wall. Tried that last time. Didn't go so well.

Although, was it really a wall?

She thrusts her hands into my hair and her tongue deeper in my mouth, and my brain short circuits.

No wall.

Table.

Counter.

Dog biscuit.

Dog biscuit?

She's grinding against my boner, and even through both our pants, I can feel how wet she is.

Muffy Periwinkle, sex goddess.

I'm getting her a damn medal. A championship ring.

A cup.

She's getting the sex cup.

She breaks the kiss with a gasp. "I'm so mad your shirt's already off. I want to rip it."

My dick violently agrees that that would be awesome, and the smile blooming on her face tells me she felt his reaction.

"I'll rip yours," I promise.

Closet.

My box of condoms is in my closet.

She pumps her hips against my straining cock and leans in to kiss me again, and I go cross-eyed.

I cannot make it out of the kitchen, much less to my closet.

I want to be inside her more than I want to play hockey, more than I want to eat fried fish when I'm stressed, and more than I want to retire on a tropical beach to spend the rest of my days swimming with sea turtles and stingrays.

Fuck it.

I'm getting us to the bedroom.

I turn, slam her into the corner of the door, and we both jolt.

"Sorry," I gasp.

She tightens her legs around me. "Bedroom."

I don't know how we make it, but we do. Muffy's still kissing me. I'm hard as petrified iron. I want to touch her skin everywhere. I want to sunbathe in the glow of her smile. I want to drown in her gaze.

I settle her on the bed, and I'm about to leave her to make a mad dash to my closet when she produces a condom from her pocket and shoves it in my hand. "Later I'll tell you how much I hate that your sweat pants have pockets and mine don't. But right now, will you please do me?"

Her hair's a crazy mass of curls. Her cheeks are pink. Her lips are swollen and parted, her breath coming fast, her eyes dark and hungry but also *happy*.

The happy was missing this weekend.

And the idea that she's happy to be here, with me, is lighting up my soul.

She is what I'm here for.

It's heavy and freeing all at the same time.

"One rule," I growl.

Her brows furrow and she shrinks for a split second before she forces a smile back. "Rules, hm?"

"No faking it."

"*Oh*," she whispers.

"Deal?"

She answers by grabbing me by the cheeks and kissing me, and suddenly, nothing else matters.

Nothing but kissing her back.

Touching her.

Learning her curves.

Stripping her out of my pants and T-shirt.

Looking at her, naked against my sheets, a blush creeping over her skin, but making no move to shield herself as I study her body, my gaze following my hands from her shoulders, down her arms, over her amazing breasts, down her gently curved belly, to that adorable belly button, the trimmed patch

239

of hair hiding her sex from me until she parts her legs, letting me take in all the wonder of her womanhood.

"You're fucking gorgeous." And I'm hoarse. Desperate to drive into her. But equally desperate that she know how badly I want her.

She's not some quick lay in a dark corner in a club.

She matters.

She raises up on one elbow, legs still parted, and tugs at the strings on my pants. "I want to see you too."

Far be it from me to tell her no for anything. I shuck my pants and toss them somewhere, fumble through rolling on the condom, and then her greedy little hands are grabbing my cock, sending sparks of ecstasy through my entire body.

"He's not broken."

I swallow hard and reach for control before her easy touch sends me over the edge and ruins this for both of us. "He was. But he likes you."

And that's all I have to say about that.

So I drop back down to claim all the kisses, my hands roaming, her fingers exploring, her legs hooking behind my back again.

I don't want to talk. I don't want to scare her. I don't want to say something I'll regret. I don't want to scare *me*.

I want to show.

I want to show her she's worthy. And beautiful. And sexy.

The Muffy I saw in Richmond? Haunted, hesitant, and hiding?

I want that Muffy to fade into the background behind a Muffy who knows she's queen of the world, and who owns it.

And if I have to use sex to give her that confidence, I'm willing to make that sacrifice.

"I shouldn't still be this horny," she gasps when I move my lips to her neck.

"Yes, you should. I'm a sexy beast."

God, her laugh is better than the crowd going wild over a

slapshot buzzer beater. "And so modest. You know that turns me on."

"You turn me on."

"Why?"

I lift my head.

She's still panting, swollen lips parted, eyes dark, but there's a serious question in them.

Why am I attractive?

I should be furious at the world for making her doubt herself, but instead, there's a selfish joy that I get to be the one who sees it. That I get to be the one to help *her* see it.

"Because you're strong." I squeeze her thigh. "You have the patience of a saint. You have drive."

Her nose wrinkles. "Not that it—"

"You keep trying long after people who don't make it to the top walk away. That's sexy." I kiss her collarbone. "And you do it because you believe in your clients in ways no one else does. You *know* it's hard. You *know* you're fighting an uphill battle. And you stick with it for them. That's fucking sexy too."

"Or crazy."

"I like crazy." I lift my head to look her straight in the eye, lining my cock up with her wet core. "And you're gorgeous too."

That nose wrinkle is getting on my nerves.

"No—" she starts.

"Your eyes have captivated me from the first moment I saw you."

She sucks in a surprised breath, and I inch into her, her swollen, hot folds welcoming my cock.

"Tell me more," she whispers.

"When you wear your hair braided, I want to grab them and wrap them around my hands and hold on while I kiss you."

"Kinky." She tilts her hips, taking me deeper, and *christ*, she's heaven.

Her pussy is where my cock wants to go in the afterlife. And every day before.

"You have the cutest ears I've ever seen."

She laughs, tightening her walls around me, and I go cross-eyed.

"And you have a magic pussy."

I thrust the rest of the way inside her. She gasps and arches into me, head back, hair spilled all over my pillow, looking every bit the goddess that she is. "Oh, god, you feel good."

"You're fucking perfect, Muffy."

And you're mine.

I pump my hips, slowly, watching every shift in her expression, looking for the right angle to make her lose her mind while my cock strains and my balls ache from holding myself back, but I don't care.

I'm trapped in her gaze, wanting to kiss her but not wanting to break this spell.

This isn't *sex*.

It's more.

"There," Muffy gasps as her eyes slide closed, her hands squeezing my shoulders, her hot, slick channel squeezing my dick. "More *there*."

I'm sweating. Every thrust, every time she grinds her hips against mine, every time she tightens her walls around me or gasps my name or tells me what she wants, it all has me on the brink of blowing my load. The dam's near bursting.

But she comes first.

She comes first.

She has one foot on the bed, her knee up, the other leg wrapped around my hips, angling herself while I slam into her to gasps of *yes* and *there* and *more*.

I'm holding her hand to the bed, our fingers entwined, the

pit of my stomach cramping from the effort of holding back while she writhes under me, chanting my name. "Oh, god, Tyler, *I'm coming.*"

"Look at me," I order.

Her eyes fly open as her walls clench around me so tight that dots dance in my vision, and I'm coming so fast and furious that all I can do is hold myself deep inside her, straining into the waves of release. "*Muffy.* Fuck. *Fuck.* So good."

"Can't... control..." she gasps.

"Don't. Let go."

Fuck.

I'm lost.

Tumbling into oblivion with Muffy.

But it's safe and warm in her eyes. Happy. Full of wonder. Glorious.

Exquisitely perfect.

She squeezes my hand and sags back into the mattress, her pussy letting go of its grip on my cock. I strain into one last spasm, and then I'm spent too, collapsing on top of her.

"So it *is* possible." Her breath tickles my ear, and I'm suddenly chuckling.

High five to Mr. Wonder Cock.

We did it.

I shift so I'm not completely squishing her, unable to keep myself from kissing her jaw, her neck, her ear. "You're a goddess."

"Can we do that again?"

"Yes."

"Today? Or do you need some time to recover? Like a week or something?"

I lift my head.

She's grinning.

She knows I don't need a *week.*

243

But Muffy teasing me while she's naked and satisfied in my bed?

I'm good with that.

I'm *perfect* with that.

I don't know what it means for tomorrow, or next week, or next month, but today?

Now? In this moment?

I've never felt more at home.

31

Muffy

TYLER GIVES GOOD SHOWER.

He's shampooing my hair, his body slick against mine, his fingers massaging my scalp, steam rising all around us and jets shooting out of the walls at all angles to keep us both warm. His lovely cock isn't hard, but it isn't soft either—it's like he has the same body organ hangover that my pampered pussy is dealing with.

How can my vagina feel so very satisfied, so very tired, so very overstimulated, and so very eager to do it all again, all at the same time?

"Did your sisters teach you to do this?" I ask him as I arch into his touch.

He snorts. "Yes, Muffy. I shower with my sisters all the time."

"I thought so. You strike me as the type."

He leans left, and I get a face full of water from the overhead spout that he's been blocking. But I'm still laughing as I sputter and spit suds out of my mouth.

I totally asked for that.

"Any more questions?" he asks.

"Ten thousand."

His face relaxes into a smile. "Good."

Rufus yowls on the other side of the shower glass. My bathroom back at Mom's house has a tub with a shower curtain, and my cat is freaking out at seeing me naked and wet, which he doesn't usually have to endure.

Pretty sure he wants to save me from the evil water. Or possibly he's having a panic attack on my behalf and needs me to save him from himself.

"Have you ever had a cat?" I ask Tyler.

"Nope. Just a dog. Boots."

"That's adorable."

"He was Staci's, really. But I taught him to beg for bacon, and he stayed with us when she went to college."

"You went to college?"

"For two years. Then I got drafted."

"What were you studying?"

"Underwater basket weaving."

I laugh, and suddenly he's kissing me. I'm completely stark naked and wet, with bubbles sliding down my face, soft and pliant everywhere he's solid muscle, and I've never felt so safe.

He knows I'm a walking disaster. He knows my biggest secrets. He knows I faked it the first time we were together, that I can be mouthy and argumentative, that I stress eat, that I'm not conventionally successful, and he's still here, kissing me like I'm the queen of sexy lady land.

"Come to the game tonight," he murmurs against my lips.

"Can't. Shift at Cod Pieces."

He growls. Like, he actually growls. I'm showering with a mountain lion who wants to suit up and take on an armored fish for me.

"It's not for the money. One of my clients is the head

manager, and she's struggling to find anyone else to fill the night manager shifts half the week."

Those electric blue eyes land on me.

"But I want to be at the game," I whisper. And I do.

I love watching him play. I'm one hundred percent in over my head right now, and I know it, because I want to spend money I don't have to get a jersey with his number on it and sit right at the glass cheering for him and telling anyone who'll listen that he's *my* man.

I'm not supposed to have a man. I'm not supposed to *want* a man.

But Tyler is different. And not because he's not a man.

He shakes his head. "You…"

I wince. I know what comes next.

Are crazy. You're crazy, Muffy.

"Do they know how lucky they are to have you?" he asks.

"They?"

"Your clients."

Okay. Not what I expected. "I'm not exactly having a lot of luck finding most of them men worthy of their time, so I don't know that I'd call them *lucky*."

He turns us so the water's spraying behind me, and tilts my head up, rinsing the shampoo out, still massaging my scalp. "You don't owe them *everything*, Muffy. You owe them your best effort to find good matches. The rest of it—"

"Muff Matchers isn't only about finding true love. It's about helping my clients love themselves enough to be able to recognize a partner worthy of their love. So the rest of it *is* important. If I'm not willing to fry some fish and clean a grease trap or two to demonstrate what a good partner is willing to do, and to validate that *all* of who they are is important no matter their job, their family, or their life mission, then all I'm doing is taking their money like any other match-making service would."

He's quiet while he rinses the rest of my hair.

And since I'm feeling weirdly exposed again, I distract myself with the sight of naked wet Tyler.

There's nothing like being in an otherwise spacious shower to make a girl realize how broad her boyfriend's shoulders are, or how solid his chest is, or how thick his thighs are.

Boyfriend.

He said we're dating.

Does that actually make him my boyfriend?

Do I *want* a boyfriend?

I want Tyler. He's somehow managed to sneak past every barrier and booby trap that I usually lay for the men who come into my life, and it's not nearly as terrifying as it should be.

"You owe it to yourself to treat yourself as well as you treat your clients," he finally says.

And *that* is exactly why it's so easy to let him in.

He's not trying to get back in my pants.

I mean, he probably is, but that's not *all* he wants.

Is it?

"Have you ever had your heart broken?" The question slips out before my filter can engage, but really, do I have a filter? Do I *want* a filter?

My mother might be her own special brand of annoying, and often accidentally insulting, but she holds nothing back, and god knows I do the same when I'm on a mission.

His gaze flicks away for a second, but he looks back at me and nods. "Once. College. I hooked up with a teammate's sister. Fell in love. Head over heels. Completely gone. Told my family. And then my teammate found out..."

I cringe. I have no idea what Tyler was like in college, but I know his reputation here. Women. Parties. Fun. "He made you break up?"

He snorts and reaches for the conditioner that his

doorman delivered with the cat supplies. "You could say that."

I snort too. "Well. You showed him. Bet he's not showering naked with a woman right now before spending the day getting ready for a professional hockey game."

"Oh, he probably is. Asshole's the one who gave me the concussion in the playoffs two seasons ago."

I squeak.

He laughs.

Rufus yowls and tries to dig a hole through the glass to get to us.

He squeezes the conditioner all over my head. "My mom got the last laugh. She put him in her show."

"*No.*"

And now he's wincing. "Not my favorite bit of hers, but she's got a point. We were best friends before he dumped me for liking his sister. What's it say about any of us if I was good enough to be his friend, but not good enough to date his sister?"

That's a question I don't really want to ponder. "Does your mom make fun of you a lot in her shows?"

He shakes his head while he gets back to rubbing my scalp and pampering the hell out of me. "Nope. I mean, she still does her zombie grandpa skit from time to time, but in her defense, I hadn't been to a funeral in twenty years, so it's not like she knew it still bothered me."

"If you've skipped funerals for twenty years—"

"I haven't known that many people who died."

I blink at him, and then we're both cracking up. I have no idea why it's funny, but I don't actually care.

Seeing him laugh is like being in on the world's best-kept secret.

Tyler Jaeger, tough-as-nails hard-ass hockey player, has an amazing laugh.

The door bangs open, and two large figures burst in. "Jaeggy! Breakfast time!"

"Your apartment's got egg all over it, Jaegs. What's up with that?"

I shriek.

Tyler shoves me in the shower corner and spins toward the door, blocking my view, but his hands are covered in conditioner and there's enough on the floor that everything's slippery and I'm suddenly sliding to the ground.

"Get out," he snarls.

"Whoa. Didn't know you weren't alone." Is that Rooster? Oh my god, is that Rooster Applebottom? *Can he see my muff?* I'm squatting on the shower floor, knees up, peering through Tyler's legs, which are spread because that's what men do.

They spread their legs and widen their shoulders and glare and look terrifying, except I'm peering at Rooster and Connor Klein and can't entirely make them out because Tyler's dangly bits are a little in the way.

Related: I'm probably not supposed to be turned on by this angle of Tyler's anatomy, but I can't look at his package at all without hoping we make it back to the bedroom before my morning dates.

Appointments.

Not dates.

Appointments.

"We'll go wait in the living room," Connor offers.

Mist is raining down on me. I'm hiding my boobs with my thighs and my vagina with my hands and ankles, which might not be all that effective.

Plus, Tyler's giving them a full frontal through the foggy glass, but then, they're probably naked together all the time.

And now it's getting *very* hot in here as I contemplate an entire team of naked Thrusters.

Not that it's not already hot.

Hello, Tyler's ass. I really could bounce a quarter off his cheeks.

"Leave," he says to our unexpected bathroom guests.

"But *breakfast*," Connor replies.

"And bunnies," Rooster adds.

Tyler makes one of those growly noises that has me getting damp between my legs again, and not because we're in the shower and I'm sitting in a puddle. "Drop the keys on your way out. Why do you even have keys to my place? *I don't have keys to my place.*"

"Fourth of July?" Connor says.

"We're keeping the keys," Rooster announces. "Might need us to rescue you from the demon cat one day. Or to have that threesome."

"*Out!*"

"C'mon, Jaeggy," Connor says. "It's not like you ever have women here. We didn't know you meant she moved into your *bedroom*. We just wanted breakfast."

The door shuts, but neither of us moves.

At least, not for a minute.

I do take the opportunity to give Tyler's ass a test squeeze.

Kinda want to bite it, if I'm being honest. I think I could from this angle.

He turns, and *hello*, Tyler's penis.

It really is lovely. And it's growing before my eyes.

"Muffy—"

His voice is strangled like me *looking* at him is making it hard for him to stand up. I wrap one hand around his thickening cock and stroke it, my other hand cupping his balls, and he makes a noise that might be a *fuck*, but it's not fully intelligible.

He's literally growing in my hand, and it's making my pussy throb.

"Time—skate—go—" he grunts.

Yeah, and I have things to do too.

But I don't want to do *things*.

I want to lick him.

So I do.

I've watched movies. I've seen GIFs. I know how blow jobs are supposed to go. But it's not like I've ever practiced.

Stick a guy's dick in my mouth?

Gross. No.

Suck on Tyler's magnificent cock?

Yes, please.

I wrap my lips around his head and flick my tongue over his salty tip, and he makes one of those delicious noises again.

My breasts are tingling. My over-exerted vagina is complaining she's empty.

"You don't have to—" he starts, and I silence him by sucking him deeper into my mouth while mist swirls around us and the spray off the shower dusts us.

It's a little awkward at first, but he's making all the right *fuck, that's good* noises, wrapping one hand in my hair, which can't be easy since it's all slicked up with conditioner, but Tyler Jaeger is an achiever.

I want to be an achiever too.

I want to give him the best blow job of his life.

I'm bobbing on his cock, sucking and licking, and it's turning me on so much that I'm spreading my own legs a little as I go up on my knees, stroking myself too.

I don't care if Rooster and Connor come back in and find us like this.

I don't care if they're still right outside the door and can hear us.

All I care about is getting Tyler off with my mouth.

But the idea of having an audience?

I jerk my fingers faster inside of myself while I squeeze his balls and take him as deep as he can go without me gagging.

"Fuck, Muffy," he gasps. "Feels so good."

He's pumping his hips into my mouth like he can't stop himself.

Like I drive him wild.

And I love it.

I love every bit of this in ways I never thought I could.

I hit my clit as I suck harder on his dick, and suddenly I'm coming all over my fingers while he groans my name and strains into my mouth, his thighs quaking. "*Muffy*, I'm there. I'm—"

He wrenches himself out of my mouth, hauls me up by my armpits, and he kisses me, a punishing, bruising, delicious kiss, while his cock pulses and spasms against my stomach, a groan emanating deep in his throat.

This.

This is trouble.

It's terrifying.

And it's also completely thrilling.

It's a *relationship*.

And despite my better judgment, I'm all in.

32

Tyler

I'M SUITING up for practice, my brain short-circuiting and refusing to remember the name of this sport I play because it's stuck back in my apartment with Muffy.

In the shower.

Her mouth on my cock while she got herself off.

I don't think a woman has ever masturbated in front of me before, and when I get home tonight, I'm asking her to do it again.

I want to watch her touch herself.

I want to watch her go breathless and mindless, those gorgeous lips parted, her eyes unfocused, her hair wild, her legs spread, her—

"Jaeger."

I blink.

Fuck.

Nick Murphy's in my face.

He's not just standing in front of the bench while I strap on my pads. He's bent down, in my face so that I can see every last pore in his skin and that nose hair that he missed when he was trimming.

He's scowling. "Are you fucking my wife's cousin?"

I stand up so we're eye-to-eye. He's already in his goal-tender chest protector, which makes him look six feet wider than he really is, and it'll hurt if I punch him there, but if he thinks he can intimidate me, he has the brains of a goat. "I'm dating my girlfriend."

"Do you even know how to date a woman?"

"Did you?"

Frey and Lavoie both snort with laughter.

"Oh, snap, Murphy," Klein calls. "Jaeggy got you there."

Nick pokes me in the chest. "I hope you fuck up. Kami's approved saving all of Sugarbear and Tooter's poop to serve to you inside your next hamburger if you so much as make one of her eyebrows twitch wrong."

"Gonna have to nix that one, Murph-meister," Rooster announces. "Friends don't let friends eat cow shit."

"They're *dogs*," Murphy reminds the room at large.

Then he does something completely unexpected.

He grins and rubs my head. "Just messing with you. Anyone brave enough to date Muffy has to deal with her mother. I can't top that kind of torture."

Ares glances over at us. His gaze drops to my crotch, then back to my face, brows up like he's asking *did it work?*

"What are you, my mother?" I ask him.

He smirks.

Can't tell you the last time I blushed in the dressing room, but I think I'm blushing now.

"Game first," he says to the room at large.

Right.

Game first.

Even if Muffy won't be there tonight, I know she'll watch the highlights reel. Can't tell me half her wardrobe is

Thrusters gear and she doesn't care what happens during the games.

You're damn right I want to make the highlights reel.

"Wait," Klein says. "If you're dating Muffy, who was the chick in the shower with you?"

I flip him off while a round of laughter and hoots go around. They *all* know I'm dating Muffy.

We talked about it *last night*.

Which means those assholes came into my place this morning *knowing* what they were walking into. "Remove those images from your brain, or I'll do it for you."

"We didn't see a thing," Rooster says. He's already in his practice jersey and skates, but instead of his helmet, he's still wearing his cowboy hat.

I'd bet money he has a stuffed Thrusty stored in there. I've seen him pull one out to hand to kids more than once after a game, though I don't know why anyone would want it after it lived in his hat.

Gross.

"We saw enough to know he wasn't alone," Klein points out.

"You cheating on Muffy already?" Nick asks.

"No. That was my sister."

An awkward silence falls in the dressing room, and I swallow a smile while I pull on my own practice jersey.

"You got issues, Jaegs," one of the guys mutters.

"Or maybe he wants some privacy because relationships are hard enough when they're all over the gossip pages," Lavoie mutters.

"Wait, what?" I say at the same time Nick moves down the bench and gets in his face. "Talk. What?"

Lavoie rolls his eyes and lifts his phone. "Gossip pages. Tyler. Your sister-in-law is *Daisy*. She went to that funeral with you. And you didn't think the rags would pick it up?"

I snag it and look at the site he's pulled up.

Dammit.

There's a shot of Muffy and me at the funeral. And another of us kissing. And a third of me holding the car door for her looking like I want to eat a piece of the metal.

The headline makes me want to eat this phone.

Mystery Girl in Daisy Carter-Kincaid's Family Circle.

"Whatever." I throw the phone back at him. "It'll get two hundred clicks, all from inside this room, and that won't be worth it for the gossips to keep digging. There's no payoff in who I'm dating. I don't sell magazines."

That's why I'm never in the gossip rags myself.

I'm never the draw.

Daisy is.

"Could help her business get some word-of-mouth advertising," Klein points out.

It could, but the idea of the public at large picking apart a business called Muff Matchers that specializes in helping women who don't fit the standard mold—let's just say I'd have to quit hockey and spend the rest of my life egging houses and getting in bar fights after I hired a hacker to track down every last internet troll.

Fuck.

That wasn't a fluke last night.

I love this woman. And I don't know what to do about it.

Tell her?

Not a chance. She'd bolt faster than a starving lion chasing a gazelle.

I don't even have any faith she'll still be at my place tonight, much less when I get back from the team's road trip out to Vegas and Seattle this week.

Lavoie and Ares settle on either side of me on the bench.

"Tell her," Ares says.

"She might want to use the story for her own purposes," Lavoie adds. "Let her make the call."

Ares grunts.

Pretty sure that's a grunt of *that wasn't what I meant and you know it.*

He thinks I should tell Muffy that I love her.

"Right," I say to Lavoie. "She's smart about her business stuff. She'll know if it's good or bad."

Ares grunts again.

Lavoie grins. "Go easy on him, big guy. It's terrifying the first time it happens."

And now I don't know if he's talking about me or the story.

Or both.

Coach walks into the dressing room. "Ten minutes, gentlemen. Applebottom, switch to white team today. Lavoie and Klein, marketing wants you for a video with Thrusty. Jaeger, medical. *Now.* You're not getting on the ice until you get your head checked."

Now I'm grunting.

I don't want to report to medical. I want to go play hockey.

Apparently my doctor's note hasn't come through yet. Fucking dead body.

But I'd still do it all over again.

I grab my phone before I head down the maze to the on-site clinic, and I text Muffy on the way.

33

Muffy

Do I have an overdeveloped sense of right and wrong, or am I so new at being the one actually in a relationship that I'm suddenly feeling like a total jerk for sitting at a bagel shop with a guy who thinks we're here on a date?

I know it's not a date.

But he doesn't.

He thinks he's here to meet Octavia Louisa, formerly an airman in the Air Force, who likes crocheting and CrossFit, and is currently studying classic literature through an online master's degree program.

He's a single dad of a ten-year-old, working some kind of technical job at a telecommunications company, divorced because he got married too young to his pregnant college sweetheart, telling me about his mom's cat without giving off unhealthy attachment vibes, and I'm rapidly deciding I could introduce him to Brianna.

Just to be sure, I accidentally spill my coffee.

And then my phone dings.

"Oh my god, I'm so sorry." I leap up, glance at my phone, realize it's Tyler messaging, and my nipples harden into diamonds.

My date's grabbing napkins and asking if I'm okay while I stand there getting wet in the panties at the mere sight of my boyfriend's name.

Boyfriend.

I have a *boyfriend.*

It's the weirdest sensation.

And also terrifying. I mean, apparently sex *is* good, but how long until he gets bored of me? Is this like a *this week* thing, or is it a *we're officially dating with the purpose of seeing if we're compatible long-term* thing?

"Octavia?"

Oh, crap. My date's said my name like seven times, and I forgot he was talking to me.

Also, I don't remember what his name is.

"Sorry," I stutter as I dive in to helping clean my mess. "Family emergency."

"Do you need to go?"

"No. It's my cousin's goldfish. He'll probably make it. She's a vet. She knows mouth-to-mouth." *Shut up, Muffy. Shut. Up.*

My date peers at me with the kind of warm concern that Brianna deserves.

Or possibly he's starting to question my mental state.

All good. This isn't a date, after all.

I manage to end my not-date soon after so I can check the message from Tyler. Before I let myself click on his studly face, though, I prep a note to my date—Steve, that's his name —to send after a while where I'll apologize for being flaky, tell him this is a weird question, but I feel like he should meet my friend Brianna?

I'm almost back to the light-rail stop before I finally give myself permission to look at Tyler's message.

And my heart nearly stops.

I call him, but he doesn't answer. No surprise. He's at practice. Morning skate. Team time. Whatever they call it.

And since I can't get ahold of him, I go down my list.

I start with Veda, who gets a text. Her dad's funeral is going viral. She should know. Someone in her circles in Richmond might notice and ask about it.

Hello, stomach dropping.

Why does Richmond still bother me?

I went, I funeral-ed, I came home with a boyfriend.

I survived. They didn't hurt me.

But I'm still breaking out in a cold sweat.

So, my next move is to call Kami.

She has experience with the limelight. Not only were she and Nick featured in a Valentine's Day promo shoot for the Thrusters last year that aired on the video boards at the arena during the game, but they were also covered on a national news channel for a feature about the personal lives of hockey players.

Forty minutes later, we're seated at the Cod Pieces franchise closest to her veterinary practice. I don't know the crew here, and that's probably for the best.

"Is this all going to blow over without me getting named and Muff Matchers coming into it?" I ask her over fried fish once she's skimmed the gossip article on my phone.

"Probably. I heard Liv Daniels is having a fling with a mystery man, so Daisy Carter Kincaid's brother-in-law dating a normal person shouldn't be interesting for long."

I don't answer.

Kami squeezes my arm. "Did you *want* the attention?"

The question makes sense. On one hand, it's free advertising if I'm identified.

But I don't want it.

And it's not the world-wide public attention that has me

frowning. It's the local attention. "I don't want anyone digging into why I left medical school," I whisper.

There's freedom in Tyler knowing. It's an unexpected gift to feel so comfortable in knowing my secret is safe with him, plus his complete support and lack of judgment make me feel like everything's okay. Or if not okay, better than it was before, even if I still get the cold chills and shakes at thinking about ever going back to Richmond. They're less chilly and shaky now. Like maybe I've been holding on to the shame and the guilt and the whole big secret for too long, when really, nothing was nearly as guilt- and shame-inducing as I've been telling myself it is.

I haven't even told my therapist that part of my story. We talk more about my parents and my feelings of inadequacy at being a normal adult with a normal job after such a big failure.

But Tyler knowing is different from the world at large knowing.

I am *not* ready for the phone calls and emails and questions I'd get.

I probably won't ever be. It's not really anyone else's business.

Kami leans closer. "You're not worried your clients would dump you over something that happened years ago, are you?"

I start to shake my head no, then stop.

Am I?

"Tyler's really mad at my mom," I hear myself say.

Kami doesn't blink at the subject shift. "Why?"

"I think he thinks she's done a lot of things to make me feel insecure in who I am and what I look like."

"How do you feel about that?"

"Probably like you feel about thinking you're the dumb one in your family?"

Kami's not dumb. She made it through vet school and

she's saved Rufus's life more than once. But her brother and sister are *uber* smart, and I know it's always bothered her when they nerd out and she can't keep up.

She drops her gaze to my chest. Pretty sure she's not making a comment on how big my boobs are, but more that I'm hiding them under a massive Thrusters hoodie.

And yes, it's Tyler's, and no, I won't stop borrowing his clothes until he makes me.

They smell like him.

I like it. This might not last long. I'm YOLO-ing while I can.

Plus, I was screening someone for Brianna an hour ago, and so it was important to dress as close as she would for a date.

"You think I wouldn't have body issues if my parents hadn't waved their own unhealthy relationships with the human shape in my face my whole life?" I guess.

"Things get rooted deep when you're little. I know my dad never meant for me to feel dumb, but I overheard him telling my mom how much he loved being able to talk to Atticus about particle physics when I was in seventh or eighth grade, and I internalized that as *I love my children who are smarter more than I love my children who don't grasp physics concepts*. It was wrong—of course my dad loves me, and he didn't say it maliciously or to hurt anyone, and since Atticus is older, of course he grasped more complicated concepts before I was mentally capable of doing the same—but that doesn't mean it didn't make me feel inferior for not being able to talk to him about his job the same way my brother could."

"She doesn't mean to hurt me."

"But she still does. And don't let your dad off the hook. He *knew* your mom was self-conscious, and he called her names anyway."

I stare at my fried fish.

It's delicious.

I totally get why Brianna wanted to lick it. And why Tyler eats it when he's stressed.

And I can't finish it, both because I'm thinking of how it will look on my hips, and also what it will do to my arteries.

But the weird part is that for once, I might actually be thinking more about my arteries.

Possibly Tyler defending my body was very, very good for me.

But why did it take *him* saying something my therapist has been trying to explain to me for years for it to sink in?

Am I putting his opinions on a pedestal because he gave me an orgasm?

Or did I have to have an orgasm for the message to sink in?

Which came first, me or my possibly improving self-image?

"Mom charged her boudoir shoot to my credit card and maxed it out," I tell the filet. It's easier than telling Kami, and I don't want to think about my self-image anymore.

"*Again*?" she gasps.

It wasn't a boudoir shoot last time—it was her buying into a pyramid scheme for herbal supplements—but I know that's not the important part. "My card got declined when we got to Richmond. Tyler had to pay for our hotel room. And then dinner. And all the gas. And he didn't complain once and he glared at me like I was insulting his manhood when I told him I'd pay him back."

"I don't think Tyler's the type who thinks a man has to pay for everything. I think he's more the type to help a friend in need and he doesn't take *thank you* well."

"I know, it's just...you do it, because we're family. And Veda did it for Muff Matchers because we were so tight in med school and she knows—anyway, we have history. Tyler and I—we don't."

"So this past year was nothing?"

"We were harmlessly flirting."

"You weren't also becoming friends?"

My cheeks are getting hot. "We were making friends."

"And now?"

"And now he's like this master conductor and my body is his orchestra and I don't want to date or get married except I could see me and Rufus living at his place forever, and I also don't know how long it'll be before Tyler gets tired of us. He doesn't want to have a girlfriend or ever get married either, except he told me this morning that we're dating and he gave me the keys to his car and he's acting like he won't *allow* me to go see my mother unless he's present to serve as a shield to absorb all of her accidental insults, even though we both know he can't order me to do anything, and I don't think it's a control thing. I think it's that he wants to protect me from getting hurt. And it feels a whole lot like what I see your parents have. And what you and Nick have. And now I'm going to hyperventilate, okay?"

Kami grips my greasy hands while I breathe through the sudden panic gripping my heart.

I know why my mom's broken.

She loved my dad with everything she had, and he left.

She wasn't enough. Her love wasn't enough.

He got tired of her, and he left.

If I let myself love Tyler with everything I have, and he leaves, I know *exactly* what my future will look like.

It'll look like my mom.

"Muffy. Talk to him."

"I can't. Kami, I told him why I left Blackwell. But I can't tell him this."

Her brows hit her hairline, and hurt flashes in her eyes.

Dammit.

This is exactly why I can't have a relationship. Even when I'm not trying, I hurt the people I love. I grip her hands tighter and lean across the table. "He fainted at the funeral home. And I felt so bad. And then he told me some personal stuff, and I'd been drinking, and—"

"It's okay." She squeezes my hands, back to being calm, rational, kind Kami who would let anyone walk all over her.

Except she doesn't do that anymore.

Not since she put her foot down with Nick a year ago.

"I'm terrified he'll hurt me like my dad hurt my mom," I whisper.

She smiles at me, and it's like being wrapped in a hug. She's not smiling because she's happy. She's smiling because she's saying *it's okay, Muffy. You'll be okay.* "My mom told me once that your parents got married because your mom fell so in love with your dad at first sight that she hid all of her quirks and made herself into the woman she thought he wanted her to be. She didn't think anyone would love her if she was herself, and after a while, she convinced herself that your dad knew who she really was deep down and loved her anyway, even though he had no clue. You don't hide who you are. At least, I don't think you do. Do you?"

I laugh, but it comes out more like a hiccup. "Believe me, if I were hiding who I am, I'd find a much more attractive package."

"You're not your mom, Muffy. And I don't know what Tyler's hang-ups are about relationships, but I know he's not your dad. He likes you *because* of your quirks. He likes you *because* you don't fit a mold. Talk to him. Tell him how you feel. And if he doesn't feel the same, you have something else your mom never had to help you get through it."

"What?" I know the answer. I have her. But I want to hear her say it.

"You have Nick. He'll make Tyler's life hell until he's begging for a trade and you never have to see him again."

I snort with surprised laughter.

But I know she's right.

I have her. And she has Nick, so by extension, I have Nick.

I also have my clients and friends. If things go south with Tyler, I'll be okay.

I will be okay.

She's right. I should talk to him.

Soon.

Maybe next week, if he hasn't kicked Rufus and me out yet.

"Thank you."

She leans across the table and hugs me, squishing the fish between us. "You're welcome. Now, can we get out of here? My boobs are about to explode. I need to pump."

From the texts of Tyler and Muffy

Tyler: If you get any messages from numbers you don't recognize, ignore them. Ignore them all.

Muffy: Why? Did you leak my number to some lonely hockey player online group that passes around good numbers for phone sex?

Tyler: In case you're unaware, it's highly uncomfortable to sit on an airplane when you have a boner the size of Mount St. Helens, and you talking about phone sex is definitely giving me a boner the size of a mountain.

Muffy: I legit always wondered if penises were actually annoying. And now I know. Thank you. Also, I hope you can breathe with that many tons of dirt and rock in your crotch.

Tyler: This is where you tell me you'd lick me until I blew like a volcano if we were together.

Muffy: Would you actually jerk yourself off on an airplane surrounded by your teammates?

Tyler: This is why airplanes have bathrooms.

Muffy: OMG. *mind blown emoji* Do guys really do that? Do they really go into the bathroom mid-flight to jack off? I am never using an airplane bathroom again. Ew. Ew ew ew!

Tyler: What if we flew to Australia?

Muffy: Depends.

Tyler: On what?

Muffy: Not IT DEPENDS. I would WEAR DEPENDS.

Tyler: Sexy.

Muffy: I should not be turned on by you being turned on at the thought of me in adult diapers.

Tyler: Fuck. And I was just getting comfortable and not worried I'd make Klein self-conscious if he happens to notice I get bigger boners than he does.

Muffy: You are such a guy. And have you ever actually seen Klein have an erection? Do you know for sure yours is bigger?

Tyler: I forbid you from thinking about Klein raising his flagpole.

Muffy: *laughing emoji*

Tyler: But you're welcome to think of my joystick as much as you want. Actually, if you wanted to think about it now and tell me you're naked in my bed and pretending I'm with you, I'd be down for that.

Muffy: Oh! I got three texts from unknown numbers. They're claiming to be your sisters. OMG! You gave your sisters my number?

Tyler: Ignore those. They're not actually my sisters. Nick's passing your number around the team and everyone's trying to get you to tell stories about me.

Muffy: The one claiming to be Allie has a picture of you with your finger up your nose when you were thirteen. *picture of Tyler dressed for hockey practice with his finger up his nose*

Tyler: That's really Rooster.

Muffy: No, that's definitely your brother in the background. OMG! The one who says she's Keely sent me a screenshot of a group text with you and your family where your dad said something about getting high and moving in with a family of otters?

Tyler: Heh. Yeah. I taught Staci how to change autocorrect functions in Dad's phone, and so she sneaks over there and replaces his favorite phrases with weird shit all the time. No one suspects her because she refuses to participate in group text messages.

Tyler: DO NOT SCREENSHOT THAT CONFESSION.

Tyler: Not that it matters. It's not really my sisters. It's Lavoie and Rooster and Ares.

Tyler: Muffy? Fuck. Where'd you go?

Muffy: Sorry. Daisy group video-chatted us all because your sisters knew you'd be denying it was actually them. OMG! They're so funny! And nice. And I can see how growing up with that much energy would scar you for life. It's like two and a half times as much energy as my mom, and she drove me crazy on a regular basis.

Tyler: Ice water has officially rained down on Mount St. Helens and it will never erupt again.

Muffy: Britney and Daisy both put some of their cats on to talk, and Rufus freaked out at all the meowing. But don't worry. I'll replace your fruit bowl before you get home. Oh! Did I tell you that one of my clients had a very successful first date this morning? I'm so excited for her. She's… well, she's a lot like me. *blushing emoji* *flower bud emoji*

Tyler: That's awesome. High five, magic matchmaker.

Muffy: It's only a first date, but they set up a second before it was over, so I'm cautiously optimistic.

Tyler: We should celebrate when I get back. Naked. With those dice that Rufus dumped out of your bag.

Muffy: OMG! I didn't know you saw those.

Tyler: Got distracted when he tried to climb the curtains.

Muffy: Those are on my list to replace too.

Tyler: Quit offering to replace things. Have I mentioned I have four sisters and I'm the baby? I didn't pick or buy anything currently decorating my place. I didn't even pick the condo. It was the default option when my sisters nixed the other options for whatever their reasons were.

Muffy: What about the TV?

Tyler: Okay, that wasn't my sisters. That was West. He was researching his own new television when he got out of the military, found one he liked, then moved in with Daisy and redirected his TV here to me since he knew mine didn't survive my move to Copper Valley and I'd been going without, whereas he had moved in with a billionaire.

Muffy: That's...wow.

Tyler: I *am* fully capable of picking things for myself. But a wise man once told me it's sometimes best not to fight it.

Muffy: Your dad?

Tyler: West, actually. He heard it from Dad first, before Dad was worn down by raising four girls.

Muffy: You're ridiculous, yet sexy and adorable at the same time. That bag Rufus emptied? It's actually my Muff Matchers new client kit. In addition to the sex dice, there are fuzzy handcuffs, a pack of cards with unique date ideas and conversation starters, eye masks, a romantic candle, lip balm, breath mints, hand sanitizer, an umbrella, and a vibrator.

Tyler: Fuck me, now I'm picturing you using a vibrator.

Muffy: I'm mildly surprised you didn't empty the drawer in my nightstand when you cleaned out my room to move me in with you. It's not like you have anything to be self-conscious about. You're definitely better than my favorite dildo.

Tyler: I'm sweating.

Muffy: So. You, me, dice, handcuffs, dildos, and vibrators? Saturday night is sounding better than I thought it would when you proposed date night on our way back from Richmond.

Tyler: Klein just asked me if I'm having a heart attack. I had to put a book over my boner. Talk to me about the umbrella. Why do you have an umbrella in your new client kit?

Muffy: It's the most phallic-shaped thing I could think of. I wanted to put in dildos but that seemed too far, even for me.

Tyler: Fuck me, you do NOT want to know the things I'm thinking right now...

Muffy: *chest selfie* Question: is this called a chelfie? Or a brelfie?

Tyler: Take the shirt off and snap another chelfie. The plane might be going down. I need to die with the image of your breasts as the last thing I see.

Muffy: Is the plane really going down?

Tyler: If I say yes, do I get a full nude?

Muffy: You, Tyler Jaeger, are a hornball.

Tyler: Only around you.

Muffy: *naked chelfie*

Tyler: God, I love your tits. You have the most gorgeous nipples.

Muffy: You remember last week, you walked into Cod Pieces and looked down your own pants?

Tyler: Yes.

Muffy: I would very much like to look down your pants right now. But I don't think I'd stop at looking. I'd want to touch you too. And stroke you. And then lick you. And suck on you.

Tyler: *gif of a man sweating profusely*

Muffy: *gif of a woman biting into a strawberry and closing her eyes in ecstasy*

Tyler: Strawberries. Fridge.

Muffy: *selfie of her biting into a strawberry with her bare breasts showing*

Tyler: Fuck. We're landing in twenty. I'll call you. If I survive that long. Gotta go before I come in my pants. *kissy emoji*

35

Muffy

IT'S SATURDAY MORNING, and Tyler's due home from his road trip any minute.

So where am I?

Back at the café next to the stuffed animal store, having a morning Muff Matchers client support group meeting.

And my mother has joined us.

"I always put out on the first date," she's telling Brianna. "That way, you know if he's worth having another date with. Go big or go home."

"And that works for you," I point out, "but everyone is entitled to do what *they* are comfortable with."

"Women shouldn't be ashamed of liking sex," she argues.

"No one's saying we should." Maren shoots a look at me that feels like a sympathetic hug, then turns back to Mom. "But, Hilda, there's a difference between not being ashamed of wanting sex, and not wanting to have sex the first time you meet someone. Some people are comfortable with one-night stands, and some people want to get to know their potential partner better before getting naked. Neither's wrong."

"I want to have sex with Steve," Brianna tells us. Mom's eyeballing the amount of cream cheese Brianna's slathering on her bagel, and I'm trying to not let my own eyeball twitch.

No one else notices. I'm oversensitive to it.

And that's okay too. I know *why*. I'm working on only changing and worrying about the things I can actually control.

I can't control my mother.

"Did you tell him that?" Julie asks Brianna.

She sniffs her bagel, smiles at it, and chomps down. "Not yet. He needs to earn me."

"High five, sister." Eugenie slaps palms with Brianna. "Way to identify what you want."

"How's school?" I ask Brianna.

She beams. "Good. I joined that study group with your friend D'Angelo, and I've never had more friends in my entire life. We're doing laser tag tomorrow."

"Aw, that's fantastic!"

And it's almost nine. I know Tyler's flight home from Seattle was supposed to land about an hour ago. He should be nearly back at his condo by now, if he's not already there.

He had the *best* game last night after a solid game two nights ago too. Rewarding him with all-day naked time is the only thing on my calendar until Monday. He's earned it.

Even if he hadn't played well, it's still what I'd want to do.

I really hate my new rule about putting my phone on do not disturb during support group meetings.

We move on to asking Eugenie how her week was, then around the circle, me trying not to fidget and jumping in every time I'm afraid my mom will say something problematic or without thinking, Maren helping because she's been doing this since she first asked me to help her find a boyfriend a year ago.

274

We've decided she's incredibly picky and possibly not in a good headspace for a man, which is only hard since most of her core group of girlfriends—including Kami—are all settling down.

It's weird to be left behind.

It's even weirder to realize I'm in her core group and I'm one of the people who might be leaving her behind. Or at least make her feel that way, even if I wouldn't ever abandon her as a friend.

I mean, assuming this thing with Tyler is serious.

I haven't exactly asked him if he sees me as the future Mrs. Jaeger, or if we're having some kind of extended friends-with-benefits-who-live-together thing.

There's a strong possibility I'm terrified to know the answer. Plus, it's only been a week.

A week. That's way too soon to start thinking about forever. I need to slow down, enjoy him as my friend and orgasm-maker, and not start acting like my mother.

Julie drifts off mid-sentence with her coffee cup halfway to her mouth, eyes going wide and aimed at something behind me.

Eugenie glances over my shoulder, and her eyes pop too. Brianna drops her bagel.

Maren gets a smug smile and pulls out her camera.

"Well, that's a sight better than coffee," Mom announces.

I'm bracing myself as I turn and check out what they're all staring at.

It briefly registers that the commotion in the outdoor seating area is Rooster Applebottom signing a woman's chest with a Sharpie, and that Duncan Lavoie is the crazy guy in just a T-shirt in the chilly morning, on one knee talking to an overexcited little kid.

I say *briefly registers* mostly because the window's not worth watching when the door is so much more interesting.

Tyler's average size for a hockey player, but he seems to

take up the entire width of the doorway. He doesn't scan the room, and he doesn't trip over any tables despite not actually looking at what's in his way as he strides inside.

Nope.

The man trains those eyes on me like he's tearing down the hockey rink on a breakaway, his only mission scoring a goal.

It's me.

I'm the goal.

Pretty sure a hockey goal doesn't come with a suddenly throbbing clit and aching breasts and a short-circuiting brain that can basically only think about the picture Tyler sent me after my shift at Cod Pieces last night, where, yes, I had one earbud in playing the game the whole time, and yes, I did accidentally yell *GOAL!* in a customer's ear in drive-thru.

But the more important thing?

That picture.

Tyler's boxers.

Tyler's *tented* Thrusters boxers.

He stops behind my chair, bends, and claims my lips in a searing kiss that I feel all the way in the ghost of me that will one day haunt this earth.

"Phew," Mom says. "Muffy, I don't know what you're sprinkling on his corn flakes, but keep it up, sweetheart. Am I having a hot flash, or is he just that sexy?"

Tyler's face twitches.

I can *feel* it.

And it's suddenly the funniest thing in the world.

I break off the kiss with a fit of the giggles, like I'm fourteen again, and I get the eyebrow of *are you kidding me?* from my gruff, broad-shouldered, hot-as-sin boyfriend.

He tugs at my chair. "Excuse me, ladies. Personal emergency. Muff will see you next time."

"Keep her as long as you want," Mom tells him. "I wouldn't mind if you knocked—"

Maren clamps a hand over Mom's mouth. "Hilda. Shut up and don't ruin this for her."

"Highly unlikely," Tyler tells her as he pulls me to my feet. He flicks that deadly gaze at my mom. "But agreed. Hilda. Shut up."

I glance at my clients.

All of them shoo me one way or another without demanding introductions.

"Sunderday—" I start, then realize that's not a real day of the week.

"We'll see you Tuesday," Julie says with a grin.

"Blank you."

Blank you?

Was I trying to bless her and thank you?

I don't bless people. What the *hell*, Muffy?

Tyler's chuckling as he wraps an arm around my shoulder, snags my coat and handbag from the back of my chair, flinging the bag across his own body like he's done this a million times even though it's bright pink, which definitely makes it more noticeable than a normal purse—for a guy, I mean—and steers me out of the café. "Is someone tongue-tied?" he murmurs.

"You are seriously hot."

"I am seriously horny. Let's go home."

Home.

Definitely not ruining this moment with questions. Not when my heart's sprouted wings and is acting like a fighter jet at an air show in my chest.

"Have fun, Jaeggy," Rooster calls.

"Don't encourage him," Duncan says, loud enough for us to hear.

A few people look our way, but Tyler's *here*, and he's solid, and he's sexy as hell, and he's taking me *home*.

I don't care who looks.

PIPPA GRANT

We reach the edge of the parking lot and he glances around. "Where's my car?"

"At home." Holy crap, does that word feel weird.

He shoots me a *what?* look.

"I grove. Got. Grove. Drove. My car." *Dammit.* I stop, pat my bag, and manage to dig into it to grab my keychain with a rubber Thrusty hanging off of it, and dangle it in front of his face. "*My conda.*"

His lips are twitching because I can't say *car* or *Honda.*

Screw this talking baloney.

I go up on my tiptoes and press my mouth to his.

Nothing else matters. I'm kissing Tyler. He's holding me so tight against his body that if I were a little less solid mass and a little more actual putty, we'd be melding into one goopy mass of overheated slime.

And I mean that in the sexy way. I swear that could be sexy.

It would still be a shame, though, because I wouldn't want anything to lessen that solid bulge pressing into my belly.

"My car," I say on a gasp as I break the kiss. "Drive. Broken."

His breath is coming unevenly too. "Your car's broken?"

"No. Me."

That earns me another grin, and then I'm being tossed over his shoulder. My car alarm goes off three rows over, and I realize he's using my fob's panic button to find it.

Smart, smart man.

I kiss him when he puts me down and tries to open the passenger door for me. He kisses me back as he tries to make me sit so we can leave.

I squeeze his ass.

He squeezes my breast.

I am no longer a woman with insecurities and complexities and a cat.

I am one flaming ball of hormones about to strip in a parking lot so I can have sex with my boyfriend in public.

"Back seat," Tyler says.

"Oh, god, *yes*. I can't wait until home."

"Back seat so *I can't touch you while I drive*."

"I don't like that plan."

"Cross my heart, Muffy, I'll get arrested with you for public indecency, but not until *after* the season."

"You clearly don't want me badly enough."

He growls, shoves me into the back seat, and shuts the door.

I'm fogging up my own window before he makes it to the driver's seat.

"Tyler?" I pant.

His gaze flicks to mine in the rearview mirror.

"I'm going to masturbate in the back seat while you drive."

My keys hit the floorboard, and he bangs his head on the steering wheel when he bends to pick them up. "No more talking. And if you don't save that pussy for me, I'm locking you out of the house."

"Spoilsport." God, I want to touch myself so bad.

"Keely's meatloaf. Staci's feet. Allie's hairbrush…"

"What are you talking about?"

"Things that don't make me too hard to drive. I need my brain so I don't drive us into a lamppost. West's gym socks. Brit's poetry. Dad loves liverwurst."

"We both just saw my mother."

"No good. I saw your mother and then I kissed you. *Fuck*, I missed you."

If my panties weren't already soaked, they would be now. But they're joined by a glow in my chest that's so unfamiliar it hurts. "That goal you scored last night? The one where you sent the puck between your legs? That was so hot."

His beard is twitching like he's clenching his jaw again,

and I want to lean forward and run my hands through his hair.

I don't, because he's right.

We need to get home and get naked.

"Dirty diapers," he mutters. "Episiotomies. Allie's morning breath…"

He's hilarious and sexy and wrong all at the same time. I squirm in my seat, letting my hand fall between my legs and telling myself it doesn't count if I'm only pressing on my clit through my jeans. "Litter boxes," I offer.

"Losing."

"Grease traps."

"Atomic wedgies."

"Banana-flavored pudding."

He shudders. "What the hell is wrong with you?"

"Banana flavoring is too far?"

"*Bananas*."

"You hate bananas?"

"They smell like my grandfather."

Oh my god, I love this man.

I shouldn't. I really shouldn't. He's smart and athletic and kind and everything a guy should be to have his pick of any woman in the entire world.

There's no way this can last.

But I can't cut myself off of him. Not when being with him feels so damn good.

And if there's any chance he'd be hurt simply because I'm afraid—nope.

Won't do it.

Seize the day. It's what I tell my clients. Even knowing I basically learned it from my mother and have always used it wrong, I still tell people that, and I should take my own bad advice.

Not bad though?

All the lessons from therapy.

You are worthy, and any man lucky enough to get the opportunity to know you had better recognize what he has.

With Tyler, I feel like he knows what he has. The bad and the good.

He's seen me at my worst. He's seen me trying to be my best. And he's seen me everywhere between.

So I'll seize the day.

I'll put everything I have into this unexpected gift of having Tyler in my life, for however long it lasts.

36

Tyler

EGGPLANT MILKSHAKES. Frozen pipes. All four of my sisters talking at once about *The Bachelor*.

Almost there.

Almost. There.

I reserved a second parking spot in the garage for Muffy's car, but it's not nearly as convenient as my spot on the first level next to the elevator, so it takes for-fucking-ever to park the car and drag Muffy to the building.

As soon as the elevator doors shut us in, we're making out like the fate of the whole damn galaxy depends on us banging it out *right now*.

"You are so sexy when you wear my purse," she gasps while I suck on her neck.

"You're fucking sexy no matter what."

She thrusts her hands down my pants. "I need your cock."

"I can smell you and I need to taste you too." I stroke her between her thighs, and *hello*, the denim is soaked.

She is so hot and horny for me, and it's making my dick strain impossibly hard again.

"Oh, god, I think I just came a little," she pants.

"Good. I'm gonna make you come all day long."

The elevator dings open.

I don't care if we dropped something in here. I'll replace it. I need her in my apartment. Naked. Riding me.

Now.

We bumble down the hallway, kissing and groping until we hit my door. I almost can't get the damn thing open, but the minute I do, Muffy flings her shirt off.

Right there.

In the hallway.

I shove her inside and haul off my own shirt, shucking my pants before the door slams shut.

She's stripped out of her own pants too, and there she is.

My Muffy, all soft curves and delicious breasts with pink lace covering her tits and pussy.

"Christ, you're gorgeous," I breathe while I trace the edges of her lingerie and stroke between her legs.

"You're just horny."

"Only for you."

Her hands are roaming all over my body, setting my skin on fire and making Mr. Wonder Cock strut like nobody's business. When she grips him and strokes, I go cross-eyed. "Fuck, Muffy—"

"Yes. Fuck Muffy. Right here against the wall, because I swear I'm going to implode if I don't have your cock in me *right now*." She drops my dick and shimmies out of her soaked lace panties, pauses at eye-level with my crotch to lick Mr. Happy, and if she puts her mouth on my cock once more, I'll be coming in her face.

I haul her up and spin her against the wall. Her legs go around my hips like she's an Olympic sex gymnast, and I don't think, I don't pause, I just slam into her.

"Oh, god, Tyler, I missed this," she gasps.

Have to be good.

Last time we tried fast and vertical, she faked it.

Won't let her need to fake it again.

But god, I can't slow down.

I'm pumping into her faster and faster while she bounces on my cock, breathless and needy. "More," she gasps. "Yes, more *there*."

Hazy darkness is creeping into the edges of my vision. If I don't come soon, I might never come again. Gonna break my dick.

Worth it.

So worth it.

I shift angles to make sure I'm grinding her clit with every thrust, and she arches her head back, knocking it on the wall. "*Tyler*."

"Fuck, Muffy, you're so damn sexy." *I love you.* "Come for me, baby. Come all over my cock."

"I—I—*Oh, god*, Tyler, I'm so close."

Her thighs are quaking. I squeeze her flesh and drive into her again and again, my own release *right there* too. "Muffy, baby, I'm gonna—"

"*Tyler!*" She screams my name, her hips buck, her legs go straight out, and she's suddenly coming all over me, squeezing my cock so hard with her magic pussy as the spasms of her orgasm take hold. "Yes, yes, *yes yes yes*, oh *god*, Tyler!"

I come with a roar, letting the dam break, so, *so* fucking good.

It's pain and perfection and pleasure, from the pit of my gut to the tip of my dick. It's euphoria.

This.

This is what I was put on this earth to do.

My vision is clearing, and *oh god*, she's gorgeous.

Grinding down on my cock while we both come, eyes

unfocused, beautiful pink tongue touching her upper lip, neck straining, breasts heaving.

We're in a bubble of ecstasy, and I'm never leaving.

Never. Ever. Fucking. Leaving.

It's Muffy.

Muffy laughing. Muffy sassing. Muffy sexing.

Her body sags, and I barely catch her as the last of my own orgasm subsides. "You're the queen of all the goddesses," I murmur to her shoulder.

She doesn't answer, but she buries her head in the crook of my neck, arms wrapped loosely around my shoulders, her breath tickling my skin in that perfect way that makes my oversensitive cock twitch.

"Muffy?"

"Shh. Just be."

Just be.

Fuck, yes.

I can *just be.*

So long as it's with Muffy.

37

Muffy

IT'S NOT weird to be living with a guy without defining your relationship, is it?

Because it's been two solid weeks of living with Tyler, with Rufus getting into everything from his tea supply— who knew he was a tea guy?—to deciding to sleep in his underwear drawer, and Tyler has yet to kick me or my cat out.

He's stopped by Cod Pieces every time he's been in town when I've had a shift that didn't overlap with a game. I've been at every home game that I haven't been scheduled to work. Given that it's only been two weeks, that means one game and two visits at Cod Pieces, but still.

I believe we'll be keeping this up for the foreseeable future.

He's suggested different motivational quotes and topics for me to email my clients about. And I've been sucked into group messages with his sisters.

This is basically a real relationship.

And every day, I wonder if things are about to fall apart, or if they'll keep getting better and better.

Take right now, for instance.

Right now, it's Friday morning. Tyler got home from a quick road trip so late last night that he doesn't have to be at the arena for anything team-related until late this afternoon. We're on the rug in front of his fireplace, soft jazz music playing in the background, playing strip poker.

He's on his side, shirtless but still in his gray sweatpants, and I'm sitting cross-legged, down to my one and only pair of lace panties.

Side note: I am not a very good poker player. Darts, yes. Poker, no. Not enough experience. Yet.

Not that I mind.

When I lose this round, I have to strip off my panties and roll the sex dice.

I really hope I don't roll to give his lips a massage, because I know for a fact that if I can get my hands on his cock, we'll end up having marathon sex for the next three hours no matter what the dice or the cards say.

"Are you in?" I ask him as I rub my own nipple with one hand and wiggle my cards at him with the other.

His gaze is trained on my nipple, naturally. "All in."

"Are you sure? I have a really good hand. You might lose."

"I'm not wearing underwear."

I fake indignation. "You came to this game in just a T-shirt and sweatpants? I'm a very serious poker player, Mr. Jaeger. I expect my opponents to *want* to win."

"I'm a very serious sex player, Ms. Periwinkle. I expect my opponent to want me to bang her senseless more than she wants to show up wearing nineteen layers of clothing to drag this out."

That wolfish smile tells me he's enjoying every bit of dragging this out.

"There were *ten* layers, and only if you count my hair tie." Yes, yes, I did count my socks and earrings each individually.

Also, I only put on earrings to slow things down if necessary.

I *like* basking in being turned on by Tyler and his magnificently talented body.

"So when you lose this round, I still don't get to see that pussy?" he asks.

"You saw it this morning in the shower. It hasn't changed."

"I'm gonna need to see proof of that myself." He throws his cards down. "I win. Strip and grab the dice."

There's a high likelihood that I'm playing wrong, since I don't even look at his cards to verify he's beat me before rising to my feet and hooking my thumbs in my panties. "Like this?"

I wiggle my hips and tease him.

His cock pulses, making the tent in his sweatpants move. "Exactly like that."

I turn so he gets a full view of my ass, stick it out at him, and sway while I slowly inch my panties down, glancing over my shoulder to watch his eyes going darker and darker with every little bit of my skin that's revealed.

The door beeps with the *someone's unlocking me* sound, and we both freeze.

That was *not* the door lock.

Was it?

Are his housekeepers coming today?

The door swings open. I squeak and drop to the floor. He bolts to his feet, lunges for the couch, and throws a throw pillow at me like *that's* going to cover me up.

"Ah, nothing like the smell of a bachelor pad in the morning," a woman's voice says.

"*Out*," Tyler snarls.

"Oh, please, like we've never seen you whacking off before," another woman says.

He throws a second throw pillow at me, then yanks on the curtains Rufus shredded and tosses the whole thing at me, curtain rod too.

"Thank you," I gasp as I crawl under the fabric.

"Oh, shit, you're here," the first woman says.

"We tried to call. Your phone says you're in the mountains. Oh my god! You found a way to trick our find-a-friend app! We thought you were hiking with Muffy." There's a pause. "That *is* Muffy, right? I can't see her clearly. Or did this just get next-level awkward?"

"*Out*," Tyler repeats.

I peer through the shreds in the curtain and see two women, both average size, one with short brown hair, the other with brown hair tucked up in a ponytail, and my heart hiccups.

His sisters.

His sisters are here.

"Told you it was a good idea to leave the kids at the hotel with the men," one says.

"Probably a good thing Mom's not here too," the other replies. "This would definitely lead to curtains matching the drapes jokes in her next show."

I trip over the curtains as I rise, wrapping them around myself. "Hi," I say.

Tyler twists his head and skewers me with a *what the fuck is wrong with you?* look.

I don't blame him.

Our options are kicking his sisters out and me rolling the sex dice to see what part of his body I have to lick, kiss, stroke, or massage, or letting his sisters stay.

This should be a no-brainer.

But my vagina isn't making this decision for me.

And the matching smiles blossoming on his sisters' faces are hitting me in the feels. "Muffy?" one asks.

"That's me."

The one with the short hair points to herself, then her sister, introducing themselves like we didn't do the same on a group video chat like ten days ago. "Allie and Keely. And we're both *so* glad you aren't an actress Tyler hired to make up a good story. Sweetie, your nipple's showing."

I bend and snag a throw pillow and cover my breast.

"Other one," Keely says.

Tyler squeezes his eyes shut and sighs a deep sigh. "What. Are you. Doing. Here?" he says through gritted teeth.

"The kids wanted to go to the planetarium and the aquarium."

"And you couldn't go to the ones in Chicago?"

His sisters share a look.

"No," Allie says.

Keely nods in agreement. "You're not playing the Indies in Chicago tomorrow night."

"And you know we don't miss Indies games."

"He used to date Gator Cranford's little sister," Keely explains to me.

"We're here to booby trap the Indianapolis bus if Gator tries to knock him out again," Allie agrees.

"The guy has a highly overdeveloped sense of revenge."

"Unlucky for him, we now have Daisy."

"Is your whole family here?" I ask.

They shake their heads in unison.

"Not yet," Allie says.

"But they will be," Keely adds.

"We really did come early to show the kids Copper Valley."

"And we thought Uncle Tyler would want to come along."

"Honest to god, we actually thought maybe you were a fake girlfriend that he planted to text and video call with us, because he *never* dates, and it wouldn't be the first time he paid a service to pretend to be his girlfriend."

I choke on air.

And for the first time since we were interrupted, I see something other than irritation flash over Tyler's face.

This is sheer pride and amusement. It's subtle—it's all in the eye movement—but there's no mistaking his mood is improving. "Best Christmas present I ever got all of you."

"You got them a fake girlfriend for yourself for Christmas?"

He flashes me a grin. "Still have the website. We can get you a fake extra boyfriend and let him talk to your mother about his complicated feelings about being in a threesome."

"You really want a threesome one day, don't you?"

"Not anymore."

Allie's smile goes so wide it has to hurt. "Awww! He's in loo—*oof*."

"Don't jinx it, idiot," Keely hisses as my heart starts an Olympic-worthy vault routine in my chest. She points at us. "So, do you really want us to go away, or do you want to hang out with us at the aquarium this morning?"

"We want you to go away and we'll get back to you when we feel like it." Tyler shifts to stand between me and his sisters, and I wonder if I'm accidentally flashing some other body part.

"Aquarium this morning without you, and we'll invade for dinner with all of the kids again at five." Allie nods. "Got it."

"Six," Keely says. "You forgot about the time change. They won't be hungry at five here."

"*Six*! Right."

"I have a team thing," Tyler says. "You're on your own."

"We know. We're inviting Muffy."

"This is *my apartment*—"

"And we love cooking and cleaning here." Keely beams. "We'll leave you a ton of leftovers."

He sighs.

I know that sigh.

It's surrender with a side of *they're right, I love their leftovers*.

Allie leans around Tyler to make eye contact with me. "And please tell me you'll sit with us during the game tomorrow. We got a party suite."

"My clients—" I start, and both women interrupt me at once.

"We have room!"

"Bring them to the party suite too!"

"Party suites are the *best* way to watch the games."

"Especially with kids."

"But we're getting babysitters."

"So we can actually watch."

Tyler heaves another sigh. "Are you done yet?"

His sisters share another look. "Yes," Allie says.

"Especially since you need to deal with your cat," Keely adds. She gives us a finger wave. "Later, taters! We'll let you get back to...whatever it was that you were doing that's clearly sweet and innocent."

"Agreed. Because I really don't need to picture Tyler doing anything not sweet and innocent."

They leave as fast as they arrived, and I peer around the room for Rufus.

"Sorry," Tyler says as he bends and lifts the sofa. Rufus darts out like he's been trapped under it for hours. "I'd say they're not usually like that, except they are. They have zero boundaries."

"Um, have you met my mother?"

His gaze locks on mine, and I tilt my brows for extra emphasis while he stands there, staring at me.

"Fuck," he finally mutters.

292

Fucking. Yes. I support that plan.

I drop the curtain and the throw pillow. "Can you super emergency lock us in so no one else can get through that fancy door?"

He's not looking at my body.

He's looking at *me*, and he looks utterly perplexed.

"What?" I wipe my face. "Tell me I'm not wearing breakfast. Do I have part of a smoothie on my forehead?"

"No," he says softly. "You just—you're fucking perfect. That's all."

My heart swells so hard and fast at the sincerity in his voice that it makes my eyes a little wet. "So far from it," I whisper.

He doesn't answer.

But he does snag the dice, toss me over his shoulder again, and carry me to the bedroom, where he locks the door, settles me on the bed, and proceeds to pick which side of the dice he wants to land up.

And when I should be sucking on his fingers, he sucks on mine. And when I should be tickling his nipples, he tickles mine. And when I should be eating his cock, he spreads my legs and feasts on my pussy instead.

If Tyler Jaeger doesn't love me, he's doing a very good job of making me feel like he does.

Neither of us say the words.

I don't think it's in us. Neither of us wanted a relationship. Neither of us wants to get married.

But he's rapidly become the very best friend I've ever had, and I don't want this to end.

38

Tyler

IT'S BEEN years since I wanted my family to meet a woman in my life, but knowing Muffy is off with my sisters at the zoo while I'm at morning skate on Saturday isn't bothering me as much as it should.

Also not bothering me?

Facing the Indies tonight.

If Gator Cranford's still holding it against me that I slept with his sister *one night* in college, when I really did think I could spend forever with her, he can fuck right off.

"How much you need me to have your back, Jaeggy?" Rooster asks while we're going through shooting practice. "You want me to rough him up right out of the gate so he's got all his anger aimed at me, or you want me to lay low so he doesn't know what hit him the first time he calls you a pussy?"

"Just play your game. I'm not worried."

"Should be," Lavoie says. "Dude acts like you knocked his

sister up with triplets and left her to fend for herself in some backwoods town without running water or electricity."

I checked in on his sister on social media for a couple years after college, and I know I didn't knock her up. She's living her best life. I'm living mine. No harm, no foul.

"Guy can't touch me," I reiterate to my teammates.

I'm floating on air.

Muffy's coming to the game tonight. She politely declined the party suite with my family since a bunch of her clients wanted to come, so they're sitting together in the nosebleed section.

It sucks that I won't see her in the front row like I did when she'd come with Kami, but knowing she's there is all that matters.

Plus, when I offered to get her tickets for all of her clients, she literally grabbed me by the balls and made me promise they'd be nosebleed tickets, *or else*.

I got the impression withholding sex was the very least that she'd do. She doesn't like feeling like she owes people, and I don't want to come home to her scrubbing my toilets in an effort to pay me back.

And I'm not one to deny the fun of the nosebleed section anyway. That's where I saw my first hockey games.

The game isn't about the seats. It's about the experience.

Lavoie sprints ahead to take his turn at shooting at Klein, who's starting tonight.

Murphy's not making noise about retiring, but he's also up there in goalie years, and the brass want to develop Connor more so we're not stuck in a bind if Murphy ever leaves.

We know it's coming, even if he doesn't. And maybe it'll take two or three years, but it *is* coming.

He's different with the wife and kid.

Looks good on him.

And for the first time in my life, I don't feel sorry for him being shackled in a marriage.

Might actually *want* what he has.

I hit the front of the line and take off to try to score on Klein, send the puck right in the five hole, and circle the net with a fist pump. "Next time," I call to my buddy.

He ignores me, because Frey's already barreling toward him from the other side.

Frey's another one with a family. Calls Gracie his wife, though if they've made it official, I didn't get an invite. She's not keen on being a princess, and Frey loves his dad and his brothers and his country, but he could care less about the whole royal-prince stuff too.

Dude has the luxury of not caring though. He's pretty far down the line of succession.

I'd give up a country for Muffy.

Fuck, I'd give up hockey for Muffy.

And that realization has me freezing hardcore as Rooster circles to join me back in line.

He grins. "Look like you got hit upside the head with the cooter stick."

"The *what*?"

"Cooter stick. You done gone and fell in *loooove*, but you don't know if it looks like love because you're in love with getting it up again, or if you're getting it up again because she's got the one cooter your dick can't live without."

Lavoie snorts in front of us. "Leave him alone, Applebutter. At least until *after* the game, yeah?"

Rooster doesn't bat a lash at his new nickname. "Not a chance, Cap'n Dunk-hat. Not if it gives him something to live for." He smacks me in the ass with his stick. "Good on you, Jaeggy. Play your heart out for her. Better'n playin' your heart out for yourself. Or for your dick. Gives a man more to live for."

"You ever been in love?" I ask him.

He grins. "Every single fucking night."

Yep. Completely the dude we all love to hate.

"You tell her yet?" Lavoie asks me.

No, I haven't told her.

This is our honeymoon period. What if it's lust and not love? What if I say I love her and it scares her away?

This is Muffy. She acts like she doesn't give two shits what anyone thinks of her, and she talks the talk when it comes to her clients loving themselves first, but she doesn't apply it very well to herself.

"You've been flirting for a year, you passed out at a funeral for her, she's living with you, she's all you talk about, she's hanging out *with your family*, and you haven't told her you love her?" Lavoie's practicing puck control while we move up in line, his stick patting the puck back and forth, but all of his attention's on me. "You don't think she's serious?"

"We hooked up because neither of us wanted anything serious."

"Jaeger. You're in something serious."

"*I* know, but I don't know if *she* knows. And what if this is just the honeymoon period? What if this all wears off next week?"

"Gotta man up and talk to her, Jaegs," Rooster says. He's spinning in a circle like he's thinking of trying out for the Ice Capades if this hockey thing doesn't work out, except he's trying to balance his stick on his chin. "Otherwise, six months down the road, she's gonna dump your ass because she's realized it's been six months and that smells like a relationship. I've smelled your socks. Don't get more attached if she can't handle it."

"Or we get six months down the road, she realizes I'm everything she's ever wanted, and all my patience has paid off." When my balls don't shrivel, I know I'm kidding myself in thinking this is a passing phase and that I'll get tired of it.

What I don't know, though, is if she's as serious as I am.

And that was the one thing that didn't work out for me the two times I tried it before.

Two.

I'm a wuss when it comes to relationships. Scared of commitment because of *two* things that happened before I was old enough to drink, hiding behind not wanting to live with my sisters for the rest of my life, when the truth is, I've been waiting my whole life for someone as fun, bright, amusing, and unexpected as they are.

Lavoie's shaking his head. "Tell her."

"And what if she bolts?"

"What if she's waiting for you to say it first and she's afraid *you'll* bolt?" He grunts. "You've met her mother. *I've* met her mother. If ever there was a woman who'd have issues, it's Muffy."

I'd slug him on her behalf, but I know he's not saying it to be an asshole.

He's saying it because it's true.

"Tonight," I say. "I'll tell her tonight. *After* we kick Indianapolis's asses, and Gator Cranford crawls out of here with his tail tucked between his legs."

Rooster punches me in the arm. "That's the spirit. Go get her, tiger."

I don't want to *get her*.

I want to love her.

Muffy

I. FREAKING. Love. Tyler's. Family.

We've hardly seen him all day, which is pretty normal on a game day. He has morning skate, team lunch, nap, then it's time for him to suit up and swagger back to the arena.

I couldn't join anyone until after my weekly client support meeting, where I have *three* clients now dating men I introduced them to, and two more unofficial members of my client roster that I've matched in my head as soon as they give me the go-ahead and sign on. Maren is still single, but I introduced her to my therapist this week, and she texted to tell me that after her first session, she's pretty sure this will be more useful than dating.

And now I've been to the zoo with Tyler's family, and we're all gathered in Daisy and West's hotel suite for dinner before the game, where Daisy's private chef is glowering at everyone while he stands guard at the roast beef station in the corner.

Apparently Cristoff needs to be shown all the love for his

food, or he threatens to feed Daisy things she's allergic to. And he's clearly not serious, because every time he references feeding her shellfish to make her blow up like a balloon, West smiles, rolls his eyes, and shakes his head.

"She can handle him," he tells me when he catches me looking confused at his amusement. "Plus, he knows what I did to the last guy who threatened my family."

I feel like there might actually be a true story there, especially when Cristoff abruptly stops muttering and eyeballs West with more than a little healthy respect, but Staci leaps in and starts asking me questions about my matchmaking business before I can press for details. She tells me she's the friend whisperer in her circle back home, and she likes to hook up mom friends who are lonely with other mom friends who've been there.

"Best match you ever made?" she asks.

"Betty and Sariela."

"You made a lesbian match?"

I nod. "Yeah, but it's not the best because it was a lesbian match. They were my first match, and it was an accident. They met at my first client support group meeting, which I did on a fluke but has turned out to be the best part of my matchmaking service. I only have like five true success stories, so helping my clients find friends on their way to also finding love is a serious boost to my confidence."

"Have you always wanted to match people?"

"I used to ship people in high school, but I never did anything about it, so after—" I cut myself off, realizing where this will go if I finish my sentence.

And now half of Tyler's siblings and a third of his in-laws are looking at me.

Waiting for me to see what came before *after*.

And you know what?

Screw it. I am who I am. If ever there was a group of people who'd accept me without question the way I'm learning to accept myself, I'd like to think it's the people who love the man who's trying to rescue me from myself.

I nod and continue. "After medical school, I wanted to find something to do to help people, and I've always felt like I didn't quite fit anywhere, so when I overheard two women talking in a coffee shop one morning about how hard it was to find guys who couldn't look past the way they had a few curves and thought for themselves and liked to do *Star Trek* cosplay, it was like I'd found my calling. I didn't have a clue who I'd set them up with, but I told them I ran a service called Muff Matchers and that I wanted to help them out."

"Wow," murmurs Staci's husband, Javi, whose infected testicles are apparently fine now, and no, I'm not thinking about that.

"That takes serious balls," Britney says, because she, obviously, is.

Everyone looks at Javi.

"Fudge you all," he mutters.

"Fudge!" Britney's twins yell together.

The rest of the kids take up the battle cry, and soon Tyler's parents are sharing a look and snickering to themselves while their children try to get the grandchildren to focus on food again.

It's fucking awesome.

They're dysfunctional in their own way, but I adore them. Every last one.

I get hugs all around when we split up at Mink Arena. They're heading to the party suite, and I'm meeting my clients at the hot dog stand across the street.

It's relatively new, but it's seriously hopping.

Mostly because whoever opened it licensed the use of Thrusty, the Thrusters' official rocket-powered bratwurst mascot, for marketing purposes, and they sell Thrusty Dogs and Thrusties on a Stick.

Not gonna lie. If I'd thought of that first, I probably wouldn't be matchmaking.

Brianna's the first to arrive, and she's dressed for the occasion. Thrusters jersey, Thrusters sweatpants, Thrusters handbag, and Thrusters bratwurst hat. Legit, the hat is like a three-dimensional stuffed bratwurst on her head, like those Cheesehead hats, except Thrusty's flying out of her forehead instead of a block of cheese eating it. "I'll get a foam finger inside," she tells me.

Maren arrives next, and she takes one look at Brianna's hat and gasps. "*Want!* Oh my god. Where did you get that hat?"

Brianna beams. "I made it."

"You *made* it?"

"Yeah. I watched some YouTube when I was bored after class while Steve was working, and I figured it out."

Now we're both gaping at her. "That's freaking amazing," I sputter.

She shrugs. "My grandpa tried to teach me how to make all my own clothes when I was growing up since the usual stuff didn't fit, so I already knew how to use a sewing machine. I never liked to before because it reminded me that I wasn't a size two."

"I love that your grandpa taught you," Maren says with a smile.

"Our family's been bucking trends since 1842."

When everyone else arrives, I pass out the tickets and we head inside.

Yes, Tyler got them for me.

I'm still sorting out the credit card issue. Namely, how I'm going to pay it all off on top of my student loans.

It's a really good thing I actually made a couple matches and have Cod Pieces for backup.

We get to our seats right as the Thrusters take the ice for warm-ups, and I get a serious thrill when I spot number ninety-one doing his usual half-lap sprint before snagging a puck with his stick and sending it flying into the empty net.

Phoebe, who's never been to a hockey game, leans around Maren, hands me her binoculars, and points. "Tell me why forty-two and eighty-two are humping the ice, and are either of them single? Please tell me they're single."

"Nick Murphy and Connor Klein. Goaltenders. They're stretching since they'll be diving all over the net blocking pucks, and they have to move fast. Nick's married to my cousin. Connor's single and loving it."

"Your cousin sleeps with a guy who can do the splits?"

Maren, who's one of Kami's best friends, makes a gagging sound. I crack up.

"It only looks like that because he has such big pads on," Maren says. "In real life, I have never once seen Nick Murphy do the splits." She sighs. "But he can get closer than I can."

"I've seen him open a jar of peanut butter," I offer.

"*Ooooh*," everyone says, and then we're all cracking up again.

I use Phoebe's binoculars to look closer at Tyler. The guys are in two lines now, moving fast as they go through a passing drill that ends with one of them shooting a puck at Connor, who's in the net now.

Tyler scores, turns, and I swear he looks right at me and grins.

Be still my heart. That's even better than the time he tossed me a puck when I was sitting with Kami right on the ice when she and Nick were quasi-dating.

I used to love coming to the games for the thrill of supporting my local team.

Now, I can't wait for this game to be over so I can kiss him.

His attention shifts back to warm-ups, turning to coast to the end of the other line, and I sink back in my chair with a blissful smile spread over my face.

Maren pokes me. "You've got it bad."

"I have it bad," I agree.

"Is he serious about you?"

"He's not kicking me out."

"But is he *serious* about you?"

I know what she's asking, and I know why. Kami had a friends-with-benefits relationship with Nick for *months* before she realized it wasn't going anywhere and dumped him. Not to say that all hockey players just like sex however they can get it, but let's be real.

The sex is definitely one of the highlights of living with Tyler.

And while Kami dumping Nick finally opened his eyes to what he had, I don't feel like Tyler takes me for granted the same way.

"I met his family. He moved me into his place and *brought my cat*. We've all heard the rumors about him hooking up with a random bunny or someone he met somewhere else, right? And he's sworn up and down almost as long as I've known him that he's never getting married. But then he tells me he misses me when he's out of town and he cooks me breakfast and he stops by Cod Pieces when I have a random shift, and it's like—"

"You're working at *Cod Pieces*?"

I open my mouth, then shut it.

"*Muffy*. Are things—" She glances at the rest of the group, leans closer, and lowers her voice. "Are things that bad?"

"No! No. I'm filling in some shifts as a favor for someone. And things are getting better at Muff Matchers. I'm screening the men better than I did last year, and the support group is going so well, and I'm on the verge. I'm seriously right on the cusp of making this *work*-work."

Maren's brows are bunched together. She knows as well as I do how badly my screening efforts failed last year, when I was letting random men sign up on my website.

I accidentally set Kami up with one of their other friends' horrible ex-boyfriends.

With the number of dating disasters my services have sparked, it truly is a miracle that I still have any clients at all.

"If you need help, call me. Understand?" Maren says.

"I've got this. I do. I'm not bailing on this the way I—the way I bailed on med school."

"I have a spare bedroom and I don't mind cats, okay?"

"Thank you, but I don't think I'm going anywhere anytime soon."

I start to smile.

She meets my eyes, and she laughs. "You really do have it bad."

Can't argue with that.

I really, really do.

But Tyler does too. He might not say it, but he's showing me that he does.

I stare at him down there on the ice, see him glance at the other side of the rink, where Cranford is glowering at him from the boards.

My stomach drops.

If Tyler gets hurt—

"Cranford won't touch him, Muffy," Maren says. "He got a twenty-game suspension after the last time he went after Jaeger. If he does it again, they'll boot him from the league, and he might have sponges for brains, and you know he'll push it as far as he can, but Tyler's safe."

"He's a *hockey player*. I don't think *safe* is quite the right word."

She smiles. "He's as safe as he can be flying across the ice and chasing a rubber puck while five other guys try to slam him into the boards. Better?"

Mostly.

But I still don't like it. Anyone willing to hold a grudge for this many years isn't someone I trust with my boyfriend.

"You want me to rough up one of the Indies after the game, let me know," Brianna says.

"I'll be there with my phone taking video," Maren adds.

"Are we supposed to cheer if they fight?" Phoebe asks.

"Yes," Maren says.

"No," I say at the same time.

"I mean, so long as it's the *other* team losing teeth," she amends.

I settle deeper into my seat and blow out a slow breath as the clock winds down on warm-up time.

The roughness is part of the game. But that doesn't mean I have to like it.

Especially with Tyler's sworn enemy out there on the ice with him.

Tyler

THE ONLY THING better than winning a game is having Muffy leap into my arms the minute I walk through the door of Chester Green's Sports Bar afterwards.

Except we lost a hard-fought game on a fucking technicality, I'm sporting a black eye courtesy of one of the Indies' left wings, who told me *Cranford says hi*, and I'm more in a mood to punch something than I am to hang out in the middle of a bar where Thrusters fans should be celebrating, but instead just eyeball those of us on the team walking in the door to join the subdued party of our friends and family who are taking up half the space.

And to top it all off, Muffy's mother is here.

"At least she's not Cranford," Lavoie mutters to me.

The Indies are starting a seven-day road trip, which means they're staying in Copper Valley tonight before heading to their next stop tomorrow.

I don't actually trust that Cranford *won't* show up here.

"Should've gone to the bunny bar," I mutter back.

Except even if my whole family could fit in the bunny bar, kids aren't allowed, and I've already spotted two little ones in the crowd waiting for us.

Muffy leaps up from her spot as we make eye contact, a million questions racing over her face. "Hey. You okay?"

"Had worse."

She looks stressed, and I don't know if it's the hard game, or if it's her mother talking to my sisters. She goes up on her toes, kisses my cheek on the side of my face that's not swelling, drops back to her heels, and tugs me toward the open seat beside her chair, calling greetings to my teammates as she drags me down the table.

"Hey, Connor. Great game. You totally got robbed. Nice goal, Duncan. Nick. You're okay, I guess."

It's so normal, my bad mood starts to lift. I squeeze her hand, and she smiles at me, which makes my heart lighten too.

Daisy's talking to the server. West's cuddling Remy, who's passed out cold. My sisters are all chattering away, most of their kids back at hotels with babysitters.

My teammates' wives and girlfriends are waiting too. Kami greets Nick with a kiss, then passes him their baby. Felicity and Gracie pull away from chatting with my mom to greet Ares and Manning. Klein's sidetracked at the bar with Athena and Cassadee, who must've heard we weren't hitting the bunny bar tonight. Rooster hasn't made it past the entrance. He's signing autographs and teasing the crowd with the stuffed Thrusty he pulled out of his cowboy hat.

I swear the dude either has stock in the toy company that makes those, or he's getting a kickback from the team for promoting them.

Dad stands and thumps me on the back. "Great game, kiddo. Tough loss, but you played hard."

"Way to not get a concussion this time," Oscar, one of my brothers-in-law, calls.

I give him a thumbs-up while Mom smothers me in a hug. "Thank god for that sweet Applebottom boy. He was even more effective than that giant Berger boy who tried to be your bodyguard last year. Where is he, anyway?"

"Rooster?"

"No, the other Berger boy."

"I'm retired, ma'am, but I'd still kick your ass in mechanical unicorn bull-riding."

Shrieks go up all around the room as Zeus Berger strides out of the bathroom hallway, pulls out a chair, sits, and then promptly crashes to the ground as it collapses beneath him.

Ares sighs and shakes his head. "Lazy ass."

"Damn, it feels good to be back here," Zeus says from the floor.

He's so tall he could still eat off the table with his ass down there.

Actually, he's so tall, he's almost as tall sitting as his wife is standing. But don't think Joey Diamonte-Berger is anything other than a badass. Even if she looks mildly green around the edges.

The wives and girlfriends converge on Joey, hugging and asking how she's feeling.

"Pregnant," I whisper to Muffy.

She sighs and looks at Maren. "You win. Can I pay you in Rufus love?"

"No, but I'd totally take you talking Brianna into making me one of those Thrusty hats."

"You bet Joey'd get pregnant?" I ask as I follow her gaze to where one of the women I vaguely recognize from Muffy's support group meeting is hugging a guy who's walked into the bar.

"Within six months of Zeus retiring," Maren confirms.

"Bet Muffy could get pregnant faster," Hilda announces. "Plus, she's got great birthing hips."

Staci and Brit both choke on their beers.

Muffy sighs. "I can also squat two hundred pounds, which will come in very handy when I toss you out a window," she mutters.

"Two hundred? That's badass." I bump her fist.

"I was playing in your weight room the other day."

"Can I watch next time?"

She slides me a smile that makes my cock twitch. "Would that turn you on?"

"It's already turning me on."

Her smile grows as she coyly pushes her hair back over her shoulder, and I suddenly don't care that we lost, or that that Indie asshole took a cheap shot at me, or even that Hilda's being Hilda.

"Who is that *fine* piece of meat?" she asks.

Muffy winces, glances back at where her mother's staring as Maren answers, "Oh, that must be Brianna's boyfriend," and suddenly, my girlfriend goes pale as a ghost.

"Muffy?"

"Rufus!" she exclaims. "I forgot to feed Rufus. That means he'll probably try to eat your shoelaces. I need to go. Feed him. I need to feed him. You stay. Have fun. Visit with Zeus and your family. Say hi to everyone for me."

"You—" I start, but I silence myself when she crawls under the table, duck-walks to the back hallway, and disappears toward the bathroom.

I look at Maren. "What the hell?"

She looks as confused as I am. "I have no idea."

Screw this.

I head toward the hallway to the bathrooms. "Muffy."

She pauses with one foot in the kitchen entrance beyond the ladies' room. "I have a rule to not be around clients and the matches I set them up with. It gets weird, like maybe they're putting on a show for me and they aren't actually as happy as they tell me they are? I don't know. I just...I can't be around clients and their matches. It's a thing."

"So you're sneaking out through the kitchen?"

"Hi, I'm Muffy. Have we met?"

Okay, that was funny. "Hold on. I'll come with you."

"No, really. You haven't gotten to see your family at all. Stay. Have fun. I'll be at home. Naked. In bed. Whenever. *Do not* walk anywhere by yourself tonight, understand?" She blows me a kiss and disappears into the kitchen, both like she's done this a thousand times before, and also like she has no idea that the words *naked* and *in bed* in reference to herself have left me with another boner that won't go away until she's helped me do something about it.

"That was weird," Maren says behind me. "Even for Muffy."

I shove my hands in my pockets to try to lessen the pressure on my woody and also to hopefully make it less visible as I turn to glance at her. "Something weird happen during the game?"

She grins. "She cheered for you every time you so much as set foot on the ice. *That* was weird."

"You're not putting that in your blog, are you?" We all pretend she's not getting the dirt for her Thrusters-obsessed sports blog, but we all also know nearly anything is fair game when Maren's around. She's usually respectful about stuff that's too personal, but we still know to watch ourselves.

"Um, duh. Yeah. I'm absolutely putting that in my blog. You're about to be outed as having a girlfriend, Jaeger. If you don't like it, you better tell Muffy you're just messing around with her. You *know* how much I like it when guys take advantage of my friends."

Considering how much joy she took in Murphy's game being in the crapper last year when he fucked up with Kami, I don't have to ask what she'd do to me.

I'm not the golden child here in Copper Valley that the town's homegrown star goaltender is.

PIPPA GRANT

You'd think a blog wouldn't have a lot of pull with the coaches, but it doesn't have to.

All it has to do is get in my head.

Two months ago I would've said it was an empty threat.

But my palms are getting itchy and there's an unfamiliar discomfort settling into my chest. "I'm not taking advantage of Muffy."

"She's not as tough as she pretends to be."

"I know."

"Kami and Felicity and Alina and I are all *way* more protective of her than she realizes."

"Good."

"Don't underestimate what her client base will do for her, even when she's hiding from seeing them with their matches. Which, yes, is weird."

I shouldn't be smiling. I know when I'm being threatened. But I also know Maren's one hundred percent right.

Muffy's way more loved than she knows.

"Don't underestimate what *I'll* do for her," I tell Maren.

Then I head down the hall to the kitchen, texting West on the way. *Muffy's tired. Long day. See you at brunch.*

He replies with an eye roll emoji followed by a fist bump emoji.

West-speak for *I know you're going to get laid, and I don't blame you.*

Hockey, the bunny bar, and Chester Green's are my three favorite things in Copper Valley.

At least, they used to be.

Miss a night hanging with my teammates and hockey fans?

The old Tyler wouldn't have considered it.

This new Tyler?

He has something more important to do.

41

Muffy

THAT WAS CLOSE.

If Brianna had introduced me to Steve, and he remembered me, I would've been caught.

He knows about Muff Matchers. Kind of. When I told him I thought he should meet a friend, I also told him I worked part-time for a small private matchmaking company that doesn't do much advertising and that my role was supposed to only be administrative work. It's highly likely that my clients will call Muff Matchers out by name at some point if their relationships keep developing, and I'm hoping that by then, no one will care how I found the guys or how I presented myself.

The ends justify the means, right?

I'm probably delusional.

Plus, I don't want to know what Tyler will do if he finds out I'm using dating apps to meet and screen guys.

Not gonna lie.

I feel like I'm cheating on him every time I open an app

and ask guys for dates, even though it's strictly professional on my end.

But since *they don't know that*, it's complicated.

And the more matches I make this way, the more likely I am to get caught.

But it's working.

So is it *really* wrong?

"Muffy."

I leap sixteen feet in the air when Tyler says my name behind me. Mist and fog are invading the city, and I thought he listened when I told him to stay and have fun with his teammates and family—you know, where he's safe if the Indies decided to go out and try to start something *off* the ice —instead of following me out, down a dark alley, and back onto the street toward his building. "*Ohmygod.*"

He grips me lightly by the elbow and tugs me away from the light-rail station I was passing as a trolley pulls up. "Are you okay?"

"I'm—I'm overwhelmed." I say it out loud and realize it's actually true. "Things don't usually go this well for this long, and right now I have more satisfied clients than I've ever had, I hadn't seen my mother in a week until tonight and I'm trying very hard to not let her get back in my head with her comments about my birthing hips, which I think is supposed to be complimentary, and I had a fantastic time hanging out with your family today even if I'm really pissed that you got a black eye in the game and I want to hit that asshole back for you. Nothing has ever gone this right for this long in my entire life."

He studies me for a moment, then nods and pulls me into a hug. "That doesn't mean anything's about to go wrong."

"You sound like my therapist."

"She sounds like a very good therapist."

I hug him back tight. It feels *so damn good* right here in his arms.

If I could stay here, in the drizzly night after a super disappointing game, but with him holding me, forever, I would die a very happy woman. He's *not* a superficial jerk who only cares about a woman's size.

He's everything, and I think he was everything before I let myself see it.

I can't deny it anymore. I don't even want to.

I am head over heels in love with Tyler Jaeger. Completely. Without question.

Not because he's handsome.

Not because he's successful.

Not because he gives me the most incredible orgasms of my life.

But because *he cares*.

He doesn't have to. If anything, he has all the reasons in the world to *not* care.

Who am I to him, really?

Considering he's still here, and all the other places he could be, I must be someone pretty special to him, and there's nothing in the world to make a woman want to love a man more than feeling complete, total, unquestionable acceptance of even her worst moments.

He's *choosing* me.

I need to choose him right back.

"Tyler?" There are so many emotions swirling in my chest, I can barely get his name out.

"Hmm?"

"Will you please—" I don't finish the sentence before someone jostles into us.

I lift my head. Tyler drops his arms and shoves me behind him. "Cranford," he growls.

A thick-necked dude with an ugly-ass scowl flexes his shoulders back. "Taking advantage of another one?"

"We're leaving." Tyler nudges me.

I grip his back belt loop and inch back toward the covered stop, where people are spilling off the trolley.

"Not gonna introduce me?" Cranford asks.

Tyler doesn't answer. He turns his back on the other hockey player, tucks his arm around me, and nudges me again, more firmly, toward the trolley. "Fuck off," he mutters over his shoulder.

I glance back too.

Cranford smiles. It's an ugly smile, one that he tops with a wiggle of the brows and then a tongue movement that makes my ovaries shrivel and hide, because *eew*.

And that's exactly what I'm thinking when I turn to look ahead again, zig when Tyler zags to get around the people departing the light-rail station, and I trip and fall into a massive concrete flower box.

42

Tyler

ONLY MUFFY.

Seriously, *only* Muffy.

The good news? Cranford disappeared into the night as soon as Muffy went down in the flower box. Not that I expected him to cause actual trouble off the ice, but I'm still happier when he's not around. Dude likes to be intimidating.

The bad news?

She'll probably have a bruise the size of Alaska on her hip from hitting the concrete wrong, someone at the trolley stop told the tabloids that I stole Cranford's girlfriend, and all of my sisters have invaded my condo after hearing about the little accident.

Could be worse.

Muffy could be seriously hurt.

"Are you sure you're okay?" Allie's asking. "I can make soup."

"How handy is it sometimes that you went to medical

school?" Brit adds. "I'd be freaking out and rushing my kids to the emergency room."

"Lots of padding and I can still walk," Muffy replies, but she winces the teeniest amount, and I want to put my fist through a wall that I didn't steer her better down the street. "You guys are so sweet to worry."

Staci smiles at her. "Worrying is basically our entire job. We're related to Tyler and West."

"On behalf of West, Ty's the bigger worry and always has been," Keely calls from the kitchen, where she's doing I don't want to know what.

Probably brewing a potion to make me more romantic for Muffy.

It's exactly the sort of thing my sisters would do.

"Out," I order.

Forty-eight women turn and glare at me.

Okay, like five of them.

Also, Muffy's not glaring. She's blushing and avoiding my eye, just like she's done since Allie banged on my door while I was trying to inspect Muffy's hip, demanding to know why people at Chester Green's were talking about me having another dust-up with Gator Cranford over a girl.

"He's such a youngest child," Brit mutters. She hugs Muffy. "We're doing brunch at a wine bar at ten, and I really hope you make it, but we get it if we're overwhelming and you send Tyler by himself."

"Does your cat always stare at the fish tank like that?" Keely asks from the kitchen doorway. Rufus is doing his thing, sitting in a dining room chair that we've placed in the middle of the living room, his back to the aquarium, peeking over his shoulder like he's afraid the fish will look back.

Didn't take long for me to realize Rufus is more of a danger to himself than he is to the fish. I like it that way.

"Yes," I answer for Muffy. "Go away."

She gives me the *don't be rude* huff. "He means thank you for being the kind of awesome sisters who care and try to help."

"Even if we're doing it in the name of not letting each other get more gossip than any of the rest of us?" Staci asks with a sly grin.

They finally leave, and by the time I shut the door behind them, Muffy's disappeared.

I find her leaning on her not-bruised hip in the middle of my bed. "I think I embarrassed myself this time," she whispers. "Who walks into a giant flower pot?"

I crawl onto the bed with her. "You're hot when you're clumsy."

She rolls her eyes and ends the massive gesture by staring at the wall over my shoulder.

"Hey. Look at me." I grip her chin lightly, stroking her jaw with my thumb until her gaze shifts to me, her pupils dilating. "You're not really embarrassed, are you?"

"No, I'm—okay, yes. No. Yes. I—*maybe?* Your sisters are all so put together, and they're so nice, and I'm basically a walking disaster. Every time I feel like I'm making progress toward being a functioning human, I go and fall in a pile of dirt. And it's not just falling in a pile of dirt. It's falling in a pile of dirt and then it being this big *thing* that meant your entire family came running to make sure I was okay, and what happens when it's something bigger than me tripping in public? Because it's usually something bigger than me tripping in public."

"I faceplanted in my Thanksgiving mashed potatoes one year because I put my chair on wheels so it would be less effort to get up when I was stuffed. And Keely got inducted into the National Honor Society in high school with her dress tucked into her underwear because none of her classmates told her she'd done it when she made a last-minute run to the bathroom before the ceremony. She gets nervous in front of crowds."

"Been there," she mutters. "But it was an amusement park and my back pocket ripped off my shorts and I didn't have another pair." Her fingers drift to my face, lingering on my cheek under my blackening eye. "And here I am being a total prima donna over tripping when you took a fist to the face."

I shuck my shirt, because this is dumb.

I know how to show her I like her exactly the way she is. "Part of the job. Show me again where it hurts so I can kiss your booboo."

She doesn't move though, and she's still carrying her wariness like it's a shield. "I'm like this *all the time*, Tyler."

This is a trap. I don't know what kind of trap, but I know it's a trap.

And her heavy sigh doesn't help. Nor does the way she leans back out of my grasp. "I just—I don't know when you'll get tired of it."

Oh. "Muffy."

Her nose wrinkles. "Never mind. Let's go to bed."

Like hell. I hook my hand behind her neck. "No never mind. Muffy. You—do you know why I've never dated?"

"Because you got burned before?" she whispers.

"Because I was waiting for you." Fuck, words are hard. How do normal people confess things like this? "I didn't know it, but I was waiting for you."

Her eyes go shiny, which makes my throat go thick.

Part of me wants to run. To hide from the truth I just dropped in the middle of my bedroom.

What if she gets bored of *me*?

She sucks in a deep breath and blinks rapidly. "Tyler?"

"Yes?"

"Will you please kiss me now?"

That I can do.

It's so much better than talking.

And so I lean in and capture her lips as I slip my hands under her shirt.

No worrying about tomorrow.

Not when I have tonight.

And if I do my job right tonight, I won't have to worry about tomorrow anyway.

43

Muffy

TYLER and I are quite the pair at brunch. I'm moving stiffly because my hip is sore, and his eye looks like he walked into a very offended, ugly boulder that's probably telling stories about what the other guy looks like right now, and we are definitely the two most casually dressed people in this wine bar for brunch.

Also?

Showers with him keep getting better. I don't know how that's possible, but it is.

So it's entirely likely we're also the two most relaxed, satisfied people in this wine bar too.

"This is the place where I accidentally set Kami up with Felicity's ex-boyfriend last year," I whisper to Tyler as our hostess guides us to the back room of Noble V. "It's the one place in the entire city that Kami's banned and I'm not. Isn't that weird?"

He grins. "Yet. You're not banned *yet*."

"Goals, right?"

It's wrong that he's even more handsome with a black eye.

Or possibly I'm a little bloodthirsty and knowing that my boyfriend can physically protect me if necessary is a turn-on.

My *boyfriend*.

He didn't flinch when I said it last night.

I've been waiting for you.

The man knows how to make a woman feel special. I squeeze his hand simply because I can.

We're not the last to arrive to brunch with his family. Staci and her family and West and Daisy aren't here yet either, and Mrs. Jaeger—*May Ella*—is frowning while she keeps checking her phone.

Allie and Keely have a coffee carafe between them that they're possibly taking turns drinking straight out of, with their families fanned out on either side. Britney's handing two of her kids coloring books while her husband hands the other two his phone.

It's like a zombie breakfast.

Without the dead bodies. Naturally.

"See the sports page this morning?" Allie's husband asks Tyler while Ty pauses to rub his nephew's head and kiss his niece's hair.

We both shake our heads.

The whole family shares looks.

Apprehension slithers up my spine, and I reach for my phone, which isn't in my pocket.

Nor is it in my bag.

At least, I don't think. It's hard to subtly reach in and dig through everything in there.

"What?" Tyler asks them as he pulls a handful of small gummy bear packets from his pockets and tosses them to the under-ten crowd, who all shriek and lunge.

His sisters get matching eye twitches, but he ignores them.

We both do, because his dad has a weird look in his eyes,

which he refuses to aim at either of us as he speaks. "Big write-up on you and Cranford and his sister."

"And?" Tyler says.

"And Amelia Cranford is still in love with you," Keely says. "According to the gossip pages, she hasn't talked to her brother since he forbade her to date you and beat you up back… How many years ago was that? Six? Seven?"

Tyler grunts and pulls my chair out.

I peer at him.

Nothing.

Totally stone-cold poker face.

And that's when the butterflies hit.

He told me he fell head over heels in love with her.

But that was years ago. Surely, he doesn't feel the same now.

That's what I'd tell my clients.

So why is it not working when I tell it to myself?

Because you know when you're the consolation prize, Muffy. You've always been the consolation prize.

"She was supposed to be on that reality TV show," Britney says to her kids' coloring books. "Which one is it? The one about competing for a husband?"

"Oh my god, I can't even keep track of them anymore," Keely says.

It doesn't matter which show. What matters is that if she's competing on reality TV for a husband, she's hot. And has a personality.

It's a rule. You can't be on TV if you're not hot and don't have a personality.

And if she wants Tyler—would she go to reality TV lengths in real life to get him?

My heart is fluttering into a panic. *Stay calm, Muffy. Stay. Calm. Tyler knows who you are. He likes you for who you are. He's not going to dump you just because someone he had a thing for way back when is suddenly into him and available and hot.*

"Mimosa?" I croak to the server as she pops in and smiles at me. "Maybe skip the orange juice part and substitute vodka for the champagne?"

"She'll have a salted caramel hot chocolate, extra whipped cream, with a shot of Baileys," Tyler corrects.

Swoon, my vagina sighs.

I'm not mad at him for changing my order. I *do* like his idea better. And not just because he had it.

He drops into the seat next to me and drapes his arm over the back of my chair. "Ignore them," he mutters.

Which isn't *I don't love her anymore and I'm not interested.*

I force a smile and reach for my water with clumsy hands.

But he knows me, and he's steadying the glass almost before the ice clinks against the side.

Be cool, Muffy. Be. Cool.

"How'd everyone sheep last night?" I blurt.

Sheep.

Oh my god.

I asked them how they *sheeped.*

"Like the dead," Allie answers.

Tyler grabs a straw and throws it at her. "Shove it."

"What? That wasn't a zombie Grandpa joke."

"Definitely not," Keely agrees.

One of the kids—I swear I knew all their names yesterday —spills a lidded cup of what I sincerely hope is apple juice, and another sticks a crayon up his nose. "Look, Mama, I gots a booger!"

I love these people. I truly do.

I steal a glance at Tyler.

He turns a soft smile my way, and that's all it takes. One slight hitch of his lips, and my pulse pulls back on the throttle and my panic chills.

He likes me.

He really, really likes me.

"Oooh, brunch time!" Daisy and West stroll into the room,

West holding Remy, who pumps his feet when he sees everyone. He sets the little boy down, and he toddles straight to Britney.

"Favorite aunt!" she crows.

Daisy slips an arm around May Ella and kisses her cheek, and I swear she whispers something that makes May Ella's nose twitch.

They both look at me, and there it goes again.

The doubt.

Things have been too good for too long. Tyler's sexy, attractive, talented ex-girlfriend still pines for him. His family is giving me weird looks.

"What the fu—udge is going on?" Tyler asks.

"Nothing," his mom says.

"It's never *nothing*."

"Tyler, are you related to the most amazing woman on the planet or not?" Daisy asks with a grin. "If it's nothing, *it's nothing*."

"It's possibly not *nothing* nothing," West says.

"Optimism, Westley." She pats him on the ass. "We're having *optimism*."

"About *what*?" Tyler asks.

And now the family's sharing more looks again, and I'm trying to pretend I'm not on the verge of hyperventilating.

Be confident, Muffy. This is okay. Tyler's not the same guy who fell in love with a woman who's not a klutzy professional disaster. He's into you despite all that. He won't leave, even if he stays out of guilt for telling you he liked you better before he knew all his options.

Apparently Allie loses their silent, mental rock-paper-scissors game, because she's the one who speaks up. "Ty, you remember this summer when we had our family reunion at the lake, and those gossip reporters showed up and thought that kid who kept collecting rocks in his pockets was with us, and then there was that massive local story about how we were hanging out with a woman who was once investigated for tax fraud at a local nursing home since it turns out she was the kid's mom, which wasn't funny but we all thought it was weirdly funny since it was the first time we really saw the full Daisy effect in our lives and we joked about how we all might as well admit now to all the weird things we've ever done that might be interesting because we're in the Daisy Halo now?"

While my stomach suddenly cramps, making my hot chocolate feel like it's an angry hurricane in there, even though it hasn't arrived at the table and I haven't actually drunk it yet, Tyler gives his sister the same flat glare he uses on the ice. "No."

"Well, this isn't nearly that bad," she finishes.

"Not even close," Britney agrees.

Keely's nodding. "It's actually really heroic. At least, it is to me."

"*What* is?" he asks.

I want to echo the question, because his sisters aren't very convincing here. Whatever this is, it's bad.

But I also kinda don't want to know.

"Muffy?" a new voice says from the doorway.

I turn, and Brianna's standing there.

With Steve.

Who's squinting at me in confusion. "Octavia?"

"Oh, good, you made it!" Keely says, making it clear why they're here.

They got invited last night after I skipped Chester Green's.

My face erupts in flames, but unfortunately, it doesn't take out the witnesses around me who will forever be able to swear by what happens next.

"Who's Octavia?" Brianna asks.

Steve points at me. "That's Octavia. We had a date two weeks ago."

I don't look at Tyler.

I don't have to. I told him I was Octavia the night that he came through the Cod Pieces drive-thru.

"Date?" he says, and I feel the chill in his words all the way through my bones.

Brianna lifts her phone. "Forget the date. Did you really auction off your virginity to pay your medical school bills?"

My vision narrows to a pinprick, and everything goes so silent, I'm not sure the world exists anymore beyond the weird gaspy noise that suddenly explodes in my ears.

It's me.

I'm a gasp. That's literally all I am.

A horrified gasp.

But is that really what I want to be? A horrified gasp living in the shadow of fear that my boyfriend, *the man I love*, will leave me now that it's public knowledge how much of a fuck-up I've been, and that his original true love, who's successful and undoubtedly gorgeous and coordinated and capable of not just walking in stilettos, but also of looking like she belongs on them, would take him back?

No.

No, it most definitely is *not*.

I suck in a breath and order the inky blackness to get the *fuck* out of my eyeballs, and as soon as the roaring in my ears subsides, I order my knees to work too.

"Yes," I announce. "I tried to auction my virginity to pay for medical school. And I go on dates. I'm on dating apps. Because it's how I find men for my clients. *I cheat to find clients*, because *so many men are assholes*. Do you know how many men I've met who only want to stare at my chest or tell me I should lose weight or mansplain how stupid things work? I refuse to let my very favorite people in the world be subjected to that. And if I sit down and talk to a guy *as me*, representing Muff Matchers, they don't take me seriously. The one thing I succeed at is failing. I am a massive success as a failure, and I don't care who knows. *I am who I am.* I do what I do. And I am *so tired* of feeling like that's not enough."

The door's open.

The door to our private room is open, and the *entire Sunday brunch crowd* heard me.

Brianna's gaping.

Steve's confused.

Some brunchers are whispering or giggling at the freak show. The Jaeger family are all tongue-tied.

And Tyler—Tyler's sitting there livid.

Completely, one hundred percent *livid.*

My heart is a punching bag and his eyes are throwing the daggers to obliterate it.

"And you can all fuck off if you don't like it," I finish.

And there you have it.

I'm done.

My career?

Over.

I cheat.

I break the rules, representing people I'm not on dating apps so that I can screen for the good ones for women who deserve love as much as, if not more than the rest of us, and I announced it to the world while dating a hockey player whose sister-in-law is among the tabloids' favorite subject.

I'll be news for exactly fourteen minutes at some point today, and everyone who matters will see it.

People who think they matter but don't—like Connie Bragowski—will see it and try to friend me on social media to pretend to care but really because she wants to feel superior and be in the middle of the drama, to tell people she saw it coming.

And Tyler?

I have no idea what I'll do about Tyler.

I just know that if he wants to be pissed at me for *doing my job*, even if I'm stretching the boundaries of *how* I should do my job, then he's not the guy I thought he was.

And maybe this is a convenient way for him to dump me so he can go back to Gator Cranford's sister.

Fine.

Whatever.

I snag my bag off the back of my chair and march to the door.

You know what?

I hope he *does* go back to her.

And when he does, you're damn right I'll take credit for that match.

No matter how much it hurts.

4 4

Tyler

FOR THE SECOND time in twelve hours, I'm watching Muffy leave me behind.

But this time, I'm so pissed I might take a chunk out of the table with my bare hands.

I need to follow her. I need to get up and follow her.

But my entire body is so tense I'm positive all I'll do is yell, and I'm just rational enough to know that yelling at Muffy right now would be a bad, bad idea.

Why doesn't she trust me enough to know I don't care if she does her job, and I will literally break *people* if they so much as look at her wrong for any of the ways that she's exactly perfect?

And who the *fuck* made her national news?

West drops into the seat she vacated while Brianna and what's-his-name turn and do the one thing I'm supposed to be doing. "Breathe, Ty."

"I *am* breathing."

"No, you're punishing the air with your nose and lungs, and pretty soon, it's gonna be too bruised for the rest of us to survive."

I snort.

"Oh, no, I'm going to faint dead away," Brit says.

Three of her kids burst into tears.

When I turn around to glare at my siblings, four more do too.

"*Down*, boy," Allie says as she gathers two of her kids up and shushes them. "None of us think Muffy's a failure, and you're being an idiot if you think sitting here is going to make her come back."

"You *do* want her to come back, don't you?" Keely says as she hands one of Brit's kids a biscuit, which is like plugging the cry hole before it bursts.

"I want her to come back," Mom says. "You were happy yesterday."

"She's *off-limits* in your show. Understand?"

Mom rolls her eyes. "The easy targets are never the fun jokes, Tyler. You know that."

"So?" West says. "You going after her, or what?"

Fuck this.

Or what.

I'm going after the tabloid who published her secrets, and then I'm going after every single person who's ever made her feel small and insignificant and like a failure.

I rise and grab my coat. "Come back for Thanksgiving," I grunt at my family.

I pass Staci and her family on my way out. "Whaaaa...?" she says. "I just saw Muffy, and—Tyler? *Ty!*"

Not worth answering.

Someone else will fill her in.

Muffy's long gone when I hit the street, which is fine with me. I'm not chasing her today.

Not yet, anyway.

It takes me forty minutes to get where I'm going, and I'm still fuming when I pull my car to a stop in front of the two-story house where my girlfriend grew up, behind an old beige Crown Victoria with custom plates that say *BADA88.*

Hilda flings the door open before I'm halfway up the walk and steps out into the chilly morning in nothing but a baggy silk robe and mismatched animal slippers. One's a sheep. The other's an elephant. Her hair's swept up like she's going to a ball, and she's plastered on full-face makeup. "Tyler! That black eye looks good on you. Are you here to ask for Muffy's hand? Because I'm not going easy on you, even though she doesn't have any other prospects. She's a modern woman. She doesn't need a man to be complete."

"Quit making her feel like a loser," I growl as I shove my way into the house.

Hilda's made-up eyebrows shoot so high they could give the ceiling a lift. "What are you talking about?"

"Somebody calling Muffy a loser, Hilda?" an old dude in grandpa pants asks behind her. "Let me at him. I got a can of mace somewhere in my pockets." He pats his thighs, then his butt, then reaches down the front of his pants and comes up with a can of whipped cream.

"What the *fuck*?" I snarl.

"Huh. Wrong can. That wasn't from your fridge, Hilda. Promise. I wouldn't steal your whipped cream. I brought my own."

"I'd let you have it, William," she replies. "Have you met Tyler Jaeger? He's boinking Muffy."

The old dude peers down his old man nose at me. "You making sure she gets her cookies first?"

"I could just look at him and get *my* cookies." Hilda fans herself.

"*I'm not here to give you your cookies.*" Jesus. "Do you have any idea how much Muffy needs you to accept her for who she is without making comments about her weight or her size or her food or what you want to do to her friends? *Jesus.* It would be like my mother using *you* as all of the material for her shows. How the hell would you feel being the butt of every joke?"

William pauses in trying to pull the cap off of the can of whipped cream.

Hilda freezes. "What are you talking about?"

"*Muffy.* Your daughter. The woman who talks tough and acts like she doesn't care but feels like she's never good enough and doesn't deserve good things. *That's* what I'm talking about. She needs you to be her mother, not the food police, and not some kind of twisted social influencer."

She's shrinking like every word is a blow, her eyes getting shiny, and I don't fucking care.

I don't. Fucking. Care.

"I don't want her to end up like me," she whispers.

"What are you talking about?" William says to her. "You're a fox." He turns a glare on me. "And if you're insulting my friend Hilda here, you should know I have a criminal record and I'm not afraid to go after your bank accounts."

"Fuck that. I know the woman who set off the dick pic virus last year. She can hack circles around you."

Both of them suck in a breath.

It pays to know the Berger twins sometimes. They move in weird, fascinating circles.

And right now, all I care about is that those circles help me help Muffy.

I point at Hilda. "Quit. Making. Muffy. Feel. Like. A. Failure."

"I don't *try* to," she says. "She does lots of good things. And she's so pretty. And she always looks so graceful even when she's dropping her phone in her oatmeal."

"Figure out how to tell her that, or you're not coming to our wedding, and you'll never meet our kids. Got it?"

She gapes at me like she's one of the fish in the aquarium Daisy got me for my last birthday.

And suddenly all of my anger is gone.

I don't care what happens to Hilda.

I care that Muffy's okay.

I don't even say goodbye. I just turn and march back out of the house. But this time, I'm pulling out my phone as I go.

Forget being mad.

Forget Cranford. Forget my black eye. Forget my family. Forget the tabloids.

Forget fear.

I love Muffy.

I fucking love Muffy. She's my best friend. She slipped into my heart a year ago, and she's stayed there, digging in deeper and deeper until everything that was right in front of me for so long is the only thing I could ever want, and it's past time I got over being afraid she'll hurt *me*.

I want Muffy.

Before I can hit Nick's number to see if Muffy's hiding out with Kami at his house, my phone rings with an incoming call from a number I don't recognize.

Normally I'd send it to voicemail, but it's local, and I don't think Muffy has her phone on her, and I have zero doubt she'd borrow a phone from a stranger if she wanted to reach someone.

I hope that someone is me. "Hello?"

"What the hell did you do to Muffy?"

The voice. I know the voice. It's— "Maren?"

"She emailed her entire Muff Matchers list, confessed to finding dates for us on dating apps since she said she *doesn't have the network* to do everything she wants to do for us the *right way*, and that she'll understand if we all want to fire her since she's probably getting booted for violating terms of service and won't be able to find us matches anymore. What. The hell. Did you. Do?"

"Where is she?"

"One, even if I knew, I wouldn't tell you, and two, if you hurt her, I will fucking *destroy* you."

"No need," I mutter. "If I hurt her, I'll destroy myself."

4 5

Tyler

I CAN'T FIND MUFFY.

She's not at my place. She's not with Kami. I talked Maren's address out of Kami, but she wasn't there either. Nor was she with Alina or Felicity, Ares's wife and the fourth member of Kami's tight-knit group of friends that Muffy's always felt like she lives at the fringes of.

There isn't an official Muff Matchers office, but I swing by Cod Pieces, where the weekend manager says he hasn't seen her and D'Angelo offers to both quit and help me look for her, and also go ninja on my ass if I hurt her.

I tell him to stay where he is and that I'll have Muffy call him later.

With Maren and Alina's help, we track down a few more Muff Matchers clients, but none of them know anything about Muffy's whereabouts.

Not even Brianna, who was the last person to see her.

"She kept apologizing, like she was sorry she had to find Steve this way for me, but I'm not mad, and neither is he," she tells me on the phone before dropping her voice to add in a whisper, "I'm glad she found him, no matter how. He's a lot nicer and more patient and interesting than any of the other guys I've ever tried to date. That was really nice of her to screen all those men on dating apps who pretend they're something they're not. It's a service more people should offer."

She's not at any of her favorite cafes.

I can't find Rufus in my condo, which doesn't necessarily mean she's gone for good—he could be hiding somewhere—but her car's gone, and based on what I know of Muffy leaving Richmond, if she decides she wants to disappear, that's exactly what she'll do.

Even if she doesn't have her clothes with her.

Or her phone, which I find lying in the middle of my bed.

Fuck.

It takes me forever, but I figure out Veda's office number. I get her weekend answering service, convince them it's an emergency, and they promise to immediately pass on the message that her best friend is missing.

And I'm out of ideas.

I'm so out of ideas that I need new ideas, so I head the one place I know I'll find people who might be crazy enough to guess where I should check next.

The bunny bar.

I bang on the knocker, and the small, rectangular hatch at eye level slides open. "Password?"

"Shaved skates."

"Wrong door." The hatch slides shut, and *what the hell?*

They changed the password.

They changed the password.

I pull up my email and flip through for a note with the new password, but I don't have anything from the bunny bar.

Seriously?

I hit my text messages and pull up the thread with Athena

and Cassadee. *Stuck outside the bunny bar. When did the pass-word change? Got a problem. I need help.*

I pace the street while I wait for an answer, and it takes a lot longer than I wish it did.

Fuck.

I'm supposed to be at practice.

Jesus.

This isn't good.

Coach is gonna kill me. Coach is gonna kill me and make me wish Cranford had finished me off. I hit Lavoie's number on my phone, and it goes straight to voicemail.

Klein's number does too.

Shit shit shit.

Goodbye, hockey career.

Goodbye, woman of my dreams.

I dial Ares last, and when his voicemail message—a single grunt—hits my ear, I spill my guts. "Ares. Fuck. I forgot it's practice time. Muffy's gone. Like, disappeared gone. I can't find her, and things went to shit because all the tabloids dug into her and exposed all of her secrets and I need to find her. I need to make sure she's okay. Fuck. *Fuck.* I think I love her. No. No, I know I love her. I love her, man. I fucking love her so hard I hurt, and I'm worried about her, and she left her phone at my place and no one knows where she is, and I don't care if she hates me or blames me—I really should've asked Daisy to make sure the gossip rags got the message that anyone who fucked with Muffy would…would… Shit. I don't even know what Daisy could do to them, but I know Muffy wouldn't be exposed like this if she was hanging out with anyone else and their family. I just—I just need to know she's okay. If you've seen her, let me know. And can you tell Coach —shit. Never mind. I'll tell him myself. I can man up. This is all on me."

I hang up and shove my phone in my pocket, ready to

turn around, get my car, and get my ass back to practice, when I realize I'm not alone.

Athena—or is that Cassadee?—is poking her head out of the bunny bar entrance.

Athena. Definitely Athena. It's the boobs. "You know you're why the password changed, right?"

"What? Why? What did I do?"

She rolls her eyes, then crooks her finger at me. "One chance, Jaeger. One. Chance."

I don't ask questions.

Instead, I silently follow her inside and down the stairs into the glittery silver, gold, and pink club.

But I don't see the bar. I don't see the lounge chairs. I don't see the puck bunny flag.

I see my heart, sitting in the middle of the room, sloshing a pink drink in a martini glass while she talks. "My next client called me to tell me her date needed bail money, because he tried to steal a chicken out of someone's backyard, and that was it, you know? Then I was like—*hic*!—Mutzy, I mean, Muffy, you need a pew land. A new gland. A—*hic*!"

"And that's when you started signing up for all of the dating apps?" Cassadee asks.

Muffy hiccups and nods.

"You are such a badass." Another bunny—is that Jami?—clinks her glass to Muffy's. "Way to stick it to the man and find a way to get what you need. How many matches have you made this way?"

"All of them."

"Woohoo, you go, girl!" I know that one too. That's Anni. With an I.

Muffy shakes her head. "I'm done. Washed up. *Hic*! Mutch Maffers is dead."

"What? *No*." Veda rises. *Veda*. Veda's here. Good. "Muff Matchers is *not* dead. Do you hear me, Muffy Periwinkle? You are doing the women of the world the best fucking service *ever* in screening out the losers for your clients, and you are *not* giving up. I forbid you."

"But I *cheated*." Muffy glares at her. "Wheaters don't chin."

Athena cocks a brow at me. "And what do you have to say for yourself?"

Jesus. I don't know how they found her, or why she's here, but I have zero doubt they're taking care of her because they knew she needed it, and that will always be what I love most about these bunnies.

In the friend way. Naturally. "Thank you for keeping her safe."

"Are you kidding?"

"I love her."

"Hm. I suppose that's a start."

I don't bother wasting my facial expressions on her, and instead step down into the sunken seating area. Muffy looks up at me, her eyes going wide, and she drops her drink in Jami's lap.

"I love you," I tell her.

She blinks.

"I fucking love you," I repeat. The bunnies scatter as I reach her and drop to my knee so I'm at eye level with this amazing, beautiful disaster of mine. "I love you when you're cuddling your cat. I love you when you're talking about your job. I love you when you're naked. I love you when you're being difficult. I love you when you're using dating apps to screen assholes for your clients, and I love how much you love them. I love you when your hair's a mess, and when you're throwing eggs all over my kitchen, and when you're taking me to funerals so you can be there for a friend in a place you never wanted to go back to. I love you when you're happy, and I love you when you're stressed, and I will *never* stop loving you, because I've been waiting my whole life to love you. You're the one and only you, Muffy, and you will always be *my* one and only. It's you. It's only you. I love you."

She blinks again. "What about Amelia Cranford?" she whispers.

It legit takes the question a minute to register, and when it does, I have to stop myself from choking on a laugh. "She's not you, Muffy. *No one* will ever be you."

"You forgot her name." Muffy's a little cross-eyed, but she's starting to grin as she pushes me in the shoulder. "*You forgot her name.*"

"I'm gonna have to tell you all of this again when you sober up, aren't I?"

"And basically a dozen times a day, every day for the rest of your life," Veda agrees.

"Kiss her!" one of the bunnies cries.

"You can use the walk-in fridge again if you want," another chimes in. "We'll keep it clear."

"And clean it afterwards."

Jesus. I'm not banging Muffy in the fridge again.

At least, not when she's drunk. Next time we're here when she's sober—if she wants to come back—might be a different story. "Can I take you home?" I ask her.

She loops her arms around my neck, leans in, and presses a wet kiss to my cheek. "No. I like it here. We're moving in. It'sh my new office. And my bedroom. Someone bring me Rufus."

"Aww, he's missing practice for her!" another woman says behind me. "That's like, *the* most romantic thing a hockey player can do!"

"No, it's way better if he misses a game."

"A *playoff* game!"

"For a funeral," Veda chimes in with a smirk.

It all bounces off, because Muffy's tugging me into a hug, her breath hot on my neck, smelling very much like a distillery crossed with a cotton candy factory. "I love you too, and that's not the alcohol talking," she tells me.

"I'm still gonna make you say it again when the alcohol's out of your system," I murmur back against her neck.

She shivers, sighs, and then—

Snores.

She snores.

Muffy Periwinkle, goddess of my world, the woman that every step of my life has led me to, and the love of my eternity, has passed out drunk on my shoulder.

And you know what?

I think she's utterly perfect.

Perfectly perfect for a guy like me.

Muffy

SOMEONE REPLACED my brain with concrete and I cannot lift my head off this fluffy bit of silky something under my ear.

Also, there's a vibrator gluing my leg to a very soft floor.

"Amoofle?" I grunt.

The vibrator meows and the floor sags and the concrete sloshes, but then gentle fingers brush through my hair, and soft lips press against my forehead, and the concrete gets a little less hard and angry.

"Hey, party girl," a familiar voice whispers. "Aspirin and water?"

I whimper.

What did I do yesterday?

Yesterday?

Today?

This morning?

Last week?

"Muffy. I need to get to practice, but Daisy and West and

Remy are staying here if you need anything, and Veda's on her way over too. I'll be back in a few hours, okay?"

I'm at Tyler's place.

I flipped out, freaked out, shut my business down, ran into the bunnies, got drunk with them, and now I'm back at Tyler's place.

I crack an eyelid open, and four Tylers swim into view. He's crouched at the side of the bed, all the blinds shut so he's shadowy and mysterious and hot, especially when he grins at me like that. "You rest more."

The Tylers all lean close so I can sniff the laundry detergent on his T-shirt—T-shirts? Are they all wearing shirts?—and I get a single kiss on my forehead. "Love you, beautiful."

And then everything's dark again.

But it's a happy, glowy kind of dark.

I slide into the dark, and everything is good, until I have no idea how many hours later when I wake up with a gasp.

Rufus is sitting on my chest, sliding onto my neck. People are talking and laughing down the hall. A small human is squealing nonsensical words. And the light filtering through the slats in the blinds has an early afternoon quality to it.

I'm at Tyler's place.

He came for me.

He found me.

Did he tell me he loves me?

Never mind that.

Did I tell him I love him?

I push Rufus off, throw the covers back, leap out of bed, and my head reminds me that we subsisted basically on alcohol and cheese yesterday, and I go down.

Am I wearing pants?

Am I still wearing my own boobs?

And why does my hip feel like my padding is bruised?

"Aw, Muffy, it's like finals week again." Veda pokes her

head into the door, smiling widely, and I'd hug her, except I won't be trying my legs again.

"What day is it?"

"Monday."

"You're still here."

"I'm quitting my practice. It's not what I want to do, and I wish I'd followed your lead out the door before med school graduation. There's an opening for a biology professor at Copper Valley University. I have an interview today."

I gape at her. "Am I still drunk?"

"No. You inspired me, actually. You're out here, doing what you want to do, making a difference on your own terms, while I—I just don't like people."

"Um, you know students are people?"

She laughs. "I know. But lecturing a roomful of possibly jaded, possibly optimistic twenty-year-olds and doing research sounds so much better than listening to everyone's Aunt Betty and Uncle Milton ask why their goiter is acting up again. At least I *know* the students won't listen to my advice, and I can actually grade them accordingly. I can't flunk someone on their cholesterol test. My dad wanted me to be a doctor with my own practice because he couldn't. I want to be a teacher because I can."

"That's—that's amazing, Veda!"

"Especially if it means I get to see you more." She helps me to my feet as the scent of fried something wafts into the room. "Also, Tyler DoorDashed us Cod Pieces."

"Oh my god, I love him." I slap my hand over my mouth, but then I whisper it again. "I love him. And he said he loves me. I don't think I drunk-hallucinated that."

"Muffy. *He passed out at a funeral for you.* The man has loved you a lot longer than he's been willing to admit it."

"Completely true." Tyler himself pokes his head into the room and smiles at me, making me warm from my toes to my split ends. He's in athletic pants and a Thrusters T-shirt, his hair barely damp like he's been to practice and come home and showered, his black eye ugly but beautiful at the same time, his grin completely intoxicating, but in the *good* way.

I could very happily have a Tyler Jaeger smile hangover for the rest of my life.

"Fries and fish?" he asks. "Veda swears it's your favorite hangover cure. If she's lying I'll toss her off the balcony."

My feet carry me to him with minds of their own, and I'm throwing my arms around him and peppering his face with kisses merely because I want to. "I love you."

"I love you more."

Veda laughs again. "So should I shut the door, or are you going to let Muffy eat her fish while it's still hot?"

She doesn't wait for an answer, and shuts the door on her way out.

And I suddenly realize why it tastes like moldy shoe leather in my mouth.

I drop back to my heels and clamp my hand over my mouth as Tyler leans in.

He tilts a brow at me over his good eye. "What?"

"I have bad breath."

"I love your bad breath. How's your head?"

"A little swishy." Sort of like my heart. Warm and swishy. But my heart's all good.

It's *all* good.

"You came to find me yesterday," I whisper. "I thought you were mad about me going on dates."

"It's your job, Muffy. I was mad that the tabloids attacked you, and that you were acting like there was anything wrong with you, and that you needed to defend yourself, and that anyone in my family might've judged you for being anything other than the determined, big-hearted, amazing woman that you are."

I drop my head to his chest. "You know I'm always going to feel a little like a disaster, right?"

"And I'm always going to be here to assure you that it's completely normal to have off days, and that you've worked harder and put more heart into everything you do than most people I know."

"Always?"

"Always."

"Even though you don't want to get married?" Yes, yes, I'm pushing it.

"It's entirely possible I've realized a life without you would be more torture than a life of commitment and regularly banging your sexy body. So now, clearly, I have to spend the next several months of my life bringing you regular sacrifices of good food and magic penis so that *you* reconsider your anti-relationship stance too. Fair warning—I play dirty. And I happen to know you like dirty, so the sooner you give up and admit you want me forever too, the better for the both of us."

I won't cry. I won't.

Okay, I'm totally sniffling up the happy tears.

And squeezing his ass.

Oh my god, I love his ass. And the way his cock twitches against my belly. And the way he's pressing his hot lips to my forehead while he squeezes *my* ass.

The door bangs open, and I leap and grab my head.

A petite, very tattooed, pixie-haired woman in cat-eye glasses eyeballs me as she flips the laptop in her hand so that the screen is facing us. "You Muffy?" she asks in a six-pack-a-day voice.

"Am I?" I whisper to Tyler.

She's a little scary.

And while Tyler's scary too, the buff tattooed guy with a buzz cut behind the woman holding what looks like my laptop is possibly even scarier.

"Yeah. This is Muffy," Tyler says with a grin.

"Good. I got your website fixed. Upgraded, even. Won't

even have to meet half these guys after their IP address goes through this little extension I installed for you. It'll pull up full criminal history right down to speeding tickets and any incriminating photos on their phones. If anyone asks, it's legal and I wasn't here."

She does that *here, take it* gesture, and Tyler grabs it from her. "Appreciate the help."

"Tell the Zeusinator we expect him in the bedroom at four PM sharp," she replies.

Her bodyguard growls.

She snickers.

And then they're both gone.

"What was that?" I whisper.

Tyler nudges me out of the bedroom. "Your site crashed. I know someone who knows someone who could fix it, and the bunnies threatened to castrate me if I didn't make the call to make it happen."

"They did not!"

"They might've. You were drunk. Can't tell me otherwise."

"Muffy!" My Muff Matchers support group is in the living room—every last member, even though it's a Monday—and they all leap to their feet when we step out of the hallway.

The pixie woman and her bodyguard are nowhere to be seen. If Tyler wasn't carrying my laptop, I'd swear I hallucinated them too.

"We're fixing your business model," Maren tells me. She and Daisy are hunched together on dining room chairs that have been pulled in near the fish tank.

"It's a *great* plan," Veda says.

She beams at Maren.

Maren blushes.

And *oh my god*.

It's suddenly crystal clear why I haven't been able to match her.

Brianna tackles me with a hug. "I'm so glad you're okay. We were super worried. yesterday."

"I have three friends who want your screening services," Julie says.

"And I have six friends who want you to write their dating profiles for them," Eugenie adds. "At first I was so pissed at that dumb gossip rag for searching out your profiles on the various apps, but then I was like, *damn*, Muffy knows how to represent us."

West shoves a bag at me. "Here. Eat. I'll fend them off until you're not quite so green."

"What's happening?" I ask Tyler as he sets my laptop aside and helps me dig out the fried fish and chips.

"Friends and people who believe in you," he replies. "Because you, Muffy Periwinkle, provide a valuable service to women who feel like they don't quite fit."

"Muff Matchers isn't a failure," Veda tells me. "It's a work in progress, like we all are."

"And sometimes you need a helping hand to figure out the best part of your business," Daisy adds.

"We're helping steer you in a little clearer direction," Maren agrees.

"One that *doesn't* put you on the streets having dates with weirdos all the time."

"Or at least quite as much."

"Not after your website upgrades."

Tyler pulls me into his lap on the couch and shoves a piece of fish in my mouth. "Eat. And be happy. And then I'm kicking all of these people out so you can get some rest before you get back to work tomorrow. Okay?"

Happy.

Holy crap.

I am. I'm happy.

Muff Matchers isn't dead. It's just starting.

My clients believe in me, apparently *more* now that they know how I've been screening their dates.

And there's a very attractive man who's not grunting under the weight of me as he feeds me my favorite hangover food and squeezes my thigh.

"Oh, and your mother called," Maren says. She and Veda share a look and roll their eyes together. "She said to tell you she's very proud of you, and that she and William and his nephew would love to take you out for lunch soon so you can tell her all about the things you've been up to with Muff Matchers."

That's weird.

Very weird.

I shift a look at Tyler.

He stares back like an innocent little lamb, and suddenly, I'm cracking up. "What did you do?"

"Anything necessary to make you happy." He winks, and I swear I fall in love with him all over again. "Fries? Or do you want me to kick these people out now?"

Remy toddles over and holds a hand out. "Fie?"

Tyler grins and hands it over, earning a massive smile from his little nephew, and there my heart goes getting all melty again.

My boyfriend—my sexy, smart, handsome, stubborn, *loves me for me* boyfriend—will make the best dad one day.

And I can't wait to share that day with him.

EPILOGUE

Tyler Jaeger, aka a groom in absolute and utter heaven

ELOPING TO VEGAS during the all-star break is the best idea I've ever had.

After my idea to propose to Muffy, of course. And the one before that, when I decided she needed to know I love her. And the one before that, when I took it upon myself to insist on accompanying her to an overnight trip where I pulled the studly move of passing out in a funeral home.

After lots of debate, I've concluded my bride never would've agreed to continue talking to me if I hadn't shown her my own disastrous side.

And speaking of disasters, my entire family is crashing this elopement, which is basically my favorite disaster ever.

The weather's warm, my nieces and nephews are running around the pool beside the gazebo I reserved, and most of my best friends on my team are here.

So are most of Muffy's clients.

So we're not exactly doing this eloping thing very well,

but if I'm going to fuck something up, I'm happy to fuck it up so that our friends and family can be here with us.

"You ready for this?" West asks me.

He's my best man, and Connor, Duncan, Nick, and Rooster are standing in as my groomsmen. I would've asked Ares, but he's occupied with all-star weekend stuff.

Freaking overachiever.

Still, it's pretty cool that the all-star stuff is here in Vegas, so he'll be around for the after-party.

"I was born into a family that made me ready for this," I reply.

He snorts in amusement. "Finally figured out what our sisters were training you for all those years?"

"Don't tell them, okay? Don't tell Muffy either. I keep letting her think she's training me herself."

He snorts again. "No, you don't."

"Okay, I don't. But she still appreciates that I don't mind buying tampons."

"Happiness looks good on you."

Feels good too.

Would I rather be out having one-night stands with puck bunnies and college chicks?

Nope.

I'd rather spend my days making Muffy feel like the queen of the fucking universe.

Seeing *her* happy is worth more than any desire to be by myself.

And seeing her succeeding in helping make other women happy is the icing on the cake.

Her adapted business plan?

Let's just say that even if Muffy's student loans hadn't been mysteriously paid off through a random act of kindness on the same day as her bridal shower, pre-empting my own plans to take care of them, she wouldn't be having any trouble making the payments now.

The band strikes up the music, and my sisters and Kami and Veda all troop down the aisle.

We really are doing this eloping thing wrong.

Plus, there are uneven numbers of bridesmaids and groomsmen.

Hilda's already sobbing in the front row. She's gotten better about complimenting Muffy and not making such a big deal out of size, but she's still outspoken and needed two warnings to quit making eyeballs at my brother.

Daisy's personal bodyguard is standing next to my future mother-in-law, though, and growls every time she glances West's way.

It's his wedding day gift to me to watch her jump.

Even Hilda knows better than to try to seduce Alessandro.

And Daisy herself is dolled up with pink hair and a silver sparkle jumpsuit today, standing in as our justice of the peace to perform the ceremony.

The band switches songs, and a woman steps to the back of the aisle, dressed in a short white dress, with jet black hair, and I choke on air.

"That's not Muffy," West mutters.

She steps hesitantly halfway down the aisle, then her gaze lands on me, and *fuck me*, if I have to go find my bride—

"Oh, fuck," Connor whispers.

"Um, hi," Amelia Cranford says.

Everyone's turning to stare at my ex-girlfriend.

"Fuck, fuck, fuck." Connor can't seem to stop saying the word.

"What the hell's wrong with you?" Lavoie mutters back to him.

Amelia looks past me, pulling the same move Muffy did the day I told her I'd be her date to Veda's dad's funeral. "Sorry to interrupt. I just need a word with my...um, my husband."

West jerks a look at me.

I look past him to Klein going the color of death.

And yeah, I kinda know the color of death.

Nick and Duncan are gaping. Rooster's cackling.

"Jaeggy, you mind if I..." Connor trails off, jerking his head toward Amelia, who's playing with her hands halfway down the aisle.

"Klein, what did you do last night?" Lavoie asks.

"I thought it was a dream." He shakes his head. "I thought it was a dream."

"Dude," Nick mutters.

And then I spot her.

Muffy.

My Muffy.

She's stepping to the back of the aisle in a white tank top, a pink veil, and cut-off shorts, a bouquet of pink, yellow, and purple flowers in her hand, cocking her head at my ex-girl-friend, who shouldn't be here, and who apparently *married my teammate* sometime since we got here.

Fuck, she's pretty.

Muffy, I mean.

Amelia looks back at her.

Muffy cocks her head and wrinkles her nose.

"Right. Sorry. I...I can wait," Amelia says.

Connor looks at me.

"By all means, go talk to your bride," I tell him.

He visibly gulps.

And Daisy gives him a reprieve. "Sit on down, sweetie," she calls. "We've got a wedding to do."

"Is that Amelia Cranford?" Allie hisses from the other side of the gazebo. "Tyler! Is that the same Amelia Cranford you fell in love with for forty-eight hours in college?"

Muffy freezes, because the band isn't playing anymore, and she could hear every last word.

Jesus.

"Oh, fuck me sideways with a hockey stick," Klein mutters. "Jaeggy. She's your *ex-girlfriend*?"

I ignore him.

My past doesn't matter.

Connor's future doesn't matter.

Okay, it does, but not at this exact moment.

At this exact moment, all that matters is Muffy. So, I stroll down the aisle, grab her by the cheeks and kiss her so soundly she's panting by the time I'm done, toss her over my shoulder, and march us both back to the gazebo. "Daisy. Marry us now. *Please.*"

"Why's your ex-girlfriend here?" Muffy whispers as I set her down.

"I don't really know," I whisper back. "And I don't care. Do you?"

"No. I mean, yes. But no. But yes. Is she single? Does she need a man?"

West chokes on a laugh. "You might be twenty-four hours too late, Muffy. Daisy, let's get these two love-birds married."

She flashes him a brilliant smile. "Dearly beloved, we're here today to get my favorite engaged couple all hitched up, and then we're having a party."

"Are you sure that's a good idea?" Keely asks.

"Shut up," Brit hisses. "Tyler's not leaving Muffy for his ex-girlfriend. Didn't you hear? She's *married*. To his teammate. Which isn't awkward at all, right?"

"She meant the part about Daisy partying," Staci mutters.

"Oh my god, is Daisy pregnant?" Allie shrieks.

"Not yet, but I have hope," Daisy replies.

I sigh.

West sighs.

My mom lets out a whoop of joy.

And Muffy starts laughing. "Oh my god, I love your family," she says to me.

"Good. You can love them for both of us."

"Seriously, Jaeger, I didn't know she was your ex-girl-friend, and I didn't know I married her," Connor mutters.

Muffy snorts with more laughter.

"Can you please get to the *I do* part?" I ask Daisy.

"Sheesh, Ty. You act like you've been waiting *forever* to get married," Brit says.

"Tyler?"

I look down at my smiling bride. "Yes, my beautiful angel who would *never interrupt someone else's wedding*?"

"I love you more than I love your family."

And that's all I need.

I'm suddenly a massive ball of smiling, dopey, heart-in-my-eyes love, completely crazy for this fascinating, surprising, hilariously awesome woman.

"Okay, Ty, do you take Muffy to be your wife?" Daisy asks.

"I do. Forever and ever. I'm only doing this *once*. And only for *one woman*. Ever."

Muffy grins, but she also wipes a little tear at the corner of her eye.

"Muffy, do you take this lughead to be your one true penis for the rest of all time?" Daisy asks.

"My one and only, I do," Muffy replies.

Fuck.

Now *I'm* getting a little hot in the eyes. I *am* her only. And I won't forget that either.

"Then by the power vested in me by the same internet service that vested my friend Zeus Berger with the power to hitch people here in Vegas, I now pronounce you husband and wife. You may kiss—"

We don't wait for permission to get to the kissing.

Which might be the story of the rest of our lives.

At least, that's my plan.

ABOUT THE AUTHOR

Pippa Grant is a USA Today Bestselling author who writes romantic comedies that will make tears run down your leg. When she's not reading, writing or sleeping, she's being crowned employee of the month as a stay-at-home mom and housewife trying to prepare her adorable demon spawn to be productive members of society, all the while fantasizing about long walks on the beach with hot chocolate chip cookies.

Find Pippa at...
www.pippagrant.com
pippa@pippagrant.com

PIPPA GRANT BOOK LIST

The Girl Band Series
Mister McHottie
Stud in the Stacks
Rockaway Bride
The Hero and the Hacktivist

The Thrusters Hockey Series
The Pilot and the Puck-Up
Royally Pucked
Beauty and the Beefcake
Charming as Puck
I Pucking Love You

The Bro Code Series
Flirting with the Frenemy
America's Geekheart
Liar, Liar, Hearts on Fire
The Hot Mess and the Heartthrob

Copper Valley Fireballs Series
Jock Blocked
Real Fake Love

Standalones
Master Baker *(Bro Code Spin-Off)*
Hot Heir *(Royally Pucked Spin-Off)*
Exes and Ho Ho Hos

The Bluewater Billionaires Series

The Price of Scandal by Lucy Score

The Mogul and the Muscle by Claire Kingsley

Wild Open Hearts by Kathryn Nolan

Crazy for Loving You by Pippa Grant

Co-Written with Lili Valente

Hosed

Hammered

Hitched

Humbugged

For a complete, up-to-date book list, visit www.pippagrant.com

---

Pippa Grant writing as Jamie Farrell:

The Misfit Brides Series

Blissed

Matched

Smittened

Sugared

Married

Spiced

Unhitched

The Officers' Ex-Wives Club Series

Her Rebel Heart

Southern Fried Blues

CPSIA information can be obtained
at www.ICGtesting.com
Printed in the USA
FSHW010548220321
79720FS